The S
Green

The Song in the Green Thorn Tree

A Novel of the Life and Loves of Robert Burns

James Barke

BLACK & WHITE PUBLISHING

This edition first published 2009
by Black & White Publishing Ltd
29 Ocean Drive, Edinburgh EH6 6JL

1 3 5 7 9 10 8 6 4 2   09 10 11 12 13

ISBN: 978 1 84502 259 4

The Song in the Green Thorn Tree © 1947 The Estate of James Barke
First published in 1947 by Wm Collins Ltd

Scottish
Arts Council

Typeset by RefineCatch Limited, Bungay, Suffolk
Printed and bound by MPG Books Limited, Bodmin, Cornwall

TO
PIPE-MAJOR
ROBERT REID
King of Pipers

"This life has joys for you and I;
And joys that riches ne'er could buy;
And joys the very best."

NOTE

I would like to assure the worshippers of Highland Mary (those Peculiars of Burns hagiology) that my treatment of her has been determined by years of sifting through and mulling over all available internal and external evidence. I am far from claiming infallibility; but I unhesitatingly claim to respect her memory, both for herself and for her association with Burns, as deeply as anyone.

There is no escaping Professor DeLancey Ferguson's verdict: "The Highland Mary we know is the creation of biographers, and should be allowed to abide in the Never-Never Land of romance. The truth about the Burns of flesh and blood had better be sought in his relations with flesh and blood women."

In the end (as indeed from the beginning) I have arrived at much the same conclusion as that reached by Professor F. B. Snyder (the most painstaking and unprejudiced investigator of the problem), and agree that his hypothesis "may fairly be accepted as the true account of the relationship." I could wish that other and more profound problems in Burns were capable of solution so satisfactory and inescapable.

In addition to the general acknowledgments made in the first novel of this work, the following concerning this novel fall to be made.

To the research work of the late Reverend Doctor Eric Robertson for putting me on the track of Mary Campbell's connection with Stairaird and the Machlin Burn.

To Mr. William Deans of Newmilns for much valuable information—especially concerning the hitherto unidentified John Arnot of Dalquhatswood; and, in this connection, to Mr. William McCreadie and Mr. Harry Gaw of Kilmarnock.

To the City Librarian and the Staff of The Mitchell Library, Glasgow, Mr. John B. Purdie, Clydebank Public Library, and Mr. James W. Forsyth of Ayr Public Library, for services that make librarians a pleasure to meet, a credit to their calling and an indispensable asset to civilised living.

To Mr. and Mrs. W. Hope Collins of Dallars House, Ayrshire, for securing me the esteemed privilege of viewing Netherplace, exploring Machlin Tower and examining the interior of the house once occupied by Gavin Hamilton.

J. B.,
Bearsden, October 11th, 1946.

CONTENTS

PART THREE

CHARACTERS

in their order of appearance
(Fictional characters are printed in *italics*)

REVEREND WILLIAM AULD, Machlin Parish minister.

JEAN ARMOUR, eldest daughter of James Armour.

JAMES ARMOUR, Machlin mason and wright.

NANCE TINNOCK, Machlin ale-wife.

WILLIAM FISHER, farmer of Montgarswood and Machlin
  Kirk elder.

JAMES LAMIE,
THOMAS GUTHRIE,
HUGH AIRD, } Machlin Kirk elders.
JOHN SILLER,
JAMES SMITH,
ROBERT BURNS.

JAMES (WEE) SMITH, Machlin haberdasher.

ELIZABETH MILLER, a Machlin belle.

JOHN DOW, host of The Whitefoord Arms, Machlin.

JOHN RICHMOND, apprentice to Gavin Hamilton.

ROBERT ALLAN, ploughman at Mossgiel.

WILLIAM PATRICK, boy-labourer at Mossgiel.

GILBERT BURNS, brother of Robert.

MRS. AGNES BURNS, mother of Robert.

JOHN BURNS, brother of Robert.

AGNES BURNS,
ANNABELLA BURNS, } sisters of Robert.
ISABELLA BURNS,

DAVID HUTCHIESON, } boy-labourers at Mossgiel.
JOHN BLANE,

WILLIAM HUNTER, tanner, Machlin.

REVEREND ALEXANDER MOODIE of Riccarton.

"RACER JESS" GIBSON, daughter of George Gibson.

ELIZABETH BARBOUR,
MARGARET BORLAND, } Machlin whores.

GEORGE GIBSON, host of Machlin lodging-house.

AGNES RONALD ("Poosie Nancie"), wife to George Gibson.

AGNES WILSON, servant to George Gibson.

REVEREND WILLIAM PEEBLES, of Newton-on-Ayr.

MRS. JAMES LAMIE, mother of Wee Smith.

JEANNIE SMITH,
JEAN MARKLAND, } Machlin belles.

REVEREND ALEXANDER MILLER.

ROBIN GIBB, Machlin Kirk beadle.

WABSTERS, Kilmarnock weavers.

DAVID BRICE, Machlin shoemaker.

REVEREND JOHN RUSSELL, Chapel of Ease,
    Kilmarnock.

ELIZABETH PATON, Largieside servant.

GAVIN HAMILTON, writer, Machlin.

DOCTOR JOHN MACKENZIE, physician, Machlin.

MARY CAMPBELL, a servant-lass.

SAUNDERS TAIT, tailor-rhymster, Tarbolton.

JOHN RANKINE, farmer of Adamhill.

WILLIAM MUIR, The Mill, Tarbolton.

WILLIAM BURNS, brother of Robert.

ROBERT MUIR, wine merchant, Kilmarnock.

THOMAS SAMSON, seedsman, Kilmarnock.

JOHN LAPRAIK, farmer-bard, Muirkirk.

MR. AND MRS. WILLIAM PATON, crofters in Largieside.

ANRA MACASLAN, Machlin dancing master.

JAMES (MAC)CANDLISH, a medical student.

ROBERT AIKEN, lawyer and collector of taxes, Ayr.

JOHN BALLANTINE, banker-merchant, Ayr.

JOHN WILSON, printer and bookseller, Kilmarnock.

MARY SMITH, wife to James Armour.

DOCTOR JOHN HAMILTON, locum in Kilmarnock.

MRS. PURDIE, aunt of Jean Armour, Backsneddon, Paisley.

ANDREW PURDIE, weaver, Backsneddon, Paisley.

DOCTOR DOUGLAS of Ayr.

ROBERT WILSON, master-weaver, Paisley.

JOHN TENNANT, factor-farmer, of Glenconner.

WILLIAM RONALD, tobacconist, Machlin.

MATTHEW MORISON, cabinet-maker, Machlin.

MRS. JOHN DOW of The Whitefoord Arms, Machlin.

ADAM ARMOUR, brother of Jean Armour.

JOHN SMITH,
AGNES AULD,   } Machlin fornicators.
MARY LINDSAY,

THOMAS MILLER of Barskimming, Lord Justice Clerk.

JAMES BOSWELL of London and Auchinleck House.

CLAUDE ALEXANDER of Ballochmyle House.

WILHELMINA ALEXANDER, sister of Claude Alexander.

JOHN ARNOT of Dalquhatswood, factor to Earl of Loudon.

GEORGE MARKLAND, Machlin merchant.

AGNES SHAW, wife to George Markland.

HUGH WOODROW, Machlin blacksmith.

JOHN WILSON, Tarbolton merchant and Masons' Secretary.

SANDY PATRICK, Kilmarnock publican.

GAVIN TURNBULL,
JOHN ANDREWS,   } Kilmarnock rhymsters.
PETER SCOTT,

MAJOR WILLIAM PARKER, Assloss, Kilmarnock.

MRS. JOHN MERRY (Annie Rankine), New Cumnock.

DAVID GAW, New Cumnock fiddler.

JOHN MERRY, Inn-keeper, New Cumnock.

MAJOR WILLIAM LOGAN, Park, Ayr.

SUSAN LOGAN, sister of Major Logan.

WILLIAM NIVEN, Maybole merchant.

WILLIE NEILSON, farmer of Minnybee.

PEGGY THOMSON, wife to Willie Neilson.

SAMUEL BROUN, uncle of Robert Burns.

JAMES DALRYMPLE, Squire of Orangefield.

JENNY SURGEONER, Machlin lass.

REVEREND JAMES STEVEN, visiting preacher.

ROBERT and JEAN, twins to Jean Armour.

PETER MACPHERSON, carpenter, Greenock.

MRS. MACPHERSON, wife to Peter MacPherson.

ROBERT CAMPBELL, brother of Mary Campbell.

DUGALD STEWART, an Edinburgh professor.

LORD DAER, son of the Earl of Selkirk.

HUGH PARKER, brother of Major Parker, Kilmarnock.

JOHN GOWDIE, theologian, Kilmarnock.

JOHN SAMSON, brother of Tam Samson, Kilmarnock.

GEORGE REID, farmer of Barquharie.

"Alas! sae sweet a tree as love
Sic bitter fruit should bear."

From: "The Ruined Maid's Lament"
By: Robert Burns⋆

⋆ But not canonical. Represents an attempt (by Hogg and
Motherwell) to "purify" a version given in the so-called *Merry
Muses*. The lines quoted are in the Bard's most characteristic
manner.

I

LOVE AND LIBERTY

ROUND BY MACHLIN TOWN

The Reverend William Auld, parish minister of Machlin, trudged down the Backcauseway. He was returning from a visit to a dying parishioner whose thatched dwelling stood along the Kilmarnock road at the north end of the town.

It was March and the weather was bleak and cold. It began to rain. Mr. Auld adjusted his cloak and pulled at the wide brim of his black hat. Then he canted his head cock-wise to the steep roof of his kirk where it rose above the bare black branches of a great ash-tree.

The roof was leaking. The previous Sunday it had rained and the drops had descended on the occupants of the Ballochmyle Loft. He might have forgotten about the leak; but he was certain Claude Alexander of Ballochmyle would remember. Aye . . . Claude Alexander! A new-comer; and the richest man in the district: sometime Auditor-General to the fabulous East India Company at Bengal! A nabob! But that was the way of things: the leak had to be above *his* head.

Mr. Auld was minded for a moment to enter the kirkyard from the Backcauseway. But he reflected on the weather, the muddy state of the ground and the lamentable fact that the clarty folk of Machlin used the kirkyard as a dung-midden, a cesspool, and, under cover of darkness, as a place for general relief. No: he would hold to the cobbles and go round by the Cross. It would add less than a minute to his journey.

As he turned right towards the Cross, he heard the tinkle of James Smith's shop bell, and turning his head sharply he saw Jean Armour in the light that streamed over the glistening cobbles from the square window. He turned on his heel.

"Is that you, Jean Armour?"

"Aye: it's me, sir."

"I was sure it was. It's wearing round to a sair nicht. Well now, my lassie: you're going round to the house? Aye: there's a good lass now. Tell your father to slip over to the kirk: I want a word wi' him anent the leak i' the roof."

"I will surely, Mr. Auld."

"Aye: you're a good lass, Jean. Run on and no' get drookit."

"Guid-nicht, sir."

He watched her as she skelped round the Cross. Jean Armour was one of his favourites. Polite, obliging, gentle—and aey with a cheery smile and a merry innocent laugh. A nice lass; and, fegs, she was growing up into a splendid young woman . . . with beauty. Aye . . . the daughters o' Jerusalem were dark but comely. Jean was black as the slaeberry; but comely. He minded the morn he had baptised her. That would be seventeen years ago anyway. He had watched her growing up as he'd watched so many others. No doubt he would marry her and baptise her children even as he had married her parents—God willing . . .

From the outside, Machlin Kirk was as ill-looking a biggin as could be seen in the West: inside it was dank and musty. There were times when it smelled like a charnel house: there were times when the smell was less pleasant. The kirk was old: how old nobody really knew; but, for a certainty, the walls had stood there for over five hundred years, so that the outside level of the yard was several feet above the floor level of the kirk.

The kirk furnishings were as drab as the masonry; some rough forms and benches served as pews and there was a number of desks for individuals of some distinction. But the most noteworthy feature of the interior concerned the peculiar arrangement of its lofts.

Mr. Auld lit a stand of candles and placed it on the edge of a communion table. The kirk stirred into life with the movements of fantastic shadows.

The kirk was ill lit at any time, there being only one large window in the north wall between the Ballochmyle Loft and the Loudon Loft and directly opposite the pulpit. On the immediate left of the pulpit, almost within reach of the precentor's desk, stood the stool of repentance, an elevated platform with a small hand-rail that could, at a pinch, give accommodation to three adults. Immediately above the place of public repentance, running the full breadth of the kirk from north to south, was the West or Auchinleck Loft: to balance it in the east was a similar loft known as the Common Loft. But whereas the underside of the Auchinleck Loft served as a roof for the vestry, the Common Loft was boarded to the floor and the portion thus screened off served the purpose of a school-house. On the right of the pulpit, and fixed at a slightly higher elevation, was the Barskimming Loft, a ridiculous and incongruous perch. Like the rest of the lofts, it had its own separate entry from the outside; and thus the genteel occupants were saved from mingling with the common herd of the congregation.

Mr. Auld turned to James Armour.

"Just above the Ballochmyle Loft, Jeems."

"Whatever you say, Mr. Auld. But, of coorse, the drip might be coming frae the ridge—and running doon. It'll mean a thorough examination, and there's nae saying off-hand just what would be needed or what the expense might be. You canna estimate on a job like that, Mr. Auld—the Session'll understand that."

"Aye . . . And you'll want payment for your examination, Jeems?"

"Weel . . . if the job's coming my way I would throw that in for nothing."

"But there'll need to be no drops on the Ballochmyle Loft this Sabbath—inspection or no inspection. We canna have Ballochmyle drookit whatever the ways o't, Jeems."

"Weel, Mr. Auld, if the rain keeps on it'll no' be lang till we see the place; and I micht be able to peg it till sic time as we get the trouble righted."

"Do that, Jeems. I'll be in consultation with the Session this verra nicht."

"I'll send over one o' the boys in daylicht to sit in the loft till we trace the hole, Mr. Auld—and then I'll just bide your orders."

"Verra well, Jeems: I'll send orders wi' Robin Gibb or Mr. Fisher—so that there'll be nae delay. Guid-nicht to you."

"Guid-nicht, Mr. Auld—and thank ye. You can lippen on me."

James Armour was the leading Machlin mason and something of a wright as well. He did a good business in the town and among the surrounding farmers; and occasionally he did important work for the gentry. Often he did work as far away as Tarbolton in the west and Cumnock in the south. He even journeyed as far away as the Duke of Argyll's castle at Inveraray. But though prosperous and a good builder, Armour was mean and grasping. He was not the man to allow any sentiment to blur his vision.

When he saw William Auld was safely across the intervening breadth of Loudon Street and heading down the Cowgate, James hurried across the yard to Nance Tinnock's howff and entered by the top door into the upper room. Nance, though usually below on the Backcauseway floor, happened to be putting an armful of peats on the fire in the upper room.

"It's yourself, Mr. Armour—it's turned a wild night."

"It has that, Nance. Aye, it has that. Bring me a gill, Nance—I'm no' biding. I've a bit job on i' the kirk; an' it's a cauld hole to work in."

" 'Deed and it's a cauld hole to worship in."

"Well . . . that'll bring no harm to your trade, Nance."

"Folk'll never want an excuse to ca' in here, Mr. Armour. I mind my mither—God keep her—saying to me when I was a bit slip o' a lassie rinsing out the pint stoups: 'As lang's folk have the fear o' God about them, they'll aey need a drink.' I'll fetch ye your gill, Mr. Armour. Aye . . . I saw Mr. Auld away roun' the corner there a wee while back; he'd be awa' up seeing Tammy Douglas: I hear he's gey near through . . ."

As Nance, a motherly middle-aged woman, shuffled down the narrow wooden stair, Armour fished out his snuff-box, inserted a spatulate thumb and conveyed a spoonful of snuff to his red-haired nostrils.

He took the drink from Nance and counted the coppers grudgingly into her hand.

"That's Holy Willie just slipped in, Mr. Armour."

The hard core in Armour's eye sharpened to a gimlet point.

"Thank ye, Nance."

"I thought I would just mention it. There's some folks better to ken as little about your business——"

"That's right, Nance. Damned, that bluidy man's jinking round every corner in Machlin. It's a wonder he's no' praying Tammy Douglas into the next warl'."

"He's a meeting wi' Mr. Auld in half-an-hour—and then he's for the death-bed."

"God forgive me, Nance; but I could never abide Willie Fisher praying on my death-bed——"

"When you're on your death-bed, Mr. Armour, you're gey glad to have anybody praying for you."

"Ah, damned, Nance, but I've a notion Willie Fisher would never pray me into Heaven—and I ken as weel as onybody a death-bed's no' to be joked about. But thank ye, Nance woman; I'll just slip out now while I have the chance. Guid-nicht wi' ye."

James Armour was one of Nance's best customers and, though she didn't like him, she was careful not to offend him. Nance found she had to practise an astute diplomacy and be ever on the alert to observe the foibles of her customers. There was no lack of drinking-houses in Machlin. There was Poosie Nancie's just across the breadth of the sward, and near it, on the other side of the narrow Cowgate, John Dow's Whitefoord Arms, the principal inn and howff in the town. But there were folks who didn't like to have their drinking habits made too public, and it was easy and convenient for them to slip in from the high ground into her upper chamber, or to jowk round the corner of the Backcauseway and seat themselves snugly in the corner of her front room.

Nance knew that none of her regulars would ever darken Poosie Nancie's door—that was for the riff-raff and passing vagrants. And though the Elbow Tavern had better accommodation than she could boast, and Ronald's meeting-house—also with its back to the kirkyard—was altogether more elegant, what with its top-floor ballroom, they were both much too public for douce drinking. But Nance knew that her greatest asset lay in her discretion: she never divulged a secret.

Holy Willie was as a man set apart. He was welcome to no howff in Machlin. Willie was the leading elder. It was his sacred duty to spy, for the glory of God, on everybody's movements; to listen to every scrap of gossip and scandal; to note every break in any of the Kirk's innumerable ordinances—and to report everything he saw and heard to Mr. Auld and his session of elders.

That Willie was a hypocrite, a sneak and a venomous-tongued liar nobody doubted—not even Mr. Auld. But Willie was feared. Behind him lay the unchallenged authority of the parish minister and the machinery of the Kirk Session. And the machinery of the Session was not to be opposed by any man in Scotland, unless he was possessed of considerable wealth and power—though even the great folks found it more convenient to have the Session working with them than against them.

Of himself, Holy Willie was as poor a specimen of manhood as Machlin could boast. He was always tippling. And though his breath, night or morning, never failed to reek of ale or spirit, he was seldom drunk to the point of incapability. He managed to dither about with brittle irritable gestures, forever peering with his weak foxy eyes, never able to look anyone or any object straight on but always from a foxy sidelong glance: his neck forever craning sideways in sitting down, standing up or walking about.

Four years previously, Old Fisher had died and Willie and his wife, Jean Hewatson, had come into possession of Montgarswood, a tidy farm lying out on the Sorn road. It was Jean and the children who did most of the farm work, since Willie was so much occupied with the work of the Lord. At the age of forty-seven, Holy Willie felt the burden of this work heavy and responsible.

Willie always took the Sabbath collections from the lofts occupied by the gentry. Access to the lofts was gained from flights of stone steps on the outside wall of the kirk. On descending these of a Sabbath, Willie would select a few small coins and, unperceived, drop them into the top of his kneeboots. It was a poor Sabbath Willie couldn't make his week's ale-money out of the pilfered offerings.

Not that he would have gone dry for lack of a copper. He could always depend on someone trying to buy off his ecclesiastical spying by standing him a drink.

Nance Tinnock didn't like Willie and she would as soon have seen the devil entering her howff. But she knew his power and knew how he had to be placated—especially for the sake of her customers. To-night she was glad to find Willie was not prolonging his stay.

"An important meeting o' the Session the night, Mistress Tinnock . . . Oooh aye. Mr. Auld and myself . . . oooh aye, and the Session. Very important business. The parish is straying from the paths of righteousness and the wicked are ettling for to flourish like the green bay tree. Like the green bay tree. Oooh aye; but the Kirk maun ever be vigilant in stamping out sin, Mistress Tinnock. Especially the sins o' the flesh . . . oooh a wicked and adulterous generation is growing up among us and we must grapple wi' them and cast them into the furnace o' correction—for the good of their immortal souls, Mistress Tinnock. For the good of their immortal souls. That's how Mr. Auld commanded me. 'Mr. Fisher,' said Mr. Auld, 'ye maun go out into the highways and by-ways and keep a sharp eye on the backsliders, so that we may yet have time to grapple wi' them for their correction.' Aye . . . and after the Session meeting there's nae rest for me. I'll need to visit Tammy Douglas and wrestle with his soul. The soul's what matters, for the flesh withereth. Aye; and the flesh is verra weak."

"Verra weak indeed, Mr. Fisher."

"Oooh aye; we maun aey be grappling."

"You'll get your reward, Mr. Fisher."

"Reward, eh? Ah—but all the glory shall be His. Amen, amen. Weel . . . I'll need to push on down the Cowgate . . . a maist important meeting the nicht . . . Ye havena seen Jamie Lamie? No, no; Jeems would be busy . . . Aye: I'll no' say guid-nicht the now, seeing how I might stop in on my road up to poor Tammy's . . . Aye, on a lang sair nicht o' a deathbed praying, a body needs a wee sensation o' refreshment . . . oooh aye."

Willie fidgeted with his plaid, folded it well about his narrow drooping shoulders and shuffled unsteadily over the cobbles—but not before he had cast a quick furtive leftwards glance towards Gavin Hamilton's back-door and Ronald's entry.

The minister's room at the Machlin manse was a square sombre room with heavy furniture and many heavily-bound leather volumes of theological writings.

Two massive pewter candlesticks supporting two thick tallow candles sat on the table at Mr. Auld's seat, and provided, in addition to the firelight, a flickering illumination.

Yet the room suited Mr. Auld, with his lofty forehead, his long pointed nose and his long square-cut jaw.

It was a bachelor's room and the room of an eighteenth century man of God. It was as square and sharp-angled as Mr. Auld was square and sharp-angled. It was wholly uncompromising as the Reverend William, stout Old Light theologian, was uncompromising.

Mr. Auld was presiding at a full meeting of the Session in Machlin. Usually they met in the kirk; but on a specially cold night, or for Mr. Auld's convenience, they met at the manse. Willie Fisher sat on his right hand. Next to Willie sat James Lamie, a strict narrow-visioned man with little imaginative faculty. Lamie was a disciplinarian who regretted that the Kirk had given up its uniquely-varied instruments of torture. For though he would not have admitted to a belief in torture, Lamie was of the opinion that physical chastisement was by far the best corrective for evil-doers. Lamie was step-father to Wee Jamie Smith, and Smith had good cause to know how devilishly he carried his theory into practice.

Next in order round the table sat Thomas Guthrie, Hugh Aird, John Siller and James Smith. They were all men over middle age. Fisher and Lamie were the active elders—it was they who kept Auld versed in every minute nicety of Machlin life.

Auld disliked William Fisher and treated him with brusque consideration. But he knew Fisher's value: his reports were very necessary and Auld knew how to interpret them, separating, often at a glance, the chaff of malicious scandal from the wheat of cardinal sin.

To-night the Session was about to compare a couple proved guilty of the heinous sin of fornication. This fornication was no less heinous in that it was pre-nuptial. That the couple had married before the evidence of their sin had seen the light of day in no way excused them.

Mr. Auld had long been made aware of the peculiar fact that, when any of the congregation had to appear on the sessional carpet for a sexual offence, he could count on a full attendance from his lay-shepherds. Indeed, no other sin so excited their holy zeal for probing into the mystery of the passionate relationship between man and woman and the theological relationship between both and the Presbyterian conception of God.

But before they began their review of the evidence—the couple would be compeared later—Robert Burns was admitted to the minister's room.

Robert, recognising Auld, approached him and handed him his certificate of character from Tarbolton Kirk Session.

Auld looked it over.

"I have here," he addressed the Session, "a certificate from Doctor Woodrow's parish for Mr. Robert Burns and his family. It is a clean bill. And what number make up your family, Mr. Burns? Perhaps you will give us some details?"

"There is my widowed mother, coming into her fifty-first year. Next to me, and sharing the tenancy of Mossgiel with me, is my brother Gilbert. He is a year younger than me—that is, about twenty-four years old. Then my sister Agnes, about twenty-two; my sister Annabella, about twenty; my brother William, about seventeen; my brother John, about fifteen; and finally my sister Isa, about thirteen years old. These, sir, constitute my family. In addition, my cousin, Robert Allan from Old Rome Forest in the Parish of Dundonald, will worship in Machlin; and I have as boys John Blane, David Hutchieson and William Patrick."

Auld eyed him with some surprise.

"And do you regularly exercise your family in religious devotion, Mr. Burns?"

"Regularly within the twenty-four hours, Mr. Auld."

Willie Fisher held out his hand for the certificate; but Auld ignored him. "Well, Mr. Burns, I extend a welcome to you on behalf of myself and the Session. You are settled, I see, in the farm of Mossgiel?"

"That is so, Mr. Auld."

Fisher said: "Your father died, Mr. Burns, not so long ago when you were in the farm of Lochlea?"

Robert nodded.

"You'll have a sub-let then of Mossgiel from Gavin Hamilton?"

"My brother and I are joint partners in the venture."

"You'll be a particular friend of Gavin Hamilton maybe?"

"I don't know what you mean."

"Oh well: we'll soon find out," said Fisher, noting the hard cold look that Auld directed to him.

"Is there any reason why I should not be a friend of Mr. Hamilton?"

Auld interposed: "The Session is not concerned with your friends, Mr. Burns. Please do not think that the Session has anything against Mr. Hamilton that need interest you. You know your religious duties, Mr. Burns, and you know the ordinances of the Kirk. I trust there will be no reason during your stay with us for the Session to have any cause to find fault with you. If I can be of any assistance to you, or you feel that you need my help or advice at any time, Mr. Burns, do not hesitate to seek me out at the manse here. And I know that the gentlemen of the Session will be only too glad in the way of their duty to be of assistance to you and your family in Mossgiel."

Robert had always regarded the Reverend William Auld as a very stern and unbending man. He watched Auld as he spoke, noted the cold fearless eye and the square purposeful jaw. But withal, he found the minister kindly and civilly disposed towards him. He thanked him and retired.

The moment he had gone, Fisher hastened to explain what he had meant by his reference to Gavin Hamilton.

"There is something of a mystery about the way Burns came to Mossgiel, Mr. Auld. From what I can gather, there was some kind of a secret arrangement in the back-end of last year atween Burns and Hamilton. There was a bit of litigation over Lochlea with David MacLure, the Ayr merchant. There has been a lot of nasty rumours anent that business that have never properly been cleared up. But I'm thinking Burns must be gey big with Hamilton to have landed so nicely into Mossgiel."

Lamie said: "I dinna like his connection wi' Hamilton. But he seems an honest-enough character by the look of him. He spoke up fair and manly enough."

Hugh Aird said: "I must say but I liked the look of him myself; and if there is ocht atween him and Gavin Hamilton it will not be long in coming to the forefront."

Auld interposed with a dry precision: "I must remind you that the Session has enough on its hands without concerning itself with idle gossip. I have had to speak before, Mr. Fisher, about idle gossip concerning Hamilton. He is not a man to be trifled with; and when we strike we must be sure of our ground. And maybe now, gentlemen, we will proceed to the business of the evening."

Leaving Auld's, Robert took the footpath behind the manse to the Bellman's Vennel and cut down leftwards to the Cross. There he paused for a moment to see if anyone was about and then crossed over to the High Street to Richmond's house only to find that John was still working at Gavin Hamilton's. He was determined not to go home without seeing one or other of his Machlin friends, and remembering that he had seen James Lamie, Smith's step-father, at the manse, he called next door, at the shop, to find James ready to put up the shutters.

"I'm glad to see you, Robin: it's a dirty sair nicht and I could do fine wi' an hour's crack round Pigeon Johnnie's bleezing ingle."

"Well spoken, Jamie; and I'm the lad to join you. I've just been afore the Session at the manse and presented my character from Tarbolton. I could do wi' a drink."

But just as Smith was about to bring out the wooden shutters from the back shop, the door-bell rang, and in came Lizzie Miller seeking a twist of linen thread.

"Have you met Miss Miller?" inquired Smith.

"I have not yet had that honour," said Robin, his speech stiffening into formal English as it invariably did on such occasions.

"Here's your chance now, Lizzie. This is Robert Burns you've heard me talking about—from Mossgiel."

Robert and Lizzie shook hands.

"I've heard quite a bit about you, Mr. Burns."

"Nothing in my disfavour, I trust?"

"Oh no . . . not yet onyway."

"Robert's a fine dancer, Lizzie. We'll need to have a set at Ronald's some night."

"That would be fine."

"I'll hold you to that promise, Miss Miller."

"Oh . . . I havena promised onything, Mr. Burns."

"I'll take it as a promise nevertheless."

"You'll enjoy Robert's company, Lizzie: I can assure you of that. What about a foursome along the Barskimming road some nicht—you could bring Jean Armour along wi' you?"

" 'Deed, I have more to do wi' my time, Jamie, than stravaig the Barskimming road in the dark. Give me my thread, if you please, and I'll be on my way. I've plenty to do if you havena . . . Good-nicht, Mr. Burns: I suppose we'll be seeing you about Machlin?"

"That you shall, madam—and I could think of a better road than the mud-track that leads to Barskimming!"

"I've no doubt. Maybe I could think on one mysel'."

Robert had noted her closely. Noted the good quality of her dress and the elegance of her silk-fringed shawl. He had also noted her regular features and the friendly light that danced in her eyes. Miss Miller was very definitely a cut above the average Machlin maiden; and she was fully conscious of her worth.

When she had gone Smith said: "You'll like her, Robin: I can see she's taken to you."

"Oh . . .?"

"She's a sharper, Betty. Cut you off by the wrists as quick as look at you—if she's no' interested."

"And who is she when she's at home?"

"Plenty of money. The father's a joiner; but he also owns the Sun Inn at the head o' the Bellman's Vennel—whaur Doctor MacKenzie lodges . . . There's a wheen o' them run thegither: Jean Armour——"

"You have a notion of Jean Armour—or was Jean Armour for me?"

"What's the odds: they're both toppers."

"I'm going to like Machlin, Jamie."

"Damned true you are. Wait till you meet them all. Apart frae the respectable dames, there's Maggie Borland, Jean Mitchell and Bet Barbour—they don't need ony coaxing. And how're things doing at Mossgiel?"

"Doing fine, Jamie. I'm reading nothing but farming books now—and I'm making a special study o' ploughs. Success in farming depends a lot on the quality of your ploughing. James Small has a maist interesting volume on ploughs. But what interest has a draper in farming problems?"

"Still and on, Robin: I'm glad to hear you're determined to make a success of your new place. You've had a lot of bad luck and I hope fortune changes for you. Mind you, I've a lot to learn in this trade. But I know you canna succeed in ony work unless you apply yourself—and what goes for the drapering goes for farming—or clerking, like Jock Richmond."

15

"That's sensible enough. Well . . . if hard work and constant application will make me a successful farmer, I'm certainly laying the foundation of a grand fortune."

"That's the shutters up now. We'll have a caup o' ale in Dow's—maybe Jock Richmond will be there waiting on us. There'll be some of the boys there onyway."

They bent their heads and hurried up by the Cross and entered John Dow's on the corner of the Cowgate. Pigeon Johnnie, as he was nicknamed, gave them a rough welcome.

Dow was of medium height. He was built like a barrel and had a coarse red face and a hard eye. He cursed and swore more than any ten men in Machlin. But though rough and violent of speech, he was good-natured and enjoyed his drink as much as any of his customers. His son, Sandy, drove the coach between Machlin and Kilmarnock.

"Weel . . . what are you twa beggars after now? How are you, Rab? A puir day for the ploughing. Writing ony mair o' yon bluidy poetry o'yours? What? Man, a poem withouten a guid swatch o' houghmagandie's nae worth o' gabbing. Gang your ways ben, Rab. Damned, you're aey welcome here. The beggars i' Machlin here are a set o' libbit cattle. Except Jamie here. Our Jamie's a beggar for the weemin, Rab—he'll hae ye on a houghmagandie ploy gin ye get better acquaint . . . Weel . . . there's your yill, boys! Draw up your seats to the bleeze—— Oh, here's Ga'n Hamilton's scrivener—looking like a bluidy ghost as usual—wha kens but you're steerin' up some sappy hizzie, Jock! It's maybe Racer Jess! Oh, I wouldna put Jess past ye, Jock. Aye: I ken fine you've your een on Jenny Surgeoner. But you're makin' a big mistake, Jock laddie. Bone Lizzie Miller, aye, or Jean Armour there." Johnnie jerked his thumb over his shoulder in the direction of Armour's house through the wall. "What's that? You're nae judge o' a hizzie. Aye, you're a puir crowd o' poachers—Geordie Gibson's jurr'll be about your stretch. What dae you say, Rab? Have you no' picked your fancy i' the Machlin jads? Mind ye, Rab: I think ye'd be a grand judge o' a ticht-hippit hizzie—and, fegs, I'll warrant you've rolled many a one in your plaidie.

Well . . . they're yours, lads, when you're young. If you canna steer them up and haud them gaun now, you'll never do it. There's an auld sang frae Carrick, Rab, that you should ken: 'Oh, gie my love brose, lassies, gie my love brose and butter, for nane in Carrick wi' him can gie a lass her supper.' "

Robert fished in his pockets and drew out a fold of paper, uncorked his ink-horn and wet the point of his quill.

"Come over that again, Johnnie—that's a new one to me."

"Damn it, Rab, dinna tell me you've missed that one? Richt then, tak' it down. I've nae doubt but you'll be able to cobble the lines a bit after your own fancy."

It was a rich song, bawdy as a bare buttock, and Pigeon Johnnie could do it rare justice.

"That's a grand song, Johnnie—if you think on more of the like, be sure to let me know."

"Another o' the same, eh, as Davit said o' the psalms? Ah, you're a randy beggar, Rab. Man, the sangs I've heard sung in this room and the verses I've heard recited—they would warm the cockles o' your heart to all eternity. I'll hae a word wi' the wife: she's a better memory for them than I hae. When she was younger, she used to sing a beauty: The Nine'll Please. I'll tell you what: you mak' a sang on the Whitefoord Arms here, and I'll see that the wife gives you the richt words o' some o' thae auld ballents. Aye, man; but nowadays they've gotten sae mealy-mouthed that they havena the same stomach for the auld ways o' putting things. Well, lads . . . I'll need to leave you: I ken you'll hae plenty to jaw about. Gie the bell a ring there, Rab, gin you want your stoup filled."

It was a pleasant room they were given in the Whitefoord Arms: a small back room, with a low boarded ceiling and a great yellow candle suspended above the table in a black iron sconce; a wide fire-place with a blaze of peats and logs on the open hearth—and a small square window looking directly across the path to James Armour's house.

It was known, and had been known for many a day, as the boys' room—where sons were in no danger of meeting with their fathers or fathers meeting with their sons. It was convenient also to the back-door, where a lad might escape into the lane and so into the Cowgate.

Smith and Richmond, William Hunter and David Brice had long used the room for their regular meetings, for though they might sometimes take a turn to the Elbow Tavern or Nance Tinnock's, or Willie Gray's in the Bellman's Vennel, or Willie Ronald's just below Nance Tinnock's—especially if there were dancing in Willie's top-floor ballroom—they invariably began their evening in the back room of John Dow's inn.

Robert was to know many a happy night there with his cronies. And to-night, stimulated by a new bawdy ballad of the old Carrick days, his mood was genial.

Already he was beginning to polish the old rough lines, but retaining all the bold unashamed uninhibited directness of the old phrases.

"I suppose I'll never learn sense. Here was I determined never to waste an hour on poetry again. There was me up in Mossgiel coming in for my meals, saying 'I will be wise,' like a bluidy idiot, and putting my nose in an agricultural treatise. And here I am! An old bawdy song and I feel like throwing every care to the winds and taking to the roads like the tinklers."

"And why not?" asked Wee Jamie. "The tinklers know how to enjoy life. I was in Poosie Nancie's once—a bit o' business took me in . . . God! you should have seen the fun they were having!"

Richmond shook his head. "You'll find only the damnedest ne'er-do-weels in Gibson's howff."

"I don't know," said Robert. "Ne'er-do-weels often do verra weel . . . Aye . . . there's many a beggar tramping the roads, bedding in a barn or dry ditch, enjoys life more than ony staid stay-at-home."

Richmond was not to be won from his position.

"On a night like this, for example? No, no, Rab. That's a romantic notion you've gotten. I'm not going to compare honest living wi' a lousy pack of cadging gangrels. They're scoundrels and vagabonds, every one o' them; liars, cheats and a damned sight worse. I'd press-gang the whole bluidy lot to the plantations—and guid riddance."

Smith was indignant: "I'm surprised at you, Jock. Trace ony o' our pedigrees back a hundred years—aye, or less—and damned few o' us came frae ony better stock than ye'll find in Poosie Nancie's the nicht—or maist nichts!"

"You're right, Jamie. There's some grand fellows amang them. Sailors maltreated by the infidels—maybe their ears cut off or a hand hagged off at the wrist; mony an old soldier crippled frae the wars . . . Oh, there're bad ones among them, just as there is onywhere. I'll warrant there's bad ones in the Machlin Kirk Session——"

"My step-father for one," said Smith. "If ever there was an evil-hearted auld beggar, it's James Lamie. A black-hearted bastard. I'm for leaving him one o' thae days. And what about Holy Willie? I'd rather mix with vagrants in Gibson's house than mix wi' yon yellow-bellied grass-snake."

"Willie Fisher? I saw him at the Session the night. But a grass-snake's harmless, Jamie; and I doubt nor Holy Willie is."

"You're right there, Rab. He's got his knife in Gavin Hamilton too—watches his every move."

"Oh! What's he got against Hamilton, Jock?"

"Hamilton and Daddy Auld dinna pull thegither—hate the sight of each other. Hamilton's strong on the New Light. Doctor MacKenzie and Gavin are gey thick on the moderates. They don't give a damn for Daddy Auld or his Session either."

"Mind you," said Robert, "when I first heard Daddy Auld thundering from the pulpit I thought he was a terror and as bigoted an Old Light outside o' Black Jock o' Kilmarnock. But when I spoke to him to-night he was damned civil. No doubt he's bigoted like the rest o' his kind; but I got the notion that he was square enough in his honesty. How do you lads find him?"

"For me," said Richmond, "he's a narrow-minded black-hearted old runt. I've never had a civil word from him. Look at Fisher! Auld listens to every slimy tale Fisher takes to him. He watches every girl and woman in the parish, and whenever he gets wind that they are in the family way, off he scuttles to Daddy Auld and, before long, they're compearing afore the Session. There isn't a dirtier rat in Machlin than Willie Fisher—unless it's William Auld that listens to him."

"That's only half true," said Smith. "Admittedly Willie Fisher's all you say he is. But d'you think Auld doesna see through Fisher? Sure he does. Auld canna go creeping through the parish—he lets Fisher do that. Fisher does all the dirty snooking for the Session. Mind you, I don't hold with it. I think it's rotten. But Auld has his way of looking at things—and that happens to be the Kirk's way. But—allowing for that—I dont' think Auld's a hypocrite. In any case, Auld's in the grip o' the Session more than you would think. I know Lamie, and Lamie would damn soon make complaint to the Presbytery in Ayr if Auld didna carry out the ordinances— especially in regard to fornication. You can see Holy Willie's jaws slavering a mile off when he discovers a good fornication. Lamie would rather gang without his brose than miss a compearing for fornication. And they're a' the same. Auld wouldna last ten minutes if he failed to compear the fornicators—you surely know that, Jock?"

"Maybe, Jamie. But I don't see you can whitewash Auld by blackening the Session. Auld can sway them whatever way he fancies. What do you say, Rab?"

"I don't know Auld well enough yet—and I don't know the Session. But I know plenty of ministers that take a commonsense view o' Kirk discipline, and manage fine without all this bluidy inquisition. I often talked wi' John MacMath, Doctor Woodrow's assistant in Tarbolton. Well, MacMath has no time for half of this nonsense—and I know he wouldna have a man like Holy Willie near him. No . . . on the question o' the Kirk, I'm all for Gavin Hamilton and Doctor MacKenzie. MacKenzie has as common-sense a view o' religion as you'll find anywhere. There's a new spirit abroad. Thinkers know that you canna make a man religious by forcing him to attend the service on the Sabbath and observe a lot of ordinances that have nothing to do with religion. Scotland's been held down by the holy trinity o' Session, Presbytery and Synod too long. Battering hell out of folk is no' letting heaven into them. And that's what the Kirk's been doing since Knox started with Mary Stewart—knocking hell out of them and fear into them. And they use the fear of hell as a hangman's whip to hold the folk in order. But folks are getting sense—aye, plenty folk never lost their sense. Take that song o' John Dow's. Take Green Grow the Rashes, Andro and his Cutty Gun, The Lass o' Livingston—and mony others. Take the Errock Stane: 'As I sat on the Errock Stane surveying far and near, up came a Cameronian man wi' a' his preaching gear. He threw his Bible ower the hill amang the threshy gerss; but the Solemn League and Covenant—' the Solemn League and Covenant, mind you . . . and you ken the rest! And they tell you that this generation's the worst Scotland ever saw! That folk are irking at the Kirk's discipline! It's plain from the auld bawdy songs that there were aey folk in Scotland had a common-sense view of religion. Only, the difference now is that among the clergy themselves there's the beginnings of intelligent revolt. And we've got to rally to the reforming clergy. Any attack on them is an attack on us; any attack on us is an attack on them. Between common-sense folk and common-sense clergy we'll make a clean sweep of all this black-hearted bigotry . . . Auld will never reform; you canna expect him at his age, especially if what you say is true about his elders. But he can be held in check. We can draw his claws if he sticks them out too far. But what has Gavin done to incur their wrath?"

"Auld claims that Hamilton owes some money that he collected for the poor. It seems he refuses to hand it over for some reason or other."

"Then it must be a good reason, Jock. Gavin Hamilton would never tamper wi' the Poor's money."

"I believe there's something about the fact that he once set off on a journey to Carrick on the Lord's Day."

"Damned bigotry!" said Smith.

"I agree, Jamie. Mind you: I think they're after Gavin just because he takes the common-sense line. And if they can let loose the holy beagles on his trail, ony scent will do. No doubt Daddy Auld has his vanity—and Gavin will have been a sore thorn in his flesh. Maybe we'll see some fun yet in Machlin. Daddy Auld and Holy Willie against Gavin Hamilton and John MacKenzie . . ."

"I don't know, Rab. You don't know Auld. He'll tramp out ony opposition without mercy. Auld can be as double-dyed as the devil. He's a bully—bark like a bluidy bluidhound—but bite? I'm no' sure except when he has all the authority of the Session behind him."

"You think that's why he employs Fisher to do his snooking?"

"I do, Rab. And Fisher's the delegate to the Ayr Presbytery. But he keeps Fisher under his thumb so that he'll never suspect just what a coward Auld really is. But to hell, Rab: we're no' here to spend the nicht discussing Auld and the Machlin Session, are we?"

"Oh, we could do worse, Jock. You see, I must get my bearings here. You forget that though I'm no stranger to Machlin I don't know the place intimately. Tarbolton I know—every stick and stone of it. Maybe I am of an enquiring turn of mind; but I like to know things. Men and their manners—living—that's a grand study, lads."

"And women?"

"Naturally. And, coming to that, there seems to be plenty to excite my curiosity hereabouts."

"Aye—they'll excite more nor your curiosity, Rab."

"That was a beauty I met the night, Jamie. Lizzie Miller, Jock—you'll ken her?"

"Fine. But she's gotten a guid conceit 'o' hersel'."

"None the waur o' that, is she?"

"Maybe no. But I don't like them when they get their heads in the air."

"No more do I . . . I know the kind, Jock. I know the proud haughty dames. I was once a silly fool thinking women were beings to be placed on a pedestal and worshipped from a distance. But that was long ago. No: proud or humble, high or low, I'll suit myself with them."

Richmond laughed.

"I've learned that lesson too, Rab. Fair game: that's what I say."

"Aye; but game: that's the point, Jock. What do you say, Jamie?"

"I like them. Only I like too damned mony of them. I can never make up my mind. I've never managed to get a walk with Lizzie Miller, though—or Jean Armour. And by God, Rab, I wouldna mind a nicht with either o' them."

"Aye . . . I can see some merry times ahead. I havena been above three times in Machlin Kirk, but each time there were two or three for the cutty stool. You have a reputation here to live up to, Jamie."

"And I fully intend to keep up the parish record."

"It's time you were started then."

"It's no joking matter, Rab," said Richmond: "they'll never get me to sit on their stool of repentance. I'll flee the town first."

"And who do you fancy, Jock? What about that nursemaid o' Gavin's—Mary Campbell, is it?"

"Mary Campbell! A Hielan bitch. I made a pass at her once and she was for howling the place down. She's pockmarked anyway."

"I thought there was something about her of a superior kind, Jock. Of course, I've only passed the time o' day with her. So she's Highland?"

"Aye—Arran or somewhere thereabouts. Sings Erse like a bluidy heathen."

"Sings, eh?"

"Aye; but it's aey the same tune. No: Jenny Surgeoner is my fancy about here."

"A nice lassie Jenny," agreed Smith. "Even if she is a few years older than you."

"She's fine," said Richmond.

"I'm glad to hear that, Jock. A good lass is worth hanging on to."

"Oh, I'm no' hanging on to her, Rab. I've no notion of getting married: that's the last straw. A pitcher o' milk's better nor keeping a cow. What about filling the stoups? Right: I'll go ben. If Pigeon Johnnie comes in he'll start blethering again."

23

"Or he might give us another bawdy song?"

"Listen! Hear that? If you were through in Poosie Nancie's here and now you'd hear bawdy songs."

Across the narrow lane of the Cowgate and through the wall came the sound of boisterous merriment.

"That's the gangrels in Poosie's! Drunk as a puggie every one o' them—and singing every bawdy song frae Maidenkirk to John o' Groats."

"Come on!" said Robin, "we'll go in and see the fun."

"What! In that lousy hole?" Richmond screwed up his fastidious nose.

"I'm willing," said Smith. "It'll be good fun."

"You'll no' get a drink in there."

"Richt then, Jock: we'll have the drink here afore we go in."

Richmond gathered the stoups and went out.

"I'll go wi' you, Rab—even if Jock doesna. There's a bit o' the snob in Jock, seeing he's clerk to Hamilton. But I'll go wi' you, Rab. I know why you want to go. Everything's grist to your mill. That's how you're a poet."

"It's no' only that, Jamie. I work hard: I try to do my best and bow my neck to the yoke of affliction. But I'm no' Job; I'm Rab Burns: Rab the Ranter. I've got blood in my veins; and, by God, it's no' stagnant. And sometimes, Jamie, I feel I canna thole another minute; then I must have company. I'm fine the now: never felt better. But I'm not always like this. And then I get depressed, melancholy. Melancholy—right down into the pit o' despair. Aye . . . and bide there for weeks. You understand that; but Jock doesna. Jock's a heady lad wi' a good grip on his senses. You and me, Jamie: chicken-hearted gulls at bottom. You've got to have a good callous round your soul to prosper in this world. And that's what you and me havena got. We're too bluidy thin-skinned and sensitive."

Richmond returned with the stoups.

"Still in the notion o' going next door? I should be getting back, Rab, and doing another hour's copying for Gavin—he's riding into Ayr in the morning."

"Please yourself, Jock. Nobody's pressing you."

Richmond went back to his copying at Gavin Hamilton's. Robin and Jamie Smith stood outside Poosie Nancie's door and listened to the merriment that rioted in the low-ceilinged room.

"Come on," said Robin. "This sounds too glorious to be passed by."

They raised the sneck of the door and went in.

THE BENMOST BORE

Gulls swarmed behind the plough; rooks followed a safe distance behind; lapwings tossed and tumbled and beat above the ponies' heads. Robert Allan, a cousin from Old Rome Forest near Kilmarnock, led the horses; Willie Patrick, the eight years old herd-boy, was brisk with his pointed wooden gaud to see that the beasts pulled evenly on the traces; Robert Burns was doubled between the plough-stilts.

It had turned a fine morning after some early rain and despite the chill wind that blew across the wide valley of the River Ayr. The valley dipped from the bare exposed ridge of Mossgiel farm and rose, far on the other side, to the soft slopes of the Dalmellington hills whose outlines stood clear against the cold sky. The hills themselves lay in pools of colour: grey-blue, dun and black, with bright patchwork depressions of drifted snow. The oblique sunlight sharpened the spurs and ridges in glittering light.

In the grey-green valley patches of gorse, whin and shrub mottled the landscape. The woodland and shaws, especially along the river's banks, were black and gold, while here and there (escaping the gilding sun's rays) a solitary tree raised the frozen ecstasy of its ebony arms.

It was a glorious scene, cold and clean-cut in its scars but caressing in its swelling contours. Nowhere else in Kyle, Cunninghame or Carrick was there to be found an equal prospect where vista merged into vista; where the eye lingeringly caressed the sweep of its own vision and no ugliness of man or of nature obtruded to mar or to blemish.

Coming down the slant of the ridge Robin would raise his eyes from the furrow and take in a sweep of the scene. It cooled his mind and strengthened his spirit.

But the cooling of his mind only served to harden its temper. Out of the memory-mist of Poosie Nancie's the images began to separate and sharpen, only to be sucked down again into the noise and clatter, the smoke and smells, the riot and dissipation of the evening.

Sometimes he saw himself sitting there with Jamie Smith on a box-seat on the far side of the fire while in the centre of the floor the gangrels danced and leapt and cursed and swore, wept and laughed and cried.

And then to a fiddler's scraping, and filled with an exultation not unmixed with Johnnie Pigeon's whisky, he had joined in a reel with a couple of tinkler-jads, linking up and down the floor with an arm in either oxter.

The songs he had heard, the scraps of tales; the slack-mouthed whore with the ready wit; the mixty-maxty muddle of uproarious merriment (with Black Geordie Gibson himself coming in threatening to throw one and all in the dung-midden if they didn't keep quiet) . . .

And the last scene with all of them lying heads and thraws on the floor, exhausted, drunk, asleep or making love; with Geordie's serving-jurr, Nancy Wilson, creeping in to lay herself down beside the sailor whose ears had been cut off by the Algerian pirates, but who doubtless had enough placks in his pocket to pay for Nancy's caresses!

Raise his eyes to the distant hills as he might, he could not rid his mind of the scene . . .

But gradually the frenzied riot of images quietened down and he began to impose an order on them. He began to extricate individuals from the mass; he was able to hold an individual in outline and hold the image static; to fill in the outline; to move the figure to his own rhythm; to rationalise the words; give them coherence, point and form; to cut away all the ragged and blurred edges; to geal the flux and then mould it; to establish a memorable rhythm; to press into a pattern . . .

And only when he set his characters in the round and heard the beat of the measure did the scene reanimate itself. And then words came with his thoughts and line tumbled and trembled on line as the thoughts were word-symbolised. The howff became intellectually efflorescent . . . Even the light in the gimlet eyes of the frightened rat, in its backward glance, outshone the light of the noonday sun until the benmost bore of his creative faculty could yield no more . . .

"By God, Robin," said his cousin, "I never kenned you plough to better measure."

Robin dragged off his bonnet and dried the sweat from his face.

"Man, Bob, I could drive a furrow frae Mossgiel to Montgomerie's and never look over my shoulder: I could tear up the clods wi' my bare hands."

"By certes, it must be grand stuff that o' Johnnie Dow's."

"Dow's my foot! Rab Burns has a spirit that's no' to be bought in ony howff; and the still's up here."

He tapped his forehead. But to Bob Allan he might have been talking Greek.

ASSURANCE DOUBLY SURE

Gilbert, who still slept with Robin, sat in their attic bedroom making preliminary calculations for the farm accounts which he intended to keep in scrupulously accurate detail.

The bedroom was reasonably comfortable. It had a rough wooden floor and the walls were partly lined. It provided adequate head-room since the thatched roof had a very steep rake. And it had the glorious boon of a four-paned glass window in the gable wall.

The window faced towards Machlin and it was possible, through the beech tree branches, to catch a glimpse of the Machlin lum-reek drifting against the background of distant hills.

Through the wooden partition was a smaller bedroom occupied by cousin Bob Allan and Willie Burns. Access to the bedrooms was gained by a wooden stairway set along the inside wall of the kitchen and this made for warmth, privacy and convenience.

Gavin Hamilton had made an excellent job of his alterations to the old farm-house and, by comparison, Lochlea seemed a miserable house. The kitchen and the spence, divided by a full partition, were bigger and brighter and there wasn't another tenant-farmer in the West who could boast a better house—or poorer soil.

Gilbert set down the principal items in his labour cost. Rob and himself, not counting any perquisites, at £7 per annum. Robert Allan at £5 10/- (Allan would have bed and board, a suiting of hoddin grey, two pairs of brogans, three fair and two fast-day

29

holidays in the year); Nancy and Bell would be entered at £4 10/- each; Isa at £2; Willie would get £4 for his first year and the orra lads, John Blane, David Hutchieson and William Patrick, he set down at 30/-, 25/- and 20/- respectively. As perquisites they had their bed in the stable loft, food, suitings, stockings and footwear.

A wages bill coming up for £40 was a heavy liability—and there would be extra help needed at harvest. They would need to practise a strict economy and everyone, would need to pull their weight. For the first five years things would be difficult . . .

Gilbert put away his papers in a stout wooden box and went downstairs for his supper.

His mother was sitting at her usual place by the fire knitting. The girls were busy sewing (Isa was crimping the linens for the Sabbath visit to Machlin Kirk); John was whittling away with a piece of ash in a half-hearted attempt to fashion a plough-handle; Willie Patrick, bright-eyed and red-cheeked, a stocky little fellow of nine summers, was peeling potatoes for the morrow's dinner.

"Come on now, Willie: hurry up with the tatties and get across to your bed. If you don't get to your bed you canna expect to get up in the morning."

"Aye, Mr. Gilbert. D'you think I've enough tatties done noo, Mistress Burns?"

"They'll dae fine, son—on you go. You can tak' a farrel o' bannock wi' ye."

Willie put past the potatoes (the big pot was left on the hearth ready for the chain in the morning), grabbed his bannock from the table, and with a civil good-night escaped to the stable loft.

Mrs. Burns looked up from her knitting to Gilbert, who had taken the stool Willie Patrick had vacated.

"I suppose Rab'll be awa' doon to Machlin?"

"I suppose so."

"He hasna taen Willie wi' him?"

"It's no' likely. Robin's got business in Machlin. I'll wait a bit for Willie. If Robin's not back I'll do the Reading myself."

"That's right, son: your father never missed a Reading as long as he was able."

"Aye . . . but there's nobody I've heard can do the prayer like Robin . . . Put by that stick, John: you're only making a hash of it."

"Rab said the last one I made was a' richt."

"Well . . . if it pleases him . . ."

Isa placed a freshly-crimped linen bonnet on her head. She peered in the narrow mirror. The action annoyed Gilbert. He rose up.

"I'll see to the horse," he said and went out.

As he approached the stable he heard the boys' shrill laughter. He quickened his pace, threw open the door and shouted: "Quiet there! Get to sleep."

Back came Robin's voice.

"Please for laughing, Mr. Gilbert."

When he came down the ladder he found Gilbert in a black mood.

"Don't annoy yourself, man. The laddies need a bit fun—they'll only be young once."

"You're spoiling them. How d'you expect me to order them about their work when you're aey playing the goat wi' them?"

"Man, Gibby, dinna get notions like that into your head. You'll win more work out of them wi' kindness than ever you'll do wi' a harsh word."

"You know best, I suppose. We're waiting on you for the Reading."

"Oh, bide your hurry: I'm no' forgetting. How about the tale of Joseph and his brethren?"

"I wish you'd be serious, Robin."

"It's easy to be serious, Gibby: any damned dolt can be serious. Listen, Gibby: I've written a whole series of songs . . . the best I've done. Come on, let's get the Reading over and I'll sowth them over to you."

"I've a damned sight more to worry me."

"You can worry the morn—all day if you like. Listen! When lyart leaves bestrow the yird, or, wavering like the bauckie-bird, bedim cauld Boreas' blast; when hailstanes drive wi' bitter skyte, and infant frosts begin to bite in hoary cranreuch drest . . ."

"Oh, come on then: let's get on with the Reading."

The reading of the scripture chapter over, they were back once more in the steading.

"What's your sang about this time?" asked Gibby.

"It's a collection of songs and verses—a cantata, I suppose you would describe it. The theme is love and liberty; so Love and Liberty will be the title of it."

"Let's hear the verses."

"Not so fast, Gibby. Jamie Smith and I went into Poosie Nancie's one night——"

"Poosie Nancie's! That was an ill place to visit. No decent body would think of venturing in there. The place smells bad enough frae the outside——"

"The inside smells a damned sight worse. You can see the smell. If the place was ever quiet enough, I'll warrant you could hear it too. But what a life goes on in there, Gibby! Aye, there's all kinds of riff-raff and scoundrels; blackguards and bitches; and maybe worse. But there's something else there too, Gibby. The unfortunate are there—the rejects and the misfits o' human society. Yet, Gibby, that's no' the half o' it. There's liberty there. A curious kind of liberty: perverse you might think. But liberty for a' that. Men and women there have chosen that way of life, the gangrel, begging life, because it's the only way of life that gives them freedom. The freedom to live as they want to live, as their hearts and minds dictate or prompt; and that's liberty. And liberty is ever a glorious feast. You may say that it's liberty at its lowest level. I'm not prepared to gainsay that. But liberty has got to begin at some level. You and me, Gibby! What do we ken about liberty? It's no more to us than a word, an ideal, an aspiration: something we like to dream about . . . Something we hope to attain some day, somewhere. But the best o' the gangrels yonder have gotten it here and now, while they live and as they live—and they live it to the hindmost challenge of their blood; and where the spirit calls they allow no cold prudence to restrain . . .

"And why should they? The bare doup of existence is all there is atween them and death; and the crust of life has to be snatched and eaten in the flight of the moment."

Gilbert was becoming deeply interested. When Robin was in a rare mood like this, it was entrancing to listen to the quick, nervous flow of his thought. But often the thought passed too quickly into words; and then Gilbert had to interject in order that he might understand.

"But surely, Robin, your gangrels dinna think about liberty as you do? Are you not thinking things for them?"

"Aye! But there you've hit it, Gibby my boy! It's the poet's task—and privilege—to think things out for folk that canna think them out for themselves.

"But for all that, the gangrels have their thoughts. You can tell that from their songs. Even if they hadna songs you could tell their thoughts from their actions . . .

"I watched them wi' Wee Jamie. And God, Gibby, but it was glorious watching. They danced, they sang, they drank, they whored, they fought and quarrelled . . . They even made speeches! But broken or maimed, or hirpling to the grave they knew how to enjoy life, how to relish the flavour of existence. I even danced wi' them myself, for you ken how music fires my blood and sends me leaping, light-foot, to the measure——"

"You danced wi' gangrels!"

"You've seen me enjoying a crack wi' Jean Glover as she passed by on her way to Tarbolton or Killie: would you dance wi' Jean if you got the chance and the fiddler was snapping sparks frae the thairms?"

"Jean Glover's a byornar woman, Robin. You would hardly class her as a gangrel."

"You could class Jean Glover as a thief and a whore. She tells me she's seen a wheen o' the correction-houses i' the West here for being no less . . . But it's no' how folks are classed by their supposed betters that matters: it's what folk are."

"I understand that fine; but what has all this to do wi' your cantata?"

"Just this, Gibby. Out o' the lowin fire o' life that was blazing on the hob o' Poosie Nancie's, I caught the red-hot embers of the thought that kindled it—Love and Liberty! I've blown the embers into glowing words and music so that they who can read and can sing may kindle the fire o' love and liberty in themselves."

"That's the greatest idea you've ever had, Robin. I doubt if you could have a greater. Come on! I'm impatient to hear what you've made of it all."

"Listen then! Ae night at e'en a merry core o' randie, gangrel bodies in Poosie Nancie's held the splore, to drink their orra duddies: wi' quaffing and laughing they ranted an' they sang, wi' jumping an' thumping the vera girdle rang.

"First, niest the fire, in auld red rags ane sat, weel braced wi' mealy bags and knapsack a' in order; his doxy lay within his arm; wi' usquebae an' blankets warm, she blinket on her sodger. An' aey he gies the tozie drab the tither skelpin kiss, while she held up her greedy gab just like an aumous dish: ilk smack still did crack still like ony cadger's whup; then, swaggering an' staggering, he roared this ditty up:—

"And you ken the tune o' this ditty as well as I do: Soldier's Joy.

"I am a son of Mars, who have been in many wars, and show my cuts and scars wherever I come: this here was for a wench, and that other in a trench when welcoming the French at the sound of the drum.

"Of course, Gibby: wi' a lal de daudle chorus. And note how the three crotchets o' the same note—dum, dum, dum—fit the sound 'of the drum.' Then back on to the verse again.

"My prenticeship I past, where my leader breathed his last, when the bloody die was cast on the heights of Abram; and I servèd out my trade when the gallant game was played, and the Moro low was laid at the sound of the drum.

"The castle o' El Moro, Gibby, Santiago de Cuba, stormed in 'sixty-two.

"I lastly was with Curtis among the floating batt'ries, and there I left for witness an arm and a limb; yet let my country need me, with Elliot to head me I'd clatter on my stumps at the sound of the drum.

"And now, tho' I must beg with a wooden arm and leg and many a tattered rag hanging over my bum, I'm as happy with my wallet, my bottle and my callet as when I used in scarlet to follow a drum.

"What tho' with hoary locks I must stand the winter shocks, beneath the woods and rocks oftentimes for a home? When the t'other bag I sell, and the t'other bottle tell, I could meet a troop of Hell at the sound of a drum.

"He ended; and the kebars sheuk aboon the chorus roar; while frighted rattons backward leuk, an' seek the benmost bore: a fairy fiddler frae the neuk, he skirled out Encore! But up arose the martial chuck, an' laid the loud uproar.

"And now, Gibby, for a great song sung by the Martial Chuck to that haunting melody—for it is something more than a tune— Sodger Laddie! I confess it's a melody that aey brings the tear to my eye. And I've written words worthy, I think, o' the lilt. The Martial Chuck was there in Poosie's. A great figure of a woman: even in the wreck of her days. A woman, grey-haired and hag-worn though she was, who still carried herself with pride and spoke with greater pride of how she had been born in the barracks and how, of all the loves she had ever known—and her unashamed confession was that she'd kenned many—her greatest and fondest love would ever be her sodger laddie—or maybe ony sodger laddie!

"You might think, Gibby, as I thought when I first clapped eyes on her, that it was sad to see such a woman reduced to such straits and such company. But damn the fear! She didna feel degraded and she didna feel sorry for herself, and she was far from bewailing her lot. I'm only sorry now that I didna get more o' her story. There were a thousand love songs in that woman, for I could well believe that she had had a thousand lovers. She must have loved many a son of Mars, for her features bore the ravaged traces o' Venus's battlefield . . . Ah! but a glorious and gallant old warrior-dame, the Martial Chuck. Listen to her song.

"I once was a maid, tho' I cannot tell when, and still my delight is in proper young men. Someone of a troop of dragoons was my daddy: no wonder I'm fond of a sodger laddie!"

Gilbert had long ceased to be aware of time. He seemed to tread a timeless air as he dandered slowly by his brother's side listening to him chanting the words in a soft cadence to the tune's wistful measure. He could see the Martial Chuck almost as clearly as Robin had seen her; and he thrilled to her tale though he knew only too well that had he seen her for himself, and not as she was transformed by Robin's genius, he would probably not have given her another glance.

And even as he listened enraptured, Gilbert marvelled at this strange gift of genius that had somehow been so richly bestowed on his brother. No wonder he could so transform everyday creatures when he transformed himself in the process. What a transformation there was from the man who, but two hours ago, had been sky-larking with the bits of orra laddies in the stable loft!

But there he was at his cantata again—the song about the sailor without any ears . . .

They had walked so far that when they saw the lights glowing in the small windows of the Tarbolton buts and bens they knew it was time to retrace their steps. Till now, they hadn't been conscious of the distance they had travelled.

As it was, Robin was on his last verse.

"This is the grand final chorus, Gibby. See the smoking bowl before us! Mark our jovial, ragged ring! Round and round take up the chorus, and in raptures let us sing: A fig for those by law protected! Liberty's a glorious feast. Courts for cowards were erected: churches built to please the priest!"

"You'll get hung for that, Robin."

"Damn the fear! That's how to write, Gibby; that's how to sing! If that doesn't make the blood leap in your veins you should give up living. Come on, man: what d'you think? I know it's good: let's hear what you've got to say."

"Robin . . . I've told you before . . . you're a genius . . . God Almighty there's never been stuff written like that. How do you do it?"

"How? I don't know, Gibby. It comes to me . . . Oh, there's plenty to do to take off the rough edges . . . that'll come: I may work on this cantata for years . . . It's when the mood's on me . . .

I'm free now to say what I like: to sing like the lark. There's nothing to hold me back now . . . Aye, and I work the better for this, Gibby: twice as well."

"Aye . . . you've worked well. Bob Allan told me the other day that he was sure you shoved the plough harder than the pownies drew it."

"To hell: I wouldna see the brutes in my gait when the mood's on me. It'll be a bad day for you, Gibby, when I stop my verses."

"I'm sorry, Robin, if I sometimes speak a bit harsh——"

"Ah, for Godsake: maybe somebody's got to speak wi' authority. I'll leave that to you: I've been doing that since ever we came here. When they ask me: 'Will I do this or that' I say: 'You'll better see my brother.' "

"So I've noticed . . . I wonder, Robin, if we're going to pull through here?"

"Of course we are. As long as we keep our health and strength, what's to hinder us?"

"Nothing, I suppose."

"Aye . . . But maybe like me you get a cold shiver sometimes? Whenever things begin to go well you're always wondering when Fate's coming along to dang you down—is that it?"

"Something like that. I canna escape into poetry like you."

"Escape? Maybe that's what it is. But it's not a foolish escape, Gibby. If I could only believe that one day I could win through to print—guid black print . . . But maybe that's not to be . . . And yet when I think on Bob Fergusson . . ."

"Still, Robin . . . poetry's a chancy thing; and a man never got his bread by it. We've set our hand to the plough here on Mossgiel——"

"Right! I'll never go back on that. I'll not let the verses run away with my sense. I made the resolution when I came here that I would say farewell to the muse. Maybe that was a bit drastic. Damnit, man, I feel the better of writing. I get a strength by it. I've been more intoxicated with my own thoughts than ever I have been with Tarbolton nappy or Pigeon Johnnie's Kilbagie . . ."

"You havena had much Kilbagie?"

"No . . . I've little stomach for hard drinking, Gibby."

"And we've less money."

"I can enjoy a pint of ale . . . and maybe an odd drop o' Kilbagie. But once I go over that my stomach revolts . . . The truth is, Gibby—though I know you don't believe me—I don't like drinking. And yet it's only in the howff that folk can forget the bluidy slavery o' their days—and give vent to their free thoughts. And if some o' them have to swallow a good gill or two o' Kilbagie afore they thaw—well, that's how it is. There's no good in thinking that we can live here like hermits, Gibby, even though we may have to work like galley slaves. You'll need to come down to Machlin and get acquaint with some of the lads there. Aye, and some of the lassies too. Wee Smith has a fine-looking sister . . . But, damnit, Machlin's full of fine hizzies as you've seen at the kirk—a damned sight better nor Tarbolton."

"We'll not be in any position to get married for a long time, Robin—mind that."

"Mind? Am I ever likely to forget? But that's no reason for denying yourself female company. You see what's happened to our own sisters . . ."

"Are you still keeping up with Lizzie Paton?"

"I see her back and forwards . . . how?"

"I was just wondering."

"Oh?"

"Just wondering . . . I've said nothing and I mean nothing."

"I've nothing to hide. I like Betty and she was a damned good lass to us in Lochlea."

"I never said she wasn't."

They lapsed into silence.

Robin was worried about Gilbert's reference to Lizzie Paton. He had seen quite a lot of Lizzie recently and he was sure no one had seen them. Now he was wondering how much the canny Gilbert knew.

There had been times when he had worried about Lizzie. As long as William Burns had lived they had not consummated their love. But once he had got settled into Mossgiel there had been no cause for restraint; and consummation had taken place.

It was difficult to analyse the peculiar sense of freedom he felt now that his father was dead, now that he was head of the house and answerable only to himself for his actions. But that he felt free in a way he had never felt was not to be denied. His relationship with Lizzie was an earnest of this new sense of freedom.

And now that he had got over the first flush of writing his cantata on Love and Liberty he was conscious of a surge of spiritual strength.

Freedom and strength were flowing in him; whether he ploughed the sour acres of Mossgiel or broke stones by the road-side it mattered not. He had a world to conquer; and he would conquer it or die in the attempt.

The world that opened to him now was the poet's world, the world of Nature and of Man awaiting artistic recreation—even as he had recreated the world of Poossie Nancie's howff.

There had been moments when he had doubted his powers though he had never doubted his vision. Now he doubted neither.

He hadn't been deceiving Gilbert when he had said he would work. He would work as he had never worked—harder than he had worked after his failure at Irvine. But he would work at his poetry too. He would turn everything he saw and felt into poetry. And he would enjoy himself in the process.

He would succeed. He would show Gilbert, show his mother, show Lizzie Paton and John Rankine and Willie Muir . . . aye, and Gavin Hamilton and his good friends in Ayr . . . show all of them the real Rab Burns that had too often been diffident and shy and self-doubting—deferring always to those who were older and supposedly better learned. There was more than one light hiding under his bushel . . . Hadn't he held his own and more than his own in his debates with Gavin Hamilton and Doctor John MacKenzie? He had out-talked them, out-argued them in politics, religion, philosophy and literature. And they knew it. Smith and Richmond were fine fellows and the best of cronies—but he could wind the two of them round his pinkie—and they knew it. Oh, he wasn't conceited about it. He had a better brain than any of them: why should he make any attempt to deny this to himself?

Aye, and he could win any lass he set his heart on. Only now he was beginning to comprehend all he had learned in the arms of Jean Glover. He had a way with the lassies; and there was no sense in denying this either.

No good in denying the fact that women meant as much to him as food and shelter. He was a man now. It was time for him to play a man's part.

Yes: life was good no matter what kind of jad fortune turned out to be. He would only live once: so he would make the most of it.

Strange, though, how he hadn't really fallen in love with a lass. He could love them all. But was this normal? Maybe he had loved Jean Gardner: maybe Annie Rankine. No . . . for a time he'd loved Jean Gardner; but Jean meant nothing to him now: so his love for her couldn't have been very deep. Annie Rankine? He would always have a warm side to Annie. And yet he had no twinge of regret that Annie was getting married to some far-out relation and would presently be settling down as Mrs. John Merry in the change-house at New Cumnock. Good luck to her—she was one in ten thousand . . .

Maybe some day his heart would tell him when he had met the woman he would love beyond all other women? John Rankine had said his heart would tell him. Maybe John Rankine would be proved right in this as he had so often proved right . . .

Meantime there was Betty Paton; kind sweet sonsy Bess! with a body that warmed the blood and a heart that was as kindly and warm as it was innocent of guile.

Betty! But already there was Lizzie Miller. And Lizzie beckoned in a different way from Betty.

Ah, but damnit, they were all different—and all desirable. And he desired them all.

Was love something to be chained to one woman—and for all time? Could love be real love and confine itself to one human heart? Was not love an emotion that grew on what it fed?

And what of the douce ones who sneered at this as mere liber-tinism? To the devil with them! Senseless asses, the lot of them. Solomon, the wisest man in the old world, had loved the lassies. Hence his wisdom . . .

When a man had done his day's darg and the sun went down into the west and the gloaming-hour was stealing over the land, what more natural than a man should seek out a maid to take to his bosom? That was blood drawing to blood . . .

But not blood alone. A man had a brain as well as a coursing of red blood. And there were things you could say to a lass in the canny hour of evening you could say to no other being. Tender passionate words came to a man then—and they had to be said or whispered as much as any other words that came to the tongue.

Life ranged from the midden-heap to the silent moon and back again. The blood hammered and pulsed on the gates of the brain and the brain fired the blood and sent it surging through the body. Then the body sent it back again more urgent, more clamant than ever till there was only one end to the struggle—and the struggle ended in a woman's arms: ended, began, and ended and began all over again. Thus it had been in Eden's bonnie yard and thus it had been down the long trail of history . . . and it would be so to the end.

Of course that's how it had always been and that's how it was now. Babylon or Jerusalem; the well of Machlin or the well of Bethsheba. The daughters of Jerusalem or the daughters of Coila.

Robin was glad he was achieving clarity on these matters: a clarity glowing with conviction. Where before he had known hesitation he was now bold in his certainty. And this certainty and conviction gave him boundless strength and unlimited mental energy.

Why! he had spun out the essential web of *Love and Liberty* in a day's ploughing and got it down on paper in a couple of nights' writing! True, there were thoughts there that had lain in his mind since the days as a boy on Mount Oliphant he had watched the beggars in their flapping rags tramping bare-footed the dusty summer loanings. But it had taken that night with Smith in Poosie Nancie's to bring it all forth in a gushing of words and music.

It was but three months since his father had been laid in Alloway Kirkyard. Only a few days ago he had been boasting how he had laid poetry aside, how he never read any books but farming ones. And here he was with a set of verses that made everything he had written look like the babblings of a bairn.

As they entered the brooding courtyard of Mossgiel and his collie came bounding to meet him, Robin said:

"I'm determined on being a good farmer, Gibby. And I'm determined on being a good poet."

"You're both already, Robin. I've been thinking: coming along the road. I've been thinking you've got gifts Fergusson never had— and Allan Ramsay wasn't fit to lick Fergie's shoon. And I've been thinking Shenstone and Beattie and Pope are no' worth bothering about. I've been thinking a lot of things, Robin. I've seen a change come over you since we left Lochlea——"

"Since we buried William Burns?"

"Aye . . . You and I have had our words, Robin. Sometimes I just didna see the road you were travelling . . . After all, Robin, I have my own road to travel and I'll have to travel it my own way. But I've said it afore; and if I'm saying it again it's because I've more conviction now than ever I had. You're a great poet, Robin . . . and I'm proud o' you. And if there's a better farmer for your age in Kyle or Cunninghame I've yet to hear about him. And I'm no' forgetting that, but for you, we'd no' be in Mossgiel the night. God alone knows where we'd have been . . . I'm saying all this, Robin, because I know you and me's no' always going to see eye to eye."

"How's that?"

"Because you're you and I'm me. Only I want you to mind that though we do differ about many things, below it all I'm proud you're my brother."

"Well . . . Gibby: you've got me speechless. But, damnit man, what have I done to deserve all this?"

"Plenty. But I've been thinking—and I had to speak while I had the courage."

"Courage?"

"Aye: you're no' an easy man to speak to, Robin."

"Me?"

"You, Robin. When you get your brows down I'd sooner meet wi' Auld Nick. You might as well face that, Robin, and it'll maybe save a lot o' misunderstanding later on. Don't think you're an easy man to get on with. You see, very often your thoughts are no' with us. And when they're no' it would be worth anybody's life to try and find out where they were. Do you know there's weeks on end you never speak to your mother?"

"Hardly that . . . but often there's nothing much to talk about. Mother's no' a talkative woman."

"No? She can talk plenty. However, I've had my say, Robin— said more than I ever meant to say. But . . . I'm glad I said it."

"Thanks, Gibby: so am I. What you've said's fully interesting: aye, fully interesting. Anyway up to bed: I'll take the dog a turn to the top of the ridge: I've a notion to see the moon coming up over the moors."

THE HOLY FAIR

He had risen early, for he could feel the breath of the morning creeping in under the eaves; and the patch of sky framed by the window was incredibly fresh: its translucent blueness seemed to shine from another and purer world . . .

He rose, pulled on an old working sark and held to him with his belt an old pair of grey breeks. He crept downstairs and let himself out into the morning. The dew was cold to his bare feet and the slight breeze played round his bare legs, for he had not fastened his breeks at the knees . . .

He climbed to the brow of the ridge, climbed into the rising sun already glinting its glorious light over the Muirs of Galston. The hares, unused to being disturbed so early, were loth to abandon their breakfast. They limped rather than ran down the green dew-drenched furrows. Above them, larks burbled and warbled joyously.

The breeze lifted the locks on his lifted head as he stood on the ridge, hands deep-thrust into his pockets, and snuffed into his lungs great gulps of the sweet caller air . . .

The land stretched and heaved and folded itself into the morning mist: a kindly green prosperous land of ripening crops and glistening lime-washed farm-biggins. On such a morning it was difficult to believe that folks could be poor and labour-driven; for Eden could not have looked more pleasant on the morning of its creation.

The dew glistened everywhere: on the eared corn and the bearded barley; on the blades of grass and the silvered thrissles; on the green thorn spray and the brown oaken twigs.

And then it flashed into his mind as he looked down the white trail of the Kilmarnock road that this summer Sunday morning was the day of Machlin Holy Fair. And what a day for a holy fair: there hadn't been a day like it this summer!

This would be the first time he would celebrate the sacraments under Daddy Auld. Again he snuffed the caller air in large refreshing draughts . . .

After an early breakfast, Robin watched the folks droving in from Tarbolton and Kilmarnock and all the innumerable tributaries that fed these main roads.

Holy Fairs had always attracted enormous crowds wherever they were held. This one at Machlin promised, on such a fine Sunday, to attract the largest crowd Machlin had ever known. No doubt Daddy Auld's popularity as a preacher had much to do with it. But the attractions of Machlin were not to be despised. Its howffs were famous for bannocks, cheese and ale . . .

Robin walked down the road with his family. But soon they were separated by the surge of worshippers pressing forward and by the need to give way to the young bloods of the parish who loved to gallop their mounts and make a display of their horsemanship. Some of the older folks journeyed in a variety of horse-drawn vehicles from tumbling-carts with crude disc wheels to the latest in carriages and box-traps.

No pilgrimage to Mecca of flowing robes in a dust of burnt sienna could have rivalled the motley procession that crowded the narrow streets of Machlin.

The men were dressed soberly enough. There was much hoddin grey and blue Kilmarnock bonnets; but there was some good braidcloth of funereal black and near-black and head-gear of heavy felts and black beavers. Yet the men were splashed with colour too, for many carried their lunches in red, green and yellow napkins. Among the gangrels, beggars and nondescripts could be seen an odd blue coat with brass buttons or a faded yellow waistcoat heavy with buttons and tarnished embroidery—relics of cast-off gentility.

It was the women who were most prodigal of colour. Shawls of every hue were given an airing. The lassies, of course, trudged with bare feet and bare legs, though they all carried stockings and shoes in their hands so that they might be reverently and decently clad when they entered under the sacred roof.

Separated from the family, Robin feasted his eyes on the spectacle and found it much to his taste. Here was a riot of human spectacle; and he was determined to let nothing escape him. One day he would put it all down in a poem just as Fergusson had set down the spectacle of Leith Races.

As arranged, he met Smith, Richmond, and Hunter the tanner at the Cross and exchanged greetings.

"Well, lads," he said, "this is going to be a glorious day: there'll be fun here and plenty gin this multitude are given physical and spiritual sustenance. Have you an idea what theological talent is to be holding forth from the tent?"

Smith, no doubt from table-talk with James Lamie, was able to supply some information.

"Black Jock Russell frae Kilmarnock will be here; Sandy Moodie o' Riccarton; George Smith o' Galston; Willie Peebles frae Ayr—There's a wheen others I forget."

"That's the main artillery, eh? If I'm no' mistaken, the first shots are about to be discharged."

At the main entrance to the kirkyard a preaching-tent was erected. The tent was a simple structure of wood and canvas and merely gave the preacher protection from the elements and served as a rostrum. Moodie from Riccarton, an adjoining parish to Kilmarnock, had taken up his stance. He looked like some monstrous Punch without his Judy.

The crowd surged towards him. He was the first speaker and was due to prepare the first tables. Very soon the kirk doors would be thrown open and the first hundred communicants would surrender their communion tokens to the elders at the door and pass in to the tables where Daddy Auld would preside.

Behind the closed doors Auld was holding a last-minute conference with his elders.

"You've a sweatin' day afore you, Mr. Auld. Oooh aye: a sweatin' day. There's twa thousand souls i' Machlin the day: that'll fill the tables a good score times. But blessed wark and a great refreshment in the Lord!"

"You're certain we have laid in enough wine, Mr. Fisher? I could wish folks would bide in their own parishes and not descend on us like a plague o' locusts——"

"Ah! but the folks weel ken that the chance o' receiving the host frae you, Mr. Auld, is an occasion not to be missed. There never were crowds like this in your predecessor's day."

"Persons, Mr. Fisher, stand in no special grace before the Lord. An ordained minister is an ordained minister; and it is against Holy Writ that there should be preference—or any countenance given to vain likes and dislikes . . . Is that Mr. Moodie I hear i' the tent? Now understand: I want a careful scrutiny o' the admission tokens. Admit no man or woman on whatever pretext unless he or she delivers up the token. And see that the gentles are no' kept beaking i' the sun too long. There are numbers of the ungodly among the rabble. Some of the mechanics frae Kilmarnock have an unco spleen against their lawful betters—and I want no scandal i' the kirkyard. I trust you'll keep an eye on things—especially you, Mr. Fisher. Maybe you'll seek an opportunity to mingle wi' the multitude and give me your report."

And yet Auld was human enough to feel satisfaction that his personality was such that enormous crowds were drawn to Machlin on the occasion of a Holy Fair. This satisfaction was in no way modified because his intelligence told him that the presence of such a throng of humanity was bound to lead to excesses, depravity and profanity.

For all that he wished the day over. His would be a long tiring ordeal. There would be no rest nor thought of rest until the day was far spent.

Though it was nearly a quarter of a century since Alexander Moodie had been translated from Tulliallan Parish on the banks of the river Forth, he could not suppress a wave of cynicism passing through him as he viewed the heterogeneous mass of Ayrshire humanity that thronged the kirkyard. Around the tent was a tight-packed mass of worshippers, solemn and lantern-jawed in their solemnity; but over their heads he saw people sprawling among the gravestones, gathered in groups about the open space beyond and gyrating slowly about the Cross. Worse: he could see a crowd already besieging the top door of Nance Tinnock's howff . . . Well: he would give them the neat spirit of the doctrine—and there would be no mealy-mouthed evasions in his preparation. He would give Russell something to out-roar when he took his stance . . .

Racer Jess, the swift-footed, half-witted daughter of Poosie Nancie and her husband Black Geordie Gibson, had already taken up her stance at the Loudon Street entrance to the kirk-yard. Her bare elbows leaned on the warm turf-dyke. Beside her were Bet Barbour and Maggie Borland, Machlin's youngest and most desirable whores. Bet and Maggie rested their shoulders to the dyke and kept their eyes open for any likely lads that might be passing.

There were many strangers in the town with good money and warm blood, and they looked forward to a busy and profit-able day.

"See that beggar there wi' the yalla napekin?" whispered Bet.

"Whaur——? Him crackin' wi' her wi' the scarlet shawl? What about him?"

"Gie him the by. It took me an hour to get rid o' him ae market-day. An' a damned mean runt forby."

"I'll watch him," said Maggie, as her eyes narrowed to cunning slits.

Suddenly Racer Jess gave her leg a smack. "Thae beggaring clegs!" she cried in a loud, shrill voice that immediately brought scowls on the faces of the pious gathered round the tent.

"Keep your bluidy trap shut, or ye'll hae the Black Bonnets chasin' us!" hissed Bet, and dug her elbow in Jess's gaunt ribs.

Jess spat on her finger and rubbed the spittle over the puncture in her thigh.

"I've had tippence frae Holy Willie afore noo," she sniffed, and began clawing the lice at the nape of her neck.

James Armour, across the Cowgate behind the Whitefoord Arms, lectured his large family in the shade of curtained windows.

"We will go across for the third tables: I have arranged that with Mr. Auld and Willie Fisher. Now, look neither to your right nor your left but come in ahint me. There's a rabble frae a' the airts here to-day; and I'll have no mixing among them. Now, Jean: I've warned you! There's no outing the day. On a day like this decent folk bide within the four walls o' their own house."

Jean was disappointed. She would have liked to have taken a turn with Jean Markland, Lizzie Miller and Jean Smith to taste the excitement that even now she felt pulsing through the stone walls of their dwelling. She could feel the heat of the sun beaking on the kitchen window. But she sighed and drew a demure countenance: she knew only too well that her father's word was law.

Jean knew how dismal the Machlin Sundays were. She was a sweet lass with a soul that sang like a choir of finches: her spirit bobbing joyously on the green spray of life.

Folks were surging into Machlin: the drowse of animation filled the twisted streets and the timbre of young men's laughter rang in the air like the peal of bells.

Jean's blood beat on the boundaries of her maidenhood—beat only to be beaten back. Not yet was it strong enough to triumph against the black glower of her father's authority or undermine the gloomy tradition of a gloomy Sabbath . . . The flesh tingled and exulted; but the vestments of the Sabbath were grimy and sour with the stale sweat of denial—the denial of a long-delayed sacerdotalism.

Jean's heart fluttered beneath a quivering breast like a bird in the snare: she bowed her head in resignation.

Across the gushet of the Cowgate, George Gibson was congratulating his spouse, Poosie Nancie, on the prospect of a record day's business. Gangrels, whores and whoremasters were flocking into the town and promised good business for the howff. His serving-jurr, Agnes Wilson, was thinking of the amount of business she might do against her own account.

Even John Dow, who had a ribald blasphemous contempt for orthodoxy, welcomed the Holy Fair for the business it would bring him, and the excitement it would give to the day.

But there were many folks in Machlin who resented the influx of strangers—especially the undesirable riff-raff. They were careful to lock everything that could be moved behind the safety of their doors—even to the fowls on their midden-heads.

Only the less-respectable elements of the Machlin folks would allow their children to venture out into the streets—and they were liable to stern rebuke from the Session for doing so.

The douce folks did not vaig the streets but held to the preaching-tent until it was their turn to take their place at the communion tables with Daddy Auld.

And the douce who liked their theology strongly laced with the astringency of Auld Licht doctrine were well served by Moodie. He had a rare edge to his tongue and he used it to slashing effect. He lingered long and luridly on the terrible damnation that awaited the sinners and backsliders; and he painted the burning lake and the boiling brimstone in singeing simile and malodorous metaphor: tidings, indeed, of salvation.

Many of his audience swayed and groaned and not a few wept bitter tears of repentance. But Moodie would not relent, nor did he offer any hope of easy access to the state of grace. His tidings were of thundering and universal damnation for all but the elect—and even they were brushed aside with scant courtesy.

Robin and his friends moved down Loudon Street to catch the drift of Moodie's discourse. There was a crowd of spectators gathered around the kirkyard entry. Maggie Borland and Bet Barbour winked and leered in the manner of their profession at Robin and his friends.

Robin listened for some time to Moodie's harangue. Then they decided they would go in and join the throng with a view to securing an early table. Once they had partaken of the host, they would be free for the rest of the day. As communicants of Machlin Kirk, they were entitled to some priority in the matter of access to the tables. So they dropped their pennies into the collection-plates, supervised by two elders just inside the entry, and made their way into the kirkyard.

Robin was in no scoffing frame of mind. But Moodie's bitter denunciations galled him. It was a day of magnificent sunshine. Under the sun-dappled shadow of the great ash-tree, Moodie's contorted face, spitting and spluttering a sulphurous spleen, was harshly irrelevant. While Robin's sympathy and rich humorous interest was warmly roused by the quaintness and variety of the human scene, his spirit rebelled at the savage sourness of the philosophic theology of the Kirk.

It seemed to him that men like Moodie were the real enemies of life—not the irreverent gangrels and the poor whores like Racer Jess and Bet Barbour. Racer Jess might be lost to God: she was not wholly lost to life. And in so far as she was lost, she was more the victim of society and the operation of its mildewed moral laws.

But Moodie and his ilk were lost to God and man. They poisoned the well of life at the source. Neither love nor hope nor charity was compounded in their philosophy: the famished tiger of denial snarled from the hollow confines of their narrow breasts; and the serpent of Thou-shalt-not lay coiled in the recesses of their dark minds, the head of unreason ever poised to strike with sterile negation.

How he wished for the privilege of mounting that rostrum, and delivering a different message to the snuffling souls shrinking under the lowered brow and shifty eye of superstition and fear. How he would exhort them to cast out fear, shake off superstition and beg them to rejoice in the sun and the glory of human fellow-ship. It was a soured priest who had said that the heart of man was deceitful and above all things desperately wicked. The deceit and the wickedness sprang from decayed moral concepts festering in the mind. Cleanse the mind of the suppurating sores of mental passion gone to putrefaction and what sweet hozannas of rejoicing would flow spontaneously from the human heart!

And so there was something of contempt and rebellion smouldering in him as he passed from the warm sunshine into the dank mustiness of the kirk and took his place at the table.

Mercifully, Auld was brief—and business-like. His exhortation was cold in its Calvinistic logic; in his fencing he enumerated the cardinal sins that barred the communicant from partaking the sacrament; but he wasted no breath on any piddling peccadilloes. He broke the bread and passed it down the tables and gave them pause to compose themselves to the solemnity of the ordeal. Then he dismissed them in a benediction of quiet dignity and sincere strength.

Give William Auld his due, he seemed neither fool nor hypocrite. He might be cold in his square-cut logic; but the coldness sprang from the discipline of an ordered mind.

Yet Robin was dissatisfied. Auld was neither bitter nor hysterical; but for all that it was obvious how the shackles of his mind kept his emotions in a rigid and unbending thrall. To Auld there could be no deviation from the logic of doctrine: predestination predetermined the inexorable law of human conduct. Deviation led to disintegration; and disintegration was as the rush of Gadarine swine down a steep place into the sea.

It took him some time to throw off his mood of philosophic introspection. They wandered at leisure about the kirkyard. Some were eating their lunches; and the gay napkins spread out among the tombstones gave a carnival touch to the incongruous surroundings.

Among the forms and benches, placed in an irregular semi-circle in front of the tent, lads and lassies were whispering and giggling and some quiet tickling and tentative cuddling was in progress . . .

They decided they would have a drink of ale; and on such a day they decided that, at this stage, it would be best to visit the Elbow

Tavern, since the Elbow was farthest removed from the press and surge of the crowd.

But the Elbow was crowded with customers who had much the same idea as themselves; so when their caups were filled they made their way out and sat down on the grass to enjoy their drink.

"It's a wonderful business," said Robin. "The sublime and the ridiculous hand in hand."

"There's little sublimity about a Holy Fair," said Smith. "It's just a rabble: Auld Nick himself couldn't distinguish the pious from the pagans."

Hunter the tanner, a strong raw-boned fellow with a direct turn of mind, said: "Religion and houghmagandie gang thegither—and I'll warrant the hizzies are in grand fettle what wi' the heat—and the exhortations."

"Aye," said Richmond, "it's the old old story. Did you ever hear how Poosie Nancie defied the Session? She was cited to compear for habitual drunkenness—and for keeping a bawdy house. By certes, Nancie faced up to them! Told Daddy Auld she had aey drank and aey would as long as she was able. Auld told her she would be barred the communion table. Nancie said she had a table o'her own and let them try to bar her from that."

"And was she barred?"

"Auld saw to that: said her foolish talk wasn't worth answering. But Poosie didn't give a docken; and she'll be rakin' in the siller the day."

"So Poosie doesn't give a damn about her immortal soul?"

"You see for yourself, Rab. And she kens fine what her own daughter, Racer Jess, is up to—no doubt she taught her the trade. But what can the Session do? Geordie and her are sunk as low as they can sink—they can't sink them any lower."

"And yet their howff brings more happiness to the gangrel-bodies than any blasts on the gospel horn."

"You're right there, Rab: folk are no' as scared o' the horn as they used to be."

"Damned man, Jamie: I have a feeling that they never were."

"Ah, I don't know: folks are still sair hadden doon by the lads in black. It's all right if you're cut off like Geordie and Poosie but can still make your living for all that. But the Session can still draw the heels from you. Just fall foul o' them and you'll damn soon see."

Robin listened to their talk. He had his own ideas; but to-day he was keeping them to himself. This was the day for catching manners living as they rose—and they were rising like trout in a hatch of may-flies.

Folks were continuing to jowk out and in the Elbow—all kinds and conditions of them. The older men were discussing the Holy Fairs of former days. Some were turning over the theological arguments of Moodie and Peebles and all were agreed that Moodie was doctrinally sound on damnation. Others were particularly critical of the host. Poor stuff was the verdict. The shortbread of the olden days was far better and gave a man a tastier chew to wash down wi' a good slooch of claret. It was a gey fushionless stuff Auld went in for nowadays—no fire to it worthy of the solemnity of the occasion. Aye: a good sacrament was worthy of a good host—and Auld was fully scrimpy with his bread.

The young men lay on the grass and watched the passing scene or listened to the talk of men who came and sat beside them. But it soon became too hot to lie in the open, and this, combined with inactivity, began to irk them. Smith, Richmond and Hunter were due back at their homes for a bite of lunch, and though there was nothing to prevent Robin walking home the odd mile to Mossgiel he did not want to break his day. Finally he agreed to go home with Smith and share his bite. Lamie would be busy assisting Auld: they would have no need to fear the shadow of his company.

"As like as no', Rab," Smith confided to him as they sauntered round to the Cross, "Lizzie Miller'll be in to have a crack wi' my sister Jean: there's something wrong if she doesna land in our house on a Sabbath after service."

When they got round by the kirk the scene was busier than ever. William Peebles from Newton-on-Ayr was laying forth from the tent, polite, pernickety, dreadfully Anglified and sourly sarcastic. Mr. Peebles was uncertain of his dignity but by no means uncertain of his dogma. He was an intellectual: he liked to talk over the heads of his audience.

Robin noticed that folk grew tired of him and there was a continual coming and going on the fringe of his audience.

But though a large crowd was still within the precincts of the kirkyard, there were more folks than ever crowding Loudon Street—especially round the Whitefoord Arms and Poosie Nancie's; on the Green between the kirkyard proper and the Cross many hundreds were seated eating their carried lunches—the women handing out cheese and bannocks to their husbands and families. Many were the good douce honest folk sitting there in their Sabbath braws; many were the lads and lassies talking and joking quietly or being introduced to mothers, fathers and acquaintances.

It was but a step from the Cross to Smith's and Richmond's and Robin was glad to get in out of the heat and turmoil of the day to relax in Lamie's elbow-chair.

Mrs. Lamie was a motherly edition of her son James; but it was obvious that Lamie was something of a cloud on her life: she was tight-lipped and repressed.

There was nothing repressed about her daughter Jeannie.

She had all Jamie's wit and intellectual perception. She had already met Robin and she was glad to see him.

"And what d'you think of our Holy Fair in Machlin, Rab?"

"Well . . . I didn't see many Machlin folks out and about, Jeannie."

"No . . . they have to get off the streets for the strangers. Have you been at your table?"

"Yes . . . I've got that by for another year."

"You'll be glad?"

"I'm no' sorry."

"I'm afraid you're no' much better nor a heathen, Rab?"

"Well, Jeannie, when I see the grand specimens of civilisation sitting about the Machlin Kirkyard listening to the highly-civilised skirlin' o' Mr. Peebles, I wouldna say but that maybe you're richt . . ."

Later, after they had had their bite, Jean Markland and Lizzie Miller came in to sup a dish of tea and exchange the gossip of the day. Lizzie, whose father was proprietor of the Sun Inn at the head of the Bellman's Vennel, was a young lady of consequence; and as Jean Markland's father was a merchant of standing, they were beyond censure from Lamie—indeed, he was socially proud that they were friendly with his step-daughter.

Jamie had once tried to make up to Lizzie but had met with little success—probably his stature was against him. For Jean Markland he had less regard. Jean was a plain lass, honest and with a very sweet disposition—but her sex was not manifest in the way that appealed to him.

Robin, however, was immediately in his element. Lizzie continued to be haughty in her rejoinders: she was attracted to Robin and she tried not to show it. Jean Markland, however, liked him from the moment he opened his mouth. And though she didn't say much, she smiled at him in an open friendly manner whenever their eyes met.

Jamie said: "Your father'll be losing a heap o' siller the day, Lizzie: him no' opening the Inn to the crowd."

"We can do bravely without their siller."

"That's an uncommon sentiment."

"We happen to be uncommon people, Mr. Burns."

"Come on, come on," said Jeannie Smith, "we'll have none o' this Miss Miller, Mr. Burns. Plain Lizzie and Rab'll do fine among friends."

"I prefer Eliza to Lizzie—if you don't mind."

"Eliza by all means," said Robin. "Neither Lizzie nor Betty becomes you. Eliza has a flavour of its own—and it suits you."

"She'll get nae Eliza from me then. She's been Lizzie to me since ever she ran to the school."

"But Jeannie: there's a sonnet of itself in Eliza—a fine Sunday sonnet—nice and genteel in the fine English of Shenstone. I must try it some day."

"There's no occasion for sonnets, Mr. Burns—besides, poetry shouldn't be discussed on a Sunday."

"No more than public-houses should be opened?"

"Not on Communion Sunday."

Jamie said: "It's a lot of hypocrisy if you ask me. The multitude must be refreshed."

Jeannie said: "Wait till Mr. Russell from Kilmarnock starts and that'll be refreshment enough for everybody. You could hear him up in Mossgiel, Rab."

"With the wind in the right quarter I believe you could, Jean. It's a pity we couldn't all take a turn up the road . . ."

"You forget the day, Mr. Burns."

"No, Eliza: neither the day nor the night."

"And what's the night got to do wi' it, Rab?"

"You should know, Jeannie, that what cannot bear the light of day must have recourse to the light of moon or stars."

"Fegs, Rab, but I wouldn't trust you myself gin the moon was up."

Mrs. Lamie, who came in with the masking-pot hot from the kitchen hob, said: "That's no way to be talking on this day, Jeannie—if James Lamie heard you . . ."

"What's the odds, mother? You'll have a dish o' tea, Rab?"

"Thank you, Jeannie."

Eliza said: "Are you no' thinking of getting married, Mr. Burns?"

"The idea never crossed my mind until I saw you, Eliza."

"That doesna say much for the rest of us," said Jeannie Smith.

"Well . . . I have hardly the fortune to be another Solomon."

"If you ask me, Rab, men must have been gey scarce in his day else he would never hae got a' the women he did."

"I think," said Eliza, "that they must have been low creatures."

"Not so, Eliza: they were dark and comely—and poets wrote songs in their honour."

"No' as good songs as yours, Rab," said Jamie. "You bide a wee, Eliza—Rab'll put a verse or twa on you that'll make you the talk o' the parish."

Eliza blushed. "If you do, Rab, I'll never speak to you again."

"Fegs, Lizzie," said Jeannie: "you havena been doing much speaking to him so far. Still . . . I wonder you don't get married, Rab—seeing you're so much o' a poet."

"And why should poets get married more than other men?"

"Oh, you ken what poets are!" She turned to Jean Markland. "We do: don't we, Jean?"

"I think it must be wonderful to be a poet—and I dinna think a poet should get married."

Robin was interested. "Why?"

"I don't know . . . I think it would spoil everything—when he was young anyway."

Eliza was jealous of Jean Markland's remark. "I think marriage would put a lot of nonsense out of their heads."

"Aye: and put a lot o' new nonsense in," said Jeannie Smith.

Robert was still interested in Jean Markland. "And who's your favourite poet, Jean?"

"I like all that I know . . . Maybe Allan Ramsay?"

But the conversation was becoming too dull for James Smith.

"Ach, Rab can write better poetry than ony o' them. What about taking another turn round the town: we're missing all the fun—and we don't want to miss Black Jock . . . come on!"

"Aye: on you go—and I hope Mr. Russell puts the fear of death into the pair of you, for you could do with it."

In taking his leave of them somewhat reluctantly Robin said to Jean Markland: "Maybe some other day, Jean, we'll continue our discussion of the poets. Allan Ramsay was one of my first poets—and I still have a warm heart to him."

When they were gone, Jean Markland said: "I can't get away from Rab Burns' eyes. Did you see how they glow . . . and change . . . I never thought a man could have eyes like that."

"Aye," said Jeannie. "No wonder he's a poet. But sometimes I think he should have been a lassie."

"Oh, I think that's a terrible thing to say, Jeannie." Eliza was shocked.

"Oh, I don't mean he's a Jessie. He's a man all right. 'Deed, he's too much of a man. But he'll lead ony lass that falls in love wi' him a queer dance."

"How d'you mean, Jeannie?"

"You shouldn't need to ask me that, Lizzie. I'll warrant there's no' a lass in the parish but would like a hug frae him."

"Oh, that's disgraceful——"

"Aye . . . and you more than ony of them, Lizzie."

Outside, the sun, now beyond its meridian, beaked mercilessly down on the town. Sparrows dusted themselves in the kail-yard dust. From the thatches, seen against the still blue of the northern skyline, heat waves radiated in broken coils. It was an August heat and the earth's pores cracked to drink it in.

The multitude was seeking rest and comfort. It was too warm to vaig the streets in their heavy Sabbath cleadings. Hundreds were asprawl the open space between the Cross and the kirkyard. Many were sound asleep. Amid the drowse of lazy half-hearted conversation could be heard the drone of snoring.

The Reverend Alexander Miller, a physical dumpling of a man, was peching Presbyterian orthodoxy from the preachingtent. As he was still awaiting a call to a kirk and was filling in his time assisting ordained ministers, he was careful to give no offence. But since he was neither hot nor cold in his Calvinistic zeal, he greatly displeased the orthodox, who promptly spewed him out of their mouths. Many, finding that the fushionless flavour lingered notwithstanding, hied themselves off to Nance Tinnock's to see what effect a caup of ale might have.

Young Willie Peebles had been hard enough to thole with his Anglified pomposities, even though he had been doctrinally sound. But the sermon-tasters relished something more than sound doctrine: they responded to vigour, violence, high colour and thundering exhortation.

Podgy Miller, lacking the safe anchorage of a kirk and lacking either a deep faith or a solid conviction in Auld Licht doctrine, was pathetically destitute of vigour and colour; nor could he roll any thunder into his periods.

He hummed and hawed, peched and grunted and dabbed the sweat-beads from his brosy face with a yellow napkin. The crowd shuffled and drifted away. Damned, what was the Word coming to when gowks bound up like harvest frogs were let loose on such a day to gulder and guddle . . . Lord send Black Jock Russell from Kilmarnock to put worthy tongue on Holy Writ, set the cheek of Faith by the jowl of Works and come down with a thundering clap on the doup of Deliverance.

And still the flaming girdle of the sun beat down its rays on road and roof, ledge and lintel, orthodox and unorthodox, lad and lass, man, wife and bairn . . .

Still the crowds flocked to the communion tables. Old Robin Gibb, the beadle, sweated and groaned and called to the Black Bonnet supervising at the tent: "Fire away there: the fifteenth table is filling up and there's nae end till the wark."

A bunch of mechanics from Kilmarnock, bent on a day's outing and some fun with the lassies, came bundling into the kirkyard from Nance Tinnock's. They staggered across the ground, picking their way between the sleeping and resting communicants, and making bold remarks to such lassies as attracted their fancy.

They stood for a moment listening to Mr. Miller. They were eating whangs of cheese and farrels of bannock. Suddenly, with a derisive laugh, a long stooping squint-eyed lad threw the heel of his cheese in Miller's face; his comrades followed suit. With ribald laughter they rushed out the entry and narrowly escaped colliding with Black Jock, who had just arrived to wind up the preparations and put a finish on the day's good work.

The advent of John Russell, a great burly black-browed man in the prime of his life, saved the situation for Mr. Miller, who was now completely demoralised.

Russell wasn't long in sizing up the situation. In no time he had mounted the rostrum. The crowd now gathered thickly round the tent. There was much thrusting and pushing to get a good position; for though there would be no difficulty in hearing him, it was added entertainment to watch the contortions of his massive face and note the flail-like movements of his powerful arms or the fore-hammer blows of his clenched fist crashing on the wooden anvil of the tent.

Robin was standing at the Cross conversing with Smith and a young Machlin souter, David Brice, when Russell mounted the rostrum.

Brice, who was of an age with Robin, was a good lad. He often joined the company in John Dow's and proved an intelligent and entertaining companion. He was well-read in philosophy and favoured an extreme rationalism with an extreme radicalism in politics.

"When you look about you," he was saying, "and picture this assembly complete wi' wings and harps, you see how clean ridiculous is the idea of a personal immortality."

"Exactly," said Robin. "But can you see them gracing Cloven Clootie's haunts?"

"And it's a pity you canna. It would be worth while making the journey just to see them."

"But mind you," added Robin, "the fear o' hell's a hangman's whip to hold the wretches in order. Moodie kens that. And, by certes, he kens how to lash them wi' it."

"Look about you," said Brice: "a grand day o' sunshine: you couldna wish for a better. See what man wi' all his boasted reason does wi' it! Look at them! If that's no' superstition I don't know the meaning o' the word. I'd give a lot to hear what David Hume would say about them. No wonder they prate on the efficacy o' faith: it's a blind man's faith."

"A blind man wi' a blank mind, Dave."

"You've hit it, Jamie."

"And yet," said Robin, "it's a rich scene—glorious! Damnit: it's heaped up and running over wi' drama—the human comedy. We Scots are a great folk: the Bible and a bawd gang thegither wi' us. You canna get away from it. I'll warrant there's more minds running to houghmagandie than are reaching out to heaven. There'll be more bairns conceived the night than in ony other night of the year. It's in the air: you can feel it."

"I can feel that way ony nicht withouten a holy fair, Rab."

"So can I, Jamie—but that's no' what I mean. You can't stir the soul without stirring the flesh."

"But why bring in the soul—that's only superstition."

"No . . . I'm not with you there, Dave. Oh, I know what you mean—philosophically. And as to immortality, I'll no' dispute wi' you. Ah, but there's a soul for all that. There's a something that's no' just the heart and no' just the mind either. A blend of the two that goes beyond either one of them: we don't know its beginning or its end or how rightly it affects us. But in all times of doubt and difficulty . . ."

A great roar blasted from the tent. It was followed by a rapid succession of verbal explosions. Then great billowing waves of oratory surged through the dozing streets and crashed against the sun-baked walls of the dwellings until they finally dissipated themselves in the open countryside.

The first explosion shook Machlin to its foundations. The wide-awake trembled in fear. Many of those sleeping and dozing about the kirkyard and the Cross started violently from their sleep, many fearing that the last trump had sounded and that judgment-day was upon them in blazing riot; others feared that they had wakened from their long sleep to find themselves in hell and that the sergeant-major of the damned in person was drilling the raw recruits.

Burns closed his lips slowly on an unfinished sentence and stared incredulously in the direction of the tent.

"I'll warrant," said Smith, "that opening roar was heard in the Chapel of Ease at Kilmarnock itself."

"I've heard Black Jock give mony a bellow, but a sound the like o' that I never heard from man or beast—it's down-right diabolical. What in God's name has gotten his dander?"

Black Jock was inspired. He would put such a fear of hell-fire and damnation into them as would do them for another year. He would teach them to approach the communion table with a light step and a careless heart! Before he was finished he would have them crawling there on their bended knees begging forgiveness between their weeping, wailing and gnashing of teeth.

Another bellow and a frightened cur came tearing round the corner of Loudon Street in a shower of dust and pebbles, tail thrust between its legs, as if pursued by a pack of wolf-hounds, and almost reversing its anatomy in a frenzied attempt to turn into the sanctuary of the Backcauseway. As it skidded broadside on the heat-burnished cobbles, it emitted such a howl of undiluted terror that an intoxicated communicant, staggering out of Nance Tinnock's low door, swore to his dying day that it was no common mongrel but Auld Hornie himself, flying from the wrath to come in the shape of a mad dog.

At the far-away corner of the town, snug in the Elbow Tavern, men started from their seats: not a few, in their nervous apprehension, jittled the ale from their trembling caups. An ancient worthy of many a Holy Fair raised his ale to his lips but didn't wait to drain the dregs: he gave his whiskers a back-hand brush: "That's Black Jock roarin'; by certes the gospel horn'll get a blast noo—let me round to the tent for Godsake: I wadna miss this for a' the yill in Machlin." Grabbing his thorn stick, he fought his way out of the ben of the tavern amid curses, groans and lamentations.

In the back room of John Dow's, Holy Willie, seeking a quick refreshment, was so demoralised by the roaring blasts that smote his ears from across the narrow width of Loudon Street that he threw open the window and let himself out head first into the back lane, much to Jean Armour's amusement, as she watched through a chink in the curtains.

Bet Barbour, engaged in amorous dalliance with a young Galston farmer in Ronald's loft (where his horse was stabled) shivered and flung her arms round the suddenly-stiffened, upward-craning neck of her customer.

But as the blasts rumbled and reverberated through every neuk and crannie of Machlin, they raised fear, despondency, terror, ribald merriment, blasphemy, holy rapture and maudlin hysteria. Horses nickered in their stalls, cattle lowed, dogs howled and the birds of the air fled the boughs and the thatched roofs.

Daddy Auld speeded his benediction (his immediate flock were ill at ease) and mopped his lined and haggard face with a large napkin which he drew from the tail of his coat. He was feeling the burden of his seventy-five years. He called to old Robin Gibb, the beadle:

"Steek the door, Robin. Mr. Russell will hold the multitude for a while yet."

"He will that, Mr. Auld. Would you no' care to streek yourself in the vestry for ten minutes like. It's sair wark, Mr. Auld, and it would be no sin to rest in your labours."

"No sin, Robin; I might even close my eyes for a few minutes and seek the blessing of the Lord. But," and here he dropped his arms listlessly, "with Mr. Russell holding forth i' the tent . . ."

"Come awa' ben, Mr. Auld. Aye . . . I've heard mony a grand voice—and whan you first cam' to Machlin, Mr. Auld, you could gar the auld bauks dirl—but the likes o' Black Jock . . . You ken, sir: I hae found myself wondering if it was a'thegither just the thing: y'ken—a wee shadie loud for a proper reverence."

"Robin, man, I'll confess that thought has occurred to me too—atween ourselves: strictly atween ourselves. But the Lord moves in a mysterious way His wonders to perform. And doubtless in giving Mr. Russell siccan a pair of byornar lungs He meant him to put them to good use. If you'll leave me, Robin, I'll rest a while in the cool and dark o' the corner here."

"I've a wee sup o' Kilbagie, Mr. Auld—it'll set you up against the next table——"

"Just as you say, Robin. And keep the door steekit till I call you."

Outside, the greatest concourse of communicants of the day was gathered round the tent. In Loudon Street about the jammed entry a great crowd of godly and ungodly, gangrels and unco guid, milled and jostled in the hope of viewing the preacher.

The host of the Whitefoord Arms thrust his head and shoulders out from his upper bedroom window to enjoy a grandstand view, when a pigeon, frightened from her last clutch of the season, dropped a gowpen of scalding lime on the crown of his bald head. With a howl of rage, Johnnie shot himself back into the room, carrying the lower sash of the window on his shoulders.

But Black Jock was only getting into his stride, finding the weight of his eloquence.

"What must it be to be banished for ever from the presence of Almighty God? You'll be cast into everlasting fire. And whatna bed is there! Nae feathers, but fire; nae friends, but furies; nae ease, but fetters; nae daylight, but darkness; nae clock to pass awa' the time, but endless eternity; fire eternal aey burning and never dying awa'. It shall not be quenched day or night. The smoke thereof shall go up for ever and ever. The wicked shall be crowded like bricks in a fiery furnace. Good Lord, what a world of miseries hath seized on miserable sinners! Their executioners are devils; the dungeon fills; the earth stands open; the furnace is burning to receive you. O how you poor souls will quake and tremble! Every part of your body will bear a part in the woeful ditty: eyes weeping, hands wringing, breasts beating, heads aching with voices crying. The Judge is risen from His glorious seat. The saints guard Him along, and the sentenced prisoners are delivered to the gaolers. Shrieks of horror shall be heard. What woes and lamentations shall be uttered when devils and reprobates and all the damned crew of hell shall be driven into hell never to return. Down you go! howling, shrieking and gnashing your teeth . . . What wailing, weeping, roaring, yelling, filling both heaven and earth. O miserable wretches!"

"I canna stand it," said Brice. "There's neither reverence nor decency in such uncivilised bellowing."

"But it's grand entertainment," said Smith. "You can see the folk are enjoying themselves: they've been waiting all day for this."

"Aye," said Burns: "Moodie only whetted their appetites."

But there was no consoling Brice. "I never had any appetite for a bellyfu' o' brunstane—and that's all the sustenance Black Jock has to offer. What d'you say for a walk along the Barskimming road?"

"Might as well," said Smith. "There's no' a howff in Machlin you could get a quiet drink the day. By certes, they're raking in mair siller nor the kirk."

"Do none o' the Machlin belles appear the day?"

"None—barrin' Racer Jess and two-three whores, Rab."

"I half thought I might have clapped eyes on this Jean Armour you're aey talking about. For all the times I've been in Machlin I seem to have missed her—except what I see o' her beneath her shawl i' the kirk—and that's little enough to pass judgment on."

"Dave, here, has a notion o' Jean.

"Half Machlin seems to have a notion o' her."

"Aye; but there's no' a sweeter lass in Machlin, Rab."

"Well, Jamie, I'm lippening on you to get us acquaint—if Davie doesn't object."

"I'm no' committed, Rab. James Armour wouldna have me for a good-son. I'm only a poor cobbler wi' heterodox opinions—he'd sooner set the dogs on me."

"Well, Dave, if Jamie and you are for a dander, I think I'll edge into the crowd here: I'm in the notion to hear Black Jock out."

The sun was going down into the west in a richly-earned blaze of glory, and the gloaming was beginning to muster in the woods and shaws; and cruisies and candles were being lit in many Machlin homes ere Daddy Auld broke the last host and gave his final benediction for the day.

The crowd had largely dispersed and the Machlin streets were beginning to resume their Sabbath quiet. True, the howffs were still doing a roaring trade and John Dow had not given over his bluster-ing blasphemy. But, though timid and shy, peace was creeping back into the village now that Black Jock's last bellowings had rumbled away out of earshot.

Willie Fisher and James Lamie accompanied Daddy Auld home with the collection—they would make an accurate and final accounting to-morrow night. Meantime they had to make their last round of the howffs, clear them of those who still lingered at the ale, and note the names of any who might be drunk so that they could be brought before the Session in due course.

Robin had come on Betty Paton in the crowd round the tent. Now they trudged home in the gloaming. Betty's household duties at Largieside had prevented her attendance at Machlin till late in the afternoon—she had been fortunate indeed to get admitted to the second-last table.

"I was sure I would see you, Rab. I was sure you would wait for me."

"You would have been disappointed if I hadna waited?"

"Aye . . . it's a long tramp hame—by your lane."

"There's plenty going that road."

"But I ettled to come hame wi' you, Rab."

"Maybe I ettled the same way. God! what a day it's been. My ears are still dirlin' wi' Black Jock's roaring and blasting."

"You dinna think hell's like yon, Rab, do you?"

"Hell? There's no such place, lass. And even if there was, you would never see it."

"There must be a hell, Rab."

"Even so . . . I'm saying you'll never see it. God's no' waiting to cast you into the lowin' pit: God's nae monster, Betty, even if He did create Black Jock in His image."

"That's a terrible thing to say, Rab. But fegs, I think Black Jock's father had mair to do wi' it than the Almighty."

"Or maybe his mither?"

"Maybe them baith."

"What if any o' the elders hear us laughin'—you're a terrible man, Rab."

"You've got to laugh, Betty—or go mad. It's been a glorious day."

"Will you write a poem on it?"

"Now what made you think that?"

"Och, I ken you. I can tell by your eyes when you're thinking on a poem: there's a smoke like . . . like reek passes ower them—as if the sight was far away. I watched you when you were listening to Black Jock—but you werena right listening, were you?"

"Ah, you're a witch, Betty . . . Aye, I'll write a poem on Machlin's Holy Fair—some day."

"It'll be a guid yin."

"It'll be a' that."

"Will I be in it?"

"No . . . you'll no' be in it. Just Racer Jess—and two-three whores."

"And why will I no' be in it, Rab?"

"Because you maun aey keep something to yoursel' you scarce wad tell to ony."

"What does that mean, Rab?"

"It means that you and me will round off the day low down in the broom yonder ayont Lochlea. That's if the midges dinna bite the——"

"Wheesht, Rab, wheesht: you mauna say words like that. D'you think maybe we should?"

"I've stopped thinking, Betty. Look at the night! You can feel the gloaming creeping along the marrow of your bones even as it creeps along the sheughs—even the throat o' the hoolet is soft wi' it. That's how Nature smoothes away the wrinkles from the brow o' the hard world. The canny hour at e'en, lass—and my arms about my dearie."

"Dinna, Rab, dinna—or we'll never see the broom the nicht."

THE HIGHLAND MAIDEN

The summer passed and harvest came in the late autumn. It was a gloomy harvest at Mossgiel. Robin had bought the seed that spring, and he had bought badly. Not that he was to blame. The seed had looked good and Gilbert had thought it excellent. Alas, it returned very poor crops.

In such a situation they were helpless. Gilbert worked at his accounts and showed that, bad though the position was, it was not disastrous: by cutting expenses down to the bone they would be able to survive the winter.

Still, their first harvest since Lochlea was a failure, and Robin and Gilbert were despondent.

Robin's visits to Machlin became more frequent. He experienced an overwhelming desire for company, for conversation. He needed employment for his intellect, needed something into which he could bite his mental teeth.

Nor were Richmond, Smith, Brice or Hunter always the most satisfactory company. In many important respects their intellectual world was narrow and circumscribed. Not that they were ignorant. Smith had excellent wit and native shrewdness; Brice could argue all night about David Hume; Hunter was sweepingly radical in his political opinions; Richmond was a mine of accurate information on a host of matters . . .

But there were times when Robin relished the more mature conversation of men like Doctor MacKenzie and Gavin Hamilton.

This back-end he enjoyed many a conversation in Gavin Hamilton's study at the end of a hard day's work.

The political situation of Great Britain was much discussed. William Pitt had become Prime Minister in December, 1783, as William Burns had fretted on his death-bed. Now his resounding victory at the polls was the subject of much speculation. Robin, Hamilton and MacKenzie expected much from Pitt by way of reform.

But Scottish affairs were not neglected in their discussions, and though Henry Dundas, Pitt's henchman, was not yet the official uncrowned King of Scotland, his ironic title of Henry the Ninth was in the immediate offing.

Nobody but the privileged few in Scotland trusted Dundas, even though Pitt depended more and more on the votes of the Scottish M.P.s who were in Dundas's pocket and who, since they owed him their political existence, obeyed his every whim.

Burgh and ecclesiastical reforms were the order of the day in Scotland, and the public prints, *The Caledonian Mercury* and *The Scots Magazine*, were filled with items of reforming news.

Robin had long been an insatiable reader of the press. There was little news, home or foreign, that escaped his attention. Hamilton and MacKenzie soon found that he was much better informed than themselves.

In his early discussions Robin was careful not to embarrass his friends with his superior knowledge. He had still to feel his way with them. He did not argue as he argued in John Dow's—or as he had debated in Jock Richards' howff in Tarbolton. He seemed to defer to his professional friends when, in fact, he was drawing them out.

But as he got to know them better and became more at ease in their company, and realised that he was infinitely better read than they were, he occasionally lifted the bushel from his light—without lifting it far enough to blind them.

One night when they had been discussing at length the need to reform the election of local government representation, he leaned across to Gavin Hamilton.

"Every man and woman who works to produce the wealth of the nation is entitled to have a say in how the nation shall be governed. But elections in the Burghs don't exist as elections: offices are held by friends and dispensed among friends. As for Scotland: we have a population of a rough million and a half; we are represented in the Westminster Parliament by forty-five members—and they are elected by not more than three thousand unrepresentative privileged landlords and their crooked nominees and agents. How then are we to talk of liberty and of the dignity of civil government when such a state of affairs exists?"

"True enough, Robert—true enough. We could do with a broader representation. But it would never do to give votes to everybody and anybody. The possession of land must ever be the basis of electoral right. What do you say, MacKenzie?"

"Much as I sympathise with Robert, I must say that I hold with you, Gavin: it would never do to give the rabble a vote. If not land, then property of some sort must be the essential qualification . . . And I think Robert agrees with us."

"The rabble! Yes; but who are the rabble? Our drunken gentles are as much a rabble as any. Worth and wealth have never gone hand in hand as far as my experience in reading or in life has gone."

"And who's to determine worth, Robert?"

"Politically you can't, Mr. Hamilton: so you are thrown back on honest labour as your criterion and yardstick of assessment. And both you, sir, and the doctor here are honest labourers of undoubted worth by the yardstick I have in mind."

"But would you include auld Robin Gibb, the bellman? I'll warrant he's honest enough—and worthy!"

"And why not? Auld Clinkum's no fool."

"Maybe; but would you say his interest in the welfare of the country was equal to that of, say, Claude Alexander of Ballochmyle?"

"Since Ballochmyle made his money in India there is no more to be said. For Henry MacKenzie in The Man of Feeling put down the last word on that subject. My own father was worth any ten Claude Alexanders—aye, or a nation of men like him."

"You've gotten some queer ideas, Robert. That's the poet in you. Your ideas wouldna work out in practice: they would turn the country upside down."

"Some day the country will be turned upside down—and it'll be found to be as practical the one way as the other. The American War turned that part of the country upside down. And the people there have found it eminently practical. Nobody can deny but that they have achieved a great political and human advancement . . ."

"That war was the cause of great misery and ruination to trade in the West here, Robert."

"The war itself was due to the headlong folly of the North administration: so much for our men of worth in Westminster—a parcel o' rogues in a nation."

"Ah! You're a wild man, Robert. I'm afeared there's a lump o' the Jacobite in you yet."

"And why not? I never held with the divine right o' kings: consequently I never held with the Stewarts. But Scotland lost more than Charles Edward on Drummossie Moor. She lost the last hope of her national independence. My forefathers were out in the Fifteen—and they were good Protestants and good Scots. They were ruined in consequence."

"Damned, you'll better put a bridle on your tongue, lad—that's dangerous talk."

"Not among friends surely——"

"No, no: you're safe enough wi' the doctor and me; but I'd have a care where I uttered siccan Jacobite sentiments."

"There comes a time, Mr. Hamilton, when care has to be thrown to the winds. I'm no Jacobite in the political sense o' the term—but I'm a damned sight less of a Hanoverian."

MacKenzie, who had remained silent for a long time, now entered the conversation.

"I'm no more Hanoverian than you, Robert. I ken fine what we lost on Culloden Moor. But there's no point in harking back to what is now lost and lost for ever. We've got to work out our destiny and our salvation along a different road. We're yoked to England.

What good will it do to thraw i' the yoke? We'll till nae soil that way. Freedom is a relative thing; and freedom and poverty are poor bedfellows. What we need is trade and industry; plenty of good hard work to make us prosperous and thriving. Poverty is the curse of Scotland: poverty—and ignorance that's bred from poverty."

"Lord God! and do you think that I don't know that? Poverty's been my lot since the cradle. My father was killed by poverty. The harder he worked—the harder we all worked—the deeper we got bogged in poverty and want. And was William Burns an ignorant man? Poverty and slavery—I was reared on them. Do the politicians raise their voices for the poor? Do the clergy? Do the gentry? The poor help the poor; and when they can't help each other they die. I've seen them die—and so have you. Politics that don't concern themselves wi' poverty are but the politics o' graft and corruption and naked self-interest. Aye: we want trade and industry; but not to make the rich richer and the poor poorer but to raise the prosperity of the whole nation."

"You put it better in that epistle you wrote to your brother-poet Sillar in Tarbolton." MacKenzie leaned back in his chair and quoted:

"I grudge a wee the great-folk's gift, that live sae bien an' snug: I tent less, and want less their roomy fireside; but hanker, and canker, to see their cursed pride.

"It's hardly in a body's pow'r, to keep, at times, frae being sour, to see how things are shar'd; how best o' chiels are whyles in want, while coofs on countless thousands rant, and ken na how to ware't."

Gavin Hamilton sipped at his whisky. With the general drift of Robin's dialectic he was in emotional agreement. But he wasn't sure that he liked the intellectual implications. It was one thing to reform society: it was quite another to turn it upside down; to make bold and sweeping alterations; to challenge the foundations of society; to make labouring-worth the criterion of social standing and consequence . . . But emotionally, yes. Why, wasn't he known as the poor man's friend? It was a good name to have; and it brought him a lot of business. Aha . . . he would do well to keep an eye on his brilliant Mossgiel tenant. He was already rousing much talk in the parish. Many douce respectable citizens were beginning to shake their heads. When James Armour had been repairing his roof the other day he had spoken very sharply about the Mossgiel farmer with the wild blaspheming tongue . . . On the other hand, Robert might be useful in attacking the Machlin Session. He had appealed against Auld to the Ayr Presbytery. He would sound Robert about it some day: a popular squib or two in his favour and to the discomfit of Auld and the Session wouldn't do him any harm.

MacKenzie, on the other hand, found Robert's arguments intellectually stimulating. He knew poverty as Hamilton didn't know it—knew it on sick-beds and death-beds; knew it in all its pain, anguish and humiliation . . . Aye, of course the wealth of the world was divided with cruel disregard for human worth and merit. It was altogether wrong that a gifted family like the Burns family should suffer from such grinding poverty. William Burns had been a remarkable man, gifted with intelligence and integrity far beyond the common run. And his sons, Robert and Gilbert, were even more remarkable . . . If Robert here wasn't shaping towards genius then he didn't know the meaning of the word. And yet there he was, slaving himself on Mossgiel when he should be studying and writing. Well . . . there wasn't much he could do about that in any financial sense: he was having something of a struggle himself. But, before the Lord, if there was anything he could do by way of friendship and encouragement . . .

Gavin Hamilton came out of his reverie, poured himself and his guests another drink, and turned abruptly to Robin.

"You're gey big with Richmond my clerk, Robert?"

"He's one of my best friends in Machlin."

"I'm not trying to pump you, Robert. I suppose he's told you of his trouble with Jenny Surgeoner?"

"I'm not at any liberty to discuss my friend's troubles, Mr. Hamilton."

"It was for his good, Robert. I was wondering maybe if you could inform me as to his affections for the lass—he's hardly in the position to marry her. Indeed, it would ruin his career at the outset. I've had a talk with him: he came to me for advice. Yet I've no wish to see the lassie wronged—the Surgeoners are a decent family. If you could help me to make up my mind on the best advice to give the lad . . . The beagles o' the Session will be on his track any day now: there'll be no escaping them unless he can get Jenny out of the way till her trouble blows past. Of course, maybe you don't know much about Richmond's affairs, Robert?"

"No . . . not his intimate affairs. And I would rather I had a word with Richmond first. But I understand he's been friendly with Jenny for a long time. I think Richmond's a man of honour in these matters."

"Aye . . . if he can afford to be a man of honour. But I notice that my nursemaid, Mary Campbell, is gey big with Jenny Surgeoner; and you're not above passing the time o' day wi' her yourself, Robert. If you can find out the way the wind lies, I'll see what I can do for Richmond. You'll be doing him a good service."

MacKenzie rose with a feigned tiredness, and Robin saw it was time for him to go. He bade a respectful good-night to his host, saluted the doctor and let himself out into the garden.

It was then he met Mary Campbell. They exchanged greetings.

"Come into the Tower here, Mary: I want a word wi' you."

"With me, Robert? I couldna go into the Tower and it night."

"Just for a few minutes. I have Mr. Hamilton's permission to have a talk with you; but it had better be private and the old Tower here's as convenient and private as you could wish."

Mary Campbell saw he was serious and the two of them slipped over to the old Tower of the Melrose monks that Hamilton used as a store. Inside the Tower it was impenetrably black, so they stood in the doorway.

"It's about Jenny Surgeoner, Mary. You're in her confidence, aren't you?"

"She's a nice lass Jenny."

"Is she in love with John Richmond?"

"In love? I'm sure I don't know now."

"Mary: what you tell me will go no further than this old wall. I may be able to do your friend Jenny and my friend Richmond something of a good turn."

"But what would I be knowing, Robert? There's very little I'm knowing about yourself when I think of it."

"And whose fault is that? But you'll get to know me, Mary: I'm not hard to know."

"You're a nice lad, Robert, I'm sure."

"You know you can trust me?"

"But what would I have to be trusting you about?"

"Mary: you'll have to trust me just as I'll have to trust you. Do you know about Jenny and my friend Richmond? Maybe you don't like Richmond?"

"I never said a word against him."

"Forget Richmond then: I see you don't admire him. But you like Jenny. Right! You know Jenny will have to mount the cutty stool with Richmond—with or without him?"

"The poor girl—and I never knew. Och, I'm not surprised either: but the poor girl . . . Does Mr. Hamilton know?"

"Soon the whole parish will know. Jenny never said a word to you?"

"I knew she was worried——"

"Mary: if Richmond doesn't marry her—how do you think she'll take it?"

"Oh, the scoundrel! He wouldn't be disowning the lass and her in her trial and sorrow."

"Listen, Mary. Richmond's no scoundrel: he'll do what's best. But if they don't love each other——"

"Of course Jenny loves him. She would never——What am I saying? I don't think we should be talking about this. I know nothing about such things."

"You haven't sat in Machlin Kirk and listened to Daddy Auld haranguing the poor devils on the cutty stool without knowing how things are likely to turn out for Jenny. Mind you: it's none of our business. But both Mr. Hamilton and myself would like to help as much as we can. There's not much I can do; but there's no end to the good Gavin Hamilton could do—if he knew the right way of things. Maybe, you see, it would be better if Jenny went away somewhere till her trouble blew over . . ."

"Till her trouble blew over . . .! Why has it always to be the lass who has to be going away somewhere? Would you ask a lass to go away, Robert?"

"No . . . I wouldna do that, Mary. But . . . sometimes things are difficult—as they may be with Jock Richmond."

"It's cruel for a man to send a lass away in her trouble. And the man who would do that is nothing but a heartless scoundrel."

"I agree, Mary: I agree. But maybe if Jenny has to go away it will only be till Richmond can make arrangements to marry her—and to save her from the holy beagles like Holy Willie."

"Aye . . . but he could marry her quietly?"

"You mean irregularly?"

"They could do penance for that later on—they would be married and the lass would have some comfort in her trouble when she would be needing it most. Och, Robin: I canna see that a man could be so heartless as to deceive a lass."

Thinking of Betty Paton, Robin squirmed.

"Mary: there are many trials and tribulations in this life. The road's not always easy. A lad and a lass can sometimes be guilty of folly—if you call it folly—and maybe they don't love each other enough for marriage. Marriage isn't for a day's or a year's daffing: it's for the rest of their earthly days. Oh, dinna think I'm trying to excuse any blackguard that would deceive a lass and leave her to face her ordeal by herself. Only—it isn't always easy; isn't always best to run into marriage just because of foolishness and the weakness of a night in the gloaming."

"Aye . . . but it's seldom just the one night, Robert: you know that as well as me."

"Ah well, Mary; you and me won't quarrel about Richmond and Jenny, will we?"

"No . . . Who's your lass in Machlin, Robert? Or maybe you have one about Mossgiel?"

"I'm heart-whole, Mary. But maybe if you and me were seeing more of each other——"

"You're a terrible man. Have you not been making a poem on any of the lassies? Och, I'm sure you must have made a lot of verses?"

Robin slipped his arm under her shawl and round her thin, lithe waist, and drew her towards him. Mary Campbell did not resist. She liked Robin. She was lonely in Machlin among strange people. She missed the soft Gaelic tongue of her native Cowal, missed the Arran mountains in whose shadows she had lived so long. Folks made fun of her strange Gaelic accent—especially the young lads. But Robert Burns was different. He was so sympathetic and understanding; and there was so much that was soothing and caressing in his words; soft words spoken softly without the harsh edge of the Ayrshire folk. Almost Gaelic he could be in his softness of speech, the fine sweet words dropping like honey from his lips. Never the trace of mockery or insincerity. He was black like the Campbells: black-haired, dun-complexioned, strong and vigorous in his sturdy build. And his eyes, glowing and smouldering . . . not Highland eyes, not Lowland eyes, not a man's eyes at all. Something of the sloe eyes of a dark Campbell beauty, but with the fire in them that no lass, whatever her beauty, could ever have. It would be easy, fatally easy, to fall in love with Robert Burns. She would have to keep a fierce grip on her emotions.

His lips were drugging her resistance, sapping away her will to resist.

"Oh Robert, Robert: you must be letting me go in now . . ."

"You trust me, Mary—my Highland Mary?"

"It's myself I canna be trusting, Robert. I don't know why I let you kiss me."

"Because you know there's no harm to my kissing, Mary."

"Do you love me, Robert? You've never said you loved me."

"There's some things that dinna need words put on them, Mary. It's the heart speaks o' love: not the tongue; and lips answer in a language that canna be heard."

"You're a witch, Robert. You should have had the Gaelic on your tongue—it's the language that speaks from the heart as the English canna."

"Then I'll just have to make good honest Lallans do duty for both."

It was cold in the old Tower. Robin drew Mary under his heavy plaid, and held her tightly in his strong arms. A long sobbing sigh came from Mary; but she was happy as she had never known happiness. Yet it was terrible to love a man as she loved Robert Burns.

A MOTHER'S REBUKE

When Lizzie Paton proved with child, and the fact could no longer be concealed from the parish, tongues began to wag. Saunders Tait, still rankling in Tarbolton (Robert was now the most active member of the Masonic Lodge there) launched into a poem:

"Search Scotland all around, by Lorn, next round by Leith and Abercorn, through a' Ayrshire, by the Sorn, tak' merry turns, there's nane can sound the bawdy horn, like you and Burns. Mess John cries, 'Fornicator Poet, you and Rab Burns hae been so roit, the good tap-pickle ye hae gloyt, of Moll and Meg; Jean, Sue and Lizzie, a' decoy't, there's sax wi' egg . . .'"

It was highly relished for its vigorous bawdry in Manson's howff and was soon being repeated, with impromptu variations throughout the township and the neighbouring farms.

John Rankine learned the news from a source nearer to Largieside, and immediately announced the fact to Robert in a letter.

Robert, of course, had received the news from Lizzie herself. She had never really hoped Robert would marry her. She sensed that though he loved her as she was unlikely to be loved again, it was not the kind of love that led to marriage.

Nevertheless he had not denied her, had not sought to avoid her company; and there had been no interruption of their intimacy. Whether or not he might yet marry her, it was some satisfaction to know that he was not going to deny the child.

Robert's reactions were conflicting. He wanted to marry Lizzie immediately: by every law of God and man he knew this to be his duty. He would not shrink from doing his duty; and his emotions revolted at the thought of betraying the girl who had so generously yielded to him.

But he did not love Lizzie: he had never loved her—not to the point of marriage. The question of marriage had never been discussed between them: he had made her no promises. Nor could she for a single moment have been blind to the ultimate consequence of her yielding.

Perhaps, then, it would be a mistake to marry Lizzie: a mistake they would regret all their lives!

He debated the question with himself for many weeks. And it was a many-sided question. No matter what happened now he would have to compear before the Session and do penance on the cutty stool. For pre-marital fornication if he married Lizzie: for simple (but more heinous) fornication if he didn't.

The prospect was far from agreeable. But at least he would do penance in Tarbolton Kirk under Doctor Woodrow or John MacMath—they would be more lenient to him than Daddy Auld.

It was a damnable and outrageous business this compearing before the Session, answering all their intimate questions while they probed every detail of the affair. Worse still, the public humiliation of having to mount the cutty stool three Sundays in succession and bear the public rebuke from the pulpit.

There was no religion, no piety about such an inquisition: it would only fill the mouths of the congregation for weeks: grist to the mill of scandal-mongering.

The more he thought of the public humiliation that lay before him, the more his mood hardened and the less he thought of his responsibility for Lizzie.

He would show them. If they were prepared to brand him with the seal of fornication he would turn the role of fornicator against them. He would accept their valuation of him and defy them.

So he replied to John Rankine in rollicking vein and put the affair at its true artistic level. His was a mere poaching offence.

He'd had his sport and had enjoyed it; and so had the bonnie moorhen. No doubt the lads in black would demand their gowd guinea of a fee. But what of it? He wasn't the first: he most certainly wouldn't be the last. Life had to be lived subject to life's own laws. And when the laws of life went diametrically against the laws of the Kirk, so much the worse for the Kirk: life was greater (and sweeter) than all the kirks and all the denominations.

But the affair wasn't so easily dismissed in the family circle at Mossgiel.

Gilbert was furious: Nancy and Bell were shocked and outraged—and deeply distressed. Mrs. Burns alone remained normal. She was not surprised. She had expected something of the kind long ago. She was merely confirmed in her estimate of the character of her first-born.

The family discussed the affair in Robert's absence. Gilbert led the attack.

"It's not only himself he's disgraced. He's disgraced the family. I won't be able to hold up my head in the parish."

Nancy said: "Lizzie Paton, of all the dirty sluts!"

Bell said: "I don't know how Robin could have fallen so low."

Mrs. Burns said: "Bess Paton's no slut: she's a sensible hizzie. She's made her mistake. But I blame our Rab: he's bewitched the lassie wi' that tongue o' his. Weel: disgrace or no': he'll just have to marry her."

At this the family were up in arms.

"Marry her, mother? It's ridiculous. She's not fit to marry into the family. She's beneath him in every way."

But Mrs. Burns was an Ayrshire peasant and she wasn't to be persuaded by such talk.

"She's been beneath him the only way he kens: so she can be beneath him in the proper way; and that's by marriage. We'll hae nae bastards in the family."

"I'll never own her as a good-sister: never!" cried Nancy.

And Bell added: "If he does marry her he'll need to take her away frae here. I couldna live under the same roof wi' her."

Gilbert weighed in again. "Here we are just getting settled into the place and we get this thrust on the top of us. It puts out all my reckonings—and every bawbee's laid out in advance. Robin canna leave us like this: it would mean we would all need to give up the place. And he canna bring a wife like that here. We just canna afford a wife—and a wife and a bairn's clean out of the question. We canna think of it, mother: we just canna begin to think of it. And that's no' counting the shame o' it."

One day Mrs. Burns cornered Robert in the byre. There was no escape.

"You've been avoiding me, Robert," she began. "But you canna avoid your mither. I'll no' catechise you: I'll leave that to the Session. I'd just like to ken how you ettle for to act wi' Bess Paton?"

"I think that's my own affair, mother: I would rather no' discuss it."

"Fine I ken you would rather no' discuss it. But you're ower late in the day thinking about that. And I'm still your mither. There's yae thing, Robert: I'm glad your father's away: it would hae been a sair, sair hurt to him."

"I don't think you've any right to bring my father's name into this."

"Maybe no; but he warned me this would happen no' so long afore he slipped away . . . It's nae surprise to me, Robert; but it's been a gey shock to your brothers and sisters."

"They'll want me to marry Lizzie——?"

"No: I'm the only one that wants that. And that's what ye canna escape. You're a Broun as weel as a Burns, Robert; and you've a conscience off baith sides."

"Maybe I'll have a double dose then?"

"If ye marry the lass, Robert, you'll hae my blessing: you'll be doing what's right—and marriage'll settle you."

"You think I need settlin'?"

"I never knew a laddie that needed it mair. I ken you've nae ears for ony word o' your auld mither, Robert; but you're aey my son; and it hurts me to see the road you're travellin'. If you dinna act your part wi' Bess, you'll live to rue it. Mark my words—me that wouldna see a hair on you straiked the wrang way. If the lass was good enough for you afore, surely she means mair to you now. Neither Broun nor Burns ever had the name o' a blackgaird afore, and it'll be an ill day when you merit the dishonour. Oh, I ken you'll gang your ain gait—you were doing that long afore your faither died. But think weel what you dae, son; and seek God to guide you. It'll be nae disgrace gin you marry the lass: that's happened to better folks than you afore this. But if you jilt the lass and leave her to mither a faitherless bairn, it's no curse o' mine that'll be on you; but it's a curse that'll go doon wi' you into the grave."

"I never said I wouldna marry Lizzie—but I never said I would: neither to Lizzie nor onybody. I've made no promises one way or the other—and I'm making none."

"Weel, son: I canna say mair nor I have. But a lass like Bess doesna give herself to a man withouten she has some kind o' a promise—even if it's no' made in sae mony words."

"And would you have me ruin my life just because I made a mistake?"

"Ah, but Robin, my son: you've made the mistake ower often for it to be a mistake. And puir Bess hasna the wit to be upsides o' a man wi' a tongue like yours. You've a tongue wad wile the bird frae a bush——"

"I never deceived Lizzie Paton——"

"No . . . maybe no. You just neither looked to your right nor your left but held to your ain inclination. But it'll no' dae . . . it'll no' dae."

"I haven't made up my mind yet—it's no' easy, mother: no' as easy as you think."

"We'll leave it at that then. But whatever way you make your bed, mind it's yourself will hae the lying on't. Mind you can be poor and still look the world in the face. But it's a gey affront when you meet folk in the road and have to pass them wi' your head among your feet."

She turned and left the byre. Robert's head was among his feet. Several times he had raised his head slightly so that his eyes came level with the bowed grey-headed figure that was his mother.

She had stood there old and bent and seemingly frail, and had talked to him with a softness of tone such as she had never used to him before.

Aye: she was his mother; and he was blood of her blood as well as the blood of William Burns. And she was right: there was no escaping her forthright logic. Her logic was only to be countered by another logic—and this logic would have to be of his own devising.

That night he saddled his favourite mare, and rode back to Adamhill to consult with John Rankine.

Adamhill welcomed him heartily.

"So I'm rough, rude, ready-witted Rankine, am I? You're a hell o' a lad getting, Rab. And what's biting you? Aye . . . so that's it, is it? Put your mind at ease, Rab: put your mind at ease. The Paton lass was just like ony other heifer in the park yonder roaring for the bull. If it hadna been you it would have been another. That's the sum and substance o' it, Rab. Oh, I ken you've been runnin' aboot wi' the lass back and forward. But, since you've made no promise the one way or the other . . . In ony case, Rab, Lizzie Paton's no' the lass for you ava'. A marriage there would be a mockery. I know, I know: you dinna like the idea o' fathering a bastard into the parish . . . and between ourselves, Rab, I've had a bit twinge o' conscience that road myself. Oh, I'll no' deny it: it gars ye wonder at times . . . But still: marriage is no' to be thocht o' . . . Now, if it had been Annie, as it micht well hae been! But that's finished now. She's gotten a good man, Annie: John Merry. It's a good-going change-house at New Cumnock they fell into. You'll need to go down and see them sometime, Rab. Oh, she aey speirs after you. I'll warrant she'll aey hae a soft side to the rigs o' barley. You were a silly beggar for yourself, Rab. God, boy; but she'd have made you a grand wife . . . Now, I dinna want to see you worrying about this bit ploy; but you'll need to watch that gun o' yours or some dark night you'll be shooting the wrong bird . . . Come on, damn you: you're neither drinking nor saying a word."

Riding home, Robert felt relieved and refreshed. John Rankine had an astonishing fund of solid common sense. And no doubt he had the truth of the matter. Lizzie had been built that way, and if it hadn't been him it most certainly would have been another. For there could be no doubt: Lizzie had been as willing as he had been eager.

And yet and yet . . . There was his mother standing there bowed and grey, speaking in a voice strangely moving and sympathetic, telling him that he was a Broun as well as a Burns and that he had inherited conscience from them both.

Folk could say what they liked; but it wasn't easy to do the right thing—wasn't easy to know what was the right thing.

Maybe if he had married Annie Rankine . . . But what was the use . . . There were none of them suitable for marriage—not the marriage he wanted—supposing he knew what kind of marriage he wanted. All he knew was the marriage he didn't want.

A NEW-YEAR'S DAY

New-Year's Day of Eighty-Five came with a Saturday blink of sunshine and a touch of white frost. It was a day on which little work was done about the farm. First there was the family well-wishing. As soon as Robin and Gilbert were out of bed they were clasping hands and wishing each other all the best. Downstairs the hand-shaking went round the family. The cloud of Betty Paton was forgotten about. Even the boy John, sickly and pining (but uncomplaining) seemed to be in a cheery mood; and when the orra lads, John Blane, Willie Patrick and Wee Davoc came into breakfast sleepy-eyed from the stable loft there was a festive spirit in the air. Robin got the whisky and sugar and prepared drinks (some of them well watered from the boiling kettle till the strength of the spirit was rendered almost innocuous), and everybody got their Ne'erday dram.

There followed more toasting, merriment and jesting, till even Mrs. Burns relented sufficiently to laugh at Robin's irresistible sallies.

The good mood and excellent spirit prevailed through the simple breakfast. Eggs had been saved for boiling and they added the touch of luxury to the meal.

"Ye micht as weel be happy, weans: Ne'erday comes but aince i' the year; and them that greet, or fecht on Ne'erday will be greeting and fechting a' the year to come. And if it's the Lord's will, maybe we'll hae a better year than we had last."

"Never fear, mother," said Robin. "We'll get by a' our troubles—those of us that hae troubles. What about you, Davoc: you've nae troubles, hae you?"

"No, Maister: jist my chilblins."

"That's a pity now. But wait till the snaw comes an' I'll soon cure your chilblins."

"Na, na, Maister: they get chappit in the snaw. I like them rowed in a bit o' red flannin warmed at the fire."

"Well, I'll see you get them rowed in warm flannel the nicht, Davoc. Mother! hae you got a bit o' red flannel?"

"I'll see what I can lay hands on. But when I was a wee lassock and was sair forfochen wi' the chilblins we waited for the snaw, made a big snawba' an' rubbed them weel wi' it. It was a grand cure. It had to be: it was the only ane we kent o'."

"And what about you, Willie? Hae you mae chilblins?"

"I hae nane the year, guid be thankit, Maister Robert; but Jock Blane has twa-three meikle blae anes."

"I hae that, Maister."

"I hae big anes too," said John. "Mither, will I get red flannin too?"

"Aye, son: you'll get red flannin."

Bell said: "Ach, what's a' this fash about chilblins: we a' hae chilblins."

"Ah, but what's chilblins to you, Bell?" said Robin. "It's a life and death matter till a wee sodger like Davoc here."

Davoc's old-fashioned talk delighted Robin. His cheeks were red with the heat of the kitchen and his small bright eyes twinkled, for he was delighted with the attention he was receiving. The Mossgiel household had been gloomy this while back but now even Gilbert smiled on the table; and when Gilbert smiled it was a grand omen.

But Isa was not to be outshone by Davoc. She too was delighted that everyone seemed happy and in carefree mood.

She waited her opportunity.

"Hae you no' a poem for us seeing it's Ne'erday, Robin?"

"Noo, what kind o' poem would you want aboot Ne'erday, Isa?"

"A poem aboot Ne'erday of course."

"Just like that?"

Nancy said: "You ken he takes a' his verses to Machlin now?"

"Oh, is that the way the wind's blawing, Nancy? I don't take my poems anywhere."

"Och, I didna mean onything, Robin."

"Hae you got a poem, Maister Robert?"

"You wanting a poem too, Willie?"

Willie said: "We a' want a poem—if it's a good one—a funny one."

"Oh! So you're becoming a critic, are you?"

"Oh, come on, Rab," said his mother. "Read them a verse or twa if you've gotten something for the occasion. Then we'll redd the table."

"Well, I have a wee bit of a verse. It's about an auld grey mare. I wrote it out this morning afore I'd my clothes right on—that right, Gibby?"

"Aye—that's right," agreed Gibby with a ready lie.

"What's it ca'd, Maister Robert?"

Robin fished in his pocket and drew out the folded sheet.

"Let me see now. It's called The Auld Farmer's New-Year Morning Salutation to His Auld Mare Maggie—on giving her the accustomed ripp of corn to hansel in the new-year."

"Oooh! This'll be a guid ane."

"Wait now, wait now. Wait till you hear the first verse. A guid New-Year I wish thee, Maggie! Hae, there's a ripp to thy auld baggie; tho' thou's howe-backit now, an' knaggie, I've seen the day thou could hae gaen like ony staggie out owre the lay.

"Tho' now thou's dowie, stiff, an' crazy, an' thy auld hide's as white's a daisie, I've seen thee dappl't, sleek an' glaizie, a bonnie grey: he should been tight that daur't to raise thee, ance in a day.

"Thou ance was i' the foremost rank, a filly buirdly, steeve, an' swank; an' set weel down a shapely shank as e'er tread yird; an' could hae flown out owre a stank like ony bird."

"Oooh! that must hae been a gran' mear, Maister Robert."

"Oh, she was a topper, Davoc."

"Was she yours, Maister?"

"No, Willie . . . I'm no' just as auld a farmer as that yet. But I kenned her weel. Listen now."

Robin sat tilted back in his elbow-chair at the head of the table, Gilbert on his left hand, his mother, back to the fire, on his right. The orra boys sat at the foot of the table nearest the door. The family were all attention. It was a rare experience for them to hear Robin read one of his own compositions. And this one promised to be first-rate. But he was in such a rare good mood that anything he read would have sounded first-rate. He could have read all day and they would have listened to him, so pronounced was his ability to hold them in the spell of his mood-magic.

Mrs. Burns felt warm towards her first-born—the child she had never been able to understand—the man whose moods she had never been able to fathom, whose ideals and aspirations she had never been able to comprehend. Why couldn't he content himself sitting at his own fireside, one of the family and at one with the family. He was just a big open-hearted laddie for all his queer moods and wayward habits. Aye; and wi' Lizzie Paton to warm the bed for him and wi' a bairn to dandle on his knee he would soon find out that the fireside was better than all the howffs in Machlin or Masons' Lodges in Tarbolton. God! Listen to him and you'd think he had all the wisdom and experience of three-score and ten on the brow of him that was black and brent.

"When thou was corn't, an' I was mellow, we took the road aey like a swallow: at brooses thou had ne'er a fellow, for pith an' speed; but every tail thou pay't them hollow, whare'er thou gaed . . .

"Thou was a noble fittie-lan', as e'er in tug or tow was drawn! Aft thee an' I, in aught hours' gaun, on guid March-weather, hae turned sax rood beside our han', for days thegither.

"Thou never braing't, an' fecht't an' fliskit; but thy auld tail thou wad hae whiskit, an' spread abreed thy weel-filled brisket, wi' pith an' power; till sprittie knowes wad rair't, an' riskit, an slypet owre."

Damned, thought Gilbert, his ears tingling with the impact of the incomparable imagery and perfection of description, that's unbeatable. How by all hell's black magic and heaven's blessing does he do it? The God's own truth, every word of it. Six roods of a good March day—there wasn't another farmer in the West could add another rood to that. Go on, Rab, go on till the crack o' doom: heaven's own breath o' inspiration filling the sails of your fancy.

"When thou an' I were young and skiegh, an' stable-meals at fairs were driegh, how thou wad prance, an' snore, an' skriegh, an' tak the road! Town's-bodies ran, an' stood abiegh, an' ca't thee mad."

The laddies gurgled with delight. Willie Burns had a broad grin on his broad face. Nancy's eyes danced and Bell beamed. Robin gave a quick glance round the table to catch the expressions; he had known from the first verse that he had their interest and attention. And he had to admit, as he took a deep breath, that never before had he got so much pleasure from reading his own verse.

"In cart or car thou never reestit; the steyest brae thou wad hae fac't it; thou never lap, an' sten't, an' breastit, then stood to blaw; but just thy step a wee thing hastit, thou snoov't awa'.

"My pleugh is now thy bairntime a', four gallant brutes as e'er did draw; forbye sax mae I've sell't awa' that thou hast nurst: they drew me thretteen pund an' twa, the vera warst."

Agnes Burns bowed her grey head and clasped and unclasped her hard toil-calloused hands. Whatna kind of laddie was this she had brought into the world? Oh, but his father would have been proud to have sat and listened to him this day; and to think that last new year he had been lying on his death-bed in gloomy Lochlea. But he was better away. He could never have survived the disgrace of Lizzie Paton. How could a son of hers sit and read verses like this and betray a lass like Lizzie at the same time? He couldn't plead that he didn't understand. A mind that could think up verses like that had all the understanding it could carry. Robert, my son: if only you would take a lesson from your brother Gilbert. Ah, but Gilbert had been named after her father, Gilbert Broun: he was more Broun than Burns.

"Monie a sair darg we twa hae wrought, an' wi' the weary warl' fought! An' monie an anxious day I thought we wad be beat! Yet here to crazy age we're brought, wi' something yet.

"An' think na, my auld trusty servan', that now perhaps thou's less deservin', an' thy auld days may end in starvin'; for my last fow, a heapet stimpart, I'll reserve ane laid by for you."

John's breathing was more rapid; a bright flush was high on his cheeks; he felt so tensed and excited that he feared a coughing fit would be upon him before Robin had come to the end of his verses. And he didn't want the verses to end. If only mornings could be like this to all eternity.

"We've worn to crazy years thegither; we'll toyte about wi' ane anither; wi' tentie care I'll flit thy tether to some hained rig, whare ye may nobly rax your leather wi' sma' fatigue."

There was a pause as Robin brought the legs of his chair to the floor and folded the sheet of paper.

Gilbert thought (and his thought was echoed in Nancy and Bell): Almighty God! But what kind of man are you? There's something about you and your verses that thaws out anger and spleen and sends the flood-waters of forgiveness surging in their stead.

And then Gilbert rose, placed a hand on Robin's shoulder and gripped hard. He went swiftly to the door. There was a lump in his throat.

"Maister Robert! Will the auld farmer gie Maggie her stimpart the day?"

"Aye, Davoc lad: the Auld Farmer has a prodigious lang memory—and heapet stimparts frae here till the moon. Now away wi' you; and see what you can do to make Peggy look like a lady, for I'll need her gin afternoon—but no' too sair wi' the curry-caimb, you deil's buckie!"

THE GOWDEN GUINEA

After the holiday of the New-Year's Day, Robert applied himself with renewed vigour to the labour of the farm. This year there would need to be no mistake with the crops.

But for all his hard work on the farm there remained plenty to interest him outside it. John Richmond, after a gruelling time with Daddy Auld and the Machlin Session, had to take his punishment publicly in the kirk and mount the cutty stool three Sundays in succession—as had poor Jenny Surgeoner, already big with child.

Robert commiserated with Richmond. He was in like trouble with Betty Paton and would soon have to go through the same ordeal himself. Fortunately, he was able to have his case brought before Doctor Woodrow's Session in Tarbolton, since Auld was satisfied with the arrangement that Robert should stand in Betty's parish, the parish in which the offence had been committed.

He did not relish the idea of having to mount the Tarbolton sinners' platform; but at least none of his family would be there; and Doctor Woodrow would be milder than Daddy Auld in his rebuke.

And so it turned out. He took the stand with Betty and other delinquents, for there was always a steady flow of penitents in any parish. For all that he got his ditty from Patrick Woodrow, and the ordeal embittered him more than he had thought it would.

Calling in at William Muir's after his third appearance, he fulminated to some purpose.

"I answer a lot of damned uncivil questions; I pay a gold guinea; I stand three times like a silly sheep and get twenty-one shillings' worth of moral catechism. Now I'm free o' any further censure—free of scandal. And what for? For doing the most natural thing in the world; for doing what I was sent into the world to do . . . But I went about it the wrong way. If I'd gotten a lad in black to mumble some damned cant I'd have been married and I could have battered a bairn out of Betty every twelvemonth. That would have been holy wedlock. But because Betty and I were fond o' each other and didn't wait for canting ceremony I'm a fornicator and my name's clashed round the countryside; and Saunders Tait will be hawking round another swatch of his damned doggerel. That's Christianity for you."

"Don't worry yourself about it, lad," said Willie Muir. "Nobody pays ony attention. There's hardly a man in the parish but what's been through the same. You tak' things ower serious, Rab. When's Betty expectin'?"

"May, sometime. May or June. Oh, I'll stand by the lass. But I'm damned if I'll go through wi' ony o' their matrimony after this. They're no' having it both ways. If they're for branding me fornicator I'll give them fornication."

"Na, na: you mauna gang that airt. Let that be a lesson to you. You've made a mistake and you've paid for it. Let it rest there. There's an excuse for a lad the first time; but no' the second, Rab. For the sake of your father's guid name and memory, dinna let them drive you into open sin. It's time you were married onyway, Rab. A bastard bairn can give a man a gey sair heart—in after years. Come your ways in, lad, and hae a bite and a sup and think nae mair about it."

But Robert had good cause to think a lot about his predicament. He soon found that tongues were wagging in Machlin and at the markets in Craigie and Kilmarnock.

Two courses lay open to him. Either he must lie low and wait till the hot breath of scandal had grown cold or he must brazen it out.

His anger was too fierce to allow him to lie low; the wound to his pride was too raw to be suffered in silence; the outrage to his manhood had been too brutal for him not to lash back in self-defence.

He found in Richmond a ready audience for his bitter tirades.

"I've seen lads and lassies on the cutty stool I felt sorry for; some of them I laughed at for they needed no pity and asked for none . . . Aye: I've seen all kinds on the stool—except the rich! They never mount the stool; they never have to suffer the indignity of being called filthy fornicators, stinking whoremongers and hell-hardened harlots in the sight of the Lord. Oh no: they pay five or ten guineas into the Poor's-box and go scot-free. And a damned beg-your-pardon secret and confidential compearing they do afore the Session.

"But the likes o' you and me, Jock: we're only dirt to be made into a public exhibition. As if the bluidy canting hypocrites with their screwed-up purse-proud faces weren't the biggest fornicators o' the lot. But then they enjoy their fornication under the sanctimonious cloak of religion.

"View it how you like, Jock: their morality's rotten. It canna be a sin to love a lass or a lass to love a lad. God made us that way— or He didna make us at all. That's the common sense of it. But we can worship the Lord with our bodies, can't we? If the act of begetting life isn't an act o' worship, then damn me if I know the meaning o' the word. And by what right, human or divine, does a lecherous little runt like Willie Fisher set himself up to tell me how I'll put into use the organs that God gave me . . ."

But Richmond, though he was in the mood for solace, was in no mood for philosophical argument.

"I made a mistake, Rab . . . I'm getting out o' Machlin. To hell wi' it! I'll go and push my fortune in Edinburgh. The damned thing is that I promised Jenny: of course, I would marry her if ocht happened. I think her folk'll hold me to it—if they can. There's nothing for it but to give them the slip."

"But, Jock: if you promised Jenny you would marry her——"

"Oh, I'll send for her as soon as I get a good position in Edinburgh."

"But you love Jenny, don't you?"

"I liked her well enough. Ach: I've been a bluidy fool, Rab. You're no' marrying Lizzie Paton, are you?"

"I never promised her marriage."

"Does that make ony difference?"

"It does to me."

"Aye; but it doesna make ony difference to Lizzie Paton."

"I think it does. She kens I didna deceive her."

"I canna see it makes ony real difference, Rab."

"Oh to hell, Jock: it makes all the difference in the world. I'll see Betty right: I'll take the bairn to Mossgiel if she'll part wi' it. You don't think I'd deny her or throw her in the ditch?"

"I don't intend to see Jenny stuck either. But—I'm clearing out as soon as I can. I've got my fortune to think about. Machlin's getting ower het a girdle, Rab. Besides, there's some talk o' Jenny being sent to Paisley till her trouble blows by."

Richmond's attitude troubled Robert. But in the end he was certain Richmond would do what was right by Jenny and marry her. It was just that his trouble was fresh on him and he did not see his way clearly.

Smith, on the other hand, was more keen to listen to Robert's blistering scorn of the Kirk. It delighted him—so much had he suffered from James Lamie—to hear the lads in black smote hip and thigh. But he was also aware that there was a deeper side to Robin's revolt: that behind all his scorn there was sound argument and thrilling logic. It emboldened his thought to know that there was a case against the corrupted Calvinism of the Kirk; that the flesh wasn't something to be reviled and denied but to be accepted as part of life's glory and mystery.

But Smith had his worries. He was not so successful with the lassies as Rab or Jock. Such of the Machlin belles as he had wooed had not yielded to his blandishments. In the heat of frustrated desire he had had to turn to his mother's servant, Christine Wilson. He didn't want to tell anyone about that: not even Rab. Kirsty was no beauty and no maid. She was almost twice his age and had already borne a child to Nance Tinnock's son.

Still, Kirsty was a woman, even though she was fat, sweaty and coming forty. And when he slipped up in the dark to the attic it was possible to imagine what Lizzie Miller or Jean Armour might be like . . .

Mary Campbell took much more mollifying.

"You are not the man I was thinking you were, Robert Burns. Och, you are like all the others. And the poor lass: what is to become of her?"

"She's no poor lass, Mary; and she's far from feeling sorry for herself. Why should she? She knows I don't love her."

"Love is an easy thing for a man like you to talk about."

"Not love, Mary. Surely you can understand what I mean! I liked Betty well enough. She is a good lass; and she has no regrets."

"How can you be knowing that? It's easy for a man to say that."

"Mary! I never promised Betty I would marry her; never told her I loved her—not as a man must love the woman he marries. Oh yes: we were foolish—or unlucky. We've paid our price for it. Even the Kirk has absolved us of any further scandal. Surely you're not going to hold this between us?"

"First it was your fine friend Mr. Richmond—you made plenty of excuses for him."

"Richmond, when the time comes, will do the right thing by Jenny Surgeoner——"

"Marriage is the only right thing. But I suppose if lassies will be foolish enough to trust the lying tongues of men they will just be having to pay for their foolishness."

"But I never lied, Mary. If I'd promised to marry Betty Paton then, by heavens, I'd marry her and defy the whole world. I scorn that kind of lying, I scorn to deceive. If you are going to join with the Kirk in branding me a fornicator, then fornicator I must be."

"You're a foolish man, Robert, to be boasting of your sin."

"Hell, Mary! Do you really count it mortal sin for two young hot-blooded people, male and female—as the Lord created them— to be guilty of sin merely because they fulfilled the letter and the spirit of nature's law?"

"Och, you're confusing me with your nonsense of words—knowledge is not at me at all—the way you would be putting it. It's foolish I am to be listening to you."

"You know fine what I mean."

"And maybe even if I were knowing I would not want to know."

"Who's doing the confusing now? Mary, lass: you do understand! Betty Paton was—if you like—a piece of folly——"

"A queer folly!"

"Have you never known a moment's folly, Mary?"

"I have never had any cause to fear I might be standing in the place of repentance—nor am I likely to be in any danger. I would never be so foolish as to be trusting any man."

"Not even me?"

"You less than any man I know."

"You like me less than any man you know?"

"Maybe . . . it's because I like you more. No, no . . . don't be putting your arms round me: I can be liking you well enough without that."

"You're a rogue, Mary. You know I love you or I wouldn't be standing here telling you all my troubles and tribulations. God, Mary, but I was angry—and here you've got me soothed and quietened till you would think I hadna a care in the world. There's magic about you."

"No magic at all. I'm just a poor Highland nursemaid and me far from my own folks and they that speak my own tongue . . . You said before, Robert, that you and me were the strangers here in Machlin; but you are not the stranger I am. You don't know what loneliness is with your fine friends here—including Mr. Hamilton—and your family just a mile up the road."

"Mary, lass, you can be lonely in the midst of a tavern and all your bosom cronies round about you. You can be lonely whenever your heart's lonely—and I've known that loneliness long enough. Maybe Betty Paton crept into a corner of it . . . Can you understand that? But of course you can. Oh, I know you have another loneliness that I haven't; and if I can ease that, Mary . . ."

"Oh, Robert! Why had you to get yourself into this trouble?"

"We'll talk no more of that. It'll blow by as these things always do. If I'd known you it would never have happened. When my father lay dying . . . No one will ever know what a trial that was. It was then that Betty Paton came to Lochlea. She was a good girl. We were both lonely and we struck up an acquaintance. Many and many a time I was thankful for Betty's company—for her human laughter—for the words of kindness she had for me. That's what Betty meant to me. We needed each other in a time of trouble, when my emotions were drained to the last bitter dregs. But Betty never meant to me what you could mean, Mary—what you do mean . . . Love, Mary, is not a thing that can be ordered in its going or coming. To like a lass and enjoy her company is one thing—it's natural and right for a lad and lass to like each other. But love—whither it comes there's no knowing—except that it comes . . . There's a worthy farmer friend of mine—John Rankine o' Adamhill—said to me, years ago, that the heart would tell me when I was in love—that I would know without my brain having to bother about a yea or a nay. I never knew how right he was till I met in wi' you, Mary. There's not another lass in all Kyle, Cunninghame or Carrick like you——"

"Och, what kind of man are you at all?"

"A poor man, Mary; but an honest one. I have never deceived my enemies: I haven't it in me to betray my friends. Oh, I'm not one of your prudent cautious ones, Mary. And the only fame I long for is the glorious fame of a true poet. That and the love of a fine woman and I ask no more from heaven."

"But I am no fine woman but a poor Highland girl without a penny and without a friend; and who am I to be the fine lady of a fine poet?"

"Fine feathers and fine silks may make fine ladies—and they may well be bitches out of hell for all that. It's an honest heart and a free mind that matters; and a man is rich beyond the wealth of rubies who can clasp such to his bosom."

"You'll have my head turned on me with your talk. Look you, Robert: I'll need to be going in or Mrs. Hamilton will be giving me a terrible catechising—and her time coming near. It's the terrible place Machlin: you can't turn yourself but you see some woman or lass big with child. You would think the men-folks had nothing else to do."

"It's the national pastime, Mary: you'll get used to it.

"Och, I'll need to be getting in, Robert. And don't you be telling Mr. Hamilton—or anybody—of our meeting here."

There was a soothing, caressing quality about Mary Campbell that reminded Robin somehow of Jean Gardner. Mary hadn't the flaming beauty of Jean, but she had something of her delicate trembling passion. But there was a maturity, a balance and sureness about Mary that Jean had never known.

And there was the glamoury of her Gaelic tongue and the fascination of the quaint rhythm of her word-patterns.

In a jeering, leering world, Mary Campbell seemed to possess the quiet ecstatic chastity of a saint. Not that she suggested a saint of chastity. Mary was human and she was a serving-lass. She lived in the midst of too much elemental passion and had too much healthy passion of her own to have any ignorant or false notions of chastity.

Robin loved her. But he knew that he could love any woman who was young, attractive and lively in her conversation. He was, indeed, in love with womankind, and womankind were crowding in on his life in Machlin—attractive, urgent and upsetting to his responses.

But, for the moment, Mary Campbell engaged his keenest response.

THE TWO HERDS

In March the Reverend John Russell of Kilmarnock and the Reverend Alexander Moodie of Riccarton disputed their parish boundaries. At least the dispute now came to a head, for they had been bickering and snarling about the boundaries for a long time.

Black Jock was, of course, the holy terror of Kilmarnock. The wabsters' wives there, when they heard Black Jock coming on his rounds, would gather their brats from the street and retire behind a snecked door.

Jock never sallied forth among his flock without his sturdy thorn stick; and he was not above applying it vigorously to the back and sides, head and shoulders of any of his flock who occasioned him any offence—real or imagined.

The Reverend Moodie, on the other hand, for all his Auld Licht sententiousness, had some fragments of laughter about him. There were times when he not only enjoyed a mild joke but could take part in one himself.

It is true that Moodie had always had a healthy respect for Black Jock. The Kilmarnock priest, well supported on his sturdy shanks, and his great barrel of a chest giving him a bull-like air, was an awe-inspiring figure. But when mounted on his saddle-backed mare and his great feet hanging low in the stirrups, Moodie could never resist a quiet smile at the corners of his mouth.

And so, coming home from a Presbytery meeting one afternoon and jogging down the long High Street of Kilmarnock,

101

Moodie withdrew the straw from his mouth and, on an irresistible impulse, applied it to the flank of Black Jock's mare.

Now the mare considered it indignity enough to have to bear the dead weight of her master without having to submit to the indignity of being tickled with a straw. She had recourse to a series of antics that almost unseated Jock. The children laughed delightedly and the adults grinned broadly.

Black Jock had caught a glimpse of Moodie's straw. But for the time and place he would have dismounted and given Moodie the fright of his life. As it was, he drew his heavy eyebrows an inch lower—and as far as Moodie was concerned they remained lowered.

Now, called to settle the dispute before the magistrates of the town, Moodie and Russell faced each other in an atmosphere of violent animosity.

Moodie may have been the aggressor in so far as he jocularly undermined the dignity of his colleague in the High Street; but to-day the tables were turned and Russell came into the attack like a wounded boar.

At Mossgiel, Robert had heard something of the preliminary bouts between the worthy herds and, being in the mood to relish any circumstance that would discomfit them, rode the eight miles into Kilmarnock to enjoy the fun.

He had formed the habit when attending the Kilmarnock market-day of dropping into the howff of Robert Muir, the wine-merchant, and they had become good friends.

"Damnit," said Muir, "if you're for the meeting, Robert, I think I'll leave the place to the lass here and take a step down with you. It'll be grand entertainment. Black Jock's ready to trail the guts out o' Moodie: so they tell me. Fair raised he is, and dunching mad like a bull."

"Aye, come on," urged Robin.

The fun was indeed glorious. So glorious, in fact, it broke every standard of Christian conduct known to the West.

Ultimately, under some sharp cross-examination from Moodie, Russell lost his temper completely, and his maniacal bellowings could be heard all over the town. Folks in the court-room began to tremble.

It had been bad enough when Russell had shouted "villain" and Moodie had shaken a lean fist and countered with "hypocrite."

"Liar!" now roared Jock. "Liar! you damned lump o' Satan. I'll teach you to shak' your fist in my face. You're a liar, sir: a treble and quadruple liar when you stand there and threep down my throat that I baptised in your parish——"

Finally, just as Russell was about to make a physical attack on Moodie, several magistrates rushed in between the disputants and brought the ridiculous and unseemly proceedings to an abrupt closure.

Robert and Muir returned to the howff feeling richly rewarded. They were joined by Tam Samson, the worthy Kilmarnock seeds-man and noted sportsman.

Tam was about the most kenspeckle figure in the town, a great wag and wit and mocker of the holy high-flyers. Truth to tell, Tam was something of a militant agnostic, and, though not a weaver, shared many of their more radical opinions.

"By God, Mr. Burns," he cried, clapping Robin heartily on the shoulder, "I'll warrant you hae gotten some inspiration the day. Damned, but I'm disappointed though. They should hae let Black Jock and Moodie settle the dispute physically."

Robin said: "He would hae finished Moodie—he's by far the older man. But you're right, Tam—the twa best herds in a' the West howling at each other like bluidy tigers would be inspiration enough for any poet. Don't worry—the lines are clinking in the back o' my mind even now. I'll be back in Killie next market-day wi' a swatch o' good rhyme for your entertainment."

Samson was a red-faced, burly man, who, for all his girth, was extremely agile on his feet. He had a ready tongue and a heart of gold. Robin liked him immensely—much in the way he liked John Rankine and Willie Muir of the Tarbolton Mill.

Robert Muir, on the other hand, was of the same age as Robin. He was thin, pale and of an intellectual cast. He liked an argument, loved poetry and women and was radical in his politics. The pair had taken to each other from the moment they had met.

Muir said: "When you think that Moodie and Russell are the kind o' men elected by the flocks—and the auld rams of the flocks at that—there's something to be said for patronage."

"There's everything to be said for patronage. If it wasna for the lairds there wouldna be a New Light minister in Ayrshire."

"Aye . . . damnit, Mr. Burns, but New Licht or Auld Licht they're damned kittle craws to hae aboot the place. A roaring bull like Black Jock's no' civilised and hardly decent. But some o' your New Licht billies are too mealy-mouthed to say boo till a goose."

And so they argued and debated over their drink; and more cronies came in and Robin was introduced as the rhyming farmer from Machlin-way.

The Kilmarnock men were different from the Machlin men as both differed from the men of Tarbolton and the men of Ayr. But the men with whom Robin became friendly had this in common: all of them had intelligence enough to know how life should be enjoyed. They were honest, good-natured and fond of good company. Almost to a man they were fond of the song and ballad literature of their district: none were tainted with the canting hypocrisy of the Auld Licht fundamentalists.

Robin's visits to Kilmarnock were not so frequent as he would have wished, but when he visited the weaving town—as when he visited Auld Ayr—he made the most of his time.

And soon there was a core of worthy men there who welcomed his visits and provided an ever-ready chorus to his latest swatch of verse.

When he returned to Robert Muir's with his satire, *The Twa Herds*, he was immediately besieged for copies.

Tam Samson roared his delight at what he considered the two best stanzas.

"What herd like Russell telled his tale? His voice was heard thro' muir and dale; he kend the Lord's sheep, ilka tail, o'er a' the height; an' telled gin they were sick or hale at the first sight.

"He fine a mangy sheep could scrub; or nobly swing the gospel club; or New-Light herds could nicely drub and pay their skin; or hing them o'er the burning dub or heave them in."

Afterwards Robin enjoyed a quiet meal with his host.

"You know, Robin," said Muir, his eyes flashing, "when I stand ben there and hear you read your verses I feel as if I were being liberated—as if something in me wanted to take wings and fly—no, soar, soar away into the light o' the sun. I canna find words to describe what I mean. Why the hell should you be wrestling atween plough-stilts? You were meant for something better. Damnit, Rab, you've gotten a head on you there's no' the equal in Ayrshire. No: I'm serious. I'm no' the man to flatter onybody: I'm telling you the truth. And that's Tam Samson's opinion too. And between you and me, there's no' a shrewder man in Killie than Tam Samson. There's naebody deceives Tam."

"You've all been more than kind to me. But, Robert lad, a man canna live by rattlin' down the rhymes on a sheet o' paper. They lighten the load o' life; but they don't fill the wame."

"They don't—worse luck. But there must be some way, Rab—there must be some way you can earn your corn without the drudgery o' a tack o' sour land. But for the minute I just canna think what road you could turn to get things easier."

And indeed there was no way. There was no deviation from the road that lay ahead of him.

But for all that Robin had never been happier. Every day he was finding his feet more firmly on the solid earth of reality. The circle of his friends and acquaintances was growing wider—and he was enjoying the rich experience of his varied contacts.

And strangely enough he was enjoying life the more because he was working harder than he had ever done. He enjoyed his infrequent breaks. He came back to the plough reinvigorated. No doubt Mossgiel was slavery; but it was a different slavery from the Mount Oliphant of his youth and the Lochlea of his early manhood. For too many long weary years he had slaved without remission and with little hope of betterment.

Now he had hope and the capacity for rich enjoyment. No longer did he fear that the world would crush him into poverty and insignificance.

He would conquer his corner of the world and set all fear at defiance. He had writhed under the lash of the Kirk and had flushed at the sneers of the unco guid. But he had found their measure, and now he was cracking the whip of searing satire on their rigidly-righteous backs. Best of all, for so doing, he was winning approbation and warm-hearted approval from the men he loved—and what a balm this was to his injured pride!

DISCHARGE TO CARE

Robin's circle of friends continued to grow. As a consequence his self-assurance developed into a happy, warmhearted confidence. The tide of inspiration mounted in his heart: his head was a riot of ideas and fancies.

Hearing a song that he liked at a house-party one evening, and finding that the author was none other than John Lapraik of Muirkirk, his heart went out in a great gush of warmth for a brother-bard. Was this not the same Lapraik who had married John Rankine's sister?

He would write Lapraik a poetic epistle. No sooner did the idea come into his mind than his hand itched for stumpie and a sheet of paper. It was grand to think that there was a rhyming comrade of such excellence no farther away than Muirkirk. He would invite him to Machlin and they would have a drink together and exchange ideas.

So down into the ink-horn went the newly-sharpened stumpie and down on the sheet of paper went the epistle.

The First of April, 1785, and the warmth of spring in the air with briars and woodbines budding green . . . and in the gloaming the whir and chirrock of the partridges . . . in the early light of the morning the hare, long-eared, peat-brown and saffron, loping across the dew-drenched lea . . .

What a joy to get it all down in the order of words, rhyme and metre forming among the words with the ease of breathing.

The image of auld Lapraik was before him. An older edition of John Rankine—kindly, sweet-tempered, with a long stretch of rich human experience behind him. A poet; obscure like himself; working in the fields by day; night-time by the cheek of the blazing ingle turning a quiet verse or two over in his mind, or maybe committing them to the discipline of ink and paper. A man after his own heart. None of your learned conceited bores with their insufferably stodgy college-talk. A man amongst men, sharing their labours, their joys and their sorrows.

A set o' dull, conceited hashes confuse their brains in college-classes, they gang in stirks and come out asses, plain truth to speak; an' syne they think to climb Parnassus by dint o' Greek.

Lapraik would like that. Aye: John Lapraik of Muirkirk would welcome this epistle. There was one sure guide to that: he was enjoying the writing of it himself. And it was a great joy to be writing heart-felt lines after so much thrashing of the clergy.

And Lapraik was bowled over by the epistle when it reached him, and he made the journey of fourteen westward miles to Machlin and met Robin by arrangement in the back room of Johnnie Dow's.

"Let me look at ye, Mr. Burns. Damned, the verra man—every inch and bit o' ye. You'll be coming thirty?"

"Twenty-six."

"Just a lad yet. Man, I wondered at your epistle; but now that I see you, I think I understand. Robert Burns—aye, the verra same. I mind John Rankine o' Adamhill telling me about a lad that had come into his parish . . . aye, John had a great word o' ye, Robert. Damned, and John's nae bad judge o' man or beast or a growing crop."

"John Rankine's been a good friend to me."

"Well, I'm proud to meet ye, Robert—even if ye'd never kenned John Rankine."

"No prouder than I am to meet you, sir. And it's only right that bards should meet over the common bowl and swop their wares."

"Aye, well . . . there's sense in that. Mind you: I'm no' much o' a bard; but I've aey had a hankering after a sweet sang and guid-goin' ballad. But you seem to hae gotten a grand knack o' stringing rhymes thegither."

"Aye: just a knack, John."

"Like ca'ing a shoe on a pownie—only it's a hantle-sight rarer."

"And a hantle-sight more important."

"In a way, Robert—after a manner o' speaking. It doesna fill the wame."

"No . . . But was it ever otherwise; and did bards ever stop singing because their bellies were empty?"

"Ah, my lad; but that's what neither you nor me can tell. An empty purse and a toom meal-poke are bad companions for ony bard. Fegs, ye'll no' sing much on an empty stomach—and ye'll no' sing lang. Ah, you're young, lad. Ye ken little or nothing about the ways o' the warld. Mind ye: when you're young and hae your health and strength you fear nothing—God, man, beast or devil. I ken all about it. Oh fegs, aye. But it's a different story when ye get up in years and misfortunes crowd round ye—you're no' just so able to dance a hornpipe at the crossroads o' the warld. No: a damned wee corner does you in many ways. And then maybe a sang comes into your mind—or maybe gin you are gifted that way you mak' one up for yourself."

"Maybe you're right, John. Don't think I'm ignorant of poverty and hardship and misfortune—they've been my constant companions through life. But, as you say, for all that I'm at the hornpipe stage and feel I could never dance myself done. But tell me how you first came to write your songs—and tell me how you like poor Bob Fergusson."

And there they sat over gill and ale, the young bard and the old bard. Gradually Lapraik became mellow and unbosomed himself to Robin, telling him of his joys and his sorrows—and the happy days of auld lang syne; brooding bitterly on the failure of the Douglas and Heron bank that had driven him to the edge of ruin, and a spell in the debtors' gaol; telling him too how little love he had for the way folk were living in the present: men and manners going, as they were, to the devil. And the lassies! the best of them nowadays were getting as bold as tinkler-jads and the dress of them getting clean out of hand with their coloured silks and ribbons. But it seemed, when Robin questioned him, that silks or satins or good homespuns, high-kilted and low-kilted, houghma-gandie had always been houghmagandie; that lad and lass had changed but little in their essential ways whatever might be said of their outward manners . . .

And then later on Jamie Smith, Jock Richmond and Tanner Hunter came in, and they gave the old bard a toasting and singing that brought tears of sentiment welling to his eyes.

Still later, Holy Willie, going his round of the ale-houses to see that folk were warned of the approaching hour beyond which it was censurable to be abroad and doubly censurable to be carousing, put his sly head round the door.

In an instant Richmond, who bore him an undying grudge for unmasking his offence with Jenny Surgeoner, pounced on him.

"Come in, Mr. Fisher, come in, sir. You're right welcome, Mr. Fisher. We have a rare guest here—a bard from Muirkirk. Come right in, Mr. Fisher, and make his acquaintance."

Holy Willie's eyes went pointed and foxy. He never knew what these damned young blackguards were thinking and plotting. But Lapraik interested him. He was curious to know why he had come down from Muirkirk and what could be the nature of his business in Machlin.

Fisher edged himself sideways through the door (but he never entered a room otherwise) and stealthily drew the sneck.

"It's getting fully late," he began. "I don't know that I should be sitting down."

"Now, Mr. Fisher, sir, who could have a better right to sit down . . . ?"

And so Holy Willie's fears were allayed, and as soon as he had a caup of ale inside him (topping the day's drink) he was at his ease.

Not that Willie was ever completely at his ease: going about the Kirk's work in Machlin as Willie Fisher went about it did not allow for any ease.

Richmond winked at Robert, who had picked up his cue.

"I came on a poem here, Mr. Fisher, that sings the grace and glory o' the eldership of the Scottish Kirk . . ."

"Indeed now, Mr. Burns: that's a pleasant change. Ayeum: a pleasant change. The verses didna come frae Muirkirk by ony chance?"

"No' that airt, Mr. Fisher—at least not that I ken o'—and I don't think the Bard o' Muirkirk kens about them either."

"Just so. Well . . . let's hear a verse or twa, Mr. Burns. It'll be a great pleasure, I'll warrant ye, hearing a lift given to the Kirk's elders."

"Well . . . gather your attention, Mr. Fisher. O Thou that in the Heavens does dwell, wha, as it pleases best Thysel, sends ane to Heaven an' ten to Hell a' for Thy glory, and no' for ony guid or ill they've done before Thee!

"I bless and praise Thy matchless might, when thousands Thou hast left in night, that I am here before Thy sight, for gifts an' grace a burning and a shining light to a' this place."

"Aye: that's verra nice, Rab," said Holy Willie, "verra nice indeed—I'm glad to see that you're taking up wi' a better kind o' verse than you hae been of late. Oooh aye: that's a verra nice verse, Rab. Fire away, fire away: I'm listening."

It could never be said that Willie Fisher ever relaxed the sacerdotal sourness of his countenance sufficiently to beam. Yet the Machlin lads had never seen such a look of satisfaction on his face. His foxy eyes were narrowed, but not as a fox would narrow them in fear or cunning. Rather were they narrowed as a housedog's, and it going to sleep on the hearthrug.

With a honeyed but grave cadence to his voice, Robin continued to intone:

"What was I, or my generation, that I should get sic exaltation? I, wha deserved most just damnation for broken laws sax thousand years ere my creation, thro' Adam's cause!

"When from my mither's womb I fell, Thou might hae plunged me deep in hell to gnash my gooms, and weep, and wail in burning lakes, where damnèd devils roar and yell, chained to their stakes.

"Yet I am here, a chosen sample, to show Thy grace is great and ample: I'm here a pillar o' Thy temple, strong as a rock, a guide, a buckler, and example to a' Thy flock!"

"Ah man, Rab," Willie sighed, "come ower that last verse again. Man, I misdoubt but I've wronged you. From what I've gathered in my work for the Session about the clachan, I had ratherly come to the conclusion that you had not just such a high opinion of the Kirk's servants. Aye, man, Rab: you'll be a credit to Machlin yet, and to Mr. Auld's parish. I trust, Mr. Lapraik, that you'll carry the news o' this back to Muirkirk. There are enemies, sir, o' the Kirk everywhere nowadays, and there's much backsliding. Oooh aye: it behooves every honest man to defend the doctrines and ordinances o' the Kirk and to grapple wi' the sinners so that they may be brought to a full repentance—aye, a full repentance, Mr. Lapraik."

But John Lapraik, noting the winking of the lads, eyed Holy Willie with some curiosity. He had known many sanctimonious hypocrites in his day, but he reckoned that Willie Fisher was a unique specimen.

"Weel, Mr. Fisher, folks aboot Muirkirk hae enough to do to mind their ain business. But I maun allow that I hae a byornar interest in Rab's verses here."

"Oooh aye; oooh aye: let's hear you then, Rab."

Robin said, without batting an eyelid: "I'm glad you like the verses, Mr. Fisher. Maybe they havena the polish or elegance of the best English, but I think you'll agree that the billie who wrote them down knew what he was about?"

"Oooh aye . . . Now I wonder who could hae made them up? You'll need to pen me off a copy, Rab: I understand you have a grand fist wi' the quill."

"Surely, surely, Mr. Fisher. But we'll better see how our anony- mous versifier proceeds wi' his extolling o' the virtue of the lay herd.

"But yet, O Lord! confess I must: at times I'm fashed wi' fleshly lust; an' sometimes, too, in warldly trust, vile self gets in; but Thou remembers we are dust, defiled wi' sin.

"O Lord; yestreen, Thou kens, wi' Meg—Thy pardon I sincerely beg—O, may't ne'er be a living plague to my dishonour! An' I'll ne'er lift a lawless leg again upon her.

"Besides, I farther maun avow—wi' Leezie's lass, three times, I trow—but, Lord, that Friday I was fou, when I cam near her, or else, Thou kens, Thy servant true wad never steer her."

As the verses had proceeded, Willie Fisher had grown more and more apprehensive. Suddenly the shafts struck home with deadly and devastating accuracy. He scrambled up from the chair, knocking it over.

His face was white and twisted with outraged terror. He raised his clenched fist in the air.

"Ye'll roast in hell for this, Rab Burns: you're a damned black-guard, Burns: a damned blackguard. Oh, that I should hae lived to hear siccan blasphemy——"

He raced to the door and clawed at the sneck, screaming with impotent rage. The lads howled with derisive laughter.

"Ye'll roast in hell, Burns, ye infernal blackguard. I'll tell the Session on ye—the whole damned lot o' ye——"

Willie Fisher escaped into the passage and they could hear him scurrying along the passage and clawing at the front door.

When they had dried their eyes and John Dow had come ben to see what the stir was about, Robin had regained control of himself.

"Puir Fisher," he said, after an explanation to Dow. "I never saw a fish so nicely hooked."

"Bad cess to him," said Dow. "But I'll need to hae a copy of thae verses, Rab. Damned, they maun be unco powerful when they put the fear o' death on Holy Willie. I thought he'd seen a warlock the way he flew at the door."

Later in the evening, when the lads had gone and Robin had taken a regretful leave with the old bard from Muirkirk, John Dow brought him ben a night-cap of steaming toddy and sat down with him by the dying fire.

"Weel, sir," he began, "what think you o' Rab Burns?"

"I kenna what to think, Mr. Dow. I'm byornar taken up wi' him: I'll tell you that much."

"Aye . . . there's damned few in Machlin ken what to make o' Rab. Whiles I dinna richt ken mysel'. Afore I got weel acquaint wi' him I thocht him a damned dour devil—and when he gets into one o' thae black moods o' his wi' his black brows lowered and his meikle black een glowing—damned I think he's a dour devil still. Ah, but it's seldom we see him in his black moods here. And man, when he's in the tidd there's naebody to equal him. It's a man like me kens. I see a' manner o' folks in the way o' my trade. Back and forwards like, I maun hae met half the folk in Scotland and the big feck o' the folk i' the West; but I've met nane could set out the burned side o' his shin wi' Rab Burns. Man, you've nae idea o' the variety o' his conversation—and he has a crappin' for a' corns forby. Politics, religion, the state o' Europe and Ameriky—damned, but he's fully strong on Ameriky—books, philosophy, poetry—ony damned thing you care to mention, Rab'll wade in wi' a swatch o' conversation that hauds a'bodies spell-bound . . . Aye, and mak' up a poem or twa-three verses just while you stand. The one time you'll find him standing at the Cross there in grave debate wi' Gavin Hamilton and Doctor MacKenzie, and the pair o' them listening wi' bent heads and cocked lugs—damned, you wad think they were lugging it to some grave college professor. The next time he'll be ben the room here wi' twa-three o' thae run-devils, singing and reciting and garrin' the rafters dirl wi' their merry on-goings. Damned, or you'll find him leaning on the corner o' Poosie Nancie's across the Gate there, speirin' the breeks aff a wheen gangrel-bodies or copying down a verse or twa frae an auld carlin and her resting her meal-poke on the kirkyard dyke outbye . . . Neist he's awa' daffin' wi' the lassies—damned, but he's half-a-dizzen danglin' the noo—aye, and I'll warrant fidgin-fain to get ahint the bush wi' him. Oh, he's a fell billie is our Rab. Aye, damned, but that tongue and that giss-quill o' his'll be the death o' him yet. There's a wheen folk in Machlin gotten their birss up against him—the unco guid especial. Aye and they'll get him yet—and when they get him they'll lay him by the heels. You see, he's too damned shairp i' the wit for them: like thae verses on Holy Willie. To hell, man! Stuff like that fair lashes them to their knees—blisters the hide on them. Aye: afore the week's out the half o' Machlin'll hae thae verses aff by heart: you canna blame them. Then they'll get to Daddy Auld's ears—and what goes in the yae lug o' Daddy doesna come fleein' out the other. Na, na: it bides there till Daddy has a need for't. I'm just waiting till he coups one o' thae Machlin queans and wow! but the Session'll come down on him howling like a pack o' beagles. And by God, sir, aince Daddy Auld gets him on the cutty stool fornest the congregation, he'll gie him a noble curry-combing. Aye, and it's a bluidy shame when you think on't, sir, for say what you like about Rab Burns—and damned a'bodies can say plenty—there's nae bad in him; headstrong and foolish for his ain sake, maybe; but damn the evil part about him . . .

"Aye . . . he's had a hard life the same Rab Burns. There he is up in Mossgiel working like a bluidy ox, him and his brother Gilbert . . . aye, and the auld mither and the dochters too. And yet, by God, half the time he walks about as if he owned the earth and hadna a care i' the warld."

John Lapraik eased his stiffening knee joints and Dow added some hot water to his toddy.

"I find your discourse fully interesting, Mr. Dow. You see: Rab Burns is a poet—I'm a bit o' a bard mysel'—but that lad's a poet in a way there hasna been in Scotland in your day or mine. And guid kens it's a fell unchancy thing to be a true poet. The warld, Mr. Dow, has sma' place for a poet—and nae reward for him. Oh, gin the warld's in its cups it'll laugh wi' him and throw him a bawbee in the bygane—providin' he kittles their fancy with a swatch o' flattery; but gin he rouses them wi' the lash o' his rhymes, they'd as lief clod him wi' stanes into the gutter."

"Aye, damned; but poets are weel-thocht o' too?"

"After they're dead. Oh, they crown them all right in the hinderend; but they crucify them first."

PRIDE OF PARENTHOOD

May was fresh and fair as a young bride—smiling up and down the heights and hollows of the land.

The song of acceptance was rich in Robin's throat. Each day seemed to bring him greater zest to appreciate the miracle of life— especially the miracle of life that bubbled in his own heart. Nothing worried him now, nothing oppressed him. He was master of himself, sure of himself and able to express himself with assured mastery.

Everywhere he went he made friends—and enemies. He cared nothing for the enemies. For the friends he cared everything; and he responded to them with generous loyalty. Perhaps had he been wiser, more prudent, more cautious and cunning, he would have restrained himself—making sure that he received more than he gave.

But he had ever been scornful of the sly cunning ones of the earth, had ever despised the mean and over-calculating. He gave as he would be given to: richly, abundantly and in full measure.

And as he loved so did he scorn. His contempt for all that was base, unmanly and ungenerous was a blistering contempt. So he made enemies as well as friends. But he feared no one.

On the second last Sunday of May he called on John Rankine of Adamhill. As he rode over from Largieside he was in a queer see-saw mood of exultation and depression.

That afternoon Betty Paton had become a mother and had made him a father by giving birth to a daughter.

He had made the journey over to Largieside with some tokens of goodwill: some meal, a ewe cheese, a pound of tea—and a gold guinea.

He had spoken softly and tenderly to Betty as she had lain exhausted on the chaff bed. Hers had been a natural and easy birth, and though she was in no broken torment she was exhausted and weak.

Her father had been civil enough: fatherless bairns were not unknown to Willie Paton and he liked Rab Burns for the honest way he owned to the child. Betty's mother had been less friendly even though she blamed her daughter for her predicament more than she blamed Robert Burns. But well might he come bearing gifts! It wasn't him who would have the care and trouble of bringing up the brat.

But before he left he had assured all of them that as soon as the baby was weaned he would take her to Mossgiel and have her reared as one of the family. Betty would be relieved of her burden and be able to seek work again in service. And as the Patons were desperately poor they had to acknowledge the generosity of the offer.

But as he rode over to Adamhill, the practical details of the ultimate arrangement ceased to bother him.

He was a father: this 22nd of May, 1785! He was coming into his seventh and twentieth summer the father of as sweet a baby daughter as had ever been born to any man.

He had no regrets that the child was illegitimate, for the good reason that he did not and would not draw any line of difference between children born in or out of wedlock. For him all children were legitimate—whatever the parents might be.

No: he had no regrets. He knew joy and exultation and great heart-throbs of manly pride.

And then came the fear. What did the future hold for this child who was his—who would be his more than she would ever be Betty's? A lass had a hard struggle and a more uncertain future in life than a lad. Would she grow like a flower—or would she be cursed with that plainness that would never stir the blood of men and raise raptures in a lover?

What indeed did the future hold for this newly-born entity of female flesh and bones and the intermingling of Burns blood and Paton blood?

If his fortunes didn't change—and there seemed little hope of that—the future might hold little but hard work and hungry days . . .

But he was a father; and oddly enough there was more joy in being a father than in being a poet—or in being a lover. It seemed that the conscious pride of fatherhood was the greatest thing a man could know.

"Weel, Rab," said John Rankine, as he dismounted in the court of Adamhill farm.

"Behold a proud father, John. Bess threw me a fine daughter this afternoon: I'm just over from Largieside."

They shook hands with mutual fervour.

"Man, Rab: I congratulate you—bastard bairn though it be. Lord, I never saw a man so set up on such an occasion. Most sinners prefer to keep silence—or deny their guilt. But, save us, here's you riding round the kintraside prouder nor Lucifer: holding your bastard bairn—as it were—up to the parish and asking for their blessing! Damned, Rab, but I've got to admire you: come awa' ben and we'll drink to the occasion . . . What are you naming the bairn?"

"Bess—the same as the mother. We couldn't do better—or fairer."

John Rankine shook his head.

"Sometimes I think I understand you, Rab: nane better. And then you say or do something that clean knocks the pins frae me."

"I don't know, John. Did you think I would deny my own flesh and blood, throw Bessie to the Session beagles and slink down the dyke-side whenever I saw onybody?"

"No: damned no, I didna, Rab. No' you. Maybe that's why I never had ony fear wi' you and Annie. But there'll be an unco clash through the kintraside about this."

"Let them clash, John. Aye; and the more they clash the better I'll be kenned. I stood on the cutty stool and took what they handed out to me. I've satisfied their laws and their ordinances. What more do they want: what more can they want? Fornicator they called me! Well, John, there's two ways o' being that. The wee lass that's been born to Bessie and me's been dearly bought—aye, but sweetly bought too, John. Many a merry night we had thegither, Bessie and me; and if this dear-bought Bess is the fruit o't, why in heaven's name should I not rejoice?"

"God, laddie, rejoice a' you ken since that's how you feel."

"Listen, John: when I wrote you off the verses you were so proud of, my tongue was in my cheek. Then I thought—in my head—that I didn't give a damn . . . I'd be the rantin' dog the daddie o't—and that would be that. Aye: as a young rantin' dog to an auld rantin' dog that had seen the day! And I wouldna have it otherwise twixt you and me. But when I saw Bess lying down there with the bit bairn in her oxter—my bairn, John—then there's another side to it. And a better side. Damn it, John, I feel I could do the same service for half the queans in the parish and still be in the right of it."

"Ah, you're a daft beggar, Rab. God kens the gate you'll go yet. But it'll be a byornar one. I'm aey telling you that, Rab. Aye . . . and I suppose this will bring forth another verse or twa frae you? Aye: I can tell by the look on your face that the lines are clinking in that head o' yours already. Come on: another drink an' out wi' them!"

Robin rose from his seat and stood with his back to the fireplace.

"I do have a verse or two, John, jingling in my mind. They're no' polished—and maybe I'll never polish them. I dinna mind them being a bit rough, though, for all honest, homely things are rough."

"That's a true statement, lad; and what are you thinking for a title? Your titles are aey worthwhile."

"A Poet's Welcome to His Bastard Wean? Or a Poet's Welcome to His Love-Begotten Daughter?"

"The first, the first—but that's just my own fancy."

"And then maybe, for a sub-title: The First Instance that Entitled Him to the Venerable Appellation of Father? Something like that—I'll need to think it over. And now for the verses, such as they are.

"Thou's welcome, wean! Mishanter fa' me, if thoughts o' thee or yet thy mammie shall ever daunton me or awe me, my sweet, wee lady, or if I blush when thou shalt ca' me tyta or daddy!

"What tho' they ca' me fornicator, an' tease my name in kintra clatter? The mair they talk, I'm kend the better; e'en let them clash! An auld wife's tongue's a feckless matter to gie ane fash.

"Welcome, my bonnie, sweet, wee dochter! Tho' ye come here a wee unsought for, and tho' your comin' I hae fought for baith kirk and queir; yet, by my faith, ye're no unwrought for—that I shall swear!

"Wee image o' my bonnie Betty, as fatherly I kiss and daut thee, as dear and near my heart I set thee, wi' as guid will, as a' the priests had seen me get thee that's out o' Hell.

"Gude grant that thou may aey inherit thy mither's looks an' gracefu' merit, an' thy poor, worthless daddy's spirit without his failins! 'Twill please me mair to see thee heir it than stocket mailins.

"And if thou be what I wad hae thee, an' tak' the counsel I shall gie thee, I'll never rue my trouble wi' thee—the cost nor shame o't—but be a loving father to thee, and brag the name o't."

When he had finished John Rankine raised his head. He was moved.

"Ah, Rab, Rab! How you can turn the tables on the Black Craws o' the kirk! They'll crucify you for that! And yet could there be onything bonnier or more natural-like? That's just how it should be. But you're the first man I ever heard tell o' to put it that way. What goes on in that head and heart o' yours is beyond ony ordinary understanding. And you composed a' that riding over frae Largieside?"

"No' quite, John. I had the feeling it was going to be a lassie—and I've been thinking on the lines for days."

"Aye . . . You had nae thocht to marry the lass—and yet, damn it, you love her!"

"Aye . . . of course. I couldna hate her, could I? But don't let's go into all this again, John. Marriage wi' Bess would have been a failure—and that's that."

"I'll say nae mair, Rab. Damned, but life's a queer mixty-maxty o' ups and downs and throughhither perversities. It doesna seem yesterday but down in the peat-bog you were giving us your satire on the Ronalds o' the Bennals. You were just a lump o' a laddie then, Rab. Now there you stand a full grown man and the proud father o' a bastard bairn . . . Are you coming ben for a bowl o' brose afore you tak' the road?"

SECRETS

Despite the disapproval of his family for his disgrace with Betty Paton, Robin was in high spirits all that summer.

He worked hard on the farm as long as there was work to be done. But the moment he could win free from labour he did so.

For the most part he sought the company of his Machlin cronies, Smith, Richmond, Hunter and Brice. But he took care not to neglect the company of his landlord Gavin Hamilton and his doctor friend John MacKenzie.

Indeed, he neglected none of his friends and never failed to attend the masonic meetings in Tarbolton; enjoy a bite and a crack with the Muirs of the Mill or call on the Sillars of Spittleside.

Maybe he would stay late in Kilmarnock on market-day and enjoy the company of his friends in Robert Muir's howff—especially genial Tam Samson and old John Gowdie, whose book was exciting a great deal of controversy in the West and was coming to be known as Gowdie's Bible. His visits to Ayr were less frequent, for it was a hard ride into the town and a much harder and uphill one coming back; but he did pay an occasional visit there and kept in touch with Bob Aiken and John Ballantine and other good friends like Willie Chalmers the writer and Willie Logan the fiddler.

And in between times he managed to keep in touch with the Machlin belles and enjoy a night with Mary Campbell.

But Mary was a difficult lass to court; and she was determined not to submit to Robin until she had secured a definite promise of marriage from him. Yet she loved him in a way that gave her little rest and caused her much foreboding agony. She lay in bed at nights and wondered how she could make him marry her—for she was sick of service and longed for a corner she could call her own.

There were times, however, when Robin felt the need to be by himself. Sometimes he would wander off alone and explore the physical nature of his Machlin environment. He delighted especially in wandering along a river bank—especially the wooded banks of the Ayr, the Fail, the Lugar and the Stincher.

He needed those lonely walks. The running water had a fascination for him: it stirred and yet soothed his creative moods. And his creative moods were deep and intense and came over him in waves.

Ideas flashed and fused in his mind and often a poem would come to birth in a sudden frenzy of creation that left him wondering and amazed, delighted and exalted.

When he was alone he was conscious of tremendous power—a power that in itself could not be shared with anyone. This power was generated in his secret self, a deep inward self so secret that even he did not know of its real nature and the extent of its boundaries.

It was a power that sometimes men like John Rankine and women like Mary Campbell sensed, but which he was incapable of revealing to anyone and which was only revealed to himself in creative flashes.

When the mood left him free for a time he was glad to seek human fellowship and taste the social hour in the Machlin taverns where men were warm and human, and, in a warm gush of words, a man might relieve the inward tension of spirit and know that thought was bounded in channels of blood and bedded in warm flesh; know that the world was not a dark mystery moving towards the illimitable darkness of eternity but the laugh of a maiden breaking in the sunshine, or the seal of lips warm and red in a gloaming of ecstasy—a silken thread spun from the sensation of experience.

But he had always been happy thinking—and never had his thoughts been happier. Now he knew with a crystal clarity such as he had never known what it meant to be a poet and how much of a poet he was.

There was nothing vain in the egotism of this knowledge. He measured himself with men and with women; he measured himself with life and with letters and knew that, in his supreme moments, he was not wanting—that the strange fusing of will and imagination that was called genius was as much his as it had ever been any man's.

There was one lass in Machlin who loved him—who longed to know him as other girls knew him. She watched him as he sat in the kirk of a Sabbath: she got glimpses of him as he strode about Machlin; and both the sight and the thought of him suffused her with a pleasurable glow that sent the blood coursing through her vigorous body and induced a spiritual buoyancy that refused to be suppressed.

Sometimes she blushed so violently at the mere thought of him that she had to find an excuse for hiding herself.

Her friends talked much of him—Jean Smith, Jean Markland and the Miller girls. They had pretended—with the exception of Jean Smith—to be horrified at his exploit with poor Betty Paton of Largieside. True, it was a commonplace exploit and not one to be taken too seriously—all men were like that and some women had to be unfortunate. But Robert Burns was different—and this difference had to be met with disapproval. It would never do for girls to admit they might somehow be in the category of the unfortunate in so far as he was concerned.

She had been consistently unfortunate in not meeting him when he visited Jean Smith's; and when she had gone across to a night's dancing in Ronald's ballroom, it had been the nights when he had been elsewhere.

Sometimes she heard her father talk about him to her mother; and she was not at all surprised to find that her father spoke of him in terms of strong disapproval.

One night, coming back from the dancing, he demanded to know if she had ever taken up with him. She blushed so furiously at that, that James Armour immediately suspected the worst.

"I'm warning you, my lass," he had said, "if ever I hear of you making up to that damned blackguard I'll break your legs for you. He's made a mock of every decent body about Machlin—he runs aboot with a wheen blackguards like Richmond and Wee Smith, that coarse tinkler Tanner Hunter and that infernal atheist Brice—and when he's not running wi' them he's colleaguing with Gavin Hamilton and Doctor MacKenzie, wha egg him on to more blackguardism—though what they see in him more nor beats me. Now I'm warning you, Jean."

Jean liked her father. True, she was well aware of his weaknesses and his petty vices. But for all his choleric temper he was essentially a kind man to his family and worked hard for their comfort and well-being.

James Armour had just topped his fiftieth year and his wife Mary (who had been a Machlin Smith) was but five years his junior. They had been married twenty-four years and in twenty-two years of child-bearing she had borne him eleven children. She hoped that she would bear no more. Robert the baby was almost two years old, and she prayed that he might live. Twice already she had borne him a Robert and they had both, like her first Mary, died in infancy. If the baby died she did not think she would be able to bear him another.

As Jean was the second eldest of the family (and the eldest girl) and was coming into her twentieth year, she had known a hard life. It seemed to her that her mother was always pregnant—or suckling a new-born infant.

But she had acted so long as nursemaid to her mother and the younger members of the family that she had grown to accept her lot. And she had come to accept the fact, to which all Machlin women gave testimony, that a woman's main task in life was either to bear children or to nurse the children of those who did.

As this seemed to represent the law of nature and of man and was universally fulfilled, Jean did not rebel against it.

But indeed there was little rebellion in Jean. Despite the drudgery of her days, her disposition was unbelievably sweet. It was this invariable sweetness of temper, combined with the warmth of her physical get-up that made her her father's favourite daughter— and indeed a general favourite with all who knew her in Machlin.

She sang well—she had a sweet clear note—and she was always singing. When she wasn't singing she was laughing; when she wasn't laughing her eyes sparkled with good-natured merriment.

Jean Smith was perhaps her greatest confidante in Machlin— though she had a specially warm affection for Jenny Surgeoner.

But to Jean Smith she could unburden herself with ease and confidence.

When they were alone together they often discussed Robert Burns. Jean Smith had a notion herself of Robert though she had sense enough to realise that Robert was not for her.

"I've tried to bring the pair o' you thegither, Jean; but it's a business you canna rush—no' wi' Rab Burns. If he sensed I was trying to make a match, he'd be off at the toot. And then, you see, he's gey big wi' Heilan' Mary Campbell ower at Gavin Hamilton's."

"She seems a nice enough lassie Mary Campbell."

"Oh aye—in a Heilan' kind o' a way: you canna trust thae Heilan' bitches: they're that damn cunning, Jean. Cunning and sleekit."

"Aye, I've heard that, Jeannie. But d'you think there's onything atween them?"

"Oh, Rab'll watch himself, dinna worry. Though what he sees in her I dinna ken."

"You never see them gaun thegither?"

"Oh, they've been seen. But you see: that's the cunning bit. She doesna want to be seen wi' him: doesna want to get a bad name."

"But why should she get a bad name, Jeannie? Surely no' because o' Betty Paton in Largieside?"

"Well, that doesna help, Jean—no' wi' the likes o' Mary Campbell. Mind you: Rab doesna hide onything about Betty Paton. Of course, that's Rab ower the back: he doesna hide onything. He let me read a poem he made up on Betty's bairn—as proud as a peacock he is about it."

"And what way did he no' marry the lass?"

"You see, he didna love her—and he didna promise her onything. That's the beginning and the end o' it as far as Rab's concerned. Oh, Rab's a funny fellow: but then I suppose that's the poet in him. But you canna help liking him, Jean."

"Do you really think he's a poet, Jeannie—a real poet, I mean?"

"Oh well: maybe no' just a real poet. Mind you: I dinna ken either. He's gotten a terrible knowledge in that head o' his. You'd wonder where he'd gotten it all—and him little better nor a working ploughman."

"They tell me his brother Gilbert's the same?"

"A nice fellow, Gilbert Burns—a proper gentleman. But he hasna onything like the life about him that Rab has. He's awfa staid and proper-like compared wi' Rab—of course I don't know him so well."

"His sisters look awfa quiet sitting in the kirk."

"They've nae life at all up there in Mossgiel—and afore they cam' to Mossgiel it was worse. They're as puir as kirk mice. The young one, Isa, has a bit of life in her; but baith Nancy and Bell are gey soured."

"I aey think they're a maist respectable family."

"Oh, they're a' that. Naebody can say a word against them. Och, but that farm o' Gavin Hamilton's keeps them slaving frae dawn till dusk."

"Well, Rab seems to get about a lot."

"Rab works as hard as ony o' them, believe you me. But he kens how to enjoy himself too. You see: he likes company, Jean. Oh, he's just as fond o' the men as he is o' the lassies."

"I wish I could meet him, Jeannie. But I don't seem to have ony luck. I wonder why my father doesna like him. He got on to me the last night I was at Ronald's dancing. He doesna like the company he keeps—not even your brother, Jeannie, though what he can have against James I don't know. And he said Davie Brice was an atheist. Oh he was angry about Rab Burns!"

"Ach, don't worry about that: there's a wheen o' the auld folk in Machlin don't like him. You see: he's an incomer; and then he's written a wheen o' verses against Daddy Auld's crowd. You'd hear about the verses he made up on Holy Willie? Oh, they gave Willie Fisher a terrible showing-up. No wonder the elders and their cronies are mad about it. When auld Lamie heard about it, he was going to take a stick to our Jamie if he was ever seen wi' Rab again. Ach, but Jamie kens how to deal wi' Lamie. He's gaun to tak' a room for himsel' doon the street. But here, Jean—that's a nice man that's set up the Latin class here. A great friend o' Rab's—it seems they used to go to school thegither in Dalrymple—James Candlish is the name. You havena heard your father speaking about him, have you?"

"I know the man you mean, Jeannie. He's biding in the Bellman's Vennel. No: my father never mentioned him. But I didna ken he was a friend o' Rab Burns?"

"Pack and thick thegither. He's going to bring him round some Sunday after kirk and introduce me. He's at the Glasgow College, no less. He's got some verra fine friends has Rab, despite what your father says."

"Aye, but it's gey hard, Jeannie, when you get the blame o' keeping him company when you've never even spoken to him."

"Ah, but I'll need to see what I can do, Jean. I know Rab would like you."

"Do you, Jeannie—honest?"

"I wouldna mislead you, Jean. I know you're set on him. But if I thought you hadna a chance I would tell you. And mind you, if I thought I had a chance myself I wouldna introduce you. No' that I can promise onything, hen. Men are funny creatures when they come to pick on a woman for marriage: half o' them are just daft. And I believe Rab Burns'll be the daftest o' the lot. The men that are maist socht after are the ones that go and marry the silliest women. Oh, I don't say Rab Burns'll marry a silly woman, but you just never know, Jean, so I can't guarantee onything. I ken he'll like you and that's a'."

"But why are you so sure he'll like me?"

"Ach, havers, Jean: everybody likes you: you can see the way men look at you. Ach, even Daddy Auld's got a soft side for you.

128

And you ken fine you could have lads in plenty if you wanted them—and if your father didn't shoo them off whenever they look at you. I don't believe it's Rab Burns he hates so much as the idea that he'll run off wi' you and get married: he doesna want to lose you, Jean."

"I ken he doesna want to lose me: neither does my mither."

"Don't let your parents stand in your way, Jean: they didna let their parents stand in their way when they were like you and me."

"Has Rab been out wi' Lizzie Miller?"

"Ach, Lizzie Miller's only a bairn: that doesna mean a thing. He's been out wi' Jean Markland too for that matter; but Jean kens fine he's no' serious . . ."

And so Jean Armour wondered and dreamed about Robin till she was in love with the idea of him; but it was only to Jeannie Smith that she confided. And Jeannie, being a good girl, never betrayed her confidence.

THE MEETING

It was in Ronald's at the dancing Jean Armour got her first close view of Robert Burns. He had come into the ball just as a set had finished. Jean was standing in the far corner with a group of lassies. She felt the blush rising deep from her bosom and instinctively she edged behind her friends for protection. But with eyes peeping over a convenient shoulder she watched him closely.

He was a handsome figure. He had buckles to his shoon, a white linen cravat and a coat of blue cloth with large metal buttons. His black hair shone in the candlelight, and his great dark eyes set in his swarthy cleft-chinned face glowed with intense animation.

A group gathered round him and he was immediately drawn into a set for the next dance. Anra MacAslan shook his fiddle at him. Jean excused herself and sat with a couple of friends and watched. No doubt: for all his sturdy thick-set build he could dance with a light abandoned step. He fairly leapt to the measure of the reel.

Unfortunately someone opened the door towards the end of the dance and his collie, Luath, came bounding down the floor to meet him.

"This dog will be the death of me!" she heard him say. "If I could get a lass to follow me as faithfully I'd count myself a happy man."

He excused himself, bowed grandly to his partners and went out with the dog. To Jean's disappointment he did not come back.

Some weeks later her father was building a barn over on West Mossgiel and Jean, hoping she might meet Robin somewhere on the road, volunteered to carry a hot bite of food at mid-day to her father and her brother John.

Luck was with her. Coming back to the village she met him leading a horse from the Machlin smiddy.

Robin saw her approaching and for a moment wondered who she might be. Then he knew it was Jean Armour. When they met, Jean was blushing furiously and her head was lowered.

"Ah, Miss Jean Armour!" saluted Robin as he halted the pony. "And where have you been, my pretty maid? Oh, don't hang your head, lass: it's no' a shame to be seen speaking to me."

Jean looked up, almost afraid that the agitation in her heart would betray her. "We havena met yet, Mr. Burns——"

"We've met now! And believe me there's no time like the present. Where, tell me, if it's a civil question, have you been hiding all this time? My friends are your friends: they all speak so highly of you and chant your praises. Yet why haven't we met until now? My good friend Jean Smith promised to have you round when I was calling; but there seems to have been some difficulty attending this business. Ah, but I think I can guess the reason, Miss Armour."

"Oh, there was no reason—Mr. Burns."

"You're reason enough—aye, more than enough. Here have I been praising the belles o' Machlin—and missing the jewel o' them all. Wait till I see Jeannie Smith—the scheming rogue."

"Jeannie Smith had nothing to do wi' it."

Robin was feasting his eyes on Jean. God! but she was a comely lass—and what a figure of a girl. He could feel desire pulsating from her in radiating waves.

He lowered his eyes to the ground where her feet, small and square with evenly-spread toes, were placed in the grey dust.

His eye travelled upwards. He had already noted the sway of her carriage as she had advanced, noted the breath-taking perfection of the scrieve of her leg. Now he admired the perfect symmetry of her limbs, the bold but vigorous delicacy of their moulding. He had seen many fine limbs in his day; but indeed none of the girls he had known had been in any way defective in this respect. But there was no need to dispute the physical supremacy of Jean Armour's limbs. High-kilted like the maidens of her day, he could trace the sweep of her thighs through the lightness of her gown.

Skilled as he was in female anatomy and every curve of clothing flesh, he quivered to the sudden impact of her presence. She was broad-shouldered, wide-chested and high-breasted. The sweep of her neck, moulded upwards from her bosom, was exquisitely achieved. Her face was open, frank and kindly, and though it was a strong face and the chin was firm, the expression of her large dark eyes softened the strong outlines and established a warmth and grace he found irresistible and indescribable. Her raven-black hair, thick and luxuriant, caught the sun and held it prisoner in a radiant mesh.

If ever a girl combined boundless physical health with every soft caressing grace of girlhood, that girl was Jean Armour. She seemed to combine in her all the physical and spiritual charm of all the girls he had known and loved. She had all Annie Rankine's intense physical vigour without a trace of her coarseness; she had all the smouldering passion of Jean Glover without any element of Jean's sexual sophistication; if she had not Jean Gardner's exquisite delicacy she had a purity of nervous health that had never been Jean's; and if she carried about her an air of rustic simplicity it was not the open simplicity of Betty Paton, for underneath this superficial simplicity Robin could sense all the deep unfathomable mystery of her sex. But, above all, there was an intense but peculiar magnetism about Jean Armour that was more subtle and more powerful than anything he had ever known. Already his blood was rioting in his veins and there was a tingling of nerves along his spine.

"Why do you blush, Jean—you're no' feared o' me?"

"I'm no' feared o' onybody: why should I be feared o' you?"

"Well spoken, Jean Armour. There's lassies in Machlin feared to look the road I'm on in case worse befalls them. I'm glad you're not one o' them."

"I dinna listen to folks' tales, Mr. Burns: I judge for mysel'."

"Well, Jean, we'll have judging. You've hidden away in the Cowgate there far too long. They tell me your worthy father's a gey strict man, and that he doesna approve o' me. But we'll need to make up for lost time. How comes it that every time I go to Ronald's dancing I meet every belle in Machlin barring yourself—and you the flower o' them a'?"

"I've been warned that you're a great flatterer, Rab. But now that you mention Ronald's, I wonder hae you no' gotten a lass yet that would be as faithful to you as your dog?"

"What! puir auld Luath here? And who told you about me and my dog?"

"Nobody told me: I heard you mysel'."

"Dinna tell me you were dancing that night?"

"You were too busy to see me."

"You'd be hiding in some corner wi' a lad."

"I was wi' nae lad."

"Don't tell me you havena a lad. I'll believe onything but that, Jean."

"Ask Jeannie Smith—ask ony o' your Machlin cronies. I don't run after the lads."

"Aye; but what's keeping them from laying siege to you? Ah, but we'll cure that, Jean. I'll tell you what. I'll be accompanying my friend James MacCandlish on a walk down the Barskimming road the night—it'll be a grand night too—so what about you and Jeannie Smith taking a dander that airt—we'll wait on you down the road . . ."

Sauntering down the Barskimming road towards the banks of the Ayr, Robin discussed many things with James MacCandlish. James was studying medicine in Glasgow. But his health had suffered and his pocket had suffered too. He was in need of a change and needed some money to pay his way; so he had come to Machlin to teach Latin during the summer vacation. He was right glad to meet Robin; his conversation and his friendship helped to lift the melancholy that had settled on him.

"But what you need most, Jamie, is the love of a good lass. There's no medicine like it for lifting the melancholy vapours from the spirit. I know what I'm speaking about. When I'm no' in love with a lass then that black bitch melancholy settles inside me and I know all the wretched tortures o' the damned. But I'm meeting a charmer the night, Jamie. She's been right here under my nose so to speak all the time; and yet till this afternoon I never got a right look at her. Of course, you havena been long enough in Machlin to know your way about. She's a Jean Armour. Bides in the Cowgate right behind Johnnie Dow's. You'll know James Armour the mason—his daughter. I've been intimate wi' a few charmers, Jamie; but Jean Armour is the jewel o' them all. Without a doubt. But the lass that'll be with her, Jean Smith—Jamie Smith's sister—now, there's a fine woman for you. Good-looking, a sterling good nature and plenty o' sound common sense. I don't want to advise with you, but you could do worse—in fact I don't know that you could do better."

"We'll see, Robin: we'll see. I believe it would suit me to get married; but I've little prospect of a steady income sufficient for that. My father's a bit disappointed in me; and he doesn't want to throw good money after bad: I've cost him a bonnie penny as it is. He certainly wouldn't help me to burden myself wi' a wife. I've a slight acquaintance wi' Jeannie Smith and I must say I'm taken wi' the lass."

"Well: now's your chance to get her down the banks o' the Ayr and see what you can make o' her."

"And d'you think you've met the right lass in this Jean Armour, Robin?"

"Well, Jamie, that's a question I once would have answered you offhand. You see: once or twice already I've thought I had the right one, but the fates were against me. And like as not, just when I think I've got Jean Armour where I want her my damned star will wheel in its course. So I'll live for the day, Jamie, and see what the fates decree. My trouble, you see, is no' in getting a lass but in deciding what lass is the right one. There must be some lack o' ballast in me, Jamie, for the damned truth is I could fall in love wi' ony good-looking lass in the parish."

"You've changed greatly since the old days when you were in Mount Oliphant."

"For the worse, eh?"

"Oh no, Robin. In some ways you havena changed a bit. We were only laddies then. But when I knew you first we werena interested in the lassies."

"We didna know what life meant then; and I was stuffed full o' that damned idiot piety that blighted all my young days. You see: I used to believe in the moral cant the humbugs and the hypocrites used to preach. But as you grow up you're no' long in discovering— if you've oony sense at all—that Calvin's holy well is full o' a lot o' damned dirty ditch-water."

"Fegs, Robin, and that's one thing you do find. There's a great philosopher o' the continent—Spinoza's his name—I'll need to lend you him. He makes short work o' John Calvin's cant. A great thinker, Robin—a mind that sees right into the inmost heart o' the universe."

"Then leeze me on your Spinoza, lad. The moral law, Jamie, is a man-made law; and dry black-hearted beggars they were that made it. But nature's law! There's a different story. The man that can unfold the working o' nature's plan—that's the man God's looking for—for that's the man will be doing the greatest service to mankind."

"Spinoza's maybe your man then, Robin."

"It's a daring path to tread, Jamie—and it takes great courage to follow the path through the wilderness out into the promised land at the other end. But it's the path that'll need to be followed—and all consequence set at defiance. I've my own thoughts and I've pondered a wheen mysteries in my own way, and I've come to a lot of conclusions; but I think I know what man's chief end is here below. Here below, Jamie, for there's no certainty of anything else. Man's chief end is happiness. But man canna be happy if the rest o' his fellows are sunk in poverty and misery. Of course the individual man can know moments of happiness even as you and I have known happiness—and we can enjoy the social hour; but you understand me? Mankind cannot know real or permanent happiness when there's a fundamental unhappiness in his society."

"I agree, Robin: I agree fully. But it's difficult to see how the inequalities of life in the material sense that you mean can ever be removed."

"But then the inequalities are man-made—they are not made otherwise. And if man can make inequalities he can just as easy make equalities—otherwise an independent wish would never have been planted in the mind—nor would the early prophets have known that man was made in God's image. True enough, religion has become a mixty-maxty of oppositions and contradictions, but that's just because human life—and human ways under the inhumanity of man to man—has become just such a mixty-maxty."

"It's a queer tangle, Robin, ony the ways you look at it."

"Aye, but we maun cut through the tangle—and I canna see but that man will cut through the tangle yet, and hit on some plan to ease his burden all round. Otherwise life's but a blind ox tramping the treadmill o' a dumb destiny."

They became so interested in their discussion they were oblivious to the glory of the summer evening. It was only when they had reached the banks of the Ayr that Robin remembered Jean Armour and Jean Smith. They walked back to meet them.

Robin and Jean finally came to rest beneath the shade of a green thorn tree: Jean Smith and James MacCandlish wandered on ahead.

The tree itself was screened by a clump of whins; and at the foot of the grassy bank the river gurgled its song. Jean sat with her hands clasped round her bended knees, her small square-cut feet placed closely together, downwards-thrusting. Occasionally she raised and shook her head in order to toss back her thick rich curls. The gesture gave such a sweetness to the curve of her throat and the eager line of her chin that it captivated him.

But her every gesture captivated him and inflamed his love. He was well aware that his experience with Jean was at the blossom of its freshness. The lure of a fresh personality open for exploration was always an irresistible allure—man or woman. His interest in John Lapraik had been just as irresistible. But there had been no physical passion to it.

They had talked and talked, rapidly surveying the fields of their interests. He was intrigued with Jean's tremendous sanity. True, she was brimming over with the mysterious enchantment of her sex; she had a natural coyness, even a natural archness. But she could answer a plain question sensibly and a sensible one plainly, and both with a basic good humour that was the base of her sanity.

Above all there was nothing stupid about her, though she was keenly conscious of the limits of her knowledge and made no pretence to any element of book-learning—hence her complete freedom from any element of pretence and the snobbery of pretence.

Robin knew well that there was much in Jean that could not be revealed in the first meetings. But the outline of her personality was firm and round and it won him completely.

"Aye: you've had a hard life too, Jean—and you only coming twenty. But then you would have the misfortune to be second in the family and the eldest lass. Lucky you never knew starvation— or you wouldna have had that bloom on your cheeks—or that swell to your bosom."

"And you kenned starvation, Rab? Fegs, you don't look it. You look strong to me."

"Oh, I'm strong enough—when I'm well enough. But the years at Mount Oliphant when I was a growing laddie were hard years—and we were damnably underfed."

"We've had scant times too, Rab. Maybe no' just starvation—but gey little in the house. Sometimes my father didna get paid or had to wait out his money for a long time: I ken what a sup o' porridge and nae kitchen means in a long day—and the bairns greetin and my mither just about her time. My mither had twa Roberts before the one that's running about now; and it was nothing else but the starving she got that took them away—they had nae strength . . ."

"But that's all behind us now, Jean. Why didn't I fall in wi' you sooner?"

"You werena verra anxious for a' you say. Did you no' like the look o' me in the kirk?"

"Well, I only got a sidelong keek at the back o' your head, Jean. And your father always has the lot of you out and into the Cowgate before I can reach the kirkyard."

"Aye . . . my father's strict: he'll no' have ony o' us hanging about the kirkyard."

"And you blame me for no' falling in wi' you? But, in truth, I've only myself to blame. I've been told a hundred times—and not only by Smith or Richmond—o' your byornar beauty."

"Och, I ken'fine I'm nae beauty."

"None more beautiful in the West, Jean. And I'm no fool when it comes to sizing up your sex."

"I suppose you've had a wheen in your day?"

"I have—in a way."

"And you told them a' the same story?"

"I did."

"And they believed you?"

"They did. I was speaking the truth—for the time being."

"And you'll say that to the next lass that takes your fancy?"

"I'll be honest wi' you, Jean. If I met in wi' a finer lass than you I would. But while I am honest I can't see ony chance o' that happening. I've known many a lass in my day and I've seen thousands; but I've seen none that could top you, Jean. And believe me, I've known some real beauties."

"What about Mary Campbell?"

"What about her? Who's been telling you about her?"

"Is there onything to tell?"

"There isn't—we're good enough friends; but . . ."

"Would you say she's a beauty?"

"You're a great lass for speirin'."

"There's nae harm in speirin', is there?"

"Well, it's one way to find out . . . No: I don't think Mary Campbell's ony great beauty; but she's a fine and remarkable lass for a' that."

"Aye . . . I always got on wi' her. But she's Heilan'."

"Is that against her?"

"No: she canna help that. But just—she's no' one o' us."

"Then why the devil are we wasting the nicht talking about things that don't interest us?"

"Oh, it's interesting, Rab. You've got a great reputation for the way you flatter the lassies—you admit yoursel' you've run after a wheen—and no' only run after them!"

"Meaning?"

"You ken as weel as me."

"You mean Betty Paton had a bairn to me?"

"If that's a' . . ."

"Are you going to hold that against me?"

"I'm no' holding onything against you—or away from you. Only I don't want you to think I'm that kind o' lass."

"How can you be sure o' that?"

"Easy enough. Folk can surely wait till they're married."

"Damn few seem to be able, else there would be little use for cutty stools."

"You should know."

"Listen, Jean. Don't think for one minute I'm ashamed o' what happened wi' Betty Paton. It happened—and that was that. It can happen wi' you. Bide a wee. It can happen wi' you. And if the lad that did it was ashamed o' having done it, what would you think o' him?"

"If he didna marry me I could only think he was a rotten black-guard."

"And that's what you think I am?"

"Maybe I should think that, Rab—but I canna."

Jean suddenly lowered her head and the violent blush spread up from her bosom. She had said something she had not willed to say.

Robin knew it was a confession of love. But coming at the time it did he was almost taken by surprise. He, too, reacted in a way he had not willed. In a moment his arm was round her, his lips had found hers. He pressed her back on the soft bank.

Theirs was a long ardent embrace, an embrace that by itself was a rich and satisfying consummation. They lay in each other's arms.

"I've loved you for a lang time, Rab. I thought we were never to meet. I didna mean to hurt you wi' what I said about Betty Paton . . ."

"You couldna hurt onybody, Jean. And Betty Paton's a' by and done wi': you've nothing to fear there or onywhere else. It's you and me, Jean, from now on: you can trust me in this: you can trust me in onything. When I saw you coming down the road today I knew you were mine."

"You couldna tell that . . ."

"Something told me then, for I knew it there and then. What I'm feared o', Jean, is that you'll turn against me in the end?"

"Why should I dae that?"

"Because everything I've set my heart on yet has escaped me, has been denied me . . . And by God, lass, I want you more than I want life itself."

"I'll love you as long as you want me, Rab. It's you I'm feared will tire o' me."

He found her lips again. Across the low singing river, in the trees on the opposite bank, came the crack of a cushat's wing; beyond the trees the faint high-pitched calling of the herd-laddies bringing home the beasts. A chaffinch came and perched on a spray above their heads, rehearsed its seven merry notes and bobbed into the whins. Not far away, on the topmost birken twig, a mavis turned its spotted breast to the dying sun, and the air throbbed and pulsed with its full-throated vespers. A brown trout rose to the jigging may-flies and plopped back into the dark pool. A yellow-billed blackbird, seeking his evening meal, came unexpectedly upon the silent lovers and ricochetted into the undergrowth with shrill and strident alarm. Then the cushat returned to the nest and soon its languorous cooing, mingling with the soft song of the river, soothed and caressed the gathering shadows and welcomed the gloaming stealing under the leafy banks.

Jean was running her fingers through his soft thick hair and humming a slow strathspey. Her low rich crooning was exquisitely soothing. Robin closed his eyes in a sheer lassitude of ecstasy.

It needed only this, that there was music in Jean, to brim the cup of his contentment.

"I should have known," he said, after a long interval. "Aye, I should have known there was music in you. You've gotten the measure o' that spring to perfection."

"Have I? I like it; but I dinna even ken what it is."

"Miss Gordon's Strathspey. God! and when you sowth it slow like that—it's—it's just perfect. There's something about our Scots tunes, Jean, that melts the marrow o' my bones. Some day I'll put words on that for you."

"Will you, Rab?"

"Aye; but I'll need to ken you a lot better."

"There's no' much to ken about me, Rab. I'm no' one o' your deep, cunning kind."

"No: you're no' that kind, Jean. But you're deeper than ony o' them. There's nae stony shallows in the big warm heart o' you. A man could shelter himself in the depths o' you, Jean—aye, and know a peace and contentment beyond ony computation—beyond ony reckoning."

"You maun be a great scholar too, Rab. And I'm as ignorant as the meikle black craws in the kirkyard ash-tree."

"Ignorant? And I suppose you think the craws ignorant? The only ignorant folk, Jean, are the college-bred asses that hae gotten a bit smattering o' book lear their thin brains canna comprehend. Dinna let me hear you talk about ignorance. Even if you knew no more than the right lilt o' a tune you would have a knowledge that you couldna buy gin your Sunday stockings were filled to the knees wi' yellow Geordies."

A soft cooee came down the river to them.

Jean sat up.

"There's Jeannie Smith calling: I'll need to gang hame, Rab."

"What about the morn's nicht?"

"Aye, we'll meet the morn's nicht the same way."

"A kiss then, Jean, and a pledge for our love against a' the days to come."

They embraced in the shadow of the green thorn tree. And the strength of their pledging kiss was strong and sweet and tender.

It was a summer of love—love as Robin had never known it. The more he saw of Jean the more he loved her—separation from her became an intense physical pain. Physically and spiritually they seemed perfectly mated. There was nothing he could not discuss with her—she was completely lacking in moral inhibitions. She was as open and free as the birds that sang, as the wind that sighed in the tree-tops. He read his poems to her, when the weather was favourable, under the shade of the thorn tree that had become their favourite trysting-spot. Often she would sing to him there, for he loved her singing and was passionately fond of song. Sometimes he would ask of her past life and of the life of the Machlin folks; of Daddy Auld and his elders; of girls who had stood on the cutty stool . . .

In each other's company the hours slipped past like golden moments, and always their parting came too soon and she would have to jink her way back through Machlin and slip quietly in at the back door in case her father's suspicions would be aroused.

It was fortunate that James MacCandlish had become Jean Smith's lover, for this enabled the pair to come together and make arrangements that would not have been possible otherwise.

It was easy for Robin to pass on word through Jamie Smith to his sister Jeannie, and Jeannie had little trouble in passing on word to Jean.

But all of them had to be careful. James Lamie was a vigilant elder and James Armour was one of the most respectable citizens of Machlin: a pillar of Machlin Kirk and an avowed enemy of the blackguard Burns.

Jeannie Smith, though she was genuinely in love with James MacCandlish, always hankered after news of Robin and Jean.

"You can see that he loves you, Jean," she said to her one wet night when they were sitting sewing in Lamie's spence and Lamie himself was at an elders' meeting in Daddy Auld's. "And I can see you love him."

"You couldna help loving him, Jeannie. I couldna tell you what he's like—there just isna onybody you could compare him to. Oh and he's clever: he's a real poet, Jeannie. Some o' the verses he reads me—they're like a spell."

"Aye, heth, he's put a spell on you, Jean. Has your mither no' jaloused onything?"

"Sometimes I think she has. And yet one nicht when my father said I was galavanting too much wi' you she said I was young and needed to get a breath o' fresh air wi' the lave. She wouldna have said that if she'd been suspicious. Och, but I would leave hame rather than leave Rab—I'd go onywhere wi' him—aye, even if it meant sleeping in barns."

"You're head ower heels, Jean. I like James MacCandlish; but I wouldna leave hame unless I was married and had a house to go to."

"Of course I wouldna like to hurt my father or my mither if it came to that. My father's good to us, Jeannie—he's no' like James Lamie. And I know I'm his favourite: everybody in the house tells me that. But he's terrible strict. If he knew I was going out to meet Rab Burns I don't know what he would dae. Rab says he's no' feared o' him; but if he kent him the way I ken him he'd be feared o' him. Aye . . . but father or no' father, I wouldna leave Rab. I couldna, Jeannie: I count the minutes frae we part till we meet again."

"You've gotten it real bad, Jean. My, but you're lucky too. I used to think that's how I wad be when I fell in love—but I've had sae mony disappointments . . ."

"But surely James MacCandlish is no' a disppointment?"

"No . . . James is a real nice fellow. But you'll need to haud Rab back where I have to lead James on. I mean he hasna the push about him that Rab has—and for a' his education he hasna the same experience. You're no' five minutes in Rab's company till you feel he kens mair about you than you do yoursel'."

"Ah; but that's what I like about him—he understands every-thing—sometimes you don't even need to hint."

"You're lucky, Jean. You'll be ettlin' to get married?"

"Well . . . we havena discussed ony details. But I ken he wants to marry me—and he kens I want to marry him. Of course I know Mossgiel's no' turning out verra weel: he says there'll be a year or twa o' hard work yet afore they turn the corner."

"Weel, dinna marry into poverty, Jean, whatever you do. Poverty and a family—and you're finished. You're never able to get your head abune the midden. Mind you, I dinna want to interfere; but I ken Rab will be ill to haud—and you ken what happened to Lizzie Paton . . ."

"Aye; you're right there, Jeannie. But it's hard. Sometimes I feel I could go daft in his arms. But for Godsake, Jeannie, don't talk about Lizzie Paton: my father would kill me."

Jean Armour's strong hand trembled over her seam. Jeannie Smith eyed her keenly. She was certain Rab Burns would never be content to kiss and fondle a lass and let his courting go at that. And a lass like Jean Armour! Aye, and she had woman's knowledge enough to know that Jean's resistance would be easily overcome—if it hadn't been overcome already.

THE AGITATION OF DADDY AULD

It was James Lamie who managed to secure a copy of Holy Willie's Prayer and take it to his priest, Daddy Auld.

"It's no' only a scandal on Mr. Fisher, sir: it's a scandal on the Kirk and its ordinances. That blackguard Burns will need to be dealt wi', Mr. Auld: he'll need to be made an example o'. And you ken better nor me, Mr. Auld, how grievous a sin it is to write ony verses against the Kirk. We've had blackguards enough in Machlin afore now, but nane that took to writing down their blackguardism and passing it round the parish."

"Is it being passed round the parish, James?"

"I'll warrant ye it is, Mr. Auld. There isna an ale-house in Machlin nor a change-house twixt here and Ayr on the one hand and here and Kilmarnock on the tither that hasna seen a copy o' this infernal piece o' blasphemy."

"Is this copy in Burns's hand of write?"

"No: it isna, unfortunately: it was wrote down for me by Andrew Noble, wha'll verify ilka dot and stroke of it."

"And what is the parish saying about it?"

"Weel, of course, Mr. Auld, it goes without saying that decent folks are outraged wi' it—and black affrontit. But them that are weak in their judgments are snared by it. Aye, fools gowk and laugh, Mr. Auld, and the ribald and profane are meikle set-up wi' it."

William Auld held the sheets in his hand but he did not read the lines. He seemed curiously detached—almost abstracted.

"This will not be the only—production—of Burns's that is circulating or has already circulated the parish?"

"More's the pity, Mr. Auld. Aye, he's been sending a feck o' ill-gotten rhymes and verses through the clachan—but nothing so diabolical as this."

"I want you to get me copies o' everything you can lay your hands on, James. I'll read this ower privately and let you know my mind on't later. I won't say I havena had complaints, James—Mr. Armour spoke strongly to me on several occasions."

"Aye, and well micht James Armour dae that, Mr. Auld, for if what I hear's true this blackguard's keeping company wi' Armour's dochter Jean!"

The paper crinkled in Auld's bony hand. There was a cold flash in his eyes.

"What say ye, James? Is this gossip?"

"Weel, I havena seen ony signs mysel'—nor has Mr. Fisher; but I heard frae a source that they were seen in company frae the banks o' the Ayr ayont the Barskimming road-end."

"We maun hae better evidence than that, James; but I charge you to keep your eyes open—aye, and your mouth ticht shut. I'll wait your intelligence wi' some impatience, James; and maybe now you'll leave me to get on wi' my duties, for I hae much to do anent the preparations for the August sacraments."

When Lamie had excused himself and withdrawn, William Auld moved over to his seat by the window and held up the sheets so that the evening light might strike them to advantage.

The priest of Machlin was not an illiterate man, nor was his reading confined to theological works, though these formed and had formed the bulk of his reading over many years. But he had from time to time lightened his labours by dipping into a literature which, though classical, was nevertheless of a secular and profane character.

The impact of the poem on his moral and literary consciousness was electrical. He erected himself with sudden angularity from his chair and began pacing the room. This was not the work of any rustic rhymster, not the thought of any rural hind; neither was its meaning fired by the stimulation of alcohol. Here was a bold vigorous mind tearing away every mask of deceit and hypocrisy. A devilish mind, a diabolical inspiration, but with a diabolical truth. This was indeed Willie Fisher, weak, vain and self-righteous. Burns had penetrated into the soul of the man, but in a manner that laid violent hands on the very rock of the Kirk's foundations. Here was a danger in the parish he had never suspected. Against this danger the menace of Gavin Hamilton and John MacKenzie was mild and inoffensive. Burns would require to be handled with the utmost caution. There was no point to be gained in hailing him before the Session. He would make fools of men like Lamie and Fisher—it would only drive him to greater excess of sacrilegious profanity.

For a moment Daddy Auld toyed with the idea of seeing him privately—of reasoning with him; aye, of grappling with him. But finally he dismissed the idea and sat down and re-read the manuscript.

Auld had seen many years and he had gathered much wisdom in the ways of men and women. He seldom misread a character. Nor was he easily shocked. He knew Fisher's worth—and his worthlessness. No doubt he had been guilty of fornication—in mind if not in body. But Fisher did valuable work in the Lord even in his weaknesses: aye, because of his weakness. And it would be foolish practice to expose an elder if his sins could be dealt with privately and circumspectly. Nor would it be politic to rush at a man of the mental calibre and temperament of Robert Burns: it would only drive him head-long into the arms of anti-Christ. Aye . . . and no doubt there was much of an unsavoury nature he knew about the Kirk's servants. It would be folly to enrage him. Yet he must be dealt with.

Auld ruminated. Ah, Jean Armour! He again shot up in agitation. Jean Armour! A pity it might have to be Jean. She was a fine girl. A man like Burns would almost certainly corrupt her—he might even seduce her.

He trembled at the thought. Lord forgive him: his own thoughts about Jean would not bear the strictest investigation.

But Lord grant that his love for her, his affection for her, was but fatherly affection. He had baptised her; he had catechised her; he had watched her grow up into magnificent maidenhood. She was the flower of his parish . . .

And here was the possibility that even now Burns was holding her in his arms—or worse.

William Auld poured himself a measure of whisky and drank it off without ceremony.

Ah, there was no purpose in blaming Jean. This Burns had youth, a fine appearance, a charm of manner . . . On the several occasions he had spoken to him he had given evidence of a singular refinement of education and address—but he was a fornicator. He should have insisted on him compearing before his Session for that offence with the girl in Largieside . . .

Should he have a word with Jean? James Armour might resent that. He was a choleric man James and very strict with his family. The whole thing might be mere gossip. If Jean were forbidden to see Burns she would be brought the more to his side: he had never known such bans to work otherwise. And if he were to anticipate matters by speaking to James Armour there was the practical certainty that he would visit her with sudden physical brutality. He must spare Jean that.

There was nothing remotely immoral about William Auld's regard for Jean. Neither he nor Jean were responsible for the fact that he had long looked upon her as fulfilling—somehow—his need for a daughter. His life had been incomplete without a daughter—a daughter like Jean Armour.

Mr. Auld sent his niece, the widowed Mrs. Campbell who acted as his housekeeper, across the path to the Bellman's Vennel to send some likely lad in search of William Fisher.

It was late in the evening before Holy Willie made his appearance. Auld saw he had been drinking. He closed the study door and drew the sneck in a way that Fisher did not like: he knew Auld's every gesture.

"You've been tippling again, Mr Fisher?"

"It's dry work, Mr. Auld, tramping the parish——"

"Enough, sir. There's no need for you to sin your immortal soul within these four walls. You know well enough that I am deceived in no particular about you. The Lord has the hairs of your head numbered; but I myself have a fair notion of their accounting, sir. I am in no mood to be lenient with your evasions and equivocations. Sit down."

Fisher sat down on the edge of the chair indicated by the long index finger. He bowed his head: he knew what was coming: he was in for a moral and spiritual drubbing.

"I have lippened on you, Mr. Fisher, to keep me acquaint in every detail of the comings and goings in the parish. I'll not say more than that, for you ken your duties well enough. In consideration for your weakness, Mr. Fisher, I have been correspondingly lenient. Far ower lenient it seems. You've been keeping things frae me, Mr. Fisher!"

"I can think o' nothing, Mr. Auld."

"I'll no' warn you again, Mr. Fisher. Were you my own flesh and blood it would mak' nae difference. And if I hae to discipline you, Mr. Fisher, I warn you you'll never lift your head again in this parish. Now, sir: what hae you to report on Robert Burns?"

"Burns in Mossgiel, Mr. Auld? Oh, a blackguard, Mr. Auld, a bad, black-hearted blackguard!"

"Your evidence, Mr. Fisher?"

"Aye, aye . . . evidence! Somebody's been clyping on me, Mr. Auld: somebody's been clyping on me."

"And what wad they hae to clype, Mr. Fisher?"

"Well now . . . eh . . . well: he wrote an ill set o' verses on me, I'm given to understand."

"You are acquaint wi' the verses?"

"God forbid, Mr. Auld, that I should be acquaint wi' ony siccan blackguardism."

Auld thrust his hand into his inner pocket and produced the manuscript.

"I hae a copy o' the verses here, Mr. Fisher, gin ye want to refresh your memory?"

Fisher began to shake violently: he bobbed uneasily on the edge of the chair.

"The Meg that you lifted your lawless leg upon is Meg Gaw your serving-lass?"

"It's a lie, Mr. Auld—a black lie. Oh that a servant o' the Lord should be held up to such wicked mockery!"

"And Lizzie's lass—now wha micht Lizzie's lass be an' she werena your dairy-lass?"

"I had Lizzie's permission tae wrastle wi' her dochter, Mr. Auld: she was backsliding sair wi' her catechism."

"Burns indicts you o' a verra different wrastling, Mr. Fisher."

"Mr. Auld, sir! You wadna heed that blackguard's opinion afore the sworn word of your ain elder——"

"Enough, man: I forbid ye to sin away the shreds o' your sair-tashed soul in my presence. Why didna ye report this to me at the onset? Why?"

"It's—it's a black dishonour, Mr. Auld; but I had meant to tell ye and seek your counsel."

But Auld was merciless. He reduced Fisher to tears till the poor devil fell at his feet and begged his mercy. When his victory was complete, Auld poured him a glass of whisky.

"Drink this up, sir, and take a hold on yourself. Now I think we understand one another, Mr. Fisher. You'll keep baith your een on Burns frae now on and you'll report to me immediately you see ony signs. Aye, even if ye hae to wauken me in the middle o' the nicht. And I want every detail you can gather on Jean Armour's movements . . . But if ye go about this business in ony clumsy fashion I'll hae ye up afore the Presbytery in Ayr. Ye'll keep your eyes and your ears weel open and your meikle slack mouth tichtly shut—aye, ye could dae waur nor hae a guid hasp on't. I'm giving ye a last chance to redeem yoursel', Mr. Fisher."

Fisher was shaken to his miserable depths, but the whisky began to warm the spunk of his courage. He was profuse in his thanks; but Auld cut him short.

"Every detail, Mr. Fisher—every little detail. Overlook nothing at your peril."

"Ah weel, Mr. Auld, I ken nocht about Burns and Jean Armour: he's been fell big wi' Hamilton's nursemaid, Mary Campbell. He was big wi' Jean Smith too: aye, an' wi' Lizzie Miller, Jean Markland—aye, but there's no' a lass i' the parish safe frae his lusts. There's a wheen blackguards in Machlin here, Mr. Auld, as ye weel ken—but Burns is the ringleader withouten doubt. Oooh aye: we should manage to lay him by the heels almost ony month now."

"Bring me a report the morn's nicht, Mr. Fisher—about this time—unless you're on the track o' something special."

And so the pact was made between Holy Willie and his minister, Daddy Auld.

But before he went to bed that night Daddy Auld had another perusal of the manuscript. Something warned him that here he was in the presence of a mighty force both of intellect and of passion; and he felt in his bones that he would not have his sorrows to seek in dealing with either of them.

He placed the manuscript in the bottom of his wooden, iron-bound deed-chest, and locked it away.

Aye, there was no doubt but that the Lord moved in a mysterious way, His wonders to perform. Aye; but the Devil was ever lurking in the shadows—and in the corners of men's desperately-wicked hearts—waiting on the chance to pounce upon the unwary and the ungodly.

On this sobering reflection, Daddy Auld went soberly ben the house to eat his supper.

THE COURSE OF LOVE

Mary Campbell knew that she had lost Robin for a lover. He never made an assignation through Jock Richmond that they should meet together in the Tower. It was high summer, of course, and that was difficult; moreover, she had her work cut out with the birth of another son, Alexander, to Mrs. Hamilton. There were indeed many good reasons why she could not see him in a way convenient to them both; but yet she knew he was no longer interested in her as he had been.

From Gavin Hamilton's desk in Machlin Kirk she could watch Robin; and she saw that his eyes never wandered far from the back of Jean Armour's head. She knew what the look in his eyes meant. Yet there was not a breath among the Machlin folks that he was in love with Jean Armour or that he was courting her.

Mary Campbell was sad and her sadness bordered on melancholy, and this gave an added chastening refinement to the already chaste lines of her features. Robin had been such a fine lover, such a sweet-tempered, gentle fellow in his loving—and this despite the physical robustness of his passion.

Mary knew she had gambled and lost. Against the vigorous rosy-cheeked health of Jean Armour's beauty she had no counter-attraction. Against her upsurging sexual dynamism and the deep-flowing allure of her personality she had no availing asset.

She knew no anger against Robin for his neglect of her: only a gnawing and forlorn regret that she had been dropped from his arms.

Maybe if she had yielded to him she might have held him. And yet with the thought of Lizzie Paton in her mind she doubted if he would ever be held against his inclinations.

But there was always the doubt—doubt that could never be resolved.

Robin was too deeply in love with Jean Armour to have thoughts for any other lass. But he did not deliberately exclude them from his mind. Had he met Mary Campbell he would have explained himself so that Mary would not have been hurt. Besides, he would have had no wish to estrange her. By now he had learned the art of keeping something to himself—or he thought he had. Every day it was becoming clearer to him that to enjoy life in its essentials it was necessary to be diplomatic about inessentials. He might even have denied Jean to Mary Campbell if that denial would have spared her feelings. And even leaving Mary Campbell out of the reckoning, it might be well to deny Jean, for though at this stage the denial was inessential, it was doubly essential that nothing should be allowed to spoil his relationship with Jean.

It was for this reason that he did not discuss her with his Machlin friends and was careful not to drop the slightest hint to Gilbert.

But he could and did discuss the matter with James Mac-Candlish. James was in love after his own fashion with Jeannie Smith. His fashion was cautious and lacked the fire of deeply-roused emotion. But he loved Jeannie and had made up his mind that as soon as his studies were completed and he was settled in his profession he would take steps towards marriage.

It interested him greatly to hear Robin talk about Jean. But he was also envious. He felt he must be missing something vital when he saw Robin's extraordinary animation. He recognised too that of the girls Jean Armour was by far the more vital and beautiful. But her vitality made him afraid of his own manhood, whereas it challenged and intoxicated Robin's. Maybe it was the poet in him that made the difference; but it was impossible to separate the poet from the man. Every element in Robin's being seemed to quiver and glow in Jean's presence—even when he talked about her. There was no doubt that Robin in love, as Robin out of love, was an exceptional being: a being whose possibilities were infinite and quite unpredictable.

He would stand for an hour at the small window in Johnnie Pigeon's back room watching Armour's window for a pre-arranged sign from Jean. As soon as he got the message he wanted he would become strangely animated, leave down his ale untouched and without a word to any of them leave the room.

Smith and Richmond were used to him now and they had sufficient wisdom not to chaff him in any way. They were excellent friends; but there were times when he seemed to belong to an entirely different world—a world of which they had no cognisance and no right of entry.

One evening when Robin had left suddenly Smith said to Richmond:

"You ken, Jock: Rab's got the pick o' the Machlin fillies: he could ride ony one o' them whenever it took his fancy. And what does he do? Settles on the finest filly in Machlin."

"Would you say Jean Armour's the finest?"

"I would; and so would you. But the damned thing is you and me are ruled out. He's head ower heels in love wi' her—I never saw onything like it. And if you or me were as much as to look at her he would see the reddest of us on the spot."

"Robin's no' so daft: he kens what he's after. He'll soon tire o' Jean Armour."

"Damn the fear, Jock. And why the hell should he tire o' her? I've dreamt aboot Jean Armour—ach, I couldna tell you how I've dreamt; I had Jean picked out at the school. I used to try and tousle her then, but she was as strong as an ox. But Lord, Jock, what an armfu'; it makes my marrow melt to think aboot her. Rab's the luckiest beggar in the West—and he kens it. He'll never tire o' Jean Armour: to hell, it would be unnatural. But if he ever did, would I mak' a dive for her!"

The fact that Robert did not see fit to discuss his love for Jean in any detail with his cronies did not offend them; but it tended to make Jock Richmond a bit sour. Jock had had his fun with Jenny Surgeoner. It hadn't been all the fun he had wished—and the drubbing he had got from the Session and by Daddy Auld from the pulpit still rankled with him.

He was still thinking of going to Edinburgh, and to this end Gavin Hamilton was agitating himself on his behalf. But Edinburgh would only be a temporary escape. Jenny's father had made him promise—and in Auld's presence—that he would send for Jenny and marry her just as soon as he could make a living for her.

In this mood Jock Richmond re-acted with little emotion to Robert's courting. Moreover, he knew that if Robert fell foul of James Armour it would be a sorry day for him. Richmond reckoned it was much safer if less romantic to pass a bawbee or two to Maggie Borland . . .

WOOED AND MARRIED

Before summer had ended and harvest had begun Jean yielded to Robin. She yielded because she could no longer resist the clamour of her blood.

Twice, to her surprise, Robin had argued her out of yielding. "No," he had said, "we mauna. I couldna bear it if onything came between you and me; and I'm not yet in a position to marry you. I canna live without you, Jean—indeed I canna right think how I have lived without you."

She had loved him the more for that—both at the time and on reflection. But the night came when neither of them could resist. Lying under the green thorn tree in the lazy warmth of late August gloaming . . .

She had sung to him that night softly and low with a golden cadence in her crooning. He had asked for the tune she had first sung to him, the song that he had said was hers. The crooning had crazed his senses; and his blood had hammered for release.

But no emotion she had ever experienced had engendered such an ecstasy as when later he had rested his head on her bare bosom and she had pressed him tightly to her as great spasmodic sobs had shaken him.

Then she knew all the wells of her strength and how much he really needed her. It was strangely exulting to realise that Robert Burns, with all his learning and knowledge and wonderful poetry, for all his passionate strength and positive masculinity, could be brought with complete acceptance to her bosom like a child. She had something to give him no one else could give him—not so completely.

And Robin knew that of all the women he had known none was so completely balanced and integrated as Jean Armour.

There was no other woman with whom he could so unutterably and finally relax: no other woman who so completely responded to and satisfied his physical and emotional desires. And it was this wholeness of Jean that refreshed him so completely; restored and refreshed him since their intense personal magnetisms fused, complemented and created fresh dynamic resources.

"Rab," she said, when he had recovered sufficiently to sit up, "I suppose we'll get married some day; but if ocht happens . . . what will I dae?"

"We're married now, my dear, in the only way I ken: the only way nature kens; married here by mutual consent beneath this green thorn tree this third day of September seventeen hundred and eighty-five years, Anno Domini. What little legality's needed to make our marriage binding in the eyes o' society is easily complied wi'. So we'll just comply wi' it now."

He fished in his pocket for a blank sheet of paper. He wrote unhesitatingly:

This certifies that I, Robert Burns, farmer in Mossgiel, and Jean Armour, spinster of the Cowgate, Machlin, do hereby take and acknowledge each other as husband and wife; and that we do so in full knowledge of the solemnity and sanctity of the occasion. Signed this third day of September, 1785, Machlin.

He read the declaration over, appended his signature, and said:

"Add your signature, Jean, and that makes the document fully legal and beyond all disputing. I'll make you out a fair copy in ink and you'll keep it safe hidden away."

"When I sign this does it mean we're really man and wife, Rab?"

"It wants the mumblings o' the lads in black and, in their jargon, it constitutes an irregular marriage; but it's legally binding in ony court o' law and binds us till death parts us. Not, Jean, that I pay ony heed to that. But it protects you from ony scandal, saving the scandal—as they will have it—of irregularity. Now sign it there. Aye: that's right. Now a kiss to seal the faith o' it."

They embraced with tender passion.

"But, God, lass, for what are you crying?"

Jean shook back her curls and smiled.

"My heart's fu', Rab—maybe it's a sin to be sae happy."

She flung her arm round his neck and drew him tightly to her bosom. And if they wept they were beyond all knowledge of weeping, for life in all its savage beauty could not have wrapped them in a sweeter bliss or heightened the ecstasy of the unbidden and unpredictable hour.

They walked hand in hand along the dusty road in the close-woven dusk, even as Adam had walked with Eve in Eden's bonnie yard.

Their emotions were as old as the ground they trod; as fresh as the breeze bowing the heads of bearded barley. They walked with a slow confident step, for the world was theirs: the world of emotion and fusing thought and the fusing magnetism of self-confidence in the future of their mutual love. The world was theirs, for they were the world as they apprehended it in the beatification of sense-illumined experience.

Long ago, in a night of heart-gloaming, John Rankine had told him that he would know when he had met the lass he would bring to the marriage-bed—how his heart would tell him.

He had thought his heart would never tell him. Now the heart's knowledge tingled in every cell of his being—and every cell of Jean's tingled in harmony. And so the double assurance of heart and mind fortified him against all doubt and all possibility of pessimism.

Married—and in the way a man should marry: in the fulfilling crest of physical and spiritual intimacy; in the sacredness of the emotional moment when the cold calculations of prudence are banished from the world.

He was glad now he had known so many other women before he had known Jean Armour: how else could he have appreciated her love.

And Jean was glad that Robert Burns was the first man who had loved her. She had always hoped that love, when it came to her, would come without blemish or discord—and without the cancer-seed of doubt sown in the heart.

To the happiness of their inviolate oneness was added a mutually-interpenetrating happiness that was beyond the computation of their hearts and minds.

In the bliss of such core-deep happiness there was no lodgment for the prudence of care and the concern of worldly wisdom.

And the future could whistle over the lave of its own fortune.

2

PASSION WITHOUT PRUDENCE

TWO BLACK BONNETS

Holy Willie and James Lamie were in sore straits. William Auld was in a black mood these days and they could not satisfy his demands for information about Robert Burns and Jean Armour.

The autumn had come and gone. Harvest had been a disaster: wind and rain had laid the unripened grain flat on the sodden rigs. Many small men were ruined and cast into bitter poverty and want.

Holy Willie had much personal trouble on his hands and ecclesiastical worries weighed heavily with him. In a night of lashing rain he sat in a corner of the deserted Sun Inn at the head of the Bellman's Vennel and lamented to James Lamie.

"Aye, it's a sair time, Jamie: a sair time for poor folks to be holden down. Mr. Auld should hae mair thocht for the bad hairst."

"Ye ken fine, Willie, that Mr. Auld can think o' naething but that blackguard Burns. Bad enough him writing yon verses on yoursel', Willie; bad enough in all Christian conscience to put down you blasphemous lines on Mr. Russell o' Kilmarnock's quarrel wi' Mr. Moodie o' Riccarton; but it was past all honest or decent reckoning to hold the Holy Fair up to siccan byornar abuse. That's what's gotten Mr. Auld's dander—the Holy Fair."

"Thae verses on the Holy Fair! I pled wi' Mr. Auld to tak' them afore the Presbytery in Ayr. We have authority for that. I got the Session Clerk in Ayr to write me out a copy. Listen to this: what could be plainer? 'In case any person or persons at any time shall find, hear or see any rhyme or cockalane, that they shall reveal the same first to an elder privately, and to no other; and in case they fail therein in revealing the same to any other, that person shall be assumed to be the author of the said rhyme and shall be punished therefor conform to the Acts of the Kirk and the Laws of the Realm.' That's plain enough, isn't it? But he wadna hear tell o't. And why that, will ye tell me?"

"Mr. Auld has his reasons."

"Damnit, Jeems—the Lord forgie me that I should swear—I hae the notion whiles that Mr. Auld has a bit sneaking regard for that blackguard."

"I confess I've had that notion myself, Willie. But no—no, it'll no' work. He means to catch him wi' Jean Armour. Ye see it micht be difficult to *prove* that Burns wrote the Holy Fair."

"Aye, we havena managed to get a copy in his ain hand o' write."

"And then Mr. Auld has little stammick to bring ony scandal about Machlin Holy Fair fornenst the Ayr Presbytery."

"There's sense in that now. Aye, Mr. Auld's gotten a grand head on him."

"Aye; but he's gotten a sair tongue on him too, Willie, as ye well ken. He wants to get Burns trapped wi' Jean Armour—and then, by certes, he'll smash down on him."

"Oooh aye—the Session'll smash down on him. The Session, Jeems; and *we* are the Session."

"Aye . . . but we havena got Burns yet, Willie; and that's what's eating Mr. Auld."

"Just so. Aha! But can we be certain that Burns is fornicating wi' Jean Armour?"

James Lamie lowered his ale and looked incredulously at his companion.

"Certain? Man, Fisher, hae ye taen leave o' your senses? I midoubt nor you're better versed in the signs than I am. I misdoubt than there's a man in Machlin kens the signs better."

"Signs! Aye, aye, signs; but what does Mr. Auld want wi' signs? He wants evidence. And neither you nor me has caught him in the act yet. And it's the act, no' the sign, that matters."

"Weel, there's little sign o' the act's consequences on Jean Armour yet."

"This Burns is up to every blackguard trick oot o' hell. Either that or they're no' fornicating yet. In a' my experience, Jeems, I've never kenned such a hot pair o' courters getting such an infernal length o' rope to hang themsel's."

"Ah, but ony month now and they'll hang themselves."

"Aye; but where do they do it, Jeems? Ye'd catch a ram quicker."

"And that's the surest sign o' the lot. If they hadna a guilty conscience they wadna jowk the neuks and crannies o' Machlin the way they do."

"Mind ye, Jeems, I'm mair nor surprised that James Armour hasna jaloused the way the wind's blowing. Armour just canna bide the sicht o' Burns. He'd lay hands on him if he kent."

"Man, Fisher, dinna haver. Ye ken fine what Mr. Auld has said about that. If Armour gets ony evidence afore we can lay our report afore Mr. Auld, I'll no' answer for Mr. Auld's actions."

Holy Willie shivered at the prospect. He knew how brittle was the thread that held him to Daddy Auld's esteem: he knew how disastrous would be the consequences to him if that thread should snap. And he was too much of a coward to admit, even to himself, that he was more afraid of Robert Burns than he was of the Reverend William Auld. Auld was careful to deride him behind the sanctity of his study walls: Burns had already held him up to ridicule and contempt before the parish.

"Weel then, Jeems: you and me'll need to have an understand-ing: we'll need to strike a bargain."

"Aye, man?"

"Oooh! There's nocht else for it, Jeems. We'll need to hold fast thegither on this. We can baith fail in our object—and ye ken fine what that means."

"And what d'you propose?"

"I'll tell you what I ken and you'll tell me what you ken. And between the twa o' us we'll nab them. Aye, nab them in the act."

But Lamie wasn't sure of Willie Fisher. And yet there was no disputing Holy Willie had the finest nose for scenting a houghmagandie ploy in the West. It might be prudent to have his co-operation.

"There's something in what ye say, Willie. What track hae ye o' them and I'll tell ye how I fit in."

But Willie wasn't to be caught so easily.

"Weel, there's a certain byre they hae been in the habit o' frequenting."

"Surgeoners!"

"Right! But ye wad think now, Jeems, that Surgeoner wad be aware o' that?"

"Ah, but Surgeoner's a bit dour the noo on account of his dochter Jenny."

"Then there's Ronald's stable."

"And Markland's barn. The pair o' them are big wi' Jean Markland."

"Coorse, there's a hunder places for a houghmagandie ploy, Jeems. And no' aey whaur ye'd maist expect—or when."

"They've too many damned friends sheltering them, Willie; and that's the sum and substance o' the business."

"Weel, there's your ain step-son, Jeems."

"Aye—the step-son, bad cess to him! But since he's left the house and taken a room for himself, I've little control ower him. I ken fine that Burns and him are pack and thick thegither. But he aey did my bidding till Burns cam' to Mossgiel."

"Aye; and he's no' the only one Burns has led astray. I've told Mr. Auld that. 'Mr. Auld,' says I, 'there'll never be ony peace amang the young folks o' the parish as lang as this blackguard's left to gang his ways.' Oooh aye: I gave Mr. Auld the full weight and benefit o' my opinion."

"Weel, Willie, we'll need to dae something: the position's getting fair desperate. What d'ye say if we both go after them?"

"We couldna do better, Jeems: we couldna do better."

THE PLANE OF LONELINESS

"Death, Mr. Burns, death comes to us a'. You hae my sympathy. And what age was your brother John?"

"Sixteen years."

"Aye, aye. Weel, see Robin Gibb about the arrangements for opening a lair . . . And you had a bad hairst like the rest o' poor folks?"

"Yes: it has left us to face a trying winter, Mr. Auld. We'll need to bury my brother with as little expense as may be possible."

"I can appreciate that, Mr. Burns. I see no reason to be at the expense o' the best mort-cloth."

"Thank you, Mr. Auld, for your understanding."

"You ken, Mr. Burns, I have the notion whiles that you hae gotten the wrong opinion about the ministers of the Kirk."

"I hope not, Mr. Auld."

"I hope not, Mr. Burns. The Lord has bestowed great gifts on ye, Mr. Burns: ye hae a big responsibility to see that ye use them in His service."

"To what gifts is Mr. Auld referring?"

"You're a poet. Now, it's a very responsible thing to be a poet: I think you understand what I mean by that?"

"I am at some loss to know how you judge me a poet, Mr. Auld?"

"My duties as parish priest are many, Mr. Burns. It's my bounden duty to God and His Kirk to be acquaint wi' everything that goes on within my parish boundaries——"

"And in the course of your duties, sir, you have come on some of my verses?"

"That is so. It is no part of my duty, Mr. Burns, to sit in critical judgment anent your verses; but I will not disguise from you the fact that they have occasioned me very deep distress. That your verses show ability I will not deny; that your skill as a versifier is uncommon I will not deny either; but I canna separate the wheat o' the content from the chaff o' the form. I wasna minded when ye cam' here the night to catechise you in this fashion. Indeed I'm thinking of your grief, Mr. Burns; or maybe I wad say more nor I have; but at a time o' death we are more than usually humbled and I wad ask you, Mr. Burns, to have some concern for your immortal soul . . .

"As I say, Mr. Burns, you hae gotten very great abilities—abilities that come direct frae the Almighty: it wad be a sair sin to abuse sic a gift.

"I'm an old man, Mr. Burns, and you're just on the edge o' life. Ye hae a keen and observant eye in a lang head . . . ye see things in life that do not conform to the precepts o' the Book, and you're driven, maybe by the contradiction, to see men in a' the weakness o' their mortal and sinful flesh as scoundrels and hypocrites.

"You dae wrong, Mr. Burns, to be hasty in your judgments, right though your judgments may seem to your eyes . . .

"And it's for the Kirk to chastise in the name of the Father, Mr. Burns. The Kirk in its years o' experience has ordained what a man may do and what he ma'na do. It is for the Kirk to judge and to chastise them that break its ordinances and the Lord's commandments.

"God has gifted ye wi' an insight that's given to few men; and it's on account o' this gift I'm speaking to you the way I am.

"I want ye to tak' counsel wi' yoursel'—and wi' the Lord. Ye're treading a dangerous path and it's nae mair than my plain duty to warn you o' the dangers that threaten you on ilka hand.

"I'd be loth for to censure you though you merit censure ten times ower. Censure indeed's the verra thing you're expecting frae me. Don't mistake me, Mr. Burns: I could censure you bravely—aye, and threep the ordinances o' the Kirk down your throat better than most.

"But I hae ower meikle respect for your intellect and understanding to do ony siccan thing.

"I'm content—in the meantime—to leave you to your conscience. You understand me, Mr. Burns?"

"Yes, Mr. Auld, I understand you."

"And you'll heed me?"

"I do not know what verses of mine you have seen, Mr. Auld. But I know I have written nothing in earnest or jest that has been disrespectful to you in any particular."

"I am sensible of that, Mr. Burns; but I have had to remind others than yourself that persons stand in no especial favour in the sight of the Lord . . . But I'll leave you to your cogitations, Mr. Burns. Robin Gibb will acquaint me o' the burial arrangements . . ."

Robert trudged home to Mossgiel in a sober frame of mind. The death of John had distressed him. He knew that the lad was better away; had known for a long time that death had claimed him for an early grave. But the sight of the poor wasted skeleton lying in the spence shocked him deeply.

The lad's death, coming so soon on the top of the disastrous harvest, had spread a deep gloom throughout the family.

And now here was Daddy Auld, solemn and serious, but not unkindly, rebuking him for his verses. Rebuking him in a way that was difficult to answer.

Auld was right from Auld's point of view. He could appreciate Auld's view-point; but he could not conform to it. Auld belonged to a different age, a different generation. He could see no other light than that diffused by the narrow window of the Old Light Calvinists. And that was a light he had never accepted. The only light he could acknowledge was the light of heaven's open canopy—the light that danced in Jean Armour's dark eyes and the light that had perished in the sunken eye-sockets of poor uncomplaining John.

But while he rejected Auld's friendly sermon he was touched by it. It was a curious relationship that had grown up between them, and Robert was somewhat puzzled by it.

Auld was a stern disciplinarian. Yet there had been a curious far-away sadness about his cold eyes, a curious deference in his tone. It was difficult to think of Auld consorting with such creatures as Holy Willie and James Lamie; difficult to see how Auld did not, in his secret heart, despise them.

Robert could not imagine anyone being on friendly or easy terms with William Auld; but only a fool would take Auld at any cheap valuation.

There was a plane of loneliness on which they both met. There was no one with whom Auld could consort on terms of equality either as man or priest. Robert, unlike Auld, had many warm friends and he had the happy knack of accepting them at their true level. But, like Auld, there was no one with whom he could consort on terms of equality either as poet or as man.

Intuitively rather than consciously the old priest and the young poet were aware that they shared this common plane.

FELLOW MORTAL

On the first day of November they happed the wasted frame of John Burns in the clay of the Machlin Kirkyard.

Some days later Robert was ploughing the Mossgiel ridge in a cutting wind from the hills hidden in a sleety drizzle. His eye watched the swaying coulter as it ripped the earth in order to prevent the shock that would result from the impact of a large boulder or an outcropping rock.

The cast of his mind was melancholic. The light of heaven's canopy was uniformly and sombrously grey. Only his relationship with Jean Armour remained golden. Yet life had taught him as it had taught few people that happiness and sorrow were the warp and woof of existence; for every height on life's road there was a hollow beyond. On the heights the sun shone and the prospect was golden: in the hollows lay the dark shadows of suffering and sorrow.

And as he ruminated with philosophic pessimism, his external eye never wavering from the shuddering searing coulter ripping open the grey-brown stubble, he saw the knife tear through a ball of bent and foggage, saw the twisted scramble of a brown ball of life as it tore its way free of the wreckage of its home and disappeared into the fallow lea.

It was near the rig-end. In a moment he had swung the plough on its side and Gilbert brought the team to rest.

Robin straightened his bent back and rubbed his numbed hands together. God, but it was raw and cold! He kicked the clay from his cold damp feet and walked back to the nest of the brown field-mouse.

He lifted up the woven mass of withered grasses. He separated the fibres gently with his fingers. Aye: it was a wonderful bit of work, a monumental structure for such a small creature. And yet a cosy-enough shelter, wind-proof and rain-proof, ample protection from the frost and the rain and the sleety dribble of November's gloomy days.

Aye: warm and safe till fortune's chance sent the plough through it and cast it over into the raw furrow.

And that was how life was. Man, for all his boasted reason, never knew the day when the coulter of circumstance crashed through the substance of his earthly possessions and cast him naked to wander across the bleak moorland of existence.

The trouble with man was that he built his home with dreams and visions and endless hopes as well as stone and thatch. And yet, howsoever he planned and builded, he could not insure himself against the morrow of the uncertain future.

Robert allowed the sleety wind to whisk the remaining wisps of the mouse's nest from his broad paw. He turned and moved slowly back to where Gilbert was standing eyeing him with dull curiosity.

"What were you looking at?"

"Nothing but a few wisps of withered grass, Gibby. But to the mouse that bigged them neatly and deftly into a shelter it was a home, and, for all I know, maybe something of a palace as well!"

"A mouse's nest!"

"Ah, you needn't look sae disgusted, man. The mouse is part o' life like you and me and wee Willie Patrick there. And we're a' damned poor creatures under misfortune's blasts."

"That's true enough."

"Aye, and the mouse has one big advantage over us. It may be able to look backwards, I don't know. I fancy it lives for the moment and is only touched by the present. It canna see forward, Gibby."

"Neither can you, Robin—and you can see more than most."

"Aye, Gibby; but I can think—and fear."

"Fear? Aye: you've hit it there, Robin."

"When you cast your eye down these wet sour sods we're turning over you fear want and starvation——"

"Are we never to prosper, Robin? Or are we cursed in some way?"

"Then the big feck o' folk in the West are similarly cursed, Gibby."

"Damn it, Robin, we planned all that human wit could plan to make a success o' Mossgiel."

"Planned? Aye: we planned. And you see what's come of our plans. You canna plan against the misfortune of circumstance, Gibby: no more nor a mouse . . . Turn the horse, Gibby: we can finish the rig gin lowsin time."

They turned the horses on the bleak bare ridge of Mossgiel, where the wind with a dribble of sleet blew cold across the dark valley.

Robin's outward eye was fixed on the shearing coulter. But his mind was fixed on other things. And somehow the failure of their plans, the sad dreary pointless death of John, the gloomy November day, fused with a strange unpredictable foreboding about his relationship with Jean Armour. And from the sudden fusing came the lines of poetry and the ideas were moulded in imperishable form.

Later that evening, safe in the loft above Ronald's stable and sharing a common plaid, Robert told Jean his verses. His voice was low and rich, husky yet vibrant with a deep elemental almost-impersonal sadness. Jean was profoundly stirred. The quality of his voice called into response every sympathetic nerve of femininity.

And when he came to the last verse: "Still thou art blest, compared wi' me! The present only toucheth thee: but och! I backward cast my e'e, on prospects drear! An' forward tho' I canna see, I guess an' fear!" she put her strong arms round him and held him in a tight embrace: she held him to her as she would a child . . .

"Oh Rab, Rab: I never want to leave you. I wish we could aey be the-gither and you hadna to go hame to Mossgiel. Rab: I just canna bear it when you're sad like this . . . I feel you're no' Rab Burns ony longer but somebody I dinna richt ken. Och, what am I saying? I ken you better when you're like this—only I'm frichtened I'll lose you."

"And I'm feared I'll lose you. That, Jean lass, is what I fear most of all."

"We'll never part, Rab; never, never! We'll aey be thegither nae matter what happens—richt to the end, Rab, I'll be yours. We're man and wife, aren't we—as weel as lad and lass?"

"That's the joy and the glory o't, Jean: lad and lass and man and wife. Don't let my melancholy touch you, Jean: it's something I shouldna ask you to share."

"But I maun share a'thing wi' you, Rab."

"Weel, Jean: you can see for yourself life's no' easy, and there's nae saying what's waiting for us round the corner—as long as you realise that?"

"Rab: you've mourned sair about John. I ken, though you've never said a word about him."

"Aye, you're right, Jean. Puir laddie: he was doomed frae the start. He must hae got a smittle frae my father. He pined and wasted away till there was nocht left o' him but the bare bones. I've lifted him oot o' his bed at night and carried him through to the fire for a wee bit company. God! he was nae heavier nor a three months' bairn . . . There's a something about it, Jean, I just canna put words on: a something, maybe, I dinna want to put words on. Damn it: the laddie was blameless o' ony mortal sin and yet the curse was on him and he had to waste away and die. And why? That's the cancer o' doubt, Jean, that eats away at the pillars o' ony come-easy go-easy belief in human happiness. Mind you: it wasna that I grieved for John in a way you would expect either. It was just that when we buried him there in the kirkyard I buried something within me. Damned, I'll soon be going about with a weel-filled lair o' buried things within me . . . Don't ever be tempted, Jean, to ask me to dig up the grave o' my buried thoughts; and dinna be annoyed wi' me if you see me brooding and I dinna offer to make you any the wiser about the source of my brooding; for as like as no' I couldna tell you even though I wanted. You see, Jean: it's no' every thought can be put in words and it's no' every feeling that can be put into thought—if you can understand me."

"Aye, fine I understand you. I havena much skill, Rab, at putting onything in words—but I can understand."

"Of course you can. And that's one o' the many things I love about you. There's plenty in that head o' yours, Jean. Aye: more than most; and the sense o' what's in your head is in your eyes . . . in the tone of your voice . . . in the lilting o' your singing. And there's more meaning in all that than in all the grammars that were ever printed . . .

"Oh, maybe it's just the way things have been turning out. Bad crops, bad weather, bad luck—and no right place for you and me to do our courting. Man and wife and we havena a bed to lie down in.

"It canna go on like this, Jean: that's a certainty. I had thought I was going to make a success o' the farming; but it seems that's no' to be. But what else is for me? I had been determined to make a success o' Mossgiel long before I met you. Indeed from the moment Gibby and I signed the lease in Gavin Hamilton's there, I was determined I would make a success o' Mossgiel. Aye, and give up my verses gin they threatened to stand in the way.

"But after I met you . . . in the summer there . . . lying below the green thron tree . . . I was determined beyond anything else that I would succeed as a farmer: so that I could take you to Mossgiel as my wife.

"But I'm afraid, I'm afraid it's not going to work out that way. Bad seed the first year, bad weather this year—and what next year?"

"Och, Rab, dinna worry: maybe next year everything will be all right."

"If hoping and hard work'll do it, Jean . . . But if no', then we must hit on some other plan."

"What kind o' plan, Rab?"

"I'm no' sure, lass. There's the Indies . . . Jamaica. Nobody wants to leave Scotland less than me: nobody would be sorrier to leave Auld Scotland's shore. But it seems I'll never make my fortune here: the fates are against me."

"But . . . No: you canna think o' leaving Scotland, Rab. Surely we could get on wi' little to begin wi': I'm no' asking for much, Rab . . . and I wad work hard, you ken that."

"Fine I ken, lass. But to labour to some of the bigger farmers—there's no fortune in that either—however modest the fortune would content us. No: there's nothing there but toil and endless slavery. And I'm set against you being the wife to a labouring slave. But there's a chance o' pushing my fortune abroad. I'll no' be the first driven to that extreme. At least I'll no' die o' the cold there—and if I succeed I'll be able to send for you, Jean——"

"Och, there's bound to be some road out for us."

"We'll see . . . Damned, Jean, I'm tired o' this life o' dodging Holy Willie and Jamie Lamie and the unco guid o' Machlin—to say nothing o' your father."

"Aye: my faither's goin' to be a problem. He's nae kind thoughts for you, Rab."

"I get nothing but glowers frae him. Some day you'll need to tell him we're married."

"I'll need to wait till we get some kind o' place, Rab. It wouldna be safe for to tell him the now."

"That's just what I'm aey telling you. Nothing's safe and nothing's sure and hell alone knows what's in store for us . . . Richmond canna bide it any longer: he's for Edinburgh."

"And what about Jenny?"

"He'll send for Jenny when he gets properly settled."

"Soon?"

"Soon—I hope: for both their sakes."

"And when's Jock for Edinburgh?"

"It's no' just settled . . . but as soon as Gavin Hamilton can get him fixed on a writer there . . . And Jamie Smith's no' happy here either."

"I dinna ken: Jamie's gotten a nice wee shop here: he's got nothing to fear since he took his ain room."

"He's been lying ower often in the attic bed with Teenie Wilson."

"Oh no, Rab. No' Teenie Wilson: she could be his mother."

"Well, she's been holding him to her bosom the wrong way to be his mother."

"Wee Jamie! Men are awfu' silly!"

"The women are no' far ahint them, Jean. Teenie's had a bastard bairn already—to Nance Tinnock's son Bob Weir. You can't say Wee Smith seduced Christina Wilson, can you? Of course, when she's serving wi' Mrs. Lamie, what can you expect?"

"I wouldna hae thocht it o' Wee Jamie—we were at the school thegither."

"Aye: he had a notion o' you, Jean."

"I ken."

"Oh, you ken, do you? There's more nor Wee Smith had a notion o' you, Jean—and still have."

"But you ken I hae nae notion o' onybody but you, Rab."

"Aye: I ken that, Jean."

"Rab! I was thinking: if Gilbert and your sisters were set against Betty Paton, will they no' be set against me?"

"To hell wi' Gibby and my sisters: we're married and what can they do about it?"

"Aye—but d'you think they would be against me?"

"What makes you think that? Puir Betty was nobody. But you're the daughter o' James Armour. And James Armour's a man o' substance in Machlin."

"Just because I'm James Armour's dochter?"

"No: I was joking, lass. They couldna help liking you just because you're Jean Armour."

"But Gilbert's well educated—and so are your sisters; and I'm no' educated."

"Jean lass: you'll need to get this education nonsense out o' your head. I've told you before: education in itself's nothing—just a matter o' book-lear. I know the value o' book-lear right enough—nobody appreciates it more than me—for what it's worth. But unless you know how to use it it's useless. Aye, worse than useless. Honest worth, Jean, is no' to be measured that way. Now I never want to hear you talk about not being educated——"

"But you and Gilbert can pass yoursel's wi' Mr. Hamilton and Doctor MacKenzie—I couldna."

"Jean: I could pass myself wi' ony man that was ever born—and it's no' conceit that's making me talk. Gavin Hamilton kens more about law than I ken: Doctor MacKenzie kens more about medicine and surgery than I ken. But on any other subject I could make rings round the pair o' them . . . And listen, lass, the only person you've got to pass yourself wi' is me . . . And damned, Jean, you've gotten something that all the bluidy book-learning frae here to hell and back to the moon couldna dang doon in the scales—you've got everything that makes a woman perfect—beauty o' mind and face and body—and a heart, lass, to throb in harmony wi' them a'. If I had you and a bit cosy bield and a bite to put on the board I'd be the king o' men and blest in abundance abune the lave."

"Oh Rab, Rab! I wish we were settled down somewhere: I could lie and listen to you till the cock crows in the morning."

"Instead o' parting when the howlet cries in the tree? Come on, lass: we've wasted enough time talking."

FAREWELL TO RICHMOND

November winds still nirled round the neuks and crannies of Machlin and kept folks to their firesides in the long dark evenings.

After a wet day on the Mossgiel slopes, Robert was glad to change his sodden clothes and make for Johnnie Dow's. If he hadn't an arrangement with Jean (and their meeting-nights could not always be planned in advance) there was always the off-chance that they could arrange something from the back room window.

If he couldn't see Jean there were always the lads to fall back on—or he could be sure of a welcome at Gavin Hamilton's or with Doctor MacKenzie at the Sun Inn. There was no lack of company. Each howff had its regular customers; and in almost every howff he was sure of a welcome from somebody.

To-night, however, was a special occasion. John Richmond was leaving for Edinburgh in the morning.

The farewell took place in their room in the Whitefoord Arms. Richmond was not too happy at the prospect of leaving now that the decision had been made. He would be lonely in Edinburgh and he would miss his old friends.

Robert and he supped listlessly at their caup of ale.

"I had to go, Robin: there's nothing else for it. Jenny's away to Paisley . . ."

"But you are going to marry her?"

"Aye . . . when I get settled . . . But I've got to get settled. You ken as well as I do that I canna push my fortune in Machlin . . ."

"No: there's little scope for you here. First Brice and now you."

"Have you heard how Davie's faring in Glasgow?"

"I've had a letter from him. He writes well and seems to be making headway. Brice'll get on: he's no' blate."

"No . . . as long as he keeps his mouth shut about religion. Though I've heard there's a wheen deists in Glasgow. The weavers and mechanics there are a stirring lot."

"We could do wi' a few right here in Machlin . . . I wonder who'll be next to go?"

"Jamie Smith's hinting . . ."

"That's the last straw. I don't think I could thole Machlin without Wee Smith."

"You've plenty friends in Machlin, Robin—and you've got Jean."

"Aye: I've got Jean. But I've got my fortune to look to as well as you lads."

"Are you still hankering after the West Indies?"

"Hankering? It's a desperate thought, Jock. But apart from farming, there's nothing for me in Scotland. And at least if you can work at all there's a bite for you across the seas—and no damned questions asked."

"Your fortune'll turn, Robin—and there'll be no need for you to think o' leaving Scotland. Why don't you get some o' the chapmen to see about printing off some o' your verses: they might turn you a penny."

"I'll no' deny but that I hanker after guid black print, Jock. You've heard me talk of Captain Richard Brown that I met when I stayed in Irvine? He thought some of my verses were good enough for a magazine. And I was only trying my prentice hand then. Aye; and Captain Brown told me many a tale about the Indies . . . They're a free, independent folk in the Americas. As I say, a man's man there if he can use his two hands and they don't ask ony questions about his pedigree. . . . But I'd like fine to see my verses in print."

"What about a broadsheet then?"

"No: I've higher ambitions, Jock. Stumpie's in rare fine fettle the now: I'll keep him busy for a while yet—and then we'll see."

"You havena done anything since The Mouse, have you?"

"I'm never idle. I've been going over Love and Liberty again . . . touching it up."

"But you'd never get that printed?"

"Maybe no. But I've put some o' my best work into it."

"You'll send me a verse or two when I'm away?"

"Yes, Jock. I'll send you what I consider worth your attention. I wouldna like to think we would lose touch wi' one another."

"No . . . And I'd like to get the news o' Machlin from time to time. And maybe Jamie Smith'll write me?"

"Smith'll write you, have no fear o' that. It's time, surely, Jamie and the Tanner put in an appearance?"

"There'll be plenty afore the night's finished."

"Well, I wish they'd hurry up. Wee Jamie's a feast o' good-natured fun in himself."

"He was telling me that his sister Jean and your friend MacCandlish are in regular correspondence. Is it Candlish or MacCandlish he calls himself?"

"MacCandlish when I knew him first at Dalrymple. But it seems he dropped the Mac when he went to Glasgow College. He was touchy about it when I spoke to him. A fine fellow James for all that, and I'd like fine to see him make a match o't with Jeannie Smith."

"I once thought you'd a notion there yourself, Robin?"

"Aye, well I had several notions, Jock. But Jean Armour puts them all in the shade . . . But I've a very warm heart to Jeannie Smith; and my good friend MacCandlish will get a first-rate wife in her, for she's neither deficient in heart nor intelligence . . . It's a small place Machlin; but when you get acquaint with it you realise that it has everything in human nature you could wish for. You'll miss Machlin, Jock—enemies as well as friends."

"I don't know about the enemies. I'll be more than glad to see the end o' folk like Holy Willie and Mr. Lamie—aye, and William Auld. I don't give a damn what you say, Rab, Auld's a black-hearted, narrow-minded, old tyrant. You'll maybe discover that afore you're much older."

"I don't agree wi' you about Auld. Narrow-minded, aye: that's the Old Light streak in him. A tyrant, aye: when he can get away wi' it. But black-hearted? No: I wouldna say that, Jock. Auld means well—and according to his faith he lives an honest life and—or I'm much mistaken—aey has. Oh, he's no saint is Daddy Auld: a stubborn, thrawn devil when it comes up his back. But I wouldna say he nurses much blackness in his heart—But here's Wee Jamie and the Tanner: I hear them talking to Johnnie in the passage. Let's hope they'll help us to get some o' this gloom off our spirits, for the truth is, Jock, you're no' ower keen on the morn's journey, and I'm no' ower keen to see you go."

But this was only a partial truth. Robert had a warm-enough heart towards Richmond. But Richmond only catered in his ready chorus to a facet of his nature and his needs. Richmond had been a segment of an intimate circle that centred in the back room of Johnnie Dow's. It was the break in the circle that worried him. With Brice and Richmond gone, it would be uncomfortably narrowed. They were, collectively, good fellows round the tavern table, making a set in Ronald's ballroom or for a night's collective larking with the Machlin lassies. Collectively they were witty, high-spirited, and provided an excellent audience for moments when his genius bubbled over in social mirth and social ease.

He would be sorry to lose this happy audience; sorry to move in a broken circle. But maybe things would work out better than he feared. He might be thrown back on Smith's company, but in this group there was no company on which he placed a higher value. And maybe, the way things were shaping with Jean, it would be better that way.

After all, neither David Brice nor John Richmond really knew him: they only knew a side of him. Gavin Hamilton and John MacKenzie didn't really know him either. Smith and Richmond would not have recognised him sitting in learned, though far from solemn, conversation with Hamilton and MacKenzie. But no more would MacKenzie and Hamilton have recognised him jesting and joking and singing bawdy songs in the rear of Johnnie Dow's. Nor, for that matter (though she had penetrated the heart of him better than any other), would Jean Armour have recognised him in gallant converse with Gavin Hamilton's sister, Margaret, to whom he had already addressed a highly-felicitous set of blameless verses.

Robert had long been conscious of the many-sided nature of his personality; but only now was he beginning to realise that he revealed to his friends only that side of his nature to which they could best respond. Perhaps he was not quite so conscious of the fact that, to many people in whom there was no response or whose response was out of sympathy, he was merely a dour enigma of black brow and smouldering eyes, silent, intractible.

Robin staggered up the long slow slope to Mossgiel. Johnnie Dow had stood the company a good measure of excellent Ferintosh.

Up the wide bare valley of the Ayr the west wind slobbered and sighed in cold showers of stinging rain.

He couldn't remember staggering home drunk from Machlin before. But it was only his legs that were under the influence: his head was as sober as his heart was sad. That last handshake with John Richmond had carried with it more than a hint of foreboding.

SPREADING FAME

The years, forty-six of them, sat in layers of good-natured fat on Robert Aiken's sturdy frame. No man looked less the successful lawyer and surveyor of taxes. He looked and dressed the part of a prosperous merchant with a dash of the country laird.

But if Aiken was a successful lawyer it was in spite of his legal knowledge. The truth was that he owed his success to his remarkable ability to prescribe for his clients a mixture of legalism and individual psychology that was vastly more comforting than any dry formalism.

Aiken avoided the courts: they were the last resort—when all manner of special pleading behind the scenes had failed. Not that he was afraid of the majesty of the law. When forced to extremes he could launch himself forth on a spate of forensic oratory that invariably carried the day. He had fought Gavin Hamilton's case before the Presbytery of Ayr with such rare eloquence and good humour that he had won an acquittal that remained only for the Synod to endorse.

Yet success had not gone to Mr. Aiken's head. He basked in his popularity, it is true. But it had ever been his nature to bask in the warmth of good-fellowship.

Nowhere in Ayrshire was the fellowship warmer or more pleasant to Lawyer Aiken than in the pleasant rooms of John Simson's Brigend Inn.

There of an afternoon he repaired and occupied a favourite seat of vantage among his daily colleagues, including leading personalities in the town: the provost and the magistrates, writers like Willie Chalmers, public men like the banker-merchant, dean-of-guild John Ballantine, retired pensioners like Major Willie Logan of Park, and an outer fringe of market-day farmers and visiting bonnet-lairds.

To this company he had read many of the manuscript verses of Robert Burns. On this particular December afternoon he had just finished reading them *The Holy Fair*. He had already read it over to himself several times and enjoyed its relish immensely. But this reading aloud to his colleagues had been a triumph. He had laughed himself till the tears had danced on his russet-red cheeks.

"Damned! there's a poem for you!" he concluded. "Every word the solemn truth put down wi' an edge that would cut ony Auld Licht throat in Scotland. Did you see how he preened down Willie Peebles? Just a line or two and snivelling Willie's nailed to the board. By certes, and Black Jock Russell frae Kilmarnock! The sound o' his byornar bellowin's dinnin' in my lugs yet . . .

"Aye . . . it was in this very room I first met him. Ye mind you day he cam' wi' his auld faither, John? Aye . . . the Dean o' Guild and me were thegither that afternoon. How long ago wad that be, John? No' sae long either. Aye . . . eichty-two or eichty-three. Aye, three or fower year back. And I kent that very day there was some byornar ability about the lad . . .

"Aye, damned, but the like o' thae verses hae never been wrote in Scotland afore . . .

"No: ye canna get copies. I could employ two guid-gaun scriveners nicht and day makin' out fair copies o' thae verses—if I'd nothing else for them to do . . .

"Ah, but the lad's only beginning. There's no end to what he'll write yet. What's that? Where did he get the gift?

"Where do any o' us get the gift—siccan gifts as we hae gotten? His faither was gifted, of coorse. You would agree wi' me there, John? No' a poet, of coorse. Aha! but a remarkable man. He was gardener to Provost Fergusson a while afore the provost died; had a bit holding o' ground in Alloway there; that's where Robert was born—What's that, Adamhill? Aye, man: speak up. I believe you're older acquaint wi' Rab Burns than onybody here."

John Rankine of Adamhill put down his drink.

"You're richt there, Bob. I'm no' the man for making claims to what I hae nae richt; but I think I ken Rab Burns better nor onybody."

"That's a fully big claim, Adamhill."

"It is. I heard him read his first verses. A swatch o' satire on the Ronalds o' the Bennals . . . And I saw him through a' his Degrees. And I'll see him gae further in the Craft yet. Aye . . . and my ingle-side at Adamhill has seen him mony a nicht . . . I could tell you things aboot Rab Burns you wadna credit—the lad's gotten byornar gifts. But I'll say this for you, Bob: you can put more pith into your reading o' thae verses than ony ither body in Ayrshire—barrin' the Bard himsel'. Mind you: the Bard can read his ain verses as weel as write them—damned, none better."

Bob Aiken was too generous in his nature to feel any meanness at John Rankine's claim to a longer and deeper intimacy with the Bard. But he knew both of them well enough to realise that Robert Burns would be attracted to a man like John Rankine in a genuine way.

"Damned, then, John, you maun bring the Bard down here some day so that we can a' enjoy his reading. There's nothing, speaking for myself, that I would like better."

The suggestion was warmly received by the company, and John Rankine was pressed on all hands to carry the suggestion into speedy effect.

But already the fame of Rab Burns in Mossgiel had spread beyond the ridge above Machlin. His verses were esteemed by keen intellects in Ayr and Kilmarnock; they were relished by rustic wits and village wags in many a tavern and change-house; odd verses went the rounds from appreciative tongue into appreciative ear; verses were copied out from a borrowed master-copy on howff benches and tavern tables by those who could write and could borrow a quill and a horn of ink from the landlord.

Robert did not always give away copies of his verses to those who sought them: he carefully selected the recipients for that honour; but he was never able to refuse a friend. And John Richmond, who prided himself on his scrivening (if not on his accuracy), had gone into Edinburgh with many a fair copy in the bottom of his leather and brass-bound kist.

The manuscripts came thick and fast now, for Robert was in the vein as he had never been, and it seemed that he would never exhaust the fertility of his imaginative and creative vigour.

Even Gilbert (who thought so highly of Robert's gifts and who had never ceased to marvel at the richness of his genius) had his amazement brought to the stage of the inarticulate: he could only shake his head and gape in wonder as masterpiece succeeded masterpiece.

And yet there was pain at the heart of his wonder. Poetic masterpieces might flourish at Mossgiel: nothing else flourished; and more and more they were being bogged in the down-sucking mire of poverty.

He sensed (for he had ceased for the time being to nag about it) that Robin was as sharply aware of the economic gloom as himself; that he was writing almost with frenzy against the day when disaster would overtake them all.

So deeply indeed was Gilbert immersed in the hopeless economics of Mossgiel that he failed to see the more immediate direction of Robin's source of frenzy.

THE ONLY LIBERTY

Cold blasts of wet winds ushered in the new year of Eighty-six. Instinctively, in his bones, Robin felt that this might well be the most momentous year in his life.

Everything was in a state of flux. The uncertainties were appalling. Jean might be pregnant—the hope that she wasn't grew fainter every day.

Gilbert and he had almost decided to give up the farm come the May term and divide the responsibility of the family between them.

Soon Bessie Paton would be consigning dear-bought Bess to his and his mother's care.

He was still dreaming that the only possible escape for him lay across the trackless waste of the Atlantic ocean.

He had decided that he would try his hand as author and commit his verses to the sanctity of good black print. His Kilmarnock friends—Muir, Samson, Gowdie and the good Colonel Parker—were all for it, and were keen that he should consult with John Wilson the Kilmarnock printer.

To this end he used every moment to polish up his drafts and to dash off new ones.

Gilbert was with him in his publishing project. If Robin was to go across the seas he must leave some record of his poems. Besides, Gilbert decided that he must take advantage of the fact that Robin was depute-master of St. James's in Tarbolton and get himself put through the Lodge.

Robin was delighted at the idea. It would be grand to have the honour of conferring the distinction of the Craft on his brother. If they were to part, as seemed likely, they could not part on a better memory.

He was deeply worried, at times he was profoundly agitated in mind and spirit, but he was far from unhappy. There were times when he was filled with a fierce exultation. He was at times conscious of tremendous spiritual strength. He had hammered out his philosophy of life on the unyielding anvil of experience. He knew where he stood in the measure of his essential greatness. Here he towered above any man he had ever met.

But his feet were steady on the solid earth.

Socially, however, he was a mere cypher: a poor tenant-farmer who was so scant of cash that he had to avoid the taverns on a market-day and towered above nobody.

This irked and galled him, for his nature was generous if not prodigal. To have to count the cost of every item of personal expenditure in terms of coppers drove home the state of his economic and financial destitution bitterly and unpleasantly.

Often and often in his poems he allowed this bitterness and resentment to spill over. Social, political and economic inequality was the canker of his Ayrshire world. More: it was the canker of Scotland, of Britain, of Europe . . .

America had struck her blow for equality, freedom and independence. The same blow would have to be struck here. The more he lived the truer became that glorious verse he had put in *Love and Liberty*: A fig for those by law protected, Liberty's a glorious feast; courts for cowards were erected, churches built to please the priest.

Aye: liberty was a glorious feast—especially when the only liberty he had was the liberty to proclaim it so.

DILEMMA

It was easier to see Jean in the long dark forenights. Her father was busy on a building contract in Cumnock and rode home only at the week-ends. Thus Jean had more freedom than when he dominated the fireside and when all her out-goings and in-comings had to be accounted for. And in the darkness of Machlin's twisted narrow lanes it was easier to elude the spying eyes of Holy Willie and James Lamie.

But Jean was worried. She knew she was pregnant and she feared there was no way of escaping the consequences. At any rate she knew of none; and since she and Robin were lawfully married what was there to fear?

Indeed there was plenty to fear. It was one thing to be married beneath the quivering ecstasy of the green thorn tree: it was a much different thing to stand on the paved floor of the kitchen in the Cowgate, facing her parents, and admit that she was married— far less confess that she also was with child.

The very thought of the ordeal chilled her. She didn't know how she would ever be able to face the ordeal of that confession.

She knew she was the apple of her father's eye, stern though that eye could be. And she now knew more than ever how her father hated and loathed the sight of Rab or the mention of his name.

Ever since he had read Rab's verses on Holy Willie and the Holy Fair he had been like a man possessed whenever his name was mentioned. As yet he had not the faintest inkling that she had

ever spoken to Rab. He had threatened her with frightful consequences if she ever did.

Her mother, too, echoing her father, had conceived the most
violent animosity to Rab and all his family at Mossgiel.

What they would say when they learned the truth—and the
truth could hardly be concealed from them much longer—she
dreaded to think. Sometimes this dread would freeze the marrow
of her bones and drain the rich blood from her radiant cheeks.

And sometimes her mother seemed to look at her queerly . . .

She longed to take Jeannie Smith into her confidence for the
sympathy and understanding she knew Jeannie would pour out to
her. But Rab was wise and had forbade her to utter a word until
they were absolutely certain.

In the darkness of the night they walked down the long Cumnock
road. Jean had told him that there could no longer be any doubt:
she was pregnant. She would not be able to conceal her bouts of
sickness much longer.

Though he had expected this news, its announcement struck
him with the shock of a physical blow. For some moments he
could neither speak nor think. His senses were numbed.

Jean's news could not have come at a worse time. Everything was
against him. There was no ray of light anywhere and he seemed to
be travelling down an ever-narrowing tunnel towards disaster.

But the moment the first shock of the news had passed, his
sympathy was for Jean in her immediate predicament.

"I canna see my road out yet, Jean: the future's blacker nor the
night about us. It would be easy if I'd some place to take you.
Anywhere away from the Cowgate. Gilbert and I canna win free o'
Mossgiel afore the middle of May—though we'd need to get some
place afore that. Gilbert says he'll take my mother and Bell and
maybe Isa. And I'll need to take Nancy and Willie—and maybe
Betty Paton's bairn. God! but the way's no' clear, Jean. Gilbert's
agreed to take on the whole burden if I can settle on onything in
the Indies—and send him what I can by way o' help. But how am
I to do that and lay by at the same time for you coming out?

"This is how it's been all my life, Jean. Lack o' money, lack o' gear—and cursed misfortune dogging my steps a' the time.

"And yet I canna throw the whole burden o' the family on Gibby's shoulders—that wouldna be fair, even if Gibby could support them. Of course, at the worst my sisters could go into service—you couldna get better workers about a farm—indoors or out. But that would still leave my mother and Isa and Willie.

"Don't think, Jean, that I'm no' thinking o' you first. As a last desperate measure we could make a corner for you at Mossgiel. But that would be desperate indeed—worse than death. I've told none o' them I'm married . . . Oh, not that it's onybody's business—if only I could meet the situation. Damnit, Mossgiel's as crowded as Poosie Nancie's on Race Night. You might manage a bit peace to yourself through the day; but that would be all.

"Then there's your own folks. Your father hates the sight o' me in the streets. If he met me in Nance Tinnock's he'd turn on his heel and walk out. Of course I canna blame him. He's one o' Daddy Auld's supporters. And I'm no' saying this to hurt you, Jean; but the only things that matter to your father are conformity to the outward tenets o' orthodoxy—and the gowden guineas. If I'd a good claut o' siller and was sitting smug in a weel-stockit mailen o' my own, my verses on the Calvinists wadna matter a damn . . . No: I don't blame him. He's got every right to see that the man who marries his dochter is properly provided for. And I ken from the clash o' Machlin how much he dotes on you . . .

"But there it is, Jean; and hell mend it, for I canna. Only don't rush and tell your mother for a wee while. Something might turn up yet. And if the worst comes to the worst, Mossgiel can go to hell and I'll haud to you. You're my first concern, Jean. First and last I've got to think of you and the bairn you're carrying."

NO MANNA FROM HEAVEN

James Smith was the most sympathetic of all his Machlin friends. He listened to Robin's plaint and advised him to the best of his ability. They were seated alone in Dow's back room.

"There's one thing you maun hold to, Rab, and that's Jean Armour. I'd think the world well lost for her. What can the Armours do? Kick up hell to begin wi'; but after that? They canna get beyond the fact that you're married. All you've got to do is hold out till the storm blows past."

"Aye; but why should there be any storm?"

"Oh, damnit, there's bound to be a storm. James Armour thinks he's no small fry in Machlin—and he canna abide you or me. And I ken he's got his horns in you. But as I say, what's the odds? When his wrath cools he'll be only too glad to recognise you as Jean's husband. Damnit, you canna see old Armour wanting a bastard in his family, can you?"

"No . . . I think you've got that bit right, Jamie; but I canna see Armour acknowledging a husband that canna support his dochter—canna even provide her wi' a chicken-cavey."

"To hell! Armour's got plenty siller. As like as no' he'll set Jean off wi' a good dowry. Fifty pounds would be nothing to him: never miss it. Bide your time, Rab—and do naething rash."

"I admit Jean's entitled to a damn good dowry: she's slaved well to old Armour and that old bitch o' a mother. Damned, Jamie, I canna thole that woman, though maybe old Armour's got her brow-beaten. How Jean was feathered in that nest beats me—I mean her disposition. No doubt she's gotten mair than a fair share o' old Armour's health. But Jean's nature—as far as I can make out—corresponds wi' neither the one side nor the other . . . Aye; but the dowry—that's Jean's affair. I wouldna touch a penny o' their money: they would cast it in my teeth and my bairns' teeth as long as they lived. I know that kind. No, Jamie; I'm lippening on nae dowry; and I don't think Jean is . . .

"But what about my poems, Jamie? Did you look over the last batch I gave you. If I'm to publish, I've got to publish only the best."

"Aye, Rab: I've read them again and again. But I just canna talk to you about them. They're beyond ony praise o' mine. I can only say that you get better and better, so that I canna say which verse is better than the other. I'd publish every one o' them, Rab . . . Did you speak to Wee Johnnie in Killie?"

"Well . . . I had a word wi' him. He's not enthusiastic: too damned hard-headed a business man; too keen on the cent per cent. But I must say my Killie friends put up a grand case for me: they're fair mad to see me venture into print. So Johnnie's gotten a swatch o' the Bard's best selection, to see what he thinks."

"It's a foregone conclusion, then. For aince Wee Johnnie claps his foxy een on your verses, Rab, he'll dash them into print richt away. Don't be surprised, gin you visit Killie next, to find your verses selling in the street."

"No . . . If it was as easy as that, Jamie, I'd have been in print long ago. But come now: you've got a fine critic's mind. D'you think I should print Love and Liberty?"

"Damn it, Rab, you canna go by that: that would be the jewel in the crown o' the book. That's your best work, Rab—if I had to mak' a choice on pain o' death. Your first version was magnificent— magnificent. But the way you've polished it up is beyond a' belief. You ken, Rab: sometimes I feel I'm no' fit to share your company. The sober truth is, you've gotten a brain that goes far beyond the boundaries o' Scotland. Machlin'll no' aey haud you. If your verses ever see the licht o' day they'll be the talk o' the land."

"If they get recognition and acceptance in the half-dozen parishes where I'm known, Jamie, I'll be more than satisfied."

"You may deceive yoursel', Rab; but you canna deceive me. Sooner or later the day'll come when lads like me will only be a memory to you. I mind fine the first day I met Gilbert and you in Johnnie's front room there. I thought you were a genius then and you've grown every day almost since then. I ken damn fine I'm nae numskull, Rab; but compared wi' you I'm nothing but a prattlin' eediot."

"And you think so little of me that you reckon, gin I turn author, I'll forget my old friends?"

"No, I don't mean that, Rab—and you ken I don't. I mean we're no' big enough in our minds, in our vision, in our ideas for you. Sooner or later you'll need to mix wi' men that hae ideas in common wi' you and can help you to keep your wit up to the scratch—aye, and beyond it."

"Ah to hell, Jamie: we're getting beyond oursel's. Don't be surprised if Johnnie Wilson tells me my verses are no' worth the waste o' printers' ink."

"You don't believe that, Rab?"

"No: I don't, Jamie, and if Wilson doesna print them, then I'll need to get somebody who will. I may have to sail for the Indies. And if I do, I'm not leaving without a memorial for remembrance. Hell! I've known hard days and bitter days in the West; but I've had my measure o' happiness too. I may be a pious idiot in some things, but Auld Scotia means more than a name to me. Scotland's my spiritual mither. There's a sense, Jamie, in which she means more to me than life itself. That's daft enough, isn't it? God damnit I can hardly pay rent enough for the privilege o' ploughing some of her sourest acres; I don't own as much ground as would bury me; and I may be driven from her shores like a broken bankrupt. But there's a sense where she means more to me than even Jean Armour means—and Jean's life and death to me.

"We'll have to fight for our Auld Mither, Jamie; fight tooth and nail and wi' every weapon we know. My weapon's my trusty stumpie and a horn o' ink. Aye, even across the seas I can still fight for her. Sitting down there in St. Stephen's are forty-five clowns, supposed to be representing us. You and I ken just what they represent: nothing but a parcel o' rogues in a nation. What does onybody in St. Stephen's care for Scotland? Scotland's ruled by the underhand cunning o' Henry Dundas—and Dundas doesna answer to St. Stephen's: he gets his orders direct frae Pitt: aye, and maybe beyond Pitt.

"Sometimes I think the Indies is the last place I should bury myself in. Man, Jamie, if I only had freedom and leisure to use my pen as I know it could be used, I'd turn out an ode to liberty every day I rise. Liberty's everything and everywhere: it's meat and drink, fire and water, blood and brain, a happy fireside and a prosperous peasantry, it's dancing and singing and sowing and mowing—and it's getting a wife and bringing up bairns in order and decency . . . Damned, there's an ode to liberty for every day in the year, for every year a man lives: for the more liberty mankind wins for itself, the more liberty there is to enjoy. For every seed of liberty that is sown, the ears come up seven-fold . . ."

Smith's eyes were glowing in his enraptured honest face.

"That's why you realised that the gangrels in Poosie's there had a deeper sense o' liberty in them than the dull cattle hobbled to the stake o' fear and darkness and superstition—aye, or the coward slaves that gae crawling to St. Stephen's for the bribe o' English gowd! The jovial ragged throng hae mair o' love and liberty about them and in them than a' the lads in black and the empty gowks in silks and satin, scarlets and ermine, belted swords and silver-buckled shoon. Robin man, I aey realised that was the meaning o' that glorious cantata; but now I've gotten a deeper meaning out o' it even though it's been staring me in the face a' the time. We've got to sow the seed the gangrels hae gotten in their hearts, no' in the dirty lice-crawling corners o' their stinking howffs but in the fertile furrows o' bonnie Scotland—aye, and wherever the sons o' men walk on the earth. I see it now, Robin. Aye, liberty's a glorious feast—only it doesna fa' like manna frae heaven. It's got to be worked for. Robin, you canna leave us for the Indies. We need the sun o' your poetry to warm us; we need your guidance to lead us oot o' this damned wilderness o' darkness where we've nocht but Daddy Auld's farthin' dips showing us the steps backwards—no' forwards."

"I aey kenned you had the root o' the matter in you, Jamie—and your roots go deeper than most. But think on the irony o' my situation, Jamie. You say I hae light enough in my verses to guide the sons o' men: light enough onyway, to gladden them and warm them. And yet I havena enough light to show where my next step will fall in the darkness. That's a damnable mockery for you when you think it over, eh? And you and me that should be drinking the rich wine o' life—we'll need to be content wi' a sma' ale for a stirrup-cup for shank's naiggie."

"Damn the fear, Rab: I hae the price o' twa Kilbagies—and it's ower the glorious fire o' Kilbagie we'll drink the close o' this session. We havena died a winter yet—and something's bound to turn up."

THE POEM OF ONE WORD

Wee Johnnie Wilson fidgeted on his tall stool in front of his high desk. The jobbing printer and bookseller of Kilmarnock was both a craftsman and a character. Nor was he by any means a fool. He was a judge of literature and a judge of men; but he was a better judge of the profit that lay at the end of a project.

His long narrow office was a litter of papers and grey dust, and, perched on his stool, Johnnie, for all his youth, looked like some quaint hobgoblin made of faded parchment and having naught but printers' ink in his veins.

Robert leaned an elbow on his high desk in front of the dust-encrusted windows festooned with withered cobwebs and dead flies, and listened to the printer.

"Just that, Mr. Burns. Ye've some rather good poems here. Rough a bit and in need o' a polish; but genuine for a' that. Oh, you're a poet, Mr. Burns, and it's a pleasure to meet you. But d'ye think, now, that the canny folk i' the Wast here'll bang their bits o' bawbees on poetry?"

"There's keen enough competition to get copies of my verses, Mr. Wilson."

"Aye, for naethin'. Man, Mr. Burns, you're a farmer; but it's me that kens that folk like nothing better nor reading something that costs them nothing—man, that's where the pleasure comes in. But ask them to dip into their pouches and pay for what they read and their sour faces tell a different story."

"And yet books get printed and books get sold?"

"Oh aye. But there's books and books, sir. An almanac now or a book that'll give folk education—a spelling book or an instructor in arithmetic—now folk see the sense o' that and can measure the value o' their money. But poetry's a lottery and poets are kittle cattle, Mr. Burns. Nae doubt there are gentry and folk aping the gentry that can be lured into placing a volume of Pope or Beattie or Thomson alangside a volume o' genteel sermons and a ready reck-oner or the complete letter-writer, to gar their neighbours and visitors think they hae gotten a bit brush on their education. But baith Beattie and Thomson, you'll notice, write the gentry's English. Noo, the Scots dialect that you favour, Mr. Burns, canna be expec-tit for to sit crouse and canty, smug and genteel, cheek by jowl wi' Beattie's Minstrel or Thomson's Seasons. As far as guid black print's concerned, Mr. Burns, the Scots dialect is a thing o' the past."

"It may become the best of the future!"

"Na, na, Mr. Burns: dinna decieve yoursel', or mak' to hide your undoubted light under the bushel o' a dying language."

"It's the language that's still spoken in the streets o' Killie here and in the fields o' Ayrshire: it's a vigorous tongue to be a dying language."

"Aye, but the vulgar tongue and genteel print are twa verra different worlds, Mr. Burns. Mind ye: I like your Scots verses. Damned, man, ye've captured the verra sough o' guid Scots. But I'm a man o' business, Mr. Burns, and I canna allow my private whims to dictate to my public responsibilities."

"Very well then, Mr. Wilson, you and I won't quarrel about the matter: I'll need to try my luck elsewhere."

Robert reached out for the bundle of manuscript that lay before Johnnie. But Johnnie's blackened claw clutched the papers tightly.

"Now, now, sir: no' just so sudden. No' just so sudden, if you please. A thing like this canna be rushed. There's considerations."

"What considerations?"

"Steady now! You see there's a hantle o' siller behind a project like this—and the siller's a' by way o' being on the wrang side o' the ledger. Expenditure's ae thing but income's anither."

"I think I could get you guarantee enough to cover the expenditure, Mr. Wilson."

"Guarantee! Man, that's a sweet-sounding word, Mr. Burns. There's music in the sound o' it. Damned, man, that's a poem o' one word. Guarantee! Aye, now you're talking a language that poets dinna ken. I'll admit your friends hae spoken to me aboot something o' the kind. But a guarantee's a fickle thing too—a mere glowworm in a fox's tale: if ye get my meaning."

"In what form do you want the guarantee, Mr. Wilson?"

"The sicht o' guid siller's best, Mr. Burns. But I wadna say no till a well-signed bond—say, by a monied gentleman o' the toon. Now, now, ye needna draw doon your brows, sir. Just a business-like precaution. The bond need never be touched. The thing to dae wad be to get a bit bond arranged wi' me here. Then we would see aboot getting out a prospectus for your poems. A subscription-prospectus ye'll understand. Now, if sufficient o' your friends—and guid folks i' the Wast here—were signing that prospectus and laying themselves to purchase the volume should it come out, then we wad ken exactly where we stand. Exactly where we stand, Mr. Burns—which is what at the moment we hae only a gey foggy idea o'."

Johnnie patted the manuscript with a sudden affection.

"Man, Mr. Burns, there's some grand verses here, and it wad be a pity to see them lost till the warld for the sake o' a wee bit of a guarantee and twa-three dozen bills o'subscription. Hae a crack wi' your friends and I'm sure ye'll be able to arrange something to our mutual pleasement."

Wee Johnnie held out a thin blackened claw and swivelled round on his high perch.

"Guid-day to you, Mr. Burns—and dinna be lang till you're back. And if ye can dress up a bit verse or twa in polished English it'll dae your collection nae herm. An' a wee touch now and again o' a higher moral tone—like your Cottager—there's nothing improves a book sae much as a high moral tone."

Robert bade Johnnie good-day but did not otherwise reply. When he came up into the street out of his musty premises he breathed deeply of the snell air.

DISCLOSURE

The fatal day came before the blasts of January winds had blown themselves out in a sobbing exhaustion.

It was a morning when Jean and her mother had the house to themselves. Mary Smith was well-versed in all the signs; and there was a terrible fear at her heart.

"In God's name, Jean, whan did this happen . . .? Afore the New-Year! And wha's the man . . .? Rab Burns! Rab Burns! God abune us: your father'll murder ye. He'll murder ye and I'll no' can save ye. Weel micht I hae kenned ye werena vaiging aboot wi' Jeannie Smith, Lizzie Miller or Jean Markland . . . Oh, but that blackguard Burns! In the Lord's name, Jean, what possessed ye? Him abune a' . . . What's that? Married! God preserve us: married, ye say? What dirty blackguardly trick's this? How could ye be sae silly as to believe siccan rubbish——"

"But, mither, it's no' rubbish. I'll show you the lines Rab wrote out for me. He's nae blackguard, mither: you're no' to say things like that."

And when Jean showed her mother her marriage lines her mother was dumbfounded and hardly knew what to think. She knew they were irregular.

"This damned paper makes ye nae better nor a common whore. Mr. Auld'll never hear tell o' this. Ye're nae better nor Racer Jess to think ye can be married this way . . . Oh God! I dinna ken what your father'll say—or what he'll dae . . . We can

201

dae nocht about it noo—if ye'd tellt me the first month . . . And
what does your fine Rab Burns say about this?"

"Rab'll dae the richt thing, mither. He's talking about sailing to
the Indies——"

"The Indies! The Indies! The black-hearted beggar! Leavin' ye
deserted in the lurch! Your father'll send him to a hotter place
nor the Indies, believe you me . . . Oh God, Jean, I lippened
on ye. I didna think you'd be sae silly and saft. And ye canna say
your father didna tell ye what he thocht about that blackguard
Burns."

Long before James Armour came home Jean was sick with fear
and worry and apprehension. She had pinned so much faith on
Rab and on their marriage document.

She was sick with the way her mother nagged and flyted;
sick with dread at the future she painted for her; sick at the way
she upbraided her for keeping her marriage secret for so long. She
began to have doubts about the wisdom of her actions. Maybe
she had been guilty in keeping things dark, in so blatantly deceiving her mother about the company she had been keeping. She
now realised, as she had never realised at the time, how she had
lied to her parents. This, in itself, was a terrible sin, as she knew
only too well; and the remorse for all her sins was eating at her
heart.

But, above all, like a terrible cloud charged with unpredictable
menace, towered the wrath of her father.

She had always feared him. He had made himself a father to be
feared. Now she knew he had cause for righteous anger, for she
had sinned grievously against him and all that he cherished.

There had never been any hard core of resistance in Jean. All
her life she had known that the world was for men and was ruled
and dominated by their whims, their fancies and commands. She
had never in her heart or in her head attempted to doubt the
inevitability of this despotism of the male. Women were but hand-
maidens, whether married or single. Women who defied men (and
there were such in Machlin) were outside the pale of orthodoxy in
the relationship of man and woman.

Jean was no fighter, no Amazon of aggression. Yet she thought she had known what she wanted in life. She had wanted marriage. That had seemed the most natural want in her Machlin world.

What she had not hoped for was Rab Burns. Rab had been beyond her fondest hope—until she had met him. Then she had wanted him with a quiet, almost resigned, desperation. She had not expected such happiness to fall to her lot. Yet she knew that had she not got him, she would never have known abiding happiness with any other man.

The happiness of their mutual love had been flawless, had gone as deep as the source of life itself. The only ache in the relationship had been the ache that lies at the heart of all perfection.

But now she knew doubt and fear and a terrible gnawing uncertainty. And she now realised that in these last weeks Rab had been far from the assured, rock-fast lover she had known.

Now she knew why he had been worried, uncertain of the future. He had no future to offer her. His talk of going to the Indies was vague, desperate talk. His talk of taking a job as labourer to some wealthy farmer was no less vague and desperate, though there was something more homely, more comprehensible in its desperation.

But the desperation remained; for now when he should take her away and place her under his own roof-tree there was nowhere to take her.

Not that she blamed him. She could never blame him. Things had happened this way because this was the way things happened; and happenings had to be endured since they could neither be evaded nor denied.

Over the secret of herself, over the depths of a knowledge she could not articulate, Jean cowered against the imminence of the blows she knew must rain upon her.

THE FLAME OF WRATH

James Armour had ever been prone to choleric temper, for he was stiff-necked in the obdurate obstinacy of his own self-righteousness. He knew his mind; and its limitations did not appal him.

That evening in the privacy of the ben-room he listened to his wife's tale with steadily-mounting choler. It was well, he thought, that she did not plead her daughter's cause, or he would have struck her down where she stood trembling and apologetic.

What a useless bitch she was to have let all this time elapse without noticing signs of Jean's condition. In a mounting paroxysm of irresistible apoplectic fury he cursed her from his presence between vice-clamped jaws. Chilled to her marrow, Mary Armour went into the kitchen and sent Jean to him.

It was with difficulty that Jean managed to crawl into his awful presence. And when at last she looked at his eyes she saw murder there and fell on her knees.

For long did James Armour curse and revile her; and the obscenity of his abuse fell on her ears with a queer, numb savagery. And when he had emptied the outraged filth of his obscene mind on her, likening her to the most foul and shameless creatures whose teats had ever been bruised with the whoredoms of the most heinous and unspeakable harlotries, he turned his attention to the cause of her distress. Then she knew that the devil out of hell must be a saint compared to Rab Burns.

Armour's insanity roared and swirled and boiled like a mighty whirlpool in a storm of tides. Great blobs of salty sweat oozed from his burning forehead and trickled down his livid cheeks.

"But by the Almighty God above me, ye'll never live to bring a Burns-get into this world. And neither, by God, will ye tak' it wi' ye intil the next, ye hell-hardened harlot o' lust and lies. I'll kick the Burns bastard oot o' ye wi' my ain twa feet afore ye go . . .

"God damn ye for a sly, sleekit, creeping, crawling bitch o' cunning and deceitfulness. Didn't I warn ye agin Burns? Didn't I tell ye what I wad dae wi' ye if I ever kenned ye to look the airt he was on, far less speak to him? There's no' a decent God-fearing respectable man or woman aboot Machlin wad be seen speaking to him. Him! a damned ill-gotten fornicating atheist. Farmer be damned! Couldna plant a bed o' leeks in a kail-yard! No; but whan he's no' fornicating he has time enough to hold up Godly men to ridicule and mockery in a damned ill-gotten jaw o' rhyming trash. A sorry scrivener o' bawdy balderdash! And ye thocht to give him the freehold o' your maidenheid for the surety o' a worthless scrap o' paper . . . There's no' a maidenheid i' the kintraside he hasna had the spoilin' o' . . . But by God ye'll never live to compear on the Machlin cutty stool fornenst the congregation wi' that bluidy blackguard. Flee to the Indies, will he? I'll break every bane in his body, the Godless whoremaster that he is . . . Fornenst a' the gentles and lairds i' the parish too. Me that'll never be able to lift my head in the parish. Had it been a gangrel frae Gibson's howff I micht hae lived it doon. But Burns! That's a contamination worse nor the foul disorder—though I've nae doubt but he's gien ye that alang wi' the rest . . ."

Sick and shivering, outraged in every fibre of her being, terrorised in her very soul, Jean crept into the darkest corner of the house and sobbed herself dry and numb.

Slowly, as that terrible night wore on to the small hours of the morning, James Armour's awful anger spent itself. He ended in a lamentation of tears, and called pitifully on Almighty God to ease the burden of shame and sorrow that had been heaped upon him.

And then he gathered the fragments of his shattered sanity about him and began to discuss the realities of the situation with the spent shadow of his spouse.

They would have to get Jean out of the way before the Session got wind of the affair. Send her to Andra Purdie's in the Backsneddon of Paisley. Blood was thicker than water, and the Purdies would hide her till her shame was by.

But the cunning Burns! How to deal with such a cunning blackguard?

There was this marriage line. This wouldn't be got over so easily. This hadn't been written out merely to get round Jean. Na, na: Burns was too cunning a dog for that. Maybe he thought Jean would get a substantial dowry. Damned, but he'd give him dowry . . .

In the end James Armour decided that the business was too complex for him to handle. As soon as he could spare himself he would ride into Ayr and consult with Mr. Aiken the lawyer. There was no point in taking any chances with the black devil in Mossgiel.

DENIAL

When James Armour's wrath had died down and when he had had a few days' time to reflect on his trouble, he decided it would be advisable to have a word with the blackguard in Mossgiel. If they were to keep the matter secret in the meantime, it would be much better to know where Robert Burns stood and to disillusion him should he stand wrongly.

The interview took place in the spence of his Cowgate home, to which Robert had been summoned by Jean's young brother Adam. Ever since Jean's condition had been discovered she had not been allowed to cross the threshold.

James Armour, a strongly-built sturdy man of exceptionally robust health, was on his dignity. The immediate desire he had known (and which still came over him intermittently) to lay violent hands on his daughter's seducer was, for the moment, under stern control.

Robert, on the other hand, was filled with trepidation. He was being pulled in every direction and he hardly knew which way to turn. Events were piling up on him and crisis followed crisis.

He had been worried about not seeing Jean and guessed that her parents had discovered the truth of her condition. He had begun to wonder indeed if her father had laid hands on her. He was preparing to call on Jean and risk the hazard of what his visit might entail for both of them when Adam found him in the rear of the Whitefoord Arms and delivered his message.

Adam, one of the most devil-may-care laddies about Machlin, had an uncritical admiration for Robin and his friends. And though Robin questioned him cautiously, it was obvious that the lad knew nothing and suspected nothing of Jean's condition.

And now Robin faced James Armour across the blaze of his spence-ingle.

"I'll mince nae words wi' you, sir. You ken why I've sent for you?"

"About Jean?"

"Exactly: about Jean. I'll say nothing at the moment about the shame ye hae wrocht on my lassie and the shame ye hae brocht upon this house. I just want to tell you that Jean's leaving here the morn's morning and that, as far as you're concerned, you'll never see her again."

Robin bounded to his feet.

"What's that? Never see me again? You're over-stepping your duty, Mr. Armour. You understand, do you, that Jean ceased legally to be your dochter when she legally became my wife?"

"Sit down, sir, and don't dare to raise your voice in my house. Wife o' yours she never was—and never will be. D'ye think a few words wrote on a bit paper are going to be taken into account by me or ony ither respectable body? You may deceive an innocent lassie by such cheap trickery; but you're no' deceiving me."

"Mr. Armour: I can understand something of your feelings in this matter; and the fact that I canna provide my wife with a fitting home for her puts me at some disadvantage: I admit that. But you do me wrong to think that I tricked Jean in any way, or that I do not intend to make Jean my wife. I'm working on plans just now towards that end, and if I can bring them to a successful conclusion I'll be more than proud to acknowledge Jean before the entire parish."

"Aye: pride and poverty aey gang thegither. You're wasting your breath. There can be no talk about you and my dochter, sir. I'd sooner see the dogs licking her heart's bluid on the hearthstane there than married to you."

"Before we go into this any further, Mr. Armour, I'll warn you that I'm flesh and blood like any other of God's creatures, and I'll not be insulted by you or the best man living. Bear that in mind, sir, before you say something you'll have cause to regret. What in God's name have you against me—speak to me fair: speak out!"

"What I hae agin you is what every respectable God-fearing body in the parish has agin you. You're a reprobate, sir: you're damn little better nor a bluidy atheist: you're a black affront tae Kirk and State—and on the top o' a' that, sir, ye're little better nor a cadging beggar. Ye hae got it neither on you nor in you. Your fornications didna begin in this parish—but, by certes, they'll maybe end here gin I'm by wi' ye."

"Maybe you'll have the decency to remember you're talking to a fellow-craft!"

"Fellow-craft be damned! They tell me ye're depute-master o' a wheen blackguards in Tarbolton o' the same kidney as yoursel'! How the likes o' you crawled intil the Craft beats me. But watch your step, my unworthy depute-master! The Grand Lodge can deal wi' the likes o' you. It has dealt wi' your kind afore now and can again."

"Can I see my wife?"

"Wife! If you mention that word again I'll see the reddest o' ye!"

"Nevertheless I demand to see my wife. I'm not denying you're her father; but that doesn't entitle you to hold her in duress."

Knotted veins began to obtrude on James Armour's flushed temples. Still he managed to restrain himself from open violence. This dastard was as dangerous as an adder and as slippery as an eel.

"Maybe ye'll understand that my dochter has nae desire to see ye or speak to ye in this life?"

"That's one lie that can easily be refuted. Bring Jean ben here and we'll soon see whether she'll deny me or no'."

"And d'ye think it wad set your mind at rest if I proved till ye that Jean wants nocht to dae wi' ye?"

"That you know nothing about me doesn't surprise me. Nor does it surprise me to learn that you know nothing about your own daughter. Jean would as soon think of denying the Holy Ghost as deny me."

"Blasphemy comes easy to a dishonoured tongue. But we'll damn soon settle that, sir."

James Armour strode to the door, drew the sneck and called on Jean.

Robert was standing on the sheep-skin hearth rug, his fists clenched tightly by his side, when Jean, preceded by her mother, came into the room.

His jaw fell in astonishment when he saw her. She was cowed as he could not have believed a human being could be cowed. Her face was completely drained of colour and her head hung forward shamefully and ashamedly. She made no attempt to catch his eye. Mrs. Armour held closely to her side.

James Armour was playing his master card and he knew it. He watched Burns closely from the corners of his small hard eyes.

"This person here, Jean, not only claims ye as his lawful wedded wife, nae less, but claims that ye're only too willing to support him in his claim. Now just tell him, in your ain words and in your ain way and of your ain free will, what your reply to that is."

Mrs. Armour gripped Jean tightly above the elbow. She felt her wilting where she stood and was frightened she might faint away in their hands as she had already done.

Jean felt that her senses, numb though they had been for days, were threatening to leave her. She wanted to fall into Rab's arms and ask him to take her away from the livid hell of the Cowgate. Then across her tautened nerves fell the lash of her father's voice.

"Ye heard me speaking, didn't ye?"

But Robert could not restrain himself any longer. He took an impulsive step towards her. Armour took a covering step with him.

"For God's sake speak, Jean!"

"I canna—I canna help it, Rab. Whatever my father says—is true."

"You mean you deny me, Jean?"

Again the lash of her father's tongue.

"Answer, will ye?"

Jean nodded her head slowly.

"Speak up!" roared Armour.

For a brief second Jean's pained and clouded eyes flickered across Robin's gut-kicked expression.

"It wad be better if I didna see you again, Rab."

"God Almighty, Jean, d'you ken what you're saying?"

"You heard her," snarled Mrs. Armour. "And I think, James," she added with infuriating sanctimoniousness, "ye shouldna stand and hear the Lord's name taken in vain."

Suddenly in a red mist of unreason Robin's mind snapped.

"God damn the lot of you!" he roared. "If you'd rather hae your dochter a common whore than an honest wife, then, by God, you can have her. Keep her and your damned rotten stinking pride wi' her. I'll see day about wi' the whole lousy pack o' you. But mind that your hour will come, Jean Armour; the bairn you're carrying's my bairn; and the day'll come when he'll curse the hour that you tried to make a bastard o' him. Aye; but bastard's what he'll never be in spite o' a' your hell-raked plans. Tell him when he cries for his Daddy, that'll be far across the seas, that he married you aneath the sanctity of a green thorn tree—and show him the lines he wrote out for the world to witness the truth thereof—and then go out and cut your bluidy throat, for the flames o' hell'll be waiting to welcome you from now on."

He staggered blindly out of Armour's house, stumbled and staggered down the Cowgate, and held on, staggering, stumbling and shambling, down the Cumnock road. The gold and orange flames of unreason flashed behind his eyes and blinded him. An inchoate chorus hammered insanely on his aural nerve: *whatever my father says is true; it wad be better if I didna see you again.*

Mechanically, his tongue tattooed the chorus behind his parched lips on a sagging, incredulous jaw.

The truth refused to resolve itself in terms of coherence. That Jean Armour, the dearest, sweetest, kindest, most desirable lass he had ever known, his very wife, could have allowed herself to be degraded to the humiliation of denying him could not be absorbed far less accepted in these terms.

There must be a mistake somewhere—some nightmare madness that would surely pass.

Exhaustion brought him to a halt some miles down the Cumnock road. He was in a lather of sweat even though the driving rain had soaked him through to the skin.

He sat down on the sodden bank by the roadside and held his throbbing head in his trembling hands.

He hadn't sat more than a couple of minutes when he began to shiver and his teeth began to chatter violently. He rose wearily, rheumatic pains in every joint goading him as he did so.

He had no idea where he was and in the wet darkness he could see no landmark to help him to distinguish his bearings. He knew that he had come south from Machlin and that he must return there.

Gradually he became consumed with blind bitter anger at Jean's perfidy. She had betrayed him, betrayed their trust, betrayed their love and all its fervent pledging, betrayed in advance their unborn child.

At the moment when he had needed her most she had betrayed him. For surely the fates were arraigned against him. Failure on all sides, difficulties everywhere, fear and uncertainty pervading all. He'd never had any luck, never would have any luck, for he had been born under an unlucky star—a star that twinkled alluringly but led him like a will-o'-the-wisp into the morass of failure, uncertainty and miserable melancholy.

But Jean! Why had she done it? How could she do it? What had come over her? To what hellish devices had her parents had recourse that they had left her but a pale shadow of her vigorous, radiating self. Yes, they might have crushed her body. But how could they have broken her spirit and killed her honour—unless she had not resisted them. Damn her: she had not resisted them. She had fallen in with their plans. Whether willingly or unwillingly didn't matter a cadger's curse: she had fallen in with them. There was no getting round that; there was no excusing that; there could be no forgiving that—now or ever. Her damnable conduct refused to be absolved.

She had denied him.

Later in the evening he lurched into John Dow's.

Johnnie eyed him with concern.

"God Almighty, Rab, what's come ower you. You look as if you'd been dragged through the Ayr by a kelpie."

"Can you put a gill o' Kilbagie on the slate for me, John?"

Johnnie poured him a generous gill and brought it over to the fireside.

"I can aey put onything on the sclate for you, Rab. But God, lad, what's come ower you? If it's none o' my business . . . But I'd advise you to get up the road to Mossgiel and get into a warm bed. Damned, you look as though you'd seen a ghost."

"A ghost? That's just what I've seen, John—and talked wi' a ghost and twa o' the damnedest devils out o' hell wi' the smell o' brimstane still about them. There's naebody here the nicht?"

"Wee Smith and the Tanner were in a while back: they'll be awa' roun' the howffs looking for you. Damned, laddie, you're in a bad way. Will I heat up an ale for you?"

"Please, John. I'm sorry I canna tell you about this nicht's fell work."

"Say nae mair. An innkeeper kens how to steek his gab . . . it's just that I'm real sorry, Rab, to see ye in siccan a sorry plight. Draw into the bleeze there and I'll no' be a minute warming you a guid pint."

He sat crouched over the fire. The generous malted spirit began to heat his blood and thaw out the queer numbness about his heart. But the liquor sapped his strength and his anger too; and by the time he was sipping his warm ale he was ready to fall down in front of the fire and weep broken tears.

The flames wavered and danced before his eyes. Steam rose in delicate quivering spirals from his sodden clothes.

They would send Jean to Paisley. She had always said they would. Her mother's sister, married on a Machlin Purdie. God help her if her aunt was anything like her mother.

And then he remembered that Johnnie Dow had hailed from Paisley. He called to the landlord.

"What like a place is Paisley, John?"

"Paisley? Are ye thinking about making the journey? Paisley's a thrang, thriving bit o' a toon, Rab. Lousy wi' weavers. Damned, ye canna get moving for them. Weaving and a feck o' kindred trades forby. A thrang place, Rab. Plenty o' poverty and plenty o' siller. Aye, there's fortunes been made in Paisley, Rab—though I canna see you making ane there."

"No . . . I was just wondering Johnnie—just wondering."

"Weel, Rab, it's the wrang end o' the nicht to start wonderin' about Paisley. Damnit, it's bad to let wat claes dry on ye like that—I've kent folk that met their death through the same thing."

"Ach, what's the odds, Johnnie? The only happy folk are dead folk."

"G'wa to hell, man, and dinna blether. I ken you're a poet, Rab, and I ken poets are no' like common folk—else they wadna be poets. You've too mony verses to cobble yet to be talking in that gloomy way. Mind ye: I'm no' saying but what ye're richt—but folk maun put out the burnt side o' their shins for a' that. The warld's a fearsome place, guid kens; but ye mauna let the fear o't get abune the heart o' ye or ye're finished."

"Ah, the world's all right, Johnnie: it's the folk that are in it. Aye: so man was made to mourn——"

"Damn ye, Rab, get awa' hame out o' this. What's in ye'll keep the cauld out o' ye till ye win Mossgiel. Then a guid bowl o' het gruel and into your bed. I'm no' having your death on my hands. There's plenty it wadna matter about; but ye ken as weel as me that you're an entirely different proposition. Come on, now! I ken ye dinna like to leave the ingle-cheek——"

"I'm going, John. And my thanks to you for your kindness. Good-night to you."

Johnnie Dow knit his brows. He had seen the Bard in many a mood; but this mood was new to him. Something had gone wrong somewhere—something far wrong. Johnnie Dow had a deep affection for Robert: he shook his head slowly and went ben the house to discuss his feelings with his wife.

They were bedded by the time he got home. This was usual. The family had little social intercourse with Robert. He got up in the mornings; he worked; he came in for a meal; sometimes he retired to his loft; if not, he went back to work or talked with Gilbert in the stable. At nights when the farm work was over he changed himself and went out. Mostly to Machlin, but he visited much in the district, and his masonic and social ties often took him into Tarbolton.

What he seldom or ever did was to draw his chair into the fire and make himself one of the family circle.

The family had grown used to this—regretfully. In every social respect Gilbert was the head of the house. More and more did Robert become an enigma to his mother: he was a being entirely outside her range of human experience. She could rarely, and at best only partially, enter his world. Again and again Gilbert explained to her that Robin was a poet—a wonderful poet—and therefore not to be judged as ordinary folks were judged. But Agnes Burns could not accept this. He was her first-born; she had nursed him at her own breast; and yet there seemed to be no bond of blood or sympathy between them. It was all very strange; always it was worrying; sometimes it was frightening; never did it make for peace and understanding between them. Maybe if William had been spared to her he would have been able to understand. But no: long before his father's death he had drifted away into a world of his own, had broken away from the fireside circle.

And so, as usual, Robin came in to a sleeping house, and by the light of the fire crept up the wooden stair to the loft where Gilbert and he shared a partitioned portion.

Gilbert wasn't sleeping. As he heard Robin come in he lit the tallow candle and sat up in bed. They had much to talk about these nights.

As soon as he entered the room Gilbert saw that something was amiss.

"What's wrong, Robin?"

"Everything, Gibby. Everything's gone wrong that can go wrong."

"Don't sit down in thae wet clothes, man. Get them off and rub yoursel' down. You canna afford to get a wetting like that."

Robin began to fling off his sodden clothes. He shivered and his teeth chattered as he stood naked and rubbed himself with a hard towel.

Gilbert threw him his night-shirt.

"Come into bed quick: I've the place warmed up for you."

Once under the pile of warm grey blankets he began to feel comfortable.

"Snuff the candle, Gibby: we can lie and talk in the dark."

For a while they lay and listened to the wail of the wind and the thresh of the rain on the thatch.

"Gibby . . . I'm . . . finished. I've been nothing but a bluidy fool a' my days. I suppose you've jaloused the relationship twixt Jean Armour and me?"

"I've guessed plenty, Robin."

"You never guessed Armour and me were married——?"

"Married?"

"Aye: in the back-end o' last year. Irregular, but legal enough: I gave her a marriage line, dated, signed and everything in order."

"Was she in the family way?"

"No . . . She wasn't then——"

"But she is now?"

"Aye: she is now. Gibby, what in God's name is there about me that's accursed?"

"What d'you mean?"

"Old Armour sent for me the night. I went and saw him. He treated me like a bluidy mongrel. Called me for everything he could lay his tongue to. Then the mother, the bluidy hag, brought ben Jean. And Jean stood there wi' her head down and denied and repudiated me in front o' the pair o' them. Said she didna want to see ony mair o' me."

"But why, in the name o' God—especially when she's wi' child?"

"They'd rather have the bairn a bastard than have me as a son-in-law. And Jean would rather mother a bastard than own me as her husband. I'm no' good enough for them. No' good enough for them! That crowns everything!"

"Had you a row?"

"Row! No' much o' a row. I told the lot o' them what I thought o' them—and breenged out o' the house. I thought I would lose my reason, Gibby—for a while I must have lost it. I was damn near Cumnock before I came round . . .

"Johnnie Dow gave me a gill o' Kilbagie and a pint o' hot ale—or I might never have won Mossgiel the night."

For over an hour the brothers lay talking over the position in which they now found themselves. Their position was desperate, how desperate only Gilbert knew. His mind mirrored the finances of Mossgiel down to the smallest detail.

Conflicting loyalties warred violently in Gilbert's emotions. He was angered and outraged at the treatment his brother had received from the Armours; but he was relieved, though he gave no sign of his relief, that Robin and Jean Armour were being separated. For Robin to have taken on the responsibility of Jean Armour, especially in her present condition, would have brought immediate disaster upon all their heads. And shamefully as Jean Armour had treated him, perhaps it would be all for the best. Gall it was, of course, for the Armours to hold them in such social contempt—Gilbert winced to think that the bareness of their poverty was so generally known . . .

But, again, coming within a twelvemonth of the Betty Paton scandal, this affair with Jean Armour wasn't going to do any of them much good. Unless, of course, Jean Armour intended to stay permanently in Paisley. Even at that, there was no guarantee by any means that the Session in Paisley wouldn't refer back to Machlin, for discipline, Robin's share of the scandal . . .

Long after the brothers had ceased to exchange words they lay pondering and worrying over the business, without arriving at any satisfactory conclusions.

On one small personal issue, however, Gilbert was relieved. On the first of March he was due to be "passed and raised" in Saint James's Lodge. It was some satisfaction to think that the Armour scandal would not be likely to have reached Tarbolton by then.

But for Robin there were no consolations. His future was as black and comfortless as it could possibly be. The only ray of hope lay in his ability to secure enough subscriptions for his poems as would convince Johnnie Wilson that there would be no financial risk about the business.

It was a weak and rather watery ray, however; and it was physical and mental exhaustion that finally blanked out his mind rather than refreshing sleep that claimed him for her own.

WAITING

Though Mary Campbell had slipped quietly away from Gavin Hamilton the previous November and had gone to Stairaird in the adjacent parish of Stair, she still worshipped for the most part in Machlin Kirk.

She was quick to notice that Jean Armour was absent from her father's desk and quicker still to learn that she had gone to Paisley.

The glances she stole at Robert Burns did not tell her what she wanted to know; but they did suggest that he was far from happy or at peace with himself and the world.

There was nothing, of course, that called for remark in Jean Armour's absence. It was not the first time she had gone on a visit to Paisley. But Mary Campbell was suspicious. She did not like to see Robert's black brows drawn with so much dour bitterness and resentment. And she noticed that he looked neither to right nor to left of him, nor yet to Daddy Auld, but into the stone wall above his head as if he did not wish in his mind to be associated with the service.

Mary Campbell knew that she still loved him; that she would love him as long as she was able to remember him.

Maybe if something had come between Jean Armour and him there would still be an opportunity for her to renew his acquaintance. Even if he never wanted to marry her, it would be grand to have his strong arms about her again, to be seared by the urgent passion of his kisses and to hear the surging eloquence of his witching words dropping so honeyed from his whispering tongue.

If only she had had him for a month longer she doubted if Jean Armour, for all her superb physical radiance, could have taken him away from her. And if ever the opportunity was given her again, she knew she would not be so foolish as to refuse him the favours he so desperately desired.

Maybe now her desire was as desperate as ever his had been . . .

Life was hard and lonely as one of the dairymaids at Stairaird. And there was never a young man to be seen who had, in the remotest sense, anything of the allure and fascination of Robert Burns.

She was on friendly terms with Jean Markland. Jean was a quiet and gentle girl who had known some of the inexplicable buffetings of fate. Jean Markland was a close friend of Jean Armour. She would seek out Jean after the service. Maybe she would invite her home for a bite and a dish of tea. She would need to find out all she could. Maybe (though she was not too hopeful) she might be able to attract Robert's attention—even if only for a nod of recognition.

THE VOICE FROM THE VENNEL

"Damn me if it isna Rab Burns himself! Put it there, you hell-begotten son o' glorious light! And what in the name o' all that's coincidental are you doing in Kilmarnock?"

They shook hands warmly and patted each other on the shoulders.

"I might well speir you the like question, John—or is it Doctor John now?"

"Aye, Doctor John Hamilton this while back. I'm down here assisting old Scobie the surgeon—and, by God, Rab, he's in desperate need o' assistance."

Robert Muir, the host, came over to their table.

"I didn't know you pair were acquaint?"

"We are, Robert. You mind me telling you of the time I was in Irvine learning the heckling? Well, John and me got acquaint in Maggie Lapper's ale-house in the Glasgow Vennel; and many a long sober talk we had on life and literature. John was the provost's son: he was studying medicine at Glesca then."

"Aye, Mr. Muir; and my worthy father, the provost, still talks about you, Robert Burns, and wonders what's become o' you. Aye; and Willie Templeton speirs at me whiles if I've ever heard ocht o' you. Oh, they'll be pleased when I tell them next time I'm home how I fell in wi' you. And what the hell's been happening to you since last we met in Maggie Lapper's?"

Robin gave his old friend a brief but racy description of how the years had passed. And then he came to the mention of his project with Wilson the printer.

"Damned, that's glorious news, Robert! Glorious! I never doubted but you had it in you. And I'll bet you think more o' Fergusson the poet now than you do o' Henry MacKenzie and his Man o' Feeling? Ah, I knew it. Bob Fergusson was the model for you. You agree, Mr. Muir? Of course you do. And I warrant you put puir Fergusson in the shade, what?"

Robert Muir said quietly: "He's put all the poets that Scotland ever boasted i' the shade, Doctor Hamilton. And though Robin shakes his head, if you ken him as well as me you'll recognise that as his modesty. But come! a cup o' my best wine to celebrate this occasion."

Over the wine Hamilton said: "So Wilson's such a glaikit cuddy that he doesn't recognise the fruits of Parnassus, eh? Never mind: I'll look him up and tell him he needna worry about his twa-three bawbees. I'll give him a' the satisfaction by way o' a bond. No, no: we'll no' see your poems held up for the small matter o' a bit guarantee . . .

"And you're thinking o' the Indies, are you? Well . . . you could do worse, but no' much. A damned unhealthy climate wi' the risk o' going down wi' a fever that would finish you off in twa shakes o' a dead lamb's tail. But if you got settled in the right quarter you might do well enough. It's high time you said good-bye to the plough, Robert. High time. Aye; and the sale o' your poems might give you enough for your passage? Well, you ken best, Robert: a man's got to forge his own destiny; and no doubt there's been fortunes made in the Indies afore now—although I'm afraid the pickings are no' what they were. I'll see if I canna put you in touch wi' some o' the reliable masters that ply the Indies ports. Captain Richard Brown? Oh, I heard he was doing well enough. I was never personally acquaint wi' him. The provost kenned him well enough. I'll speir the next time I'm in Irvine . . . Now you get that prospectus drawn up, Robert my lad, and we'll see what can be done to push it in the West here. No: I don't know how long I'll be about Killie. I'm afraid I'm like you, Robert: I havena fixed on my future; but I'm aey picking up experience. But wherever I am, Robert my lad, I'll be pushing your future as best I can: you can depend on that."

When Hamilton had gone Robert said to Muir:

"A sterling fellow John Hamilton. I never saw enough of him in Irvine; but what I saw was both pleasant and instructive. And his manner hasn't changed a bit: still the same bluff, hearty, honest fellow. The kind o' friends, Robert, that make life worth living— and a grand offset to man's inhumanity to man—aye, and fickle women. But here, now! when we're alone: I've drafted out an idea for my prospectus. I saw Johnnie afore I came in and he's put forward his own ideas. Tell me what you think. Wilson's idea is a single sheet headed: Proposals for publishing by subscription Scotch Poems by Robert Burns. The work, he promises, and I think he means it, will be elegantly printed. One volume, of course, octavo. Stitched and put together in a blue paper cover and priced at three shillings. About two hundred to two hundred and fifty pages. And he wants this sentence in: thinks it politic in a subscription work. 'As the author has not the most distant mercenary view in publishing, as soon as so many subscribers appear as will defray the necessary expenses, the work will be sent to the press.' "

"And you hoping to get your passage to Jamaica out of it? Damnt, Robin, Johnnie's a cautious chiel."

"In a way it's true enough. Even if I had no hope of turning a penny out of it, I would still pursue the project. Hell, the money's the least of it, Robert."

"I know, I know, Robin—it's just that the way Johnnie puts it tickles me. And I've no doubt but you'll turn a penny on't."

"I had a longish screed written setting out the main idea of my poems. But Johnnie says folk have no time for any kind o' rigma-role in a prospectus. The name of the book, the author and the price: that's what matters, says Johnnie. If I want to say anything I can put it in a preface to the work, should it ever get the length of publishing."

"Damn it, has he no' made up his mind to publish yet?"

"No fear, Robert: Wilson will take no risks till he sees how the subscription goes. In fact he's not too keen to print this trifle of a prospectus until he has had a word wi' Willie Parker, Tam Samson and some o' my influential backers in the town here. Aye, and this despite what's already been done. John Gowdie told me he had a long crack wi' Johnnie and a' he got out o' him was aye and imphim and we'll see, we'll see."

"You'd have thought Gowdie would have impressed him."

"To hell wi' it, Robert. Sometimes I feel like throwing the whole bundle o' manuscript in the back o' the fire. I loathe all this bluidy haggling and cautious, canny side-stepping. Every damned thing I ever set my heart on has been denied me. In fact, the more I set my heart on a thing, the surer it is to be denied. However— here's one small thing I've set my heart on. I'm determined not to let my prospectus go forth as if it were a bit o' merchandise I was selling. I've chosen a seven-line motto from Allan Ramsay. How will this do?

> "Set out the brunt side o' your shin,
> For pride in poets is nae sin;
> Glory's the prize for which they rin,
> And Fame's their joe;
> And who best blaws the horn shall win—
> And wherefor no?"

"Nothing could be neater or more to the point than that. Pride in poets is nae sin! Capital, capital! That'll get you a hundred subscriptions in itself. Courage, man, courage. Finish your wine and we'll take a dander round to Tam Samson's: I ken he's dying to see you and it'll be a tonic to both of us."

PROFESSIONAL ADVICE

But no matter what Robin did: discussing his publishing business with his good Kilmarnock friends, presiding over (and raising Gilbert) in St. James's Lodge, enjoying a social hour in Manson's howff, keeping in touch with his Ayr friends, ploughing the Mossgiel ridge, sifting all the information he could get about the Indies—there was no peace for him.

He was unable to banish Jean from his mind. He was hurt and sore, baffled and outraged. And always to cover his hurt came anger in the effort to blot it out, to overcome it. Gilbert tried to comfort him; but Gilbert's cautious comfort was of little avail. For the first time Robert Muir was conscious of a quality of recklessness in Robin's character and wondered, after the unusually hectic session they had enjoyed with Tam Samson, what lay behind his wild and whirling words.

Gavin Hamilton and Doctor MacKenzie noticed a change in him, though in their company he managed to keep a tight rein on himself. MacKenzie thought that since he had made the decision to turn author he had grown immeasurably in intellectual and spiritual stature. Gavin Hamilton merely thought that his maturity was ripening fast.

Sooner or later, Robin knew that his scandal with Jean would be dragged out into the light of the parish and he was anxious to anticipate this with a statement in his own defence.

Sitting in Hamilton's room, he gave them a cautious account of the affair and appeared to solicit their advice.

Hamilton was judicious. His own father and mother had had to appear in their parish and stand rebuke on the cutty stool for pre-nuptial fornication; and he had had a bitter resentment of the cutty stool ever since. Both he and MacKenzie regarded the stool as an outrageous relic of the barbarous days of ecclesiastical darkness and oppression. For them there was indignity in it, but no personal scandal.

But Robert's case was different: there was the social aspect of it, and, as Robert was his tenant, there was a modicum of reflection on him.

"I'm real sorry to hear all this, Robert. It isn't easy to advise you. In fact it's never easy to come between a man and a woman in an affair like this: third parties are apt to get the worst of the encounter in the long run. No doubt James Armour's gotten big notions of his consequence in the parish. I ken he doesna bear you any warmth—more for token o' what he considers your heterodox opinions. Aye: James Armour's a bitter supporter of Mr. Auld. But for all that, I doubt if he's hot for any scandal affecting his good name and the name of his dochter. Armour'll move all he kens to have the scandal glossed over. As for Miss Armour's behaviour in the matter—well, you've cause enough to feel aggrieved. It's for you to decide whether or not she's the kind of wife for you, Robin. I have my own opinion; but it would be wrong for me to give expression to it here."

"But you'll agree, Mr. Hamilton, that my marriage line was honourable enough?"

"Honourable as could be, Robin—and fully legal—outwith the Kirk's ridiculous censure. There's no doubt about the validity of your marriage to Jean Armour—if you want to press the matter. Indeed, it would take the Lords of the Session and a' the dignity o' Parliament House in Edinburgh to dissolve such a union as you have entered into. But I wad counsel caution, Robin. Bide your time. Armour doesna want you; his dochter's repudiated you and I doubt if you're ower keen yourself."

"After her damnable conduct she's no wife o' mine. No, sir: I have a pride of stomach that would not allow me to grant that she had any title to my corpus—legal or otherwise: she has put herself outside the pale of my consideration."

Over MacKenzie's long face broke a shadow of sympathy.

"Of course, Robin, it may be that Jean was bullied into submission to her father by the fear—if not the application—of physical violence. Armour is a violent man."

"I have thought of that, Doctor, as an extenuating circumstance. But intimidation does not excuse repudiation. I had made her my wife: her duty—to put it no higher—was surely to cleave to me?"

"Yes: that's true enough, Robin. But, like Gavin here, I wad counsel caution. Time has a way o' straightening out the ravels o' life—and you want to avoid taking a step now that wad commit you in a way you might regret."

"My only desire, Doctor, is that my honour should stand fair in the sight of my friends. God knows I have been many kinds of a fool in my day; but I deny with all my strength that I merit the appellation of blackguard."

Gavin Hamilton poured out a drink.

"Nobody that kens you, Robin, will ever accuse you of being a blackguard—I doubt even if Mr. Auld, who has no tenderness in his judgments, would call you that. I'm real sorry this has happened; but you can still hold your head in the parish wi' the best of them—and despite onything that the Armours may say or do. And now drink up—and here's to the success of your venture wi' Wilson the printer."

They drank to that, and Robin felt better than he had done since that fateful night in the Cowgate. Gavin Hamilton saw him to the door.

"Give me a look in as soon as you hae word from Kilmarnock: I'm aey glad to have your news."

THE REBOUND

Coming from Gavin Hamilton's and about to make his way home by Netherplace, he ran into Mary Campbell, who had just left Jean Markland's house.

"Well, well: if it isn't Mary Campbell!"

"And if I'm not mistaken maybe it is Robert Burns himself?"

"Correct, madam: Robert Burns in the flesh—and at your service. And where have you been hiding away, Mary, since you went to Stairaird?"

"It's yoursel' has been doing the hiding, Robert. But you're looking well?"

"You're looking mighty sweet yourself, Mary—though God knows you never looked any other way. But here! this is no place for you and me to be talking on the Lord's Day—and peering eyes keeking out of every window. Come: I'll walk you down to the Burnfoot."

It was the middle of March. There was a welcome glint of spring sunshine, and the air was sharp with the freshness of a new year and the certainty of rebirth. The earth was sodden with the heaviness of the early spring rains; but stippled across the grey pastures was the glimmer of summer green. The lapwings, green-crested, screamed in a plaintive passion of black and white; snipe drummed aslant the marshes; and the whaups, with inviolate dignity piercing across the barren wilderness lying beyond the boundaries of creation, vented their mating-calls like a quiver of burnished arrows shot suddenly against the sun.

And there, in the tiny pin-heads of pricked thorn-flesh, was the courtly splendour of a yellow-yorling, to brighten the eye and gladden the heart.

In shimmer of green and glint of gold and the bobbing flash of yellow and brown; in cry and call and freshing breeze, the presence of spring was manifest.

In the glory of summer and the mirk of winter he had travelled this road to the banks of the Ayr with Jean Armour. Now in the spring of sorrow and distraction he was walking the same road with Highland Mary Campbell.

For a while they fenced quietly exchanging conventional queries and answers. Mary Campbell played her part with great skill. She was determined to say nothing until he made the opening.

Eventually he made it.

"Mary! Will you come to the Indies with me?"

"The Indies, Robert? And what do you mean? You know fine, surely, I'd be going anywhere with you?"

"That's the answer I want to hear, Mary. A straight answer without equivocation—and without conditions."

"Now I didn't say ocht about conditions—don't be putting words in my mouth."

"But you would go?"

"If you wanted me to go."

"Mary, you'll never know what that answer means to me."

"But am I the only one you would want to go to the Indies with?"

"You mean Jean Armour?"

"Now you're putting words in my mouth again."

"Ah, there's no point in quibbling, Mary. You'll have heard how big I've been with Jean Armour—you're neither blate nor fool. But Jean Armour means nothing to me—indeed she means less than nothing, less than the dust."

"Maybe you've been having a lovers' quarrel—and you know what they are: just like the showers in the spring."

Robert laughed, a wry-faced, bitter laugh.

"No, no, Mary. Armour and I are finished. I'll never see her again—nor she me."

"I heard she had gone to Paisley."

"You heard that, did you? Well, Paisley's only the first stage of her journey to hell."

"What's come over the pair o' you? You were so happy together—or so it seemed."

"Yes, Mary—there were happy times. But there was a false happiness in them . . . Mary, neither you nor I belong to Machlin: it means nothing to us. It's a damned midden-hole of a place, stinking wi' pride and deceit and rotten hypocrisy. I'm tired o' it, Mary: tired o' its mean, petty ways. I want to blot the memory of it out of my mind. Across the ocean is new life and new ways of living where a fellow has an even chance to push his fortune. What happiness is there here for you or me? Nothing but drudgery and the snash and sneers of little people placed by the throw of fortune's dice to be our superiors: to lord it over us . . . I'm for printing my poems, Mary—or I'm hoping to have them printed in Kilmarnock. That'll be my answer to the sour bigots and the damned brainless upstarts that have looked askance at me since ever I came to Machlin."

"Your poems, Robert! You're printing your poems—in a book, is it?"

"In a book, Mary. And I've written some grand verses since I saw you last."

"It will be a wonderful thing now to see your name on a book of poems. Will it be dear to buy?"

"Three shillings—and value for every penny."

"I'm sure, I'm sure—and value for something that money couldna be paying for."

"You're right, Mary. Value that canna be equated in terms of cash. But that's something I owe my native land—something I share beyond the computation of any Indian nabob—or grasping Machlin tradesman. Oh, I'll be sorry to leave Scotland too, Mary: that winna be an easy parting. But I'll come back, Mary. Aye . . . someday I'll come back and claim my own. I'll own my own farm—every stick and stone of it and have all the horse and kye and implements to work it after my own will. Work for my own happiness and such as may be dependent on me—and not for rent to hand over to a factor be he generous or otherwise."

"I don't know, Robert; but I can only wish you what I've aey wished you—success and happiness in whatever you do; and health and strength to do it."

"Mary! we made a big mistake, you and me, when we didna strike a bargain in the Tower."

"A bargain, Robert?"

"You're right. Bargain's too cautious a word to describe what I mean. We should have pledged our troth then."

"Maybe we should. But, och, in my own way, I did just that."

"And I was the blind fool not to have seen that. But it's not too late to renew our pledge. Mary, I want to settle down: I'm weary of dodging and doubling; weary of the eternal snooping and prying of the holy beagles. The Indies offers the only way out that I can see. I've been making enquiries. I could get a job on one of the plantations as a kind of overseer at a commencing salary o' thirty pounds a year. A man and his wife could live well enough on that, for living is cheap and things are in abundance there. And I understand that, in a year's time, the climate is no inconvenience to white people. I can even indenture myself for my passage—and it would not be a difficulty beyond getting over to provide for yours."

"And when would you be thinking of going?"

"Oh, May, June or July. Before the summer is over. My brother Gilbert and I would want quit of Mossgiel by May—and I wouldna want to delay long after that."

"It's a big step too to be taking. And maybe there would be a going away but no coming back?"

"If we were going to happiness, to independence and freedom, what matter?"

"Yes: if we were going to happiness."

"Mary: I know this is asking a lot from you; and I have no right to seek an answer from you; but somehow I feel walking here wi' you—it seems somehow that we've just picked up where we left off . . . Forgive me, Mary, for a lot of things I'm saying . . . I've been sorely buffeted of late, and my mind's in a terrible turmoil of thoughts—aye, and hopes. For I have my hopes, Mary. I'm very low in the depths o' melancholy when hope dies away within me."

"And for what is it you hope for most, Robert?"

"Honest fame, Mary. For the recognition by those who matter of my worth as a poet—aye and for my worth as a human being. There must be recognition in the world somewhere. All I ask for is a chance to merit that fame. But even in the mere matter of publishing and printing my poems, I have to plead and bargain and make proposals. Oh, I know that folk who have money canna afford to take risks wi' it; and the more money they have the less can they risk a penny of it."

They had turned to the right before the Barskimming Bridge and were now close to where the Burnfoot Ford crossed the Ayr where the Machlin Burn met with the river. It was time to take his leave of Mary; but neither of them wanted to part.

The glimmer and glint of the sun had gone and the sky was filled with the quietude of dove grey, and the trees about the river banks were bare and melancholy.

"I'll have to run now for the milking, Robert; but it's sorry I am to be going."

"Could you not manage out for an hour in the darkness?"

"Not on the Sabbath. There are prayers and the singing of psalms on the Sabbath evening. Mrs. Graham, the housekeeper, is very strict. But maybe to-morrow night, if you were waiting quietly at the end of the byre. Later maybe we could slip into the byre if there was nobody about. I am sometimes watching a poor beast that is late in calving and the byreman says she will be bad in the calving. About seven of the clock maybe?"

And so they parted on a short but tender embrace.

Ah, she was a sweet, soothing lass, Highland Mary. Sympathetic and understanding. Maybe he would never be able to love her as he had loved Jean Armour; but then he would never be able to love anyone on this earth as he had loved her—damn her for her bitter perfidy. But then Mary Campbell had a different understanding—a deeper knowledge of the human soul. She had known suffering and loneliness: she had a deep experience of men and women in all stations of life, semple and gentle. But above all she had understanding. What would her attitude be if she knew Jean Armour was with child: if she knew he had married her? Ah, she would understand: no one indeed would understand half so well.

Maybe it was the Highland blood in her. Maybe it was because she loved him and had always loved him. She had waited, knowing that her day would come. That showed the spirit and the understanding that was in her. Aye, but still waters always ran deep—and there was no sounding of Mary Campbell's depths.

Strange, too, the way he had run into her as she was leaving Markland's . . . He hadn't intended to take more than a few paces down the Barskimming road with her . . . Yet they had just slipped into the old easy way of talking. And here he had asked her to go with him to the Indies—as his wife. Aye; and she had accepted the proposal as the most natural offer he could have made her. By the Lord! there was no limit to the faith and trust of Highland Mary.

But to-morrow night he would test her further: see just how far she was prepared to commit herself . . . If she went to the Indies she would have to go as his wife—and Jean Armour still had their marriage lines. It wouldn't be so easy explaining that to Mary Campbell . . .

But maybe there was no need to be explaining anything: the trouble all his life had lain in the fact that he had been too honest, too guilty of explaining all his innermost thoughts and laying bare the springs of his actions.

Maybe it would be better to keep something to himself. In any case, what did he know for certain about his plans? His poems might never see the light of day; his trouble with Jean Armour might yet raise a hot scandal in the parish; he might not be able to fix on a plan for going to the Indies . . .

The bitter truth was that he had nothing to tell Mary Campbell that could be vouched for and substantiated—except Jean Armour.

Jean Armour: he had walked this road often enough with her—away over there on the bank of the Ayr was the thorn tree that had sheltered their nuptial couch. The singing of her when the thorn had been green! God! what a mess he'd gotten into—and all because of his damned ram-stam impetuosity, his damned honesty, giving all he had and asking no questions but expecting to be given to even as he gave . . .

ADAMHILL'S ADVICE

Market-day in Machlin was a day of stir and bustle. About the Cross, but more especially in the Loudon Street gushet on the flank of George Gibson's howff, men and women came early with their cattle and horses, sheep and goats, pigs and poultry.

And from mid-day the place was a bedlam of animal noises, the shouting of herds and drovers and the barking of their dogs.

Farmers moved among the beasts, examined their points and, if they felt like buying, began a preliminary business of making an offer. But the haggling didn't begin in earnest till both the seller and buyer had made up their minds. Then the fun became fast and richly furious.

Much spittle was expended on bare palms before the bargain was finally and irrevocably struck. Once the hands had come together in a resounding smack and the fingers had knotted on the deal, there was no turning back. All that remained to be done was to sojourn to John Dow's, or Nance Tinnock's, or Willie Ronald's, and seal the formalities with a drink.

But many folks attended the market who were neither selling nor buying. They came to exchange information, to see old friends, to make sundry purchases and to enjoy a social hour in the taverns.

They might take the occasion to visit the tailor or the shoemaker, the saddler or the barber.

Thus it had been for generations: market-day was the secular holy fair, and everybody participated—for it was the economic festival of their existence.

And Machlin's monthly fair and market was famous all over the West country.

But, as on every social and religious or economic occasion, the divisions of wealth and the gradations of social distinction were much in evidence.

Ragged, half-starved laddies would stand for the best part of the day with their charges. Maybe they held a pair of mettlesome horses, or kept constant guard on a half dozen bullocks. Maybe the gaunt wife of a poor crofter or tenant-farmer would stand in the rain with her cow, while her husband trekked from one potential group of buyers to another, advertising its merits and soliciting an offer.

Wealthy farmers would saunter past with a quiet smile at the corner of their mouths, knowing full well that if they wanted to buy, they could always do so on their own terms.

And always beneath the bustling air of business there was the undercurrent of tragedy. Many a beast was brought to the market only under the cruel lash of necessity—especially when quarterly rents were in the offing.

But for all that, a buyer had to have his wits about him. There were rogues and scoundrels who, under the cloak of poverty and the whine of hardship, were skilled in the art of passing an unsound animal (maybe doubtfully acquired) as a sound bargain and a sterling investment.

The Bard seldom failed to visit the fairs and the markets. Here the human drama attracted and held him. And invariably in the taverns there were groups of men who provided a ready audience for his quips and his sallies and his satiric verses.

Here he renewed old friendships, and talked farming and politics and how the world in general headed for the devil.

And some laughed and cracked with him, and others lent a serious countenance to his graver discourses. Still others shook their heads sadly, or voiced their disapproval sharply, for the sheep and goats kept to themselves. There were Old and New Light farmers as steadfast in their beliefs as Old and New Light clergymen.

But if the fairs and the markets were dictated by economic necessity, they were no less popular through social necessity. Without them life would have been intolerably bare and lonely. The Bard, even in his blackest moods of depression, drew inspiration and strength from them.

Gilbert rode home from the Machlin market with John Rankine of Adamhill.

"What's this I hear Rab's doing now, Gilbert?"

"It depends on what you've heard, John: Rab's aey doing something."

"Aye, you're richt, Gilbert; but I hear talk o' him going to the Indies."

"Aye: he's talking that way, John. There's nothing hereabouts for us. Mossgiel's got a sour clay bottom."

"That's why Ga'n Hamilton got rid o't—but I didna learn that till Rab and you were settled in. Ga'n Hamilton's a' there when it comes to a business deal."

"Well, we were glad enough to get it when we did . . . And but for a bad sowing the first year and a bad harvest last year we micht hae managed."

"Damned, but the Indies is a faur-like place to go just because Mossgiel has turned out badly. I'll need to come down to the Lodge some night and hae a crack wi' him."

"You think he shouldn't go?"

"I don't, Gilbert: I don't. To hell! we havena the likes o' Rab i' the Wast. Why should he go and bury himself in the bluidy Indies? Rab's a good farmer——"

"What's he no' good at?"

"There you are! But he could make a better show at hiding his dislikes. Damned, he makes enemies whaur there's nae need to, wi' that tongue o' his. There's folks he flays to the bone wi' the edge o' his tongue. Oh, folk that need flayin', damn the doubt;

237

but it doesna dae Rab ony guid. And what are you for daein if Rab quits Mossgiel, Gilbert?"

"The family'll just need to break up, John. We'll a' need to go into service o' one kind or another. Mind you, this is confidential, John. I wouldna like ony rumour to reach Ga'n Hamilton before Robin and I had a word wi' him first."

"I'll no' breathe a word, Gilbert: you can lippen on me."

"I know, John; but whether Robin goes across the seas or no', it looks as if we'll need to break up the family. Either way it doesna look as if we can carry on."

"I'm verra sorry to hear that, Gilbert. Damned, more nor sorry. You lads havena had it easy—nor your father afore you. But the rent o' a guid farm the now's something sinfu'—downright sinfu'. To hell, man! the lairds are fair desperate for siller the now: as soon as a tack runs out they're clapping ten to twenty pounds on the rent. Aye; and they're putting the smaller tacksmen out and running the tacks thegither for mair than twice the combined rents. And you'll notice how they're on for improving their ain places—planting the damnedest fancy trees and useless bluidy bushes; and biggin miles o' stane dykes and laying out lawns and terraces and what-not. Of course, a' these bluidy nabobs frae the East Indian Company hae gotten the kintraside ruined wi' their greed for ground . . . I'm telling you, Gilbert, this bluidy planting'll be the ruination o' the land—thae plantings, when they tak' proper root and begin to grow up, 'll suck a' the sap and substance out o' the soil—aye, damned, for miles around. Weel . . . I'll no' keep you, Gilbert. Tell Rab to do nocht about the Indies till I see him. I'll be ower at the next meeting o' the Lodge if I don't see him afore then."

"I'll tell him, John. He'll be pleased to get your message. You've been great friends, the pair o' you."

"Aye; and aey will be. Guid-day, Gilbert."

HONEST MEN

Robert walked back from Simson's Inn with Aiken the lawyer. He had sat and listened for an hour to his praises being sung by men like John Ballantine and lawyers Willie Chalmers and John MacWhinnie. Then he had told them how he was thinking of publishing his verses by subscription over the imprint of John Wilson in Kilmarnock. He had been much gratified at the way they had received his news.

"I don't think you hae ocht to fear, Robert, about how your book'll be taken up in Ayr. Get out your subscription bills and we'll get you enough names to gladden Wilson's heart—and ensure the expense o' the project. Aye: come into my chambers here for a bit blether: it's a while since I've had a heart-to-heart crack wi' you.

"Aye . . . make yourself comfortable, Robert—and hae a pinch o' snuff. I hae heard rumours that you're thinking o' emigrating to the Indies. What's in your mind, Robert?"

"Oh, there's little in my mind, Mr. Aiken. Only, Mossgiel hasn't turned out too well for my brother and I—and that means for the family. We'll need to do something about it. There's worse places for a poor property-less devil like me than the Indies—or so I'm led to believe."

"Aye . . . If you were going the right way about it and had the proper influence, introductions and connections, I've no doubt you could do worse. Aye . . . It's a wonder a man like you hasna thought o' getting married. You ken, Robert, a judicious marriage has been the rock on which many a man has builded a secure and prosperous way o' life. Now, now! I'm no' suggesting that you or onybody else should marry for money. But you've reached the age o' discretion now and I canna see that there could be ony harm in a judicious look around you."

"I know exactly what you mean, Mr. Aiken; but when you've no money and no prospects, you would need to look very judiciously indeed."

"I just thought I wad mention it, Robert."

"No, Mr. Aiken, marriage is out of the question for me. I'm not in a position to keep myself, to say nothing of a wife."

"Wait till your poems come out. You'll see a big change in folks' attitude then. Man, the only thing that counts in this life wi' the majority is success. Aye; and there's damn few folk hae ony prospect o' succeeding as a poet. There's a wheen respectable families I could introduce you to in Ayr, Robert. You've got to mingle wi' the richt folk, Robert, to get on in this world."

"I'm afraid, Mr. Aiken, I wouldn't be much use mingling in the town's social circles. I'm afraid my spirit's too stubborn and independent for that. Besides, a poor tenant-farmer would be at a disadvantage with every step he ventured."

"Aye; but what I'm telling you is that there's a mighty difference between a poor tenant-farmer and a successful poet wi' a book o' rhyming-ware ablow his oxter by way o' testimonial."

"Ah, but the hypothetical volume's not under my arm yet, sir."

"No . . . Well, you were wanting my opinion on what should go into your volume. Now, I've sat behind this desk here and dispensed advice on a wide variety o' subjects baith sacred and civil. But damned this is the first time I hae been asked to advise a bard anent the publication o' his verses. But a richt congenial job, Robert my lad, a job that tak's a' the dryness aff the law . . .

". . . them a', Robert! To hell, man, you canna mak' flesh o' one and fowl o' anither. Of course I see your point. But then you needna mention names. Wilson will just put in a row o' dots where the name should be. It'll no' spoil your verses—and it'll no' give offence."

"Even Holy Willie's Prayer?"

"Certainly. Oh, a wheen o' the bigots will hae their backs up. Ah, but that'll do your verses no harm—do them a lot o' good in fact. Coorse, Robert, a lot o' folk'll ken wha you're referring to; but as long as you dinna put down the name in full, naebody can say a word to you. There's a common axiom, Robert; and you'll have heard it mony a time: ye canna hang a man for thinking.

"But, by certes, Robert, you're a hell o' a man. Some o' thae verses o' yours are beyond ony comparin' wi' onything. Och aye; Allan Ramsay and Robert Fergusson; but they just dinna measure up to you, Robert. Maybe I'm no judge o' poetry like Henry MacKenzie in Edinburgh. But I ken what I like—and mair nor that, I ken when a thing's true and when it's no' true; and yours, Robert, are—well, damned if that's possible—they're truer than life itself. They mak' me laugh and they mak' me cry. Aye, and the byornar thing, Robert, is that I'll be reading away and enjoying myself and then a bit word about the Auld Farmer or The Mouse and the bluidy tears are blinkin' in my eyes afore I ken where I am. That's what I call genius: that's the test, Robert my boy; and when you can pass that test you can pass muster onywhere. I wish I was as sure o' the success o' Gavin Hamilton's plea afore the Ayr Presbytery as I am o' the success o' your verses: aye, half as sure."

Robert bade his friend and patron good-day and rode back home to Mossgiel. When men like Aiken, Ballantine and Chalmers—well-educated and highly-respected citizens of Ayr—could so highly commend his publishing venture, there seemed no reason for any further doubt. Not that he had ever had any doubts: the doubts were John Wilson's.

If only Wilson could have been with him to-day he would have dismissed the idea of a prospectus and gone ahead with the printing.

But he would lose no more time: he would ride into Killie and tell Wilson to print off two or three dozen prospectuses right away. He could have had a round dozen of names in Ayr himself—and each of his friends there would be good for a dozen of other friends.

Robert was elated. Maybe now all the years of his thinking and reading and writing would bear fruit—and honest fame that had eluded him so long come to crown him with a wreath of bays. Even if he had to leave Auld Scotland behind him across an angry waste of grey seas he would leave some tangible token of his memory behind him.

Amidst the storm and stress of life things were beginning to take some providential shape. Only the other day he had staggered away from Armour's house feeling that the end of the world had come upon him and that the hand of man and of fate was irrevocably turned against him.

And now, to-day, he was riding home from Ayr with a light heart, warm in the thought of his many excellent friends. And warm, too, in the thought that here was one sweet girl who, whatever his circumstances and wherever he might go, was prepared to share his fate. The circle of his friends through Ayr, Kilmarnock and Machlin was wide; but at the centre of that circle stood Highland Mary Campbell, steadfast, faithful and all-trusting.

And even as he rode with the sun in his back and his face towards the rolling uplands of Tarbolton parish, behind his teeming thoughts verses were forming and taking shape.

It was a permanent source of wonder to him now how easily he rhymed. But the reason for that was not hard to seek. He had an aim now, a definite purpose. The volume he was now certain would eventually be published in Killie demanded that he give good measure—and measure of the finest quality.

Had he had the spur of such an aim years ago, he could have filled a volume every spring and autumn. True, the main ballast was already in Wilson's hands; but there were still a few items wanted to trim the cargo neatly so that the stability of the Kilmarnock barque would ride triumphantly the stormy waters of criticism.

PAISLEY BODIES

Jean Armour went sadly from Machlin: none of her friends knew she was going: they only learned when they saw her board the Machlin fly with her mother.

At Kilmarnock her mother saw her into the coach for Paisley, gave her final instructions and bade her a tearful good-bye.

Andrew Purdie and his wife Meg were kindly enough to Jean, though when Meg got an opportunity of her alone she did not mince any words about the shame Jean had brought on her mother.

She was puzzled, however, when Jean told her how she had given her marriage lines to her father.

"God, Jean: it beats me. What was our Mary thinking about? I'm no' the least bit surprised at James Armour: your father's gotten a fell temper, Jean. Then whatna low-down kind o' tinkler was this Burns when neither Mary nor James Armour wad hae ocht to do wi' him?"

"He's nae tinkler, auntie. He's a tenant-farmer in Mossgiel."

"I ken Mossgiel fine: Ga'n Hamilton had it a while. And what's wrong then: is he an ill-looking tyke or a drunkard or what?"

"No, no, auntie. He's the handsomest man in the parish! He takes a drink like the rest; but you'd never see him drunk: or like it. It's just that my father thinks he's no' good enough for me."

"God! but they're particular . . . and you in the state you are! I never heard tell o' ony sic ongauns. No: I canna believe you, Jean: there's something else."

"He had a bairn to a lass in Largieside—about a year ago."

"Huh: that seems to be a' they dae about Machlin. I never was in Daddy Auld's Kirk a Sunday but there was twa or three i' the cutty stool. You couldna marry a man yonder but had twa-three gets to somebody. Our Mary kens that brawly—aye, and James Armour."

"My father doesna like his poems either."

"Poems! In God's name what d'you mean by poems?"

"He writes poems, auntie—songs and verses. Oh, they're grand verses, auntie."

"He maun be a daft beggar. And what does James Armour no' like about his verses?"

"I dinna ken, auntie. He wrote a poem on Holy Willie: my father said it was blasphemy."

"Holy Willie! Yon wee runt . . .! You couldna write ony blasphemy on yon snooping, sneaking creature. I mind he cam' into our house one night. He was gey tiddly, I'm telling you. Syne, if he wasna ower late clearing his coat tails when he sat down and clinked a bottle o' the communion wine again the chair and broke it. And I'm sure Mary kens fine how he used to pilfer the placks out o' the collecting ladle when he cam' doon the outside stairs frae the lofts. Holy Willie! If he didna run and clype every tittle-tattle to Daddy Auld he wad be run out o' the parish. Min' you, a' the same, he's a great prayer at a death-bed. Them that hae heard him say there's nothing to touch him at a death-bed. But, certes, he wadna pray me or mine into the next world. But I suppose I'll need to wait till I see your mother afore I get to the bottom o' this, Jean."

"Auntie! D'you think Rab Burns'll be finished wi' me? My father was terribly angry. Oh, I've never seen onybody so angry: he nearly killed me. And when he sent for Rab Burns he had me in, and made me tell him that I never wanted to see him again. He cursed my father and mother and me and ran out o' the house."

"God Almighty! For a carry-on I never heard tell o' the likes! Were the lot o' ye clean mad?"

"But auntie——"

"Oh, dinna ask me, Jean. I never in a' my experience heard o' onything like that. But if your father wanted to turn the man agin you he's gone the richt way about it. Were you sair set up on him?"

"There'll never be another man like him, auntie. There wasna a lass in Machlin but was jealous o' him and me. He's no' like other men at a', auntie: honest he isna."

"Weel, dinna greet noo, lass. What's done canna be undone. Maybe things will turn out better than you think. Mind ye: the Paisley bodies clash here just as much as they dae in Machlin. Jenny Surgeoner is still here wi' her bairn. Ah, but you'll need to watch yoursel'—we hae our good name to think about and Andra's weel thocht o' in Paisley . . . But we'll see, we'll see. Dinna worry ower much the now."

"I'll no' need to bide indoors a' the time, will I, auntie?"

Meg Smith was younger in years and in spirit than her sister Mary. She had married Andrew Purdie and not James Armour; nor was it likely that she would be asked to bear eleven children as Mary had been. In her heart she thought lightly of Jean's offence. She knew that if fornication was a sin few could deny its guilt. And Jean was a lovable lassie and it was a damned shame that James Armour should have abused her. It was all right for men to talk; but if men weren't what they were there would be few lassies wi' bastard bairns. She scratched the crown of her head with a bone pin and screwed up her eyes.

"Ah to hell, Jean: I'm as guid a Christian's gaun; but I'm nae gaoler. Aye: ye'll get oot. You min' o' Bob Wilson that used to be at school wi' you? He's a guid-doin' weaver here and he's turned oot a braw lad. Gin ye set your bonnet the richt airt, ye'll maybe get a husband here in Paisley. Bob aey had a notion o' ye, Jean. An' I canna blame him: nor this daft poet Burns either. Noo stop your greetin like a guid lass. Andra Purdie's strict enough; but his temper, to differ frae your father's, is civilised. There's a lot I hae agin the Paisley bodies—but they're civilised compared wi' the Holy Willies and Holy Maggies o' Machlin."

And above her tears and her gnawing worry, Jean couldn't help wondering at the difference between her mother and her aunt.

There was a bold freedom and essential kindness about Mrs. Purdie that was not about her mother. And coarser and rougher in the tongue though she was, Jean did not doubt that she had more downright affection in her.

But Jean was tired: she had been through a terrible ordeal and she hadn't slept for nights. Nor from her mind's eye could she banish the picture of Rab Burns, his face twisted with anger and with pain, cursing them all before he left the house. She feared he would never forgive her no matter what happened now.

And what would happen now and what the future held, Jean hadn't the courage to guess, for she had no strength left to give her courage.

Andrew Purdie saw Jean was worrying. One night when he was taking off his shoes, he said: "Aye, aye, Jean: it's a sair world, God kens; but there's naebody for taking a stick to you hereabouts. There's plenty hae made the same mistake as you—aye and lived to look back and laugh at it a'."

A DELICATE MISSION

It was the first day of April, and William Auld, pacing his study floor, was in a mood of sharp irritation.

William Fisher, sitting nervously on the edge of a chair, did not dare look his minister in the face.

"There isn't the veriest shred of evidence, Mr. Fisher, that Jean Armour is with child. I know the people of this parish and I know the weakness and wickedness of mortal humans. Jean Armour has gone off to her aunt's in Paisley. So the gossips are certain she is with child. Is that all the intelligence you can bring to me, Mr. Fisher?"

"Maybe Mr. Auld will allow that the circumstances are highly suspeecious. Oooh aye; highly suspecious."

"Don't try my mortal patience, sir, with your childish babblings. What circumstances are highly suspicious? Speak out, Mr. Fisher."

"I ask you pardon, Mr. Auld; but Mr. Auld kens I'm no' the man given to hasty opinions. But you see, Mr. Auld, there was nae preparations-like for Jean Armour's departure. Moreover, she was keepit in the hoose for near a week afore she went and naebody kent she was going. Oooh aye, Mr. Auld, I think ye maun allow that's no' unsuspeecious. And Mary Smith has given gey unsatisfactory answers to the questions that hae been put to her anent her dochter's going. To one she says Jean's awa' to help her sister; to anither that she's awa' on a kind o' a holiday; to another that she hasna been keeping weel this whilie back and that the change'll dae her guid."

William Auld stood with his back to Willie Fisher, looking out the window. He clasped and unclasped his hands behind his back.

"Oooh aye; an' anither thing, Mr. Auld: them that saw her goin' said she lookit gey shilpit and as white's a ghost. But a'bodies ken, Mr. Auld, that until this happened Jean Armour was in good health—byornar health, Mr. Auld.

"And then there's Burns, Mr. Auld. He's been acting verra queerly. Of coorse, he's aey acting queerly as everybody in the parish kens. Mr. Lamie and me have keepit a strict watch on Jean Armour and him; and baith Mr. Lamie and mysel' are of the opinion that fornication has been committed. Unfortunately, Mr. Auld, we could never catch them red-handed. But as Mr. Lamie and me hae observed jointly and severally, we never knew o' a courtin' couple mair disposed——"

"Enough, Mr. Fisher: I hae nae desire to hear what you and Mr. Lamie observed. Facts, Mr. Fisher: where are your facts?"

"I'm coming round to the facts, Mr. Auld, begging your pardon for ony annoyance. I'm just trying to outline, as it were, the highly suspeecious nature o' this affair. But I think, Mr. Auld, you'll allow that it's a byornar suspeecious circumstance that Jean Armour wasna a week in Paisley than Burns—and on the Sabbath efternoon, Mr. Auld, the Sabbath efternoon and coming frae Ga'n Hamilton's nae less—should fa' in wi' Mary Campbell—Highland Mary, no' the other one—and without ony ado convoy her doon the Barskimming road to the Burnfoot."

"Where is this Mary Campbell domiciled?"

"Stairaird Farm, Mr. Auld."

"And why doesn't she sit under Mr. Steel in Stair?"

"Weel, she just left Hamilton's service in November, Mr. Auld, and there's nae reason why she shouldna worship in Machlin till communion at least. It's not unheard of to——"

"I am better able to pass an opinion on that, Mr. Fisher, than you are. I presume, Mr. Fisher, that Burns and Highland Mary Campbell are on friendly terms?"

"Friendly enough, Mr. Auld, oooh aye, friendly enough; but they havena been seen speaking thegither, kirk or market, since he took up wi' Jean Armour until Sabbath come sax days. The whilk, if Mr. Auld will allow, is a highly suspeecious circumstance."

"Aye, suspicious, Mr. Fisher. I wonder you're able to sleep in your bed at nichts for the wecht o' suspicions that must be pressing on you. But we canna compear Mr. Burns on suspicions, Mr. Fisher—nor yet Jean Armour."

"But maybe Mr. Auld will allow——"

"Mr. Auld will allow nae unfounded and unsubstantiated suspicions, Mr. Fisher, to goad him into any uncharitable and unchristian conclusions."

"I canna think how I hae given you offence, Mr. Auld—I hae tried to do my duty as ye instructed."

Auld raised a large thin hand to his lofty forehead, spanned his brow and pressed deeply into his temples.

"I'm worried, Mr. Fisher, deeply worried about this business. Your suspicions are alarming and point only too obviously to an unfortunate issue. To-morrow evening I shall moderate the usual meeting of the Session. Prepare a brief and concise statement, Mr. Fisher, and bring the matter forward in the usual way. By then I shall have determined on my course of action. But remember, Mr. Fisher, to be brief and to the point."

Holy Willie was delighted that Mr. Auld had been brought round: he regarded this as a personal triumph.

"Mr. Auld can depend on me," he uttered with such satisfaction that a great slaver of saliva trickled down his chin, which he impatiently and almost unconsciously wiped away with the back of his hand.

And for once Willie was as good as his word. His statement the following evening to the Session was not only brief but surprisingly lucid.

James Lamie, anxious to share in the glory, was more effusive, but Auld cut him short. But the Session, despite Mr. Auld's weight and authority, were not to be muzzled. They knew what was at stake. It seemed that an effective trap could be set for their archenemy from Mossgiel. They had every intention of setting the trap to their own best advantage. Daddy Auld was no fool. He knew what duty dictated, and he had no intention of shrinking from it. His goose-quill rapidly made the requisite entry in the scroll minutes under the date Sunday, 2nd April, 1786:—"The Session being informed that Jean Armour, an unmarried woman, is said to be with child, and that she has gone off from the place of late, to reside elsewhere, the Session think it their duty to investigate all the circumstances thereanent. The Session therefore appoints James Lamie and William Fisher to speak to the parents."

But Daddy Auld was far from happy about the business. The only consolation he had was that in the meantime at least he had saved Jean Armour from the attentions of the Paisley Session and had managed to throw the burden of the investigation on the shoulders of her parents. But it was saddening to think that Jean Armour might be with child to Robert Burns. Had her betrayer been any other lad in the parish he would have had a quiet word with him and obtained all the information he wanted. But they would need to move very cautiously where Burns was concerned, very cautiously indeed.

Lamie and Fisher moved even more cautiously. They foregathered in a quiet corner of the Elbow Inn to make their plans.

"Well, Jeems," said Fisher: "this is a verra delicate mission we hae been sent on."

"Aye, William, it's a' that; but we'll go thegither."

"Oooh aye: we'll go thegither. Indeed, Jeems, I'd rather that Mr. Auld had gone wi' us—or that we had summoned Armour afore the Session. It could be a ticklish business too, ye ken."

"It could that."

"Aye: it could be a verra unpleasant interview—especially if we were wrong."

"Ah, we canna be wrong: she's coupit . . . and weel coupit."

"Oooh, weel coupit, Jeems. Aha, and there's naethin'll uncoup her noo. Oooh, we'll soon hae Mr. Burns in Mossgiel in our grip—and, by certes, Jeems, it behooves Mr. Auld to chirt him sair. Though min' ye, Jeems, it's a bad thing that the mare's fled the stable. Oooh aye: I could hae gotten to the backside o' this affair wi' Jean Armour."

"Aye: I wunner how lang she's coupit?"

"Three or fower month: ye can weel reckon on that."

"Round about the New-Year! That wad throw her till, let me see . . . aye . . . eh . . . September."

"September, Jeems—or maybe the end o' August."

"Damned, Willie, but Burns has had a good run wi' her too . . . Ah well, we'll hae a run wi' him noo."

"Ah, but we'll need to move wi' speed in the matter; for I wadna be surprised that Burns tries to give us the slip."

"He'll no' be able to give us the slip, Willie: the Session can pursue him wherever he goes."

"Aye: in Scotland. But I heard a wee bit o' a rumour the nicht that the same bold Burns has been speiring about the Indies— Jamaica, to be precise. Coorse, it's nae mair nor a pointer."

"Jamaica! Danged, Willie, but we'll need to move fast—we'll go round to the Cowgate now!"

"Na, na: we'll no' tackle Mary Smith *and* James Armour. Na, na: we've got to go canny about this business, Jeems. See the mither first. Aye: and I think *you* should see her first, Jeems: you and her are better acquaint than I am. Then if need be—but only then, mind ye, will we baith see James Armour. Ye get mair oot o' the women when ye get them their lane."

James Lamie gave the suggestion the turn of his mind. He was suspicious of Willie Fisher; but he was also envious of the march he had stolen on him with Mr. Auld in reporting Jean Armour's removal from the district. As there did not seem to be any catch in Fisher's suggestion, he decided to act on it at the first opportunity. If he got all the information they wanted from Mary Smith, he would have the satisfaction of reporting to Mr. Auld.

NULLIFIED

But Mrs. Armour was more than a match for Mr. Lamie. When she answered his knock the following morning, she had already been warned that he was coming—and what he was coming about.

She received him with cold courtesy.

"Guid-mornin', Mr. Lamie."

"Ah, guid-mornin', Mistress Armour."

"And what can I do for you this mornin', Mr. Lamie?"

"Weel . . . I hae a wee bit o' business o' a delicate nature frae the Session to discuss wi' you, Mary—it micht be better if I cam' in aff the door-step."

"I'm just i' the middle o' my reddin' up, James. There's nocht the Session can hae to discuss either wi' me or mine that canna be discussed just as weel on the door-step as ben the hoose."

Lamie was taken aback. It was his experience that when he made a sessional visit of the nature he was making folk were only too glad to get him off the step and into the benmost corner of the house.

"Just whatever you say then, Mary. Is it true that Jean's away out o' the parish?"

"Has she got to get your permission to step outside the parish?"

"No . . . no . . . No' if she's just away for a day or twa like."

"That's fine then. Well, ye can tell the Session that Jean's away to visit some friends in Paisley and will be back when it suits her."

"I'm real sorry about this, Mary—but—eh—there's talk i' the parish that Jean's wi' child——"

"Wi' child! Fancy that noo! And me her mither kens nocht about it! I wonder, noo, wha could be spreading sic ill-gotten clash about the place? The Session wadna ken that, would they?"

"I'm only doing my duty, Mary; and you ken what that duty is as weel as me."

"Ah weel: maybe aye and maybe no. There's duty and duty, James. But since the Session seem to ken mair aboot folks' business than folks dae themselves, maybe the Session'll ken wha faithered this supposed bairn on Jean? I ken Mr. Armour'll be fully anxious to ken *that* when he comes hame."

"Oh, the Session has its weel-founded suspicions, Mary. But since ye say that Jean's no coupit wi' bairn there'll be nae need to look for a faither—but we can aey clap hands on one should one be wanted."

"Fegs, you're a wonderful lot o' industrious bodies, Mr. Lamie."

"We're a' that, Mistress Armour: the Lord's work in this parish needs a' the industry we can command. But I'm glad to hear what you say about your dochter and I'll report your statement to the Session."

"Ah weel then, Mr. Lamie: God's blessing on your work—and guid-morning to ye."

And with that, Mrs. Armour nipped smartly back and clapped the door shut on James Lamie's sour and discomfited face.

When James Armour came home and heard his wife's report of the visitation from Lamie his anger rose. But mounting with his anger was a sense of consternation. What was it the Session had discovered? Had Burns been blabbing? Had Jean let drop an incautious remark somewhere? Or were they suspicious without having any real evidence for their suspicions? And then James Armour bethought himself of Jean's marriage lines and his agitation mounted.

"Thae damned lines!" he said to his wife, when the children were bedded. "I'll need to dae something about them. If Jean or

Burns hae blabbed onything about them, then Mr. Auld will demand them—aye, and on penalty if they're no' forthcoming. There's nothing for it, wife: I'll need to ride into Ayr and consult wi' Aiken, the lawyer. He's a good lawyer as we ken—and verra discreet. Robert Aiken will come ower nothing: so I can tak' him fully into my confidence."

"We'll need to dae something, James. If we're brocht afore the Session I dinna ken what we'll dae."

"Session! I'm no' worried about the Session. It's this damned marriage line. God, wife, but I never thocht that Jean was such a sly deceitful bitch."

"Oh, she's no' a bitch, James—and it was that Burns that led her away."

"Aye: it was Burns that led her away; but she wouldna have been led away if she hadna wanted to be led away. She micht hae weakened in his arms, but she wasna in his arms when he was writing out this paper and she wasna in his arms when she signed it. God! it would drive a saint mad to hae brocht up a dochter the way she was brocht up for her to turn into a harlot. God! I should hae kicked the Burns-get out o' her as I threatened and *then* sent her aff to Paisley."

"James, James: dinna anger yoursel'. Ye ken fine you'll work yoursel' into a state and you'll no' be able to sleep a wink. And if you're for riding into Ayr the morn you'll need to get your sleep."

"Aye . . . But it'll be a day or twa yet afore I can ride into Ayr. Fetch me my writing things and I'll pen a note to Mr. Aiken telling him that I'm coming. Aiken's a busy man."

But it was the fourteenth day of the month before James Armour managed to ride into Ayr to keep his appointment with Robert Aiken.

Aiken received Armour in his inner sanctum in the rear of his High Street chambers.

"Not a verra nice day for riding, Mr. Armour: you can stand up to the fire here for a taste o' heat . . . Damn near the middle o' April and as wat and cauld as November. Now, sir, what can I do for you?"

"Weel, I'm lippening on you a lot, Mr. Aiken. I'm in sair trouble wi' my dochter Jean."

"I'm sorry to hear that, Mr. Armour. What age is your dochter?"

"She was twenty-one in February."

"I see. And who's the man? I trust he's no' married already?"

"That's just the verra point I've come aboot, Mr. Aiken. This blackguard that's ruined my dochter has given her a marriage line."

"Aha! Could I see the lines, Mr. Armour? So ho! Robert Burns in Mossgiel!"

"Ye ken him, Mr. Aiken?"

"Well . . . I've heard tell o' him, Mr. Armour. Writes a bit verse back and forward?"

"That's the rotten cur. And bad bluidy bawdy verses he writes by a' accounts. Now tell me this, Mr. Aiken, and tell me nae mair: what's the value o' thae lines?"

"Value? Legal enough in a way, Mr. Armour. Ye see, the secular law and the ecclesiastical law are no' just the same thing. What Mr. Auld and his Kirk Session would say about this and what Lord Braxfield in the Court o' Session would say would be twa verra different things. Where ye have coitus, as we lawyers say, wi' consent to marriage, ye hae in effect established marriage. How long is your dochter in her trouble? Twa to three months. Aha! Weel, that establishes a very awkward case, Mr. Armour. It's an irregular marriage, of course, from Mr. Auld's point of view, and doesna absolve the contending and interested parties from ony scandal: there'll be delation and censure ower that whatever way we look at it. It's a mitigating circumstance this bit paper, Mr. Armour—indeed it's a proper enough legal document: I couldna have wrote it out ony better myself. I just wish that when clients come to consult me in the like difficulty—and that's gey often I may say—there's no' one o' them but would be verra glad to be in possession o' this kind o' document."

"So it means she's married to the blackguard! Weel, it'll no' dae, Mr. Aiken. It'll no' dae: I just canna have it. This Burns hasna a sark to his back. No' only that, Mr. Aiken, but he's a notour atheist, whoremaster and blaspheming blackguard. On no account, sir, will I hae him married onto my dochter! So ye'll need to find a way o' getting round that. In a case like this, Mr. Aiken, I'm no' the man to grudge your fee."

"Hoots, Mr. Armour: we'll no' talk aboot fee. And what does your dochter say to this?"

"Mr. Aiken, sir: I'd be a poor parent and failing in my duty to tak' a betrayed lassie's opinion on a matter like this. Siccan a marriage wad ruin me as weel as my dochter. I hae contacts wi' lairds and gentles—aye, the verra nobility o' the West. A disgrace like this wad put an end to my prosperity. Besides, Mr. Aiken, ye dinna ken this hound: I just couldna thole him at whatever price. Saint or sinner, I just canna have him."

"Aye, aye: your dochter's well educated?"

"Educated? What's education got to do wi' it? She can get through her catechism and she can sign her name. She needs nae mair education nor that. She's helped her mither a' her days— aye, and she's still needed aboot the hoose. I've had eleven o' a family, Mr. Aiken; and maybe it's no' richt for a parent to hae a favourite. But if there's sic a thing, then Jean was my favourite. Aye . . . and what's mair, Mr. Aiken, if I thocht the blackguard had a bawbee to his name I'd hae it aff him."

While James Armour was making his violent statement, Bob Aiken was doing some quick thinking. He knew Armour; and he knew the mood he was in. He was a strong-willed man and his mind was bent on violence. Then there was Robert Burns. It was like him to make out a marriage line; but foolish. He did not doubt this for a moment. Had Robert Burns been in earnest he wouldn't have left his wife to face the music with her father: he would have taken her under his own roof and owned her openly. No: the Bard was no doubt regretting the existence of these lines as much as James Armour . . . Not the kind of wife for him either. No education: could hardly sign her own name: no manner of wife at all for a poet, and such a scholarly one as Robert Burns. Strange, though: he had been talking to him only the other day and he had not mentioned a word about marriage. Damned!

maybe this was why he was desperate to get to the Indies. Aye, that would be it. That being so, he might be able to do him a real good service this morning.

"Weel, Mr. Armour . . . There's several ways we could look at a matter like this. Doubtless you'll have your plans for your dochter. I mean—if she could be got away——"

"That's settled, sir. I've packed her off to Paisley to the wife's sister. There's nae point in the Kirk Session compearing her—till we canna help it. In ony case she micht get relief afore then: I've kenned the like to happen afore now."

"Very sensible, Mr. Armour. And a good choice o' a place, Paisley: she'll be hidden away there fine."

"Aye; but what about Burns, Mr. Aiken? I dinna trust him."

"I don't think ye'll have ony bother wi' him, Mr. Armour. There's nocht he can do about it. And as like as no' he'll be quite content to let sleeping dogs lie."

"Ah, but what about the marriage lines?"

"And what's your worry anent the bit paper?"

"He didna write that out for nothing—no' a practised whore-master like him. I don't want ony comeback, ye ken. As like as no' it was my siller he was after. I couldna lie in my bed at nichts and think that line could be ony way employed again me—or mine. Would it be all right to throw it in the back o' the fire?"

Bob Aiken looked at the document spread open on his desk. He had a professional objection to destroying documents that might have an ultimate use. At the same time he didn't want to do Robert Burns any disservice. There might come a day when James Armour would want his daughter married—would want the validity of this document testified. Meantime he had to be satisfied.

"I'll tell ye what, Mr. Armour. We'll cut Burns's name out of the paper: that will remove the name and source of your trouble. The document otherwise ye may keep or not, as it best pleases you. It might be handy to have by you in the event—privately, of course—of your wanting to prove to Mr. Auld that your dochter really was—well, if not exactly married, then not just in the open state of sin she might otherwise be accused of . . . You understand me, Mr. Armour?"

"Fine, Mr. Aiken, fine! But how will a' this go wi' Burns? What action could he tak' gin he was so minded?"

"Aye; but you'll make a point o' seeing Burns and telling him that the paper has been—eh—nullified. Aye, nullified—rendered useless; that evidence of his marriage—as we may call it—no longer exists. And, of course, that this is your dochter's wish as well as yours."

"I'm loth to meet wi' the blackguard."

"There are times, Mr. Armour, when we have to swallow our dislikes and act as our best interests dictate. And gin I were you, I'd lose no time in seeing him and letting him know exactly how matters stand."

Bob Aiken folded the paper and deftly tore out the portions that contained the name of Robert Burns.

"There you are now, Mr. Armour. Everything's in order. Don't hesitate or bide on ony ceremony, but just let me know should ony development take place. My professional services—such as they are—are always at your disposal."

On this James Armour and Robert Aiken shook hands, each certain they had done the right and proper thing—though from very different motives and with very different ends in view.

It was dark by the time James Armour won back to Machlin. As he approached the Cowgate he saw Robert Burns come through the kirkyard as from Gavin Hamilton's house. The beam of light from John Dow's entrance revealed him.

James Armour dismounted.

"Hold there, Mr. Burns. Aye . . . it's James Armour. I want a word wi' you, sir. What I've got to say'll no' keep ye lang. Aye . . . I'm just back frae Ayr, where I hae been consulting wi' Mr. Aiken."

Here James Armour stopped and peered cautiously about him.

"Go on, sir: there's nobody about."

"Mr. Aiken told me to tell you that he had nullified that marriage line ye wrote out for Jean."

"Nullified! What d'you mean? Mr. Aiken gave you no such message!"

"Nullified was Mr. Aiken's word for it. I dinna expect a character like you to believe me. So you can ride into Ayr and see Mr. Aiken yoursel'. But as far as I'm concerned—or anybody belonging me's concerned—I hae what's left o' the lines: wi' your name cut out o' them. And that's the legal end to that: bad cess to you!"

And with that James Armour, conscious of his mounting choler, tugged savagely at the bridle and led his horse round to the stable.

For a long time Robert stood in the side of the road unable to take a step in any direction. The news and the manner of its communicating had struck him like a blow. He felt cut to the marrow. But Aiken, Aiken . . . Why had Robert Aiken, who had seemed so much his friend, done a cruel thing like this to him? Cut his name out of the paper—nullified the document! God! was there no friendship left in the world? And what must Aiken think of him when he had done such a terrible thing? What had Armour told him? Whatever he had told him, Aiken had believed. Bob Aiken, who had been one of his most disinterested friends and his chief patron in Ayr. What kind of scoundrel and blackguard did Aiken think him now? What would Mr. Ballantine—who was now a magistrate—and John MacWhinnie and Willie Chalmers think of him when they heard Aiken's report? The hand that had been so often held out to him in the warmth of genuine friendship; the hand that had so often patted him on the back—the same hand had cut his name from his marriage lines!

This was the bitter, incomprehensible core of the matter. Aiken had turned against him. It was Armour who had turned him.

The tension eased. He moved forward.

And by God! It was Jean Armour who was at the bottom of it all. If she had only stood by him this calamity could never have befallen him.

Nor would the news of his terrible disgrace stop in Ayr. Even now it would be finding its way into every corner of Kyle, Cunninghame and Carrick. Wherever he was known, people would stop and say to each other how Robert Burns that had been in Alloway, in Mount Oliphant, in Lochlea and was now in Mossgiel, had been lowered in the dust by James Armour, the Machlin mason, and Robert Aiken in Ayr; how he had thought to marry Armour's daughter and had given her marriage lines; how both she and her family had spurned and rejected him and how Aiken had backed them up . . .

God damn and roast their rotten souls! All because of his poverty and lack of worldly gear they had ruined him. Ruined him? Killed him! Murdered him! Hell's hottest hob was too cool for them! His proposals were almost to hand; and how in the name of heaven or hell could he send them round the country-side? If a man like Aiken had turned against him who would stand by him? Who now would want to subscribe for his poems?

But surely, surely, Jean could never have had it in her heart to do all this to him, to destroy and degrade him so utterly? Surely in denying him she had never foreseen what the consequences would be?

He moved slowly, head down, round by the Cross. There was a moon low in the sky and there was light enough now to recognise anyone. The lights from the Machlin windows cast warm beams into the narrow streets. There were peals of girlish laughter in the air, and occasional raucous skirling and shouting of young men rent the village stillness with defiant but vital vulgarity. Men hailed each other on recognition, and from the howffs came the familiar merry drowse of conversation.

But Robert heard nothing and saw nothing. Nothing till the bright voice of Eliza Miller bade him good-evening.

"Oh, it's you, Eliza: I'm sorry . . . I didn't recognise you."

"Composing another poem, I suppose?"

Robert raised his hand and passed it wearily across his forehead.

"No, Eliza: poets are human beings, you know, subject to all the trials and tribulations that affect ordinary mortals."

"I was sorry to hear about Jean, Robert."

"And what did you hear about Jean?"

"Nothing . . . Just that she was away to Paisley. Her mother said she hadna been feeling well."

"You're a nice lass, Eliza, and you ken I've aey had my heart set on you; but you can lie as pretty as you look."

"I'm sorry, Robert."

"Ah! what in hell's name is the good of sorrow, Eliza?"

Eliza looked down at her toe where it tapped the ground. Robert and she had been lovers: of a kind. Many a night they had kissed and cuddled; but she thought she had lost him for ever to Jean Armour. Now Jean was in Paisley and, if all she heard were true, pregnant. And it was something more than rumour that insisted that the Armours would have nothing to do with him. Eliza loved Robert; but she was woman enough to want to know the story between him and Jean Armour, woman enough to want that triumph over Jean.

"You never come to Jeannie Smith's on a Sunday, do you?"

"No: not as often as I used to, Eliza: not as often as I'd like."

"We all miss you, Robert."

"Miss me? I'd like to believe you; but I'm not in the mood for believing anything . . . or anybody."

"I just thought you micht like to come in on Sunday. Jeannie said if I saw you I was to be sure and speir."

"Aye . . . speir! Pretty soon, Eliza, there'll be no need to speir. I suppose you all want to know about Jean Armour and me?"

"No . . . nobody wants to ken what doesna concern them."

"No? Then they damn soon will—and they'll ken it without speiring."

"You're gey bitter, Robert."

"Bitter? It's easy to be bitter. But why shouldn't I be bitter if I want?"

"There's no need to be bitter wi' me, is there? I've never been against you, Robert. We were always good friends—at least——"

"At least! Don't mind me, Eliza: you've met me in an evil hour."

"Och, come on, Robert! Let's tak' a turn down the road."

"What! You're not afraid to be seen walking wi' Robert Burns, the celebrated blackguard in Mossgiel? Take a dozen steps down the road wi' me, Eliza, and your maidenhead's as good as gone. Oh! you may take it to bed wi' you for the rest of your days—but it'll be gone as far as the Machlin folk are concerned."

"I don't know what's come over you . . ."

"It's not what's come over me—it's what's come over other folk. Thank the Lord, however, I'll soon be far enough away from the ignorant pride and black-hearted ignorance that passes for worth in this part o' the world."

"Speaking for myself, I never thocht much of the Armours. I liked Jean weel enough——"

"Did you?"

"I can only speak o' folk as I find them. I wouldn't be honest if I said I didna like Jean Armour—but that doesna mean that I don't like you, Robin. I wouldn't listen to what onybody said against you."

"And you don't mind walking down the road wi' me?"

"Of course I don't."

"Come on then. God damn it, Eliza, I don't know what I'm saying or what I'm doing: you'll need to forgive me."

"Give me credit for some understanding, Robin. It's a shame the way you've been treated."

"Just exactly what do you know, Eliza?"

"I've told you all I know. I know the Armours are against you."

"Do you know why?"

"No . . . Unless it's Jean."

"And what about her?"

"Well, you know about the Session as well as me."

"The Session? What about them?"

"Have you no' heard?"

"Hell, Eliza, I've heard nothing about the Session. What is it?"

"Of course this is only what I've heard . . . It's been reported to the Session that Jean's having a bairn."

"Who the hell could tell them that?"

"I've nae idea. James Lamie and Holy Willie are to see her parents."

"The holy beagles! Wee Smith told me nothing o' this!"

"I don't think the Smiths ken yet. My father got it very confidential: I heard him tell my mither."

"By God! they've wasted no time unloosing the houghmagandie pack on Jean. And yet? When was this, Eliza: last Sunday?"

"Must have been, Robin. I'm sorry if it's true—for both your sakes."

But his thoughts were after another hare. If Armour had been questioned—— But that was it. They had decided to mutilate the paper *before* the Session got the wind of it: the low, cunning foxes . . .

"Listen, Betsy: there's something you can do for me."

"If I can, Robin."

"Let me know whatever you learn about the Session. Wee Jamie will get to know nothing: Lamie will watch that. I've damned few friends left; but in the beaten way o' friendship at least could I ask you to do that for me?"

"Of course, Robin: you know I would do anything for you."

"The time's at hand when you'll be tested in your friendship, Betsy—aye, and tried sorely for all I know. But this much I can tell you. If anyone says I played Jean Armour false, tell them they lie. Tell them the falseness lay in Jean Armour and not in Robert Burns. Tell them that the day will come—and it's maybe not so far distant—when the Armours will be sorry they didn't bite out their tongues rather than say the things they said. Tell them it may be true that Robert Burns hasn't a change o' sark to his back but that he's still got a quick honour in his breast——"

"But what *did* they say?"

"They said plenty they had no right to say, Betsy."

"Is everything finished atween you and Jean?"

"Finished? Finished as if we had never known each other far less ever sweethearted. Finished, Betsy, in the way that only death finishes human relationship. Jean Armour's dead as far as I'm concerned."

"I'm sorry, Robin."

"So am I: that's the hellish bit about it. You ken that I loved Jean Armour?"

"And I ken she loved you! D'you no' think it was her parents that forced her away?"

"Parents! She wasn't a bairn. She was responsible for her own actions. She had no right to hide behind parents—or allow parents to influence her. Our duty to one another came first—or should have. You'll hear plenty about it a' in the days to come, Betsy: you can remember what I said."

Eliza Miller saw that she wasn't going to get the truth out of him this night—still less was he going to take her in his arms. But whatever had happened between him and the Armours, it had wounded him deeply. Indeed she began to realise that she had but a limited understanding of the man who walked by her side. But against this she felt that she knew him as few folks in Machlin knew him. To have been made love to by Robert Burns was an experience she could not put in words—not even unspoken words . . .

ANTIDOTE

When he got home that night he found a parcel awaiting him from Wilson the printer, containing copies of his subscription sheets. He opened the parcel and handed copies round the family for their inspection.

Viewing his name for the first time in print, he was conscious of an elation of spirit. There could have been no finer antidote to James Armour's bitter news.

The family read the sheet carefully. The brothers and sisters were delighted, and even Mrs. Burns, after long and careful scrutiny, seemed to be impressed. Not that she was wanting in criticism.

"Why have you changed your name?"

"Gibby and me have agreed on that, mither. Folk that don't know us call us Burness, and folk that know us wonder why we spell it Burnes. Burns is the Ayrshire spelling: so Gibby and me have agreed to use it from now on——"

"I ken your faither didna like his name changed; but I canna suppose it matters. And what d'ye dae wi' this noo?"

"We distribute copies to all our friends; and they distribute copies to their friends. Anybody that wants a copy signs his name below—and if they want more than one copy they put that down. Then we get the lists back and Wilson kens where we stand and where to send the copies to when they come out."

"And when will that be?"

"If we get enough names to cover the expense the copies should be out gin the summer."

"Ah weel, Robin: there's been a gey lot o' talk aboot this. I hope the thing prospers wi' ye."

"And so do we all, mither," said Gilbert. "We'll get enough names there's no fear. Aye: I've always told you how Robin would be famous some day. It'll no' be long now."

"I hope so, Gibby—if it'll please the pair o' ye."

Nancy said: "We'll a' be pleased. Oh, Robin: I think it's wonderful to see your name here. Scotch Poems by Robert Burns. Everybody will be proud o' you."

And certainly, as he looked round the rapt faces gathered at the fireside, he was conscious of great and heart-warming pride. He was sorry that they were so poor and their living accommodation was so dismal and confined. How grand it would have been to have had a spence like John Rankine's at Adamhill (aye, or a fine room like Gavin Hamilton's), where he could have invited a few friends. His family and his friends could have enjoyed a social evening and celebrated this the beginning of his career as poet.

The reflection passed as it had often come and passed. A deep wave of melancholy began to submerge the elation with which he had first viewed the subscription bills. He made a sudden gesture to Gilbert. The pair of them left the kitchen.

"Is there something wrong, Robin?"

"Gibby: I don't know what's going to happen. I get so tired and wearied sometimes I could throw myself down and weep. It's this bluidy never-ending poverty that depresses me. I would even go and get drunk, but I havena small change enough for that."

"Getting drunk wouldna do ony good, Robin."

"No . . . There would be the greater misery to face when I sobered up. Gibby! I don't know what I'd do without you. You know what's happened now? I saw Armour the night as he was riding in from Ayr. He told me he had been consulting wi' Mr. Aiken and that he'd cut my name out of the marriage paper."

"Cut your name out!"

"Aye. Nullified the paper. Armour said Aiken told him to tell me that."

"What in heaven's name made them do a thing like that?"

"The houghmagandie pack's been unloosed, Gibby. It was reported to the Session last Sunday that Jean Armour was pregnant. They sent a deputation consisting of Holy Willie and James Lamie to investigate. God kens what they've learned; but it's surely clear that Armour didn't want my marriage to come before them. So now my marriage is nullified—torn up. They can say it never existed."

Gilbert resented this act almost as much as Robin; resented the manner and the unfavourable implications of it. But in his heart he was relieved that Robin was not married, that he was clear of entanglement. He expressed his feeling with caution.

"It's a damnable bit o' business, Robin; and nobody can excuse it. But maybe, in the long run, you're better free o' Jean Armour."

"Maybe, Gibby. I wish I could think so. Oh, don't imagine that I would ever have taken up wi' her after the damnable way she denied me. But it hurts me, Gibby, to think they would cut my name from the paper. And Aiken that was my chief patron in Ayr! I had intended sending him a bundle of subscriptions. Now—I might as well throw them in the fire. Did you ever ken it different? When I set my heart on onything it's sure to be denied me. I've a feeling my poems will never see print. We're battling against the tide, Gibby—a tide that's aey ebbing."

"Sometimes it looks that way, Robin. But we'll need to get out your subscription bills. And I've a feeling that you're going to make a penny or twa out o' them. Wilson may be all that you say he is; but if he decides to take the risk o' printing, he sees money somewhere. I've a notion to give Mossgiel another year—see what this harvest brings anyway. If I go down then I go down—and no regrets. It's only bad luck that's defeated us so far—and our luck canna aey be bad."

"Right then, Gibby: if you think you can manage . . . I'll probably be away by mid-summer—once my poems are out. I've a notion I might make my passage out of them—or the price of my outfit. But to-morrow morning I'll start sending out my subscriptions. Gavin Hamilton, for a start."

"Don't miss Hamilton, whatever you do."

"Aye; and I'll better take the opportunity of telling him about old Armour and Aiken—I don't want him to get that news second-hand."

And so the following morning he headed a sheet of paper: Mossgiel, Saturday morn: 15th April, 1786. Then he wrote:

Honoured Sir, My Proposals came to hand last night, and I know you would wish to have it in your power to do me a service as early as anybody, so I enclose you half a sheet of them. I must consult you, first opportunity, on the propriety of sending my quondam friend, Mr. Aiken, a copy. If he is now reconciled to my character as an honest man, I would do it with all my soul; but I would not be beholden to the noblest being ever God created, if he imagined me to be a rascal. Apropos, old Mr. Armour prevailed with him to mutilate that unlucky paper, yesterday. Would you believe it? Though I had not a hope, nor even a wish, to make her mine after her damnable conduct; yet when he told me, the names were all cut out of the paper, my heart died within me, and he cut my very veins with the news. Perdition seize her falsehood and perjurious perfidy! But God bless her and forgive my poor, once-dear, misguided girl. She is ill-advised. Do not despise me, Sir: I am indeed a fool, but a *knave* is an infinitely worse character than anybody, I hope, will dare to give the unfortunate Robert Burns.

He folded the sheet, addressed it to Gavin Hamilton, and sent Willie Patrick to deliver it.

On Sunday he called in at Hamilton's to discuss his affairs. Hamilton seemed pleased to see him.

"I got your letter, Robert—and your proposals. I haven't had time yet to get them going; but dinna worry, I'll see them well filled up for you. But this is a bad business wi' Armour and Aiken!"

"You don't think me a knave, Mr. Hamilton?"

"Nonsense! Nor does Bob Aiken. There's a mistake somewhere. But the first time I see Aiken I'll put that right."

"You don't think Mr. Aiken's against me?"

"Na, na: Aiken couldna be against you. Of course, he's aey acted for Armour—You'll no' be in Ayr one o' these days?"

"Yes . . . I know I have some friends in Ayr. But I have no wish to burden them with the expense of paying postage on my proposals—so I had intended riding into Ayr with them this week."

"Good! Call on Aiken then—and hear what he's got to say. There's bound to be some explanation. Strictly speaking, neither Aiken nor anybody else can destroy a marriage line. Legally it's valid whether lost or destroyed. So I would see what he's got to say. Aiken's a lang-luggit adviser and kens what he's up to. A personal call's what you want. And what's your news frae Killie—Wilson's news?"

"Well, I've to get on with a final selection of my verses. I'm planning to fill a volume of some two hundred pages. There'll be a dedication in verse to yourself, Mr. Hamilton—if you'll honour me by accepting it."

"That's verra kind o' you, Robert. But there's more important folk than me you might bestow that honour on."

"No, sir: I am determined that you shall have that honour: no one merits it more; and it would gratify me greatly if you could see your way to accept."

"If you're determined, Robert. Maybe you'll give me a look at the manuscript—gin you have it ready?"

"That was my intention, Mr. Hamilton. I have not yet completed my draft——"

"At your convenience, Robert: at your convenience. I'll tell you what: look in to-morrow night—by then I'll have looked over such of your verses as I have in manuscript and give you my opinion on them. Maybe after that you could send them on, with such others as you can lay your hands on, to Ballantine?"

"That's good advice and I'll act on it, Mr. Hamilton. I've been busy polishing some of my earlier verses. I have done much to improve my Love and Liberty. Indeed, my manuscripts are in several hands; but I'll collect as many as I can for Ayr."

"Have you seen Doctor Douglas of the town?"

"No."

"Make his acquaintance if you're still thinking about the Indies: he has many influential connections there. Either Aiken or Ballantine will give you an introduction."

"Of course . . . Gilbert will be keeping on Mossgiel."

"That's understood, Robert. D'you think I'd let you away to the Indies and leave Mossgiel without a dependable tenant?"

Gavin Hamilton laughed; but Robin thought the laughter a bit forced. Gavin Hamilton was neither fool nor sentimentalist. But, he was human enough to feel embarrassment for the cover-up of his laughter.

"Come on, Robert: we'll hae a dram to the success o' your proposals—though if Daddy Auld knew I was drinking healths on the Sabbath he'd want me up afore the Session for rebuke."

But at that moment Mr. Auld, having heard James Lamie's report and listened to his elders' comments, made a note in his scroll minutes:—

"James Lamie reports that he spoke to Mary Smith, mother of Jean Armour, who told him that she did not suspect her daughter to be with child, that she was gone to Paisley to see her friends, and would return soon."

But even as Mr. Auld scrolled the minute (for he was leaving nothing here to the dubious phraseology of the clerk, Andrew Noble) he was doubtful if Jean would soon be back.

Mr. Auld was troubled. If he was to believe William Fisher, then everybody in Machlin knew—except Mary Smith, it seemed—that Jean Armour was with child to Robert Burns . . .

He looked round the tight-lipped faces of his assistants; and he doubted if there was one of them had any real understanding of their work—or their duty in Christ. And so he doubted if in one heart that beat there by the grace of God, there was a drop of pity for Jean Armour. Looking back across three-quarters of a century, William Auld realised that only too often had he lacked that pity himself. Even for hardened harlots there should be pity. How much more pity then should there be for Jean Armour, who had been plucked like a dove from the nest?

Still . . . pity did not save a soul from the terrible damnation of all eternity.

With a repressed sigh William Auld took up the next case.

THE HOUR AND THE MOMENT

That night Robin managed to steal an hour with Mary Campbell in the darkness and warmth of the Stairaird byre, to wrap her in his plaid and to promise to be true to her in time coming.

By this time Mary had learned her lesson. She had waited long for the opportunity of marriage and she was heartily sick of her dairymaid drudgery and the emotional bleakness of Stairaird.

This time Robert wouldn't escape her so easily: she would bind him to her by every tie she knew. She did not distrust him: rather was her faith in him boundless. She loved him. Day or night there was no escaping his influence. In his magnetic presence she was transported out of the meanness of her physical environment and transformed in her physical self.

She loved him in the ideal world of mental creation; and the chemistry of her blood responded to him in an abandonment that was clamorous and incessant.

She was not a virgin; but in her love for him she was virginal, spiritually and physically.

Her love was chaste, delicate, supersensitive, refined. She was utterly unlike Jean Armour. Jean Armour had been a virgin; but a virgin in the first red-rose flush of fecund motherhood. Jean Armour's love was full-blooded, rich, vital, utterly unashamed, completely natural and devoid of any inhibition. In the glory of her girlhood she was crowned with all the magnificence of motherhood.

But in the red glory of Mary Campbell's hair there sat no crown of fertility. In the paleness of her plain, pock-marked face there was no laughter of lively lust. There was no husky vibrance in her voice carrying an echoing undertone from an urgent womb.

Not that she was a pale mask of inhibited purity. There was fire in her, a fire that burned with a white flame. The passion that was in her did not overflow into her pores or send the flood-tide of her red blood drumming along her senses. Her passion gleamed like a knife blade sharpened to a keen point of sensation. And thus was her mind and her vision sharpened and pointed.

It was towards this gleaming knife-point of sensation that he was drawn. There was no seduction. Mary Campbell, unlike Jean Armour, gave nothing that her mind did not tell her to give. And she gave nothing that her body did not prompt her mind to give. She gave herself to Robert Burns because her body and her mind told her she must. And her experience told her that she did wisely, for there was no other way to bind such a lover as Robert Burns to her; and her heart warned her that without him the future would be unbearably empty and lonely.

And he, deep in the experience of many loves, and loving, as he breathed, with joyous acceptance, responded keenly to the tempered singleness of her integrity.

He had ceased to compare love with love. Yet he could not fail to be aware that his loves were of two main kinds. At their base was Jean Glover; but they had been suckled right and left at the breasts of Jean Glover's anarchism. Jean Glover was too like himself—anarchistic and amoral in her loving . . .

On the right stood Alison Begbie, Jean Gardner and Mary Campbell: on the left stood Annie Rankine, Betty Paton and Jean Armour.

Jean Armour queened the left as Mary Campbell queened the right. The others, like Nancy Fleming, Mysie Graham and Eliza Miller, were mere maids-in-waiting.

All this Robert knew instinctively and without the aid of categories. But John Rankine had lied to him—without knowing the nature of his lie. Long ago he had told him how his heart would tell him when he was in love with the inevitable woman.

His heart had told him Jean Armour. But what had Jean Armour's heart told her? John Rankine's wisdom had been one-sided.

Now his heart told him that Mary Campbell's was a truer love than Jean Armour's.

But could he believe his heart any longer? Was it truly an infallible guide?

He crushed Mary Campbell in his arms.

"What's wrong, Robert: what's wrong?"

"Oh—nothing, Mary . . . and yet everything . . . And you'll go to the Indies wi me?"

"Yes . . . I'll go to the Indies wi' you, Robert—or anywhere else you want me to go."

"I knew that, Mary."

"And you will marry me, Robert?"

"And how best could I assure you of that, my dear?"

"If you wrote it on the Bible I would know it was sure as God's blessing."

"Then you shall have it that way, Mary—even though the promise of my own lips is surer than death itself."

"Oh—don't talk of death: it's a black thought and unlucky."

"Right, then! Will you listen to some lines I have made up for us?

"Will ye go to the Indies, my Mary, and leave auld Scotia's shore? Will ye go to the Indies, my Mary, across the Atlantic roar?

"O, sweet grows the lime and the orange, and the apple on the pine; but a' the charms o' the Indies can never equal thine.

"I hae sworn by the Heavens to my Mary, I hae sworn by the Heavens to be true, and sae may the Heavens forget me, when I forget my vow!

"O, plight me your faith, my Mary, and plight me your lily-white hand! O, plight me your faith, my Mary, before I leave Scotia's strand!

"We hae plighted our troth, my Mary, in mutual affection to join; and curst be the cause that shall part us! The hour and the moment o' time!"

There were few women, especially at that hour and that moment of time, who could have resisted this appeal from Robert Burns; and Mary Campbell's resistance had been broken even before he began. But her fondest hope was realised and her deepest wish fulfilled.

Hurrying home along the Barskimming road, Robin was again assailed with the image of Jean Armour. Even the arms of Mary Campbell could not exclude Jean. He tried to shake the image from his mind. Will ye go to the Indies, my Mary? Aye; but Jean was in Paisley; and it was his child that lay under her heart.

What was she thinking now? What was she doing? How was she faring?

Maybe with Mary Campbell beyond the Atlantic's roar he would be able to forget her—and their child yet to be born.

Maybe Jean's bairn would be a boy. When he grew up there would be little between him and dear-bought Bess. Folk would point them out and say: There's the laddie Jean Armour had to Rab Burns and there's the lassie Lizzie Paton had to Rab Burns. Aye . . . he went to the Indies a lang time ago wi' Highland Mary Campbell. Aye . . . he used to be a tenant in Mossgiel along wi' his brother Gilbert. Gilbert was a steady lad: there's none o' his bastards running about the parish barefoot . . .

He hurried his step in the darkness and bowed his head as a blatter of spring rain swept over the fields. He could hear the sneer in their voices as they talked of him; he could see them pointing their fingers at the backs of his illegitimate children.

There was no peace for him anywhere. In the arms of Mary Campbell—yes. Mary Campbell was balm on the wounds Jean Armour and her parents had inflicted on him; but balm only for as long as Mary herself was applying the balm. Away from Mary, the rankling injustice began to smart again in the wounds.

The wind-brushed smirr of rain began to soothe him. Nature, whatever her mood, always soothed him. Wind and rain, especially the smirring of spring rain, was great solace. There was the certainty of growth in its freshness. The autumn rains had in them the smell of death and decay. The tearing, blustering west winds of winter, tossing the bare branches like rigs of barley, were winds that gave him exultation. There was nothing he loved better on the edge of a winter's evening than to take a walk by the margin of a wood or planting . . .

But at the moment there was the soothing effect of the spring rain in the spring darkness. Strange that the rain and the darkness could soothe away the trouble in his mind and the pain in his heart . . .

As he came in by Machlin, and the warm lights shone in Johnnie Dow's inn, he decided that there could be few better times to enjoy a social hour and a social glass of tippenny ale. And he was in need of physical refreshment.

CRITICS

Robert Aiken was worried: he had never before seen such reproach in the great glowing eyes of Robert Burns.

"Now listen, Robert: I know things are difficult to explain . . . now. But you maun believe me when I tell you that I never had the least notion of doing you an injury. Injury? By God, lad, that's the last thing I wad think o' doing you. I thought when I destroyed your name in that piece of paper I was doing you the best turn in the world. I thought you were in a bit o' trouble wi' Armour's lass and that if I could humour him into thinking that the marriage was nullified I was as much looking after your interests as I was looking after his . . . He told me, too, that his dochter nae mair wanted the marriage nor he did . . . And . . . damnit, Robert, you must believe that! If you had as much as dropped a hint to me that last time we were speaking . . ."

"Maybe the fault was as much mine as anybody's. But then, I never thought that Jean Armour would have denied me the way she did. Maybe I could have got over that; for there is always the possibility that she was bullied into denying me. But when Armour told me that you had cut out my name and nullified our marriage, I thought that you too had denied me . . . and that was a hard blow to me after the friendship you had bestowed on me. I confess, Mr. Aiken, I was deeply hurt."

"Aye . . . I understand, Robert my lad, and I appreciate your feelings. And what's on your mind on Armour's lass now?"

"I'm finished wi' her. She has spurned me once; but she won't get another opportunity. And there are others willing enough to share my fate, however poor it may seem in the Armours' eyes."

"Aye . . . just so, Robert. Indeed, that is so. Well, I'm glad we've cleared up the misunderstanding."

"No one more than me, Mr. Aiken. And now, sir, if I were asking you offhand what you thought was my finest poem, how would you answer?"

"Your finest? That's no' just so easy."

"The one you like yourself best of all. There must be one."

"Well, for myself, Robert, I think your Cottager is your crowning achievement. Of course——"

"Then, Mr. Aiken, I shall have the honour, when my poems come to be printed, to have The Cotter's Saturday Night inscribed to you."

"Me, Robert? Laddie, you touch me wi' that—touch me where I havena words to say just how I'm touched. But, Robert my boy, it's an honour I'll cherish a' my days—aye, and I ken my children after me'll cherish it—aye, and their children's children. But come on round and we'll get John Ballantine and see if we canna help you to mak' a grand selection for Kilmarnock Johnnie."

Half an hour later their heads were together round a table in Simson's. It was thrilling for Robert to sit and listen to his eminent Ayr patrons gravely discussing the merits of his verses. Ballantine was judicious.

"You could hardly include Holy Willie's Prayer: that would give a lot of needless offence in Machlin."

"I dinna ken, John: Willie Fisher's kent by a'bodies for miles around."

"It's one thing, Bob, to pass round a manuscript: it travels from one friendly hand to another. Besides, a thing wrote down carries less authority than the same thing set out in print. There's an authority, nay, a sanctity, about the printed word given out to the world at large that can never be about the written word."

"Aye, there's that to it, of course. What say ye, Robert: is your heart set on Holy Willie?"

"Well, it's one of my best satires—but Mr. Ballantine has spoken some grave words—and I feel there's wisdom in them."

"But would the same no' apply to The Holy Fair?"

"No . . . not if the names were left blank. But I admit The Holy Fair's in the doubtful category."

"Oh, damned, John, The Holy Fair maun go in."

"The volume will certainly be the poorer without it, Mr. Ballantine."

"Oh! don't think I don't appreciate your Holy Fair, Robert. What does Gavin Hamilton say?"

"Mr. Hamilton approves of it—and of Holy Willie too."

"Aye, Gavin'll want Holy Willie: trust Gavin. He's had a sair time wi' Machlin Session—and Daddy Auld's no' finished wi' him yet. What does your printer say?"

"I can see I'm going to have a wordy battle wi' Wilson, Mr. Aiken. Wilson has his own ideas . . . But if I can assure him that you gentlemen approve, I know it will carry great weight wi' him."

"Put us both down for The Holy Fair, Robert. Now, your Love and Liberty . . . Mr. Ballantine and me hae had mony a talk about that. Mind ye, Robert, it's a thundering bit o' work . . . but I canna see it sitting smug wi' onything else. And damn me! the polish you've put on't makes it fully bolder, eh, John?"

"Fully bolder, Bob. For private consumption nothing could be finer. It's a glorious cantata—as it were—but it couldna lie in the same bed o' print with The Cotter's Saturday Night. D'you no' agree, Robert?"

"It's my finest work."

"Yes: there's a sense in which I wad agree to that, Robert. But the philosophy of it is much too strong and challenging for ordinary reading. It's one thing, Robert, to laugh the follies of the Auld Light party to scorn; but it's quite another thing to put a magazine o' gun-powder under the foundations o' the Kirk—aye, and the State! You see, Robert, I'd like to see your volume win approval in as many quarters as possible and among all conditions of men; and you have enough and more to ensure you the plaudits of the West here—of that I'll take my oath. My counsel is to avoid offence—needless offence—and avoid like the plague all manner o' violent controversy. It is better to win the emotions to your side than inflame the passions of controversy against you. I'm certain Mr. Aiken agrees with me."

"Aye: it's sage advice, Robert my lad: sage advice. Mind: I can sympathise wi' you. There are times when I wad say print the lot and be damned to the consequences. Aye; but that wad be me speaking in my private capacity. I maun confess to a byornar fondness for whatever you pen, Robert. But then the lawyer in me gars me side wi' Mr. Ballantine when it comes to settling what to put afore your printer. Damnit, the feck o' my business is taken up wi' the conflict atween the private world o' whim and ambition and the public world o' common law and public rectitude . . . A man may take a horsewhip to an erring wife in the privacy and sanctity o' his ain house; and yet he dursna give her a clap across the mouth wi' the back o' his hand in the public thoroughfare. I think you understand that, Robert?"

But Robin understood only too well what Mr. Aiken was driving at. What both he and Ballantine wanted was a volume that would give as little offence as possible to the influential people of the West. But this would not be as easy as they supposed. He was not going to sacrifice the best of his work to that end. True enough, he had written poems in the past that he had never intended should see the sanctity of print; and there were many of his verses that were not suitable for print—being far below his own standard of poetic merit. But whether or not he was the only person in the world that liked it, he was determined not to sacrifice *Love and Liberty*. This was far and away his most ambitious work to date. He had spent a long time getting the tunes right. And glorious tunes they were. If the West was to know him as a poet, they must know him for his best work . . .

But he thanked his friends for their help and interest; and his thanks were sincere.

Securing an introduction to Doctor Douglas, he went along and interviewed him on the prospects of employment in the Indies. Doctor Douglas was only too glad to be of assistance to any friend of Aiken or Ballantine.

"The West Indies, Mr. Burns . . .? You could do worse; you could do worse. Certainly I can fix up something for you there. Through my brother Charles, sir; through my brother. Let me see now . . . Yes; a book-keeper's job. Kind of supervision over the blacks. The very thing. Just what my brother could be doing with—a dependable man. Yes, yes: I've heard my good friend Aiken speak well of you, Mr. Burns. Let me see now: let me see now . . ."

When Robin left him (after an hour's pleasant conversation), he was practically assured of a book-keeper's job on his brother's estate in Antigua. There was nothing he had to fear but the rigour of the passage out and a touch of blackwater fever when he arrived. And the salary of £30 a year was not to be despised against such trifling risks.

Doctor Douglas promised to write to his brother immediately and to communicate with him the very moment he had news for him.

Robin returned in better spirits to Mossgiel, and for the next few days he was busy addressing copies of his subscription sheets to such of his friends and acquaintances as he could not call upon. And as his work on the farm kept him busy, it was only in the evening he had any time to himself.

He wrote many letters with his proposals. Nor did he forget such old friends as Annie Rankine, who was now Mrs. John Merry of the New Cumnock Inn.

And Annie, when she got his letter, immediately showed it to her husband, who, though he did not know the Bard intimately, had already formed an affection for him. He did not know the full story of the corn rigs episode; but he knew from his father-in-law that Robert Burns and Annie Rankine had been sweethearts of some sort in their younger days.

The pair of them immediately set about securing signatures. It surprised both of them to find how widely Robert Burns was known as a poet. Though it wasn't everybody who came about the Inn that could afford to spend three shillings on a book of poetry, it was surprising to see those who were prepared to risk that sum on the strength of a snatch or two of his verses remembered from a merry night of drinking or an idle moment of resting in the harvest-field. Not a few, indeed, had been privileged to hear Annie herself singing *Corn Rigs* or reciting an odd verse on the author's pet ewe. Some were so keen to see the poems in print that, though they could not afford the money for individual copies, they clubbed together to ensure that a copy would eventually come among them . . .

Nor did Gilbert spare himself. He had many friends that Robert knew little about. Even in Machlin he had friends who were not his brother's friends, in the sense that they did not frequent his company or visit his favourite howffs. There were lads and lassies in the farms around on excellent terms with Gilbert, and he wasted little time in getting round them and soliciting their support.

Gilbert had been prepared to meet with refusals. It was not a usual thing for anyone to go around asking for subscriptions for a volume of poems and songs written by one of themselves. But again and again Gilbert was delighted to find that folks were not only willing to put down their names but were overjoyed at the chance to do so.

At night, when they were lying together in bed, Gilbert would tell Robin of his work and assure him that the book was going to be a success.

Strangely enough, when they discussed the poems that should go into the volume, Gilbert voiced the same sentiments as Aiken and Ballantine. He was against *The Holy Fair, Holy Willie's Prayer, The Prophet and God's Complaint, The Twa Herds* and *The Ordination.*

Gilbert reinforced his objections with a dash of characteristic prudence.

"You're no' away to the Indies yet. Even though you were away the morn, you've got to remember, Robin, that the rest of us will have to bear the brunt of any displeasure. You must admit that in some of your verses you go a wee bit over the score."

"Aye, maybe I do, Gibby."

"No' that they're no' good. But there are verses that sound all right in Johnnie Dow's back room that you wouldna like your mother or your sisters to read."

"Right again, Gibby; but even the sense of that might dawn on me. I'm not just such a bluidy fool as to want to see everything that I ever wrote set down in print. Besides, Wilson in Killie will as like as not be the final judge on what's to be included and what's to be left out. And believe me, Gibby, Wilson can be a right waspy wee critic when he likes. He sits perched up on his stool yonder like a hobgoblin, his wee foxy eyes darting over the paper; and nothing misses him. Whatever passes Wilson's scrutiny will be fit to be read by man or maid."

"I'm relieved to hear that, Robin. Mind you: when you wrote The Cotter's Saturday Night you set a standard that'll take some licking . . ."

"Aye; but you must bear in mind, Gibby, that even the humblest groat has two faces to it; and a footba', like the globe itself, has a face for every point of the compass. But let's get to sleep, man, for I have Wilson to face in the morning and a hard day's darg gin I get back."

"I'll do the work: it's a wee while now since you had a day off; and if you've time you can keep your eyes about you at the market and see what's being offered for a cow new calved."

HER DEAR IDEA

Sometimes he surprised himself: he was so calm and cool and at ease. There were times when he sat down and wrote a verse or two as if he hadn't a care in the world and he had all eternity in which to scribble. And then, as often as not, he would be humming a tune in such a joyful, artless manner that Gilbert would stare at him incredulously and shake his head. It seemed that the more he saw of his brother the less he really understood him. Truly, thought Gilbert, he was a man of many moods and many phases; or maybe it was just that he was a poet . . . Though why a poet in such desperate straits as Robin was in could find the heart to hum in that happy carefree manner was beyond him.

But such moments were rare. Sooner or later the thought of Jean Armour came blinding into his mind; and then he felt that it would not take much for him to lose all sense of proportion and balance. More and more Jean Armour haunted his mind; and more and more his anger at her died away in a terrible pain of longing.

If only he could see her and speak to her and hear from her own lips all that had happened to her since that day she had told her mother and that night her father had come home. Surely Jean would have an explanation for all the terrible things that had come between them.

At such times he could neither work nor rest nor speak civilly to anyone. Too often he neither saw nor heard anyone: oblivious to all that was around him and conscious only of the pain tearing at his heart.

Madness, he felt, must be something like this. And with what sanity he had left he sought to flee from his madness.

When he was in the fields by himself he would groan out loud, and relieve, to some extent, the pressure on his feelings. When the mood came over him in company (as it often did) it depended on the company whether he rose and walked out or whether he drank himself into a state where the anguish was blurred and the pain deadened.

At other times he would seek to drive the sweet ecstasy of the memory of Jean's physical love from his senses by singing the bawdiest of the old bawdy ballads, till even his bawdry-enthusiastic colleagues felt they were in the presence of a force whose whirling violence they were totally incapable of understanding . . .

The riot and frenzy of his words was unbelievable even to those who thought they knew him well: men like Smith and Robert Muir and John Rankine. But Rankine, because he knew him longest and knew him best, understood him best . . . John Rankine had strangled the poet in himself long ago . . . even when he had not understood clearly what he was doing. John Rankine had been capable in his day of mad frenzy; and he too had tried to drown it in the nappy and the reaming swats and in the arms of women and in torrents of unpremeditated words. John Rankine had some glimmer of what Robert Burns was going through . . .

John Rankine did his best to comfort him. But the Bard was not to be comforted by a flow of words, however sympathetic. He could only escape from himself in the action of his own words and deeds. He had never been used to getting drunk, for drink had never agreed with him—even when he had had the money to spend on it. Now there were friends in whose company he was not allowed to pay for drink. At the end of a session of refreshment, John Rankine was not the man to allow any one to settle the bill: to square the lawnin was at once his prerogative and his privilege: and so with a man like Tam Samson. To challenge this was to challenge the long-standing social etiquette of the West; and it never crossed the Bard's mind to challenge or question it. It had only been in the company of lads like Richmond, Brice, Hunter and Smith that each had paid their share of the reckoning—little enough though that had usually been. Sometimes, of course, men like Aiken and Ballantine would dispute for a moment over the privilege of the lawnin; but as they were both gifted with good memories, they were usually able to let their memories decide the order of precedence.

And thus it was that, from meetings in the Lodges in Tarbolton and the Sons of Auld Kille, when the labour of the Lodge was over, Robert entered keenly into the social mirth of refreshment. And but for these occasional evenings when he was able to ease the terrible tensions that gathered in his being, it is doubtful if he could have survived without an outbreak of some unpleasant and disastrous kind.

But though the tensions were relieved, they were not removed. Nothing could eliminate the memory of Jean Armour. Only in the arms of Mary Campbell did he know temporary peace. True, he had made up his mind regarding Mary. She would share his future and share it as his wife: if she lacked qualities that Jean Armour had in superabundance, she had something that Jean Armour hadn't. She could give expression to a faith in him that had been denied Jean or that Jean had never known the need to express. Mary, who had always loved him, had waited for him without complaint. This, above all, was something that endeared her to him.

Mary Campbell never for a moment guessed he was worried about Jean Armour: she reckoned he was only too glad to be free of her and the complications with the hated Armours. She was well aware that Jean was in Paisley and why she was there: she was equally aware that Betty Paton was still in Largieside nursing his first-born: a first-born of which he was as proud as if she had been born in holy wedlock. This knowledge had troubled Mary; but she had had to make the decision as to whether she wanted Robert Burns with this background, or didn't want him at all.

All the time Mary knew she had little or no choice in the matter. She was in love with him; and he was not the kind of lover who could be argued about. He had either to be accepted or rejected: there was no possibility of compromise. She had little difficulty in satisfying herself that she was glad it was so and that fate had brought him to her. That it meant giving herself to him had likewise to be accepted. It was a worry and it was a risk; but it was also fulfilment. And Mary, seeing the long stretch of barren spinsterhood before her, with the alternative of loveless and passionless marriage, was avid for fulfilment. She was passionate; but it was only when she was thoroughly aroused by Robert that she had cause to tremble and exult at the intensity of her passion.

Sooner or later she knew that she would become pregnant. But they were sailing for the Indies; and before they sailed Robert had promised he would marry her. Once aboard the vessel that would carry them to the new world, neither parents nor kirk session could call them back to answer any questions or suffer the indignity of any rebuke.

THE GALLANT WEAVER

In Paisley, Jean Armour found that life was more pleasant than she had anticipated. There was Jenny Surgeoner with whom to unbosom herself and to share mutual condolences. Jenny was a great comfort even though she was deeply unhappy since she had never had as much as a scrap of paper from John Richmond in Edinburgh. It was now that Jenny felt keenly her inability to put pen to paper. If only she could write and tell her lover how she felt and how his baby girl was thriving . . .

There was no writing for Jean. She could with some little difficulty have penned a short note to Rab. But not only had she been forbidden to do so: she knew that nothing she could write would have any influence on him. Her love for him had not diminished, though it was criss-crossed with pain, sorrow and anxiety as to the future. She could not blame him: she could not blame herself or her parents: they had been caught up in the net of circumstance and there was nothing anyone of them could do about it.

Jean's training, as well as her instincts, had led her to take a fatalistic view of human nature and human destiny. But it was not a soured nor even an unhappy fatalism. Her acceptance of whatever fate decreed or circumstance brought forth was quiet and resigned: in the intensity of her suffering she never thought to challenge.

It was this quality, when she was not suffering, that gave to her the radiance of quiet happiness and made her so popular with all who knew her.

And it was precisely this underlying quality that aroused Robert Wilson when he came to visit the Purdies. Robert was a Machlin lad who had settled in Paisley and was prospering as a weaver. So well had he prospered that he had now a shed of his own with eight looms clanking busily in it. He had gone to school with Jean. He was good-looking and much thought of in the community. He had reached the position where he could look around him for a wife. He had courted a few of the Paisley girls with a view to matrimony; but none of them had completely convinced him that they were good enough to take as a life partner.

But the moment Wilson beheld Jean Armour, and had recovered from the shock of realising the magnificent woman the chubby and cheery little girl of his school-days had grown into, he knew he was in love with her and that she was the woman he must wed.

Robert Burns he did not know; and it was a shock to discover that Jean was pregnant to him. But Jean's condition was all too common, and nothing in itself to get into a moral sweat about. Of course Wilson would much rather she had not been with child; and had she not been the woman she was, the circumstance might have weighed with him more than it did. As it was, Jean's beauty and vitality completely captured him.

Even Mrs. Purdie was not at all surprised to see the way the wind was blowing and did everything to encourage the well-doing weaver. It would be fine if she could send Jean home to her mother a lawfully-wedded wife in the eyes of God, the Kirk and all society.

It did Jean a lot of good to be paid attention by a lad like Robert Wilson: it helped her to recover much of her lost self-respect and self-confidence: to make her feel she was not an outcast from society. She agreed to take a turn up the High Street with him and to pay a visit to his weaving shed. Both her aunt and her uncle were quick to assure her that there could be no harm in it.

Robert Wilson (who was a calm, canny and cautious lad) was wildly excited at the prospect of courting Jean.

QUESTION AND ANSWER

Mrs. Burns, terribly bowed, her gnarled parchment-skinned hands lying in her lap, raised her head from the cheek of the fire and said: "Maybe ye'll tell me whaur this Indies is that you're thinking o' goin' to?"

"If you were up on the ridge there and looking towards Arran, you'd be looking for three thousand miles across the ocean before your eye sighted the islands o' the West Indies."

"And could you tell me what in God's name's takin' you awa' there?"

"Gilbert and me hae spoken it ower . . ."

"Aye; but I'm no' Gilbert: I'm your mither. Is it a lass?"

"And why should it be a lass?"

"I canna think o' ony other thing that wad tak' you awa' siccan a distance."

"Well, it's no' a lass. There's more in life than a lass."

"They've been the feck o' your life, Robin."

"I suppose I've never worked—either in the Mount, Lochlea or Mossgiel here?"

"I didna say that. I ken how hard you've worked. I ken how hard we've a' worked; and I ken we'll a' hae to work the harder gin you go awa'."

"Mossgiel canna keep us a': that's plain to be seen."

"Maybe it is; but it'll just need to keep us. However, Willie's coming on . . ."

"You don't want me to go?"

"I canna see the sense o't . . . And it's going to leave us in a bonnie habble . . . But I suppose if you're no' runnin' awa' frae a lass you'll be takin' one wi' you?"

"I micht dae that."

"Aye: I thocht that wad be it! And wha is she?"

"Mary Campbell: you'll no' ken her."

"Her that had the bairn . . ."

"No' that Mary Campbell. Highland Mary Campbell: she used to be wi' Gavin Hamilton's wife."

"A red-haired Heilan jad! Aye . . . you'll end up in the midden lookin' at the stars . . . And there'll be middens in the Indies the same as here, I've nae doubt."

"You're gey bitter, mither; but you've aey been bitter as far as I was concerned."

"Weel, you canna expect us to be onything else but bitter when you rise and leave us a' in the hole."

"Maybe you'll be in a bigger hole if I stay . . . I've arranged wi' Gilbert to send you what money I can."

"Mary Campbell'll see that you hae nae money to send hame. We'll no' be able to put the pat on the fire lippenin' on what you send us. Na, na, my son; but if you think that you're doin' what's richt there's nae good in me sayin' onything. I'm only givin' mysel' a sair heart and no' doin' you ony good . . . And what kind o' penny are you thinking your verses'll turn?"

"I've nae idea."

"No . . . nor has ony other body. But ye'll be lookin' for something?"

"I'm looking for nothing but honest fame."

"Ah weel, if it costs naebody ocht then you'll hae nae trouble getting it. And gin it costs nothing, naebody'll envy you it."

"Hae you no' a kind word for me at all?"

"Aye, plenty gin you were worthy o' them . . . Your sisters were hearing in Machlin that Jean Armour's awa' to Paisley. They're sayin' in Machlin that you bairned her?"

"Who's sayin' that?"

"There's plenty o' clash about it. But maybe that has nothin' to dae wi' you rinnin' awa' to the Indies wi' Heilan Mary Campbell?"

"It hasn't."

"Ah weel then: maybe there'll be enough black foreign hizzies for you to yoke on in the Indies . . ."

He swept his bundle of subscription bills under his arm, grabbed his hat and strode out of the house.

PARTIES AND CABALS

Mr. Auld had many worries on his shoulders. He went over his parish in his mind's eye and noted the troublesome points.

The establishment of George Gibson and his wife, Agnes, had always been a vexatious source of wrong-doing. Black Geordie was a lost soul and as bad a character as could be met with in the West. But at least he cloaked his wickedness and did not flaunt it before the parish. But his wife was a more difficult character. Not only was she drunken and dissolute: she had a savage and unbridled tongue in her head. She would have caused mischief in an empty house. She was under scandal and was barred from communion. But this did not seem to upset her. Probably she was beyond any redemption.

And yet the Gibsons performed some service to the community. There was a constant stream of gangrels passing through the town. They had to be housed somewhere, else they would become a nuisance, if not a menace, to decent Christian parishioners.

Elizabeth Black had set up a rival house to accommodate the overflow from the Gibson howff.

Between them, Mr. Auld had no doubt that there was much traffic in evil-doing. The Session would need to look closely into the business.

A certain Agnes Wilson had become attached to Gibson, and the reports he had of her were disturbing. Not only was she an open and shameless prostitute, she was something of a thief, or, at least, a resetter of stolen goods.

There had lately been an unpleasant scene in the town when she had been carried round the streets by some of the young lads, astride an undressed pole, and had suffered much bruising and injury to certain of the more private parts of her anatomy. No doubt the lads had acted thoughtlessly on instructions from their parents.

But it had been—according to Hugh Aird's report—a distressing and distasteful scene, and Gibson had got a sheriff's warrant to apprehend Adam Armour as the ring-leader.

A bad business. It was the sort of thing that would be taken up by the Presbytery in Ayr. He would rather avoid this, for it reflected on his ministry. The Session would require to take immediate steps to see that this woman was put out of the parish.

And what of Racer Jess, who had already borne an illegitimate child? And Elizabeth Barbour and Margaret Borland and Jean Mitchell? There had been harlots ever since man had first lusted after woman. And man had done so ever since the Fall.

No doubt there would always be harlots. But their paths should not be made easy by connivance and false tolerance. And they should be grappled with for the sake of their immortal souls. But especially must the young men who, out of ignorance and the lust of hot blood, consorted with them be grappled with. For the harlot could have no cause to sin if she had no one to tempt into sin.

Maybe he was due to preach another of his periodic sermons on the sin of lust and the deadly evil of harlotry. There was no doubt: the morals of the parish were in a sad state, and fornication and adultery were increasing.

In every way people were backsliding and giving way to profanity. He would have to address some stern words to his elders.

Indeed, towards this end he had scrolled out some observations. Mr. Auld perused his notes with care.

"The Kirk Session of Machlin are informed that the Lord's Day is grossly profaned in this place by both men and women, particularly the younger sort, meeting together in parties and cabals after sermon, and are seen walking and traversing the fields and highways in an indecent manner on the evening of that holy day. The Session therefore think it their duty to warn the people in this congregation, young and old, against the sin of Sabbath-breaking, and earnestly exhort parents and heads of families to command their children, servants, and all within their gates, to keep holy the day of the Lord as He has commanded, and particularly to refrain from the profanation of this holy day by idly vaiging together and by profane worldly conversation. And the members of the Session and other heads of families are desired to take notice of, and inform against, such profaners of the Sabbath, that they be spoken to privately, or censured, as the Session or Presbytery shall judge proper."

Yes, reflected Mr. Auld, there were many grievous sins being committed in the parish. But there could be little doubt that a proper and deep-seated reverence for the Lord's Day lay at the base of all Christian virtue.

And here was one of the many reasons why Mr. Auld disliked Gavin Hamilton. Not only had Mr. Hamilton set himself against him and the authority of the session; but he repeatedly disregarded Sabbath observance. Mr. Auld was certain that though this was sin enough in itself; it was, in a man of Gavin Hamilton's position, a great temptation to sin in others.

But at the thought of Gavin Hamilton, Mr. Auld got up from his desk and began to pace the floor of his study.

Hamilton must be brought sharply to book and made sharply aware that the ordinances of the Kirk and the authority of the Session could not be defied with impunity.

EXPERIENCE ORGANISED

By the end of April, spring was smiling over the land. The pastures were green and succulent and there was a healthy growth on the sown rigs. The green blush on the thorns was as fresh and as incredible as ever. The gowk had been heard in the valley, and swallows were flashing in and out of the barn door. Lapwings tossed and fretted and raged more anxiously when they were disturbed; and the whaups' wailing had now a mellow note at the heart of it. The hens were beginning to lay away; sturdy lambs enjoyed the sunshine and an abundance of ewe milk; calves no longer tottered on shaky legs, but frisked with vigour and butted their mothers' udders with over-bold affection. And though the beech, the oak and the ash had not yet broken bud, the promise of summer's richness could no longer be doubted.

Yet all the witching allure of the smiling spring did not deceive the Bard. He knew that this land, however sweet and green and pleasant, could not hold him nor give him shelter nor sustenance. The mockery of long hard bitter months lay behind that smile: they would come again when that smile had worn off. Yes: there was pain in the green magic of growth. But then, a vast impersonal melancholy had ever lain coiled at the heart of nature. And though man might escape from this melancholy by a series of man-made shifts and stratagems, he remained shackled to nature, of which he was a part.

The shifts and stratagems were occupying his full attention. His response to every over- and under-tone of nature was super-sensitive to a degree. His need to escape from the pain of nature was equally great. But indeed he now found himself in a devil's cauldron of sensation, emotion, melancholy introspection and mounting exultation. And yet, no matter what the pressure of outward circumstance upon the tension of his inward emotion, the need to organise his emotions and experiences in terms of rhyme and rhythm remained clamant as ever.

He surprised himself at the ease with which he was able, in the circumstances, to respond to the call. It seemed that the greater the pressure upon him the better the response. What did not surprise him was that, organisationally, he was master of his art. There was no need for surprise: he had served a long and arduous apprenticeship. As for experience: he had crammed a richer and deeper experience into his quarter of a century than anyone of whom he had knowledge!

And so he composed his poetry and sent round his manuscripts to his trusted friends for their criticism; and the pile for Johnnie Wilson in Kilmarnock grew imposingly.

BLACK AND WHITE

One day Gilbert, hearing him lilting an old tune, said: "I wonder whiles how it is that you can throw aside your worries so easily?"

But Robin shook his head: "I have so many worries, Gibby; but I have only one head to do the worrying. I only lay aside my worries the better able to take them up afresh.

"You saw yon two volumes of The Book I brought home from Killie the other night: you were wondering what their purpose might be? Well: since you're talking about worries, I'll let you into a secret. But this *is* a secret, Gibby, and one I will never release you from . . . You know I'm taking Mary Campbell with me to Jamaica? I've a double reason now for taking her. The good old cause, Gibby: at least that's how it looks just now, though it may be a false alarm. But Mary's leaving Stairaird at the May term and going home to prepare for the voyage. She's Highland, and her folks are even more so. Well, she's got to have some evidence of her marriage wi' me. I gave Jean Armour a bit o' paper and you saw what happened to that. But it'll no' be so easy to destroy a couple of Bibles, will it? I'll pledge her my troth on the Bibles in such a way that nobody will be able to dispute it . . . And add my Mason's mark for her father's benefit.

"But that only settles one problem in order to raise a dozen. Mary goes home to Campbeltown: I bide here. And what about the boat to take me to Jamaica? What if it comes too late for Mary? What if father Campbell takes it in his head to act like father Armour . . .?

"And you're wondering how I can cart stanes out o' this auld bawk and lilt the measure o' an auld strathspey? Or maybe you're wondering if I have any sanity left in me? Of course, Gibby, you don't need to tell me that this affair with Mary, coming so soon on the top of my trouble with Armour, will not be for my own good if it gets noised abroad. There's plenty folk wouldn't even pretend to begin to understand it. And when my own mother canna even make the attempt . . .

"As far as the world's concerned, Gibby, Mary Campbell and me just don't exist. Have I struck you dumb altogether?"

"I just don't understand you, Robin: don't understand how you can do it. Jean Armour I can understand: Jean would have tempted an archangel. But Mary Campbell? There must be something missing in my make-up: there must be some kind of reason that's been withheld from me. And I canna see Mary Campbell and a bairn in the West Indies *after* you've had time to look around you, far less *before* you've right landed. Do you mean that you want to marry her—child or no child? Do you no' think you've been driven into Mary Campbell's arms just because you were driven out o' Jean Armour's?"

Gilbert was surprised at the calmness with which he took this.

"Maybe you're right. I don't know. How should I pretend to know? I'm not Almighty God: just one of the poor creatures of His creation. All I know is that I want Mary Campbell and I don't want Jean Armour. And if both of them bear me a child within the year, don't ask me about that either. Ask God who made us both and gave us the senses and the passions such as we've got. For if I've been led astray, Gibby, then the light that led astray has been light from heaven. Or was it light from hell: or darkness, maybe? And if I have done wrong, you ken who'll have to pay for it. Who's been doing all the paying anyway: right or wrong?

"Mind you, it's a fine day: the sun's shining; and your face would make a fine study for ony philosopher. So I can talk calmly. But don't let the calmness delude you: you've seen me when I have been onything but calm. In ten minutes' time you'll maybe find that I'm not fit to be spoken to! But you know, Gibby, if honest worrying about things could really help, then not only would my problems have been solved, but everybody's connected with me . . . But since this seems to be our day for making speeches, I'll make way for you."

"No, no: I canna make speeches. But if I listened to you long enough you could convince me that black was white. I'm a human being the same as other folk; and I have my passions the same as other folk; and I like lassies as well as any other man. But I've got some sort of will-power and some sort of sense of right and wrong: I happen to think it's wrong to put a lassie in the family way before you're properly married to her . . . or even to run the risk of putting her in the family way . . . so I restrain myself and don't run any risks. It's not always easy; but you can court temptation as well as try to avoid it."

"Do you think you've ever been in love?"

"Yes: I know I have."

"No: you never put yourself to the test, Gibby. You see: the woman has a point of view as well as the man. No woman ever fell in the family way unless she wanted. At least, that's my experience . . . and the experience of plenty others. When a man and a woman are drawn together by the passion of love—or the love of passion, for it's the same thing however folk may quibble—then a third quality enters the relationship. When the steel and the tinder strike there's fire. That's a new quality, a new something that neither of the parties can generate by themselves. What you're saying is: don't come together. But the only thing to do then is to go and live on a desert island . . .

"Folk just can't help coming together: that's life. If we could rule our passions by our wills, Gibby, the problem of good and evil, pain and suffering, would be solved. For nobody would consciously will pain or evil. True, some of us have wills stronger than our passions and some of us have passions stronger than our wills. But there are others of us yet who do not find that our wills conflict with our passions but that the twain are in harmony! If you really understood my Love and Liberty you would understand that.

"The curse of morality is that it creates laws that can't be obeyed without unhappiness: so that when everybody is thoroughly unhappy, morality says they are in a state of grace! But, you see, it was man's unhappiness that drove him to make moral laws for his happiness, whereas happy men don't need moral laws . . . Damnit, Gibby, my mind's as clear as well-water the now: I could make you up a brand new philosophy where you stand. Aye: and a damned sight more to the point than half the tortured meanderings you'll find in the printed books by the learned and reverend divines."

"I've no doubt about that, Robin." Then Gilbert added in his dry way that he sometimes adopted: "But a brand new philosophy isn't going to get you out of your difficulties; and they're as old as Adam's . . ."

"Aye; and as fresh as the morn's dew that hasna fallen yet. When Eve was tempted by the serpent, the serpent was outside her. Now the serpent is inside both man and woman. And that makes a new man out of the Old Adam every time: and a new Eve out of the Old Eve. Just as we're biggin a new dyke out o' thae auld stanes. But Adam kenned nothing about dykes: just as he kenned nothing about morality."

"I give it up, Robin: I told you before you could just as well argue that black was white."

"Aye; and that would just depend on what end of morality you were looking at."

Gilbert lifted a stone and placed it on the load.

"I'm looking at the end o' this load, Robin: come on, give me a hand."

PARTING LOVE

Never did any man pack so much into his days. He was up early in the mornings and did as much as anyone the share of the farm work. And it was here that he leaned heavily on Gilbert. Where Gilbert was slow and deliberate, he was quick and decisive. He weighed up a situation in a glance and gave lightning decisions. But he left Gilbert to work out the plodding details; and Gilbert seldom acted in any decisive way without first consulting him.

Robin never realised that there was so much could be done in twenty hours (for he seldom allowed himself more than four hours of sleep). He was sensitive about the postage tax and did not like anyone to be at the expense of receiving his subscription sheet. He himself knew only too well what the expense of receiving letters could be; and often enough he had cursed the folly of worthless communications and damned their writers' stupidity. And so, with the object of saving his friends expense, and also with the wish to make personal contact, he would ride as many as twenty-five miles of an evening.

Many of these visits were social occasions, and sometimes, as when he visited old John Tennant and his family in Glenconner, he was heartily welcomed and forced to stay the night. Auld Glen (as John Tennant was affectionately known to his family and friends) was very proud of the Bard.

"Weel, Rab," he said, when he had read through the proposal sheet, "I dinna ken aught aboot the business side o' a venture like this; but I hae nae doubt as to its success. We hae copies o' some o' your verses here; and they hae been handed round till they're worn to tatters. But I could gie ye the names o' a dizzen folk that come here; and every time they come they ask if there are ony fresh verses frae you. Sae damnit, laddie, they just canna be onything else but a success. It's just a pity, though, that your father couldna hae lived to see them; for by certes, Rab, he was fell proud o' your skill o' words. Ye'll be puttin' in thae lines you wrote till his memory? Oh aye: they maun gae in whatever else comes out . . ."

The kindness he received on such visits touched him deeply. He was being made to realise, as never before, the many sincere and genuine friends he had in the West, and just how much he would miss them all when he went to the Indies.

And the quicker he could tie up his arrangements for doing so the better. Mary, caught with child, had decided that she must leave Stairaird on the servants' term day. Every minute was bringing that hour of parting nearer.

And Mary was taking it bravely. She was smiling and hopeful and determined that everything would work out all right in the end. As long as she could take home evidence of their marriage, and provided they could sail before her child was born, there would be little to worry about.

She was pleased with the idea of the Bibles. To take an oath on the Bible was binding enough on any conscience; but to write out an oath on the Book was binding beyond any possibility of breaking. Her father would never doubt the sanctity of that oath nor would he doubt the intentions and the honour of the man who thus bound himself—especially with his Mason's secret mark. It remained that their union had not been blessed by the Kirk, and she had worried and was still worrying about this. She would not be able to tell her parents about Jean Armour and how it was that her husband had the certainty of scandal weighing on him from the Machlin Session. It would be difficult to explain this to anyone who did not know Robert and the circumstances of his treatment by the Armours. And there was no doubt that her father would ask uncomfortable questions.

But Mary knew only too well that she had to live her own life and that nothing her father could do would relieve her of the drudgery of service: only Robert could relieve her of that burden. And if she could only lay down the burden of service by taking up the burden of motherhood then the burden would be of her own making and a light enough load to bear, since she was gaining a husband in the process. She would not, of course, tell her parents about her pregnancy . . . not at the outset. And maybe if the boat came soon enough there would be no need to tell them.

But the parting was at hand and still there was no news of the sailing date. It was Sunday, the fourteenth of May, in the year of Eighty-six . . . She had packed her kist on the Saturday. Securely roped, it was lying in the shelter of the cart-shed ready for the journey to catch the fly at Machlin on the Monday morning . . .

Now that she was actually going she knew something of fear . . . Robert had not yet given her the Bibles as he had promised. He had promised he would bring them this afternoon. She did not doubt him in any respect; but irrational fear could not be set aside by any lack of doubt. She was Highland and carried a load of Highland superstition in the irrational centres of her being.

The morning had been misty and cold; but now the sun had broken through and already the day was perfect in its warmth and sun-drenched freshness. With an eager heart she draped her plaid lightly about her shoulders and went across the stepping-stones that forded the Ayr, and made for the green covert where they had trysted to meet.

There were green thorns there; but their tryst was not beneath a green thorn. For some reason she could not comprehend, Robert was apprehensive of a thorn tree . . . And so it was in a sheltered nook beside the banks of the Machlin Burn that purled to the Ayr with a slow and languorous rhythm (though it sometimes fell over a rocky ledge) that their tryst was concealed and shaded with the delicate filigree shadow-tracery of small-leafed birken trees . . .

There the ferns were opening their wondrous fronds, while across the narrow stream the thorns were about to burst forth in a riot of scent-languid blossom. There, on the moss-soft grass-green bank, Mary spread her plaid and, having made certain she had not been observed, waited for her lover, her husband, and the father of her unborn child . . . Waited eagerly and with fervent anticipation for the parting hour that she knew would come . . . and pass away too soon . . .

It was like a young god that he came to her that day, coming with a lover's soft call in his throat and a wave of his arm . . . and the Bibles pressed in his other oxter. Like a young god in his light blue coat with the big buttons, the plush breeks, the white cotton hose, the buckles to his brogans, and the dazzling white of his Holland cravat . . . and the wide sweep and elegant curl to the brim of his hat. Like a young god's was the soft vibrant lover's call in the deep husky throat of him; below the brim of his hat the flash of his great burning eyes . . .

He was at her side. Down on the plaid beside her, his arms around her, his lips urgent and searing on her lips, the deft stroke of his hand upon her bosom . . . Then the quick sweet flow of his words; words that poured in passion's urgency and passion's fire-urgent sweetness; words that soothed and caressed and yet raised the deepest and most violent fire of desire . . . And in a moment she had yielded to him as she had always yielded . . .

There was a scent from the thorns across the yard of soft murmuring water . . . A heavy, indescribable effluvium that seemed to drug her senses and add an acute ecstasy to her passion, so that she was almost ready to cry out aloud in her exquisite, fine-drawn agony . . .

And then he lay with his head in the crook of her arm, breathing softly and with a rhythmic sense of delicious lassitude . . . Too early yet for him to arouse himself in a soft-spoken intelligibility of words . . . Let her enjoy and cherish this moment . . . this hour and this moment of time . . . She was pregnant: nothing could undo that now . . . nor would she want it undone . . . Now she knew why there was a continual procession of cutty-stool penitents. To men and women had been given an awareness of sensation that could not be denied . . . A sensation more clamant, more incessant, less to be denied than the sensation of hunger and want and the sensation of fear . . . This was the forbidden fruit that would not be forbade, that could not be forbidden. A paradise of passion that could not be gainsaid, even though the flames of eternal damnation licked around its outer fringes . . . This was why, since God had created man in His own image and since Adam had delved and Eve had spun, the fruit of the tree of the Knowledge of Good and Evil had to be eaten and consumed regardless of any consequences . . . And surely life, that was so terrible and wonderful, had to be terrible and wonderful in its creation and at the point of its creation . . .

And where the birken dance of sunshine and shadow played on the dappled page, he explained the meaning of his inscription: Thou shalt not swear false oaths . . . Surely here there was something that could not be denied either in this world or in the world to come . . . And there was his handwriting, bold and clear and without any trace of equivocation . . . Thou shalt not swear false oaths: but that was what the lad who had lain in her arms could never do . . .

"Our ship will come, Mary: have no fear . . . But God, lass, on a day like this it's hard to think of parting from Auld Scotia . . .! Have you no feelings that way at all? Well, maybe it is that Scotland does not mean the same to you as it does to me . . . Sometimes I think of Scotland as my Auld Mither in a sense perhaps that only poets understand . . . Maybe that's what being a poet really means: understanding history in terms of the Auld Mither . . . If Scotland were only a piece of land bounded by waters and a strip of earth between the Tweed and the Solway, then the idea would be ridiculous . . . But Scotland is more than a piece of land. It is a very particular piece of land. It's a land that has given shelter to a race of people for many hundreds of years, so that the folk here know of no other land: homeland, Mary . . . I know that for you the heights and hollows of Ayr can mean little or nothing . . . That's why I would like to see the hills of *your* homeland before I go. Ah, but that's not all of Scotland I would like to see before I cross the ocean. The Campbells were on the wrong side at Drummossie Moor . . . but that's an old story now. But I'd like to see the graves of the clansmen there. And I'd like to see the field of Bannockburn . . . and the sad field of Flodden. And yet, tied to the plough-stilts, what could I see—except what I could see with my inner eye. Oh, I could see plenty with that: too much maybe for my own happiness. Of course, I'm sorry to be leaving Scotland . . . but glad to be going with you. Strange, is it not, that I should have so many regrets at leaving and that you should have none . . .?"

"But life . . . or Scotland . . . means nothing to me, Robert, if you are not there. Wherever you are then I'm happy and can be knowing no regrets."

"Only you could say that, Mary, *and mean it*. Maybe you think that I love Scotland more than I love you? But no: I love Scotland with a son's love: not as I love the lass of my bosom . . . And that's the hell and the heaven of life, Mary . . . having two loves . . . Oh, having a hundred loves . . . Songs and the words to fit fine melodies and fine men and women to sing them: a fine land to give background to sweet singing . . . And dear companions, Mary: they're important too. Life is nothing to live it by yourself. The purpose of life, Mary, is to live it socially. What do we see in the world around us but social strife and social injustice: and how could it be otherwise when life itself is unjust at its base?

"I've given this a lot of thought, Mary; and I've had cause. I've had its injustice hammered into me since the day I was born. But social life, life based on social justice and social plenty . . . Think what a paradise this country of ours could be if only folks could be brought to see that?

"But then, you see, the values to-day are the values of money. What will men not do for money? They make themselves and everybody around them unhappy in the pursuit of money. They think that there must be some value in money for itself . . . just to have it within their grasp. But the real and enduring pleasures o' this world, Mary, canna be bought with money. You and me sitting here: we havena a penny to our names; and yet—look at the riches we're enjoying! Aye: just at this moment. The hell is that decent folks should have their guts twisted just because they don't happen to have the siller to pay for the privilege of living. And is it not a sin that it should have to be paid for, seeing it's a gift frae God and not a man-made thing at all? Some day, I'm sure, man will realise that he has been a bluidy fool wasting his life pursuing money. Maybe you think I shouldna be talking this way when this is our last time together for a while——"

"No, I like to hear you talk, Robert, for you make me understand things clearly that I've often thought about myself . . . and sometimes I have been frightened to think about them. Maybe you think that I like working here: or that sometimes I didna envy Mrs. Hamilton! I know it's a sin to be envying the big folks and that it's God's will that they should be where they are and we should be where we are——"

"No, no, Mary: you must not blame God for the way things are ordered. The rich and the poor were not made so by God—but by man. Mind you: I'm not saying that there are no good men who are rich men. It has aey been a puzzle to me that folks canna see the right way of this. You mind when the children of Israel forsook the Lord and started worshipping the Golden Calf? What do we do nowadays? When you go to the kirk on the Sabbath it looks as if we had not forsaken the Lord. Ah, but what have we done with the Golden Calf? We've melted the calf down and then put it through a stamping machine with the image o' Royal Geordie. There is no sense in bowing down to a golden calf when we can stuff it into our wallets where nobody can see it. But don't ever be tempted to blame the Lord, Mary, when it's man's inhumanity to man that makes countless thousands mourn . . . Aye: man's inhumanity to man . . . There was a Garden of Eden once: the memory of it has never died from men's minds . . . Indeed, Mary, I sometimes think that there have been many Gardens of Eden. But aey the serpent o' man's greed has entered into it and destroyed it. How many times this has happend we will never know. But we'll hae a Garden of Eden in Scotland again, never fear . . . And we'll find ways and means o' keeping the serpent out of it . . .

"But now, my Mary, there's our Garden of Eden to speak about. You understand how it's to be? I'll write and tell you as soon as Doctor Douglas and me get the ship settled on. Aye: it canna come soon enough, Mary; for me as well as you. I don't want to have to face the Session for Jean Armour; but maybe if she bides in Paisley there'll be nae need for that. I'd like to see my poems off the press; and I'll see what I can do to push on Johnnie Wilson in Killie. But if the boat comes, then we'll sail—poems or no poems . . . You'll come across to Greenock: it's almost certain to sail from there. And that should be handy enough for you seeing your uncle bides there. Anyway, you've got to keep up your spirits for you ken it'll no' be long. There's no fear that your father will turn you out should be discover how things are?"

"No: not when I can show him the Bibles . . . It's a pity, Robert, that I canna write; but maybe I could be learning? Do you think it would be taking me a long time?"

"If I had the time, Mary, I could have you writing in a week or two."

"Maybe I could be getting the session clerk or the schoolmaster himself to be writing me out a bit note to say that I was keeping all right; but I couldna be asking him to say more than that, could I?"

"If you get him to say that you'll do fine. And I won't be able to say a great deal myself, Mary. You never know into whose hands a letter might fall."

"If you just say you are well and when the boat will be sailing, that will be all the news I will be wanting."

Robert drew out from his pocket a napkin with cheese and bread and spread it on the plaid.

"We might as well have a bite now, Mary: I don't know about you, but I'm beginning to feel the pangs o' hunger; and it's a long time since I had my morning bite."

They enjoyed a last meal together, and washed it down with a lave of water from the burn.

They were both in a mood of deep happiness. There was no need to worry about time, for time had stopped for them: the cup of the day and its happiness was theirs to be drained to the less . . .

But deeper than the deepest layer of their happiness was the strange feeling that they were doomed; that however much they planned and hoped, Fate would determine otherwise; that the happiness they were enjoying now would have to be paid for in tears and sorrow in the days to come. This feeling was with Mary Campbell, for she had known much sorrow and suffering. Exile and service did not bend the mind to a deep faith in the permanency of happiness. When she was a little girl she had heard tales round the fireside of days that had been happy, days that had seemed to stretch away back to the kind of Garden of Eden that Robert had spoken about . . . days before the clansmen had gone out never to return. But she remembered tales of hunger and want and cruel killings from those days too—days before the Sasunnach speech had been heard in the clachans.

But Mary's pessimism was not at the forefront of her mind; and there was the immediacy of Robert Burns to work a very different kind of spell on her.

They had drunk their fill of love and the happiness of their companionship; and they had talked their minds empty—for the moment. They had discussed their hopes and fears, ambitions and desires; and their senses had flowed with the rapture of the hour.

But the sun went down behind the hill of Stairaird; the shadows deepened; and the night air brought a cold rustling among the leaves. The actual severance of their physical presences could no longer be delayed. The parting had to be now.

Robert had his own deep fears; but his sympathy was all for Mary's. And he knew that her fear that somehow something might intervene to destroy their future happiness was uppermost. At once his mind supplied the solution that would give dramatic point and significance to their moment of parting.

He raised Mary from the plaid.

"We'll take the pledge of our parting, Mary, across the surety of running water. It's an auld wives' superstition, sure enough, but there's little sense in scorning it for all that."

"I would like that, Robert. Always I will be hearing the music of the burn whatever else I will be hearing."

"And there's no sweeter music, Mary."

He jumped the burn and stretched his hand across: she reached out and clasped it.

"To our love, Mary, and its pledging till the day that our life-blood flows to the sea of eternal rest . . ."

Along the bosky banks the bird-song had faded and died away. And the song had died in the hearts of Robert Burns and Mary Campbell . . .

The agony of parting consumed them. How and when they would meet again was agonisingly uncertain. They could put no words on their deepest fears; but they feared deeply.

He saw her safely across the stepping-stones beside the pebbly shore below the Stairaird bluff. He saw her to the safety of the byre-gable; and he held her tenderly in a last lingering embrace.

3

FAME WITHOUT FORTUNE

JOLLY MORTALS

No-one noted the departure of Mary Campbell: not an eyebrow was raised, nor did a solitary tongue wag. In the coming and going of the Servants' Day she passed unnoticed.

But Machlin was buzzing with rumours regarding Jean Armour: not only did malicious gossip have it that she was courting Robert Wilson (there was no suggestion that he might be courting her); but it was asserted with much salacious detail that Jean, in the safety of her condition, was being generous with her favours.

These rumours, which reached the Bard in a carefully-edited form, roused him to a frenzy, and folks had to be mindful how they approached him. He cast suspicion from him with vehement indignation; but in the very act of doing so the traces of suspicion scarred his memory.

Jamie Smith, who knew so well both Jean and Wilson, was the only one in whom he could confide; and James was sceptical.

"Bob Wilson's no' a bad-looking fellow; and he's gotten plenty o' the world's gear . . . But I just canna see Jean having onything to do wi' him in that way. Coorse, you ken Jean better than I do and maybe . . . No: I would pay no attention, Robin: they're the damnedest rotten liars in Machlin—ye ken that as well as I do. But you still hae a notion o' Jean?"

"I don't know what I have, Jamie. I'm finished with her and she wi' me . . . Still, it's my bairn she's carrying. And if I thought

Wilson as much as laid a hand on her I'd tear the liver out of him. I know what rumour can do and I know what lies folk can tell."

"Weel: they ran to the school thegither when he was in Machlin: it could be honest friendship."

"Aye: it could be honest friendship: if friendship in such circumstances were likely to remain honest. Hell! how I wish my boat was settled for the Indies."

"And what about your poems now?"

"I saw my printer the other day: we'd high words. You know my dedication to Ga'n Hamilton? He was near for cutting it out of the book altogether. So he's going to slip it somewhere into the middle where it will not be conspicuous. It surprised me; but it seems that Gavin Hamilton's not just so popular at the moment. Certainly Johnnie Wilson doesna like him and neither does Tam Samson. Anyway, Johnnie says that to dedicate my poems to him will get up the backs of the Auld Lichts."

"By God! it's a fine world where a man canna print his own poems the way he wants. What does Johnnie ken about a poem onyway?"

"Oh, he's no fool . . . But you see, Jamie: the only real freedom we've got is the freedom to think. You can think what you like, and in certain circumstances you can say what you like; but the moment you appear before the public you must cease to be your private self. Then you must don the mantle o' your public self: get a false-face to put on for the public benefit. You become like a preacher or a politician: disguise yourself and gull the public behind a mask. As a matter o' fact, Jamie, I'm not sure but that the public prefer the mask to the genuine man. The functionaries o' the Kirk and State seem to prove that onyway. Still . . . I don't intend to don the mask. Maybe I'll have to sacrifice Love and Liberty and Holy Willie's Prayer; but I'll leave in enough to make sure that the public know what kind o' poet I am."

"But must you leave out Love and Liberty? 'I am a Bard of no regard wi' gentle folks an' a' that, but Homer-like the glowerin' byke, frae town to town I draw that.' "

"Dinna vex me, Jamie. I ken better than anyone just how much o' my best inspiration is in that set o' sangs and verses. I may never do anything better. But maybe, too, its impact on the unco guid would prove too much for my volume—at this stage! Wilson's opinion is that already the volume's over-loaded. Maybe I'll get a chance some day—somewhere . . . to publish what I really want— without any damned niggling interference, supervision and censorship. Still, as I say, Jamie: Wilson's no fool. He's adopted nearly all my suggestions about the printing, the style o' binding and the bits o' decoration for the text. It'll be as handsome a volume of its kind as has ever come out o' Scotland. But here: have you seen this in the Edinburgh paper? There, man: read that column about the fell doings o' The Highland Society."

Smith became red with indignation as he read how the Highland Society, meeting in the Shakespeare, Covent Garden, London, under the presidency of the Earl of Breadalbane, had concerted ways and means to frustrate the designs of five hundred Highlanders who, as the Society were informed by MacKenzie of Applecross, were so audacious as to attempt an escape from their lawful lords and masters whose property they were, by emigrating from the lands of MacDonnell of Glengary to the wilds of Canada—"in search," as Robin put it, "of that fantastic thing: Liberty."

"The damned slave-owners!" said Jamie. "Sitting smugly down there in Lunnon!"

"Aye: slave-owners, Jamie: titled Highland slave-owners! It's a wonder some o' their Lowland cousins dinna think to prevent me sailing for jamaica. For the puir devils i' the North are seeking the same kind o' freedom as I seek. But they canna get it in Scotland any more than I can. What right have I to liberty? And what right have they? You see, neither o' us hae money nor land nor property: we're only vermin. Breadalbane! Glengary! Applecross! Lord God, I'm vermin to a bit mason-body like James Armour because he could buy and sell me ony market-day.

"That's the trouble, Jamie; and aey has been. Lack o' siller, lack o' the warld's gear. Never mind the generosity o' the heart, or the richness o' the mind or the nobility o' the spirit! But a stack o' yella Geordies! There's a passport for you! It tells you plainly in the Book that a rich man just canna enter the Kingdom o' Heaven. But d'you think they're worrying about Heaven? The yella Geordies will get them onywhere on this earth—and here and now's all their concern. If I'd the money I wadna be sailing for the Indies—nor would I be beholden to Johnnie Wilson to say what he'll print o' my verses. I'd print what I wanted—and damn the consequences."

"And damn right, Robin! But I'm for getting out o' Machlin as soon as I can: I've too many enemies. If I could get a good job in the Indies I'd come wi' you."

"Come on: we'll stretch our legs round by Catrine and Ballochmyle and talk things over: it's a fine night for it."

"I canna the nicht, Robin. I'm just waiting on an agent riding doon frae Paisley wi' some shawls and silks for me: I've orders agin them. But if you're coming back this way, look in at Dow's: I'll be round about nine—the agent'll be putting up there . . ."

His steps had taken him in the direction of Ballochmyle woods and the rich green shaws of Catrine. It had been one of his favourite walks since he had come to Machlin. But wherever there were woods and running water he was happy. And now among the trees, heavy with the lushness of mid-summer, he was lost in an ageless magic. Nature was the lass that could be loved without the moral edicts of Thou Shalt and Thou Shalt Not. And yet she was a lass who revealed her secrets only to those who came wooing her: her beauty withered under the ravisher's hands . . . and the ravisher's eyes.

He laid himself down on a quiet bank in the rays of the dying June sun. Nature bathed him with the healing balm of her beauty. The stillness crept into his bones and lay softly along his heart; and a great and abiding harmony filled his soul. His thoughts became as still as a millpond, till gradually he had no thoughts and not even the gnats of transient imagery danced above the stillness. He had sunk below the level of thought; and so he was beyond the trouble of worry and the anxiety of care.

In the great green womb of Nature there are no laws of morality; for Nature is mindless and she forges no shackles of duty for those who know her love. But deep in her oneness lies the secret of Eden's bonnie yard; and the fall of man . . . a secret more elusive than the flutter of a moth in the scent of a night-rose and more real than the red rip of a claw in the silken-down curve of an unguarded belly . . .

He knew the oneness of nature: knew that all life flowed from a common source . . . and returned there; knew that the endless patterns of life were but patterns; knew that the spark in the mouse and the spark in the man were sparks from the same fire, the fire that generated all life . . .

There was nothing strange or esoteric or mystical about this knowledge that enabled him to lie quiescent on the mossy bank. It was knowledge like any other knowledge and to be used like any other knowledge. There was no need to wrap it in mystical words or to muddy the stream of thought with the confused hart-pantings of pantheism . . .

When he came out of his dwam he recalled the passage he had read in the Edinburgh paper. He came back to full consciousness with the fire of burning words lighting up his mind. His sympathy ran fierce and deep for Glengary's chattels. They were seeking what he was seeking himself: freedom and liberty and the possibility of earning a living for himself and his dependants; for the chance to live like a man and not as a slave. It seemed that wherever the sun shone, whether in Kyle or in Glengary, around the knoll of Bunker's Hill or about the Black Hole of Calcutta, it was not the caprices of nature that burdened man, but man's inhumanity to man. And it was only man who could correct the errors of man: it was only man who could assert the rights of humanity against the wrongs of inhumanity and raise, against whatever odds, the banner of freedom.

And when he had reviewed the lines in his mind he felt relieved and refreshed. The gloaming was over all the land; and the land was so hushed and still that it seemed there had never been an angry word spoken in the world, or that the blood of a brother had ever been spilled in the sacred earth in the murderous moment of a foul deed.

Coming out of the wood onto the dew-laid dust of the road, he knew, as he had always known though never with such clarity, that just as man expiated in blood and tears his fall from grace down the tortured centuries, so must he struggle in blood and tears to regain that grace.

For grace there must have been in that eternal glory of gloaming when the Great Architect rested from His labours and noted the goodness of His handiwork.

True, Genesis was the dream of an ancient poet; but was it any the less real for that? Was it any less real for being compounded of the interaction of blood and brain than a plough-coulter that was compounded of fire and inorganic matter?

As he came down in the candle-light dusk on the huddle of Machlin roofs, he was once more confirmed that dream or no dream, Architect or no Architect, man's struggle was with the here and now, and that the wherefore and the why would in the fullness of time be added unto him.

Quickening his step he made for the back room of the Whitefoord Arms. He hoped he would find company there; that he might rejoice once again in the sons of men and find an audience for his *Address of Beelzebub*.

He found a worthy audience. Cracking with the host, at the entrance, was John Rankine of Adamhill. The Bard was delighted to see him.

They shook hands warmly and Johnnie Dow clapped them both on the shoulders.

"Come in, you pair o' daft beggars, and we'll drain a measure or twa. Wee Smith's waiting ben the hoose for you, Rab . . . aye, and the Tanner, Mattha Morison, Tabaccy Ronald and a wheen ithers."

"And what the hell hae you gotten agin my respected brither-in-law?"

"Damned, I'm sorry, Adamhill. Aye: the Bard frae Muirkirk's here, Rab: clean went oot o' my mind."

"What! John Lapraik? By certes, John, but I've got a rare swatch o' rhyme ready for the lot o' them . . . By the way: I see from the Edinburgh Courant that the Lords o' the Session are still rouping off MacLure and Campbell: how did Adamhill come under the hammer?"

"It's the damnedest hell's broth o' a mix-up, Rab; but dinna get me started on David MacLure o' Shawood or I'll set fire to Johnnie's thatch. I'll tell you that story some other day when we have the peace o' our ain company."

The company were soon in a grand mood of expectation. John Rankine had announced that the Bard would give them a new poem and had told his good-brother, John Lapraik, to redd the hay-seed out of his ears in order the better to receive the treat that was coming. Ronald, the tobacconist, expressed the hope that the new verses would be strong in moral uplift and edifying content; but he was immediately howled out of order and told to go and seek the company of Holy Willie. But Ronald had no such intention. He would wait and criticise. The Bard tolerated his criticisms: when Ronald expressed his dislike he knew that he was on the right lines. And as Tabaccy Ronald supplied him with his papers, it was convenient to let him assume the role of moral critic . . .

But the Bard was in no mood to plunge straight into his *Address*: he would allow tensions to be eased and the stage to be set before he commenced.

John Rankine and Jamie Smith knew this.

"Come on, Jamie," roared the farmer: "let's hae the Fiddler's Sang frae Love and Liberty."

"Let's hae the Sailor's Sang first," cried the Tanner.

Robin looked round the company and his gaze came to rest on the bowed and quiet figure of John Lapraik.

"Where's your manners, gentlemen? John: since the lads are determined to have a sang of mine, what's your choice?"

"It's got to be frae Love and Liberty!" insisted Adamhill.

"I like a' your sangs in Love and Liberty, Robin; but if there was a woman here there's nothing I wad rather hear at the moment than I Once Was a Maid Though I Canna Tell When."

Johnnie Dow exploded on such a tremendous oath that Ronald swallowed a mouthful of ale the wrong road and, if John Rankine hadn't hit him such a blow between the shoulders as sent him staggering across the room, the probability is that he would have choked.

"I'll tell you what!" roared the host. "I'll get the guidwife ben tae sing you I Once Was a Maid; and by God! she can dae it rare justice."

The company agreed to this with genuine enthusiasm. And then Johnnie hesitated. "Wad ye gae ben and ask her, Rab? She wad dae onything for you."

Robin instantly made for the door. When he had gone Johnnie pulled a wry face. "The wife was just speaking aboot Rab the ither nicht. 'John,' she says, 'gin I had been ten year younger I'd hae had him in bed wi' me and ye could hae gaen till the attic wi' the lass.' "

Above the laughter could be heard the voice of the Tanner. "But no' the lass ye hae the now, Johnnie!"

Ronald with his Jessie-expression said: "There's no question that Robert is very popular wi' the ladies; but Mistress Dow would only be joking."

"Joking? Gae ben the kitchen and see what's keeping them. But by certes, Muirkirk, wait till ye hear her wi' that sang. Damnt, ye'll say she's the Martial Chuck herself: and I'm the only bedmate she ever kenned."

With that, they heard from the passage the merry peal of her laughter, and in a moment Robert was ushering her into the room, his arm round her shoulder.

"Now, Landlady: we havena had the pleasure of your top notes this while back. But we hae a worthy bard here frae Muirkirk, a guid-brither o' Adamhill: so let him hear what a Machlin guidwife can dae wi' a Machlin sang."

"Richt ye are then, Rab; but my range is a wee roosty wi' want o' practice."

The company gave her vigorous encouragement; and then Robert held up his hand for silence and, with head uplifted and her features composed, she sang:

"I once was a maid, though I cannot tell when, and still my delight is in proper young men. Some one of a troop of dragoons was my daddy: no wonder I'm fond of a sodger laddie!"

Most of them took up the "lal de lal" chorus in the same spirit as she had sung the verse: that is, with a balance of pride and tenderness that immediately won a hushed response for the next verse.

"The first of my loves was a swaggering blade: to rattle the thundering drum was his trade; his leg was so tight and his cheek was so ruddy, transported I was with my sodger laddie."

Once in his young days (he was now coming sixty) John Lapraik had had the notion of being a sodger laddie—then indeed had his own leg been tight and his cheek apple-ruddy. He could picture that red-coated laddie now, even as he had pictured himself then. But, by the Lord, Johnnie Dow's wife could do the song rare justice.

"But the godly old chaplain left him in the lurch; the sword I forsook for the sake of the church; he risked the soul, and I ventured the body: t'was then I proved false to my sodger laddie.

"Full soon I grew sick of my sanctified sot; the regiment at large for a husband I got; from the gilded spontoon to the fife I was ready: I asked no more but a sodger laddie.

"But the Peace it reduced me to beg in despair, till I met my old boy in a Cunninghame Fair; his rags regimental they fluttered so gaudy: my heart it rejoiced at a sodger laddie.

"And now I have lived—I know not how long! But still I can join in a cup and a song; and whilst with both hands I can hold the glass steady, here's to thee, my hero, my sodger laddie!"

And when she had finished, the Bard from Muirkirk rose from his corner and, with tears in his eyes, shook her by the hand; and then he put his arm round her shoulder and gave her a kiss on the flush of her cheek.

The gesture was greeted with applause; and the landlord went ben the passage to fetch a supply of Kilbagie in honour of the occasion. They were in for a night of it; and now that he had secured his wife's good favour he was determined that the night, in so far as he was concerned, would be worthy of the occasion.

As Robert saw they were determined to go through his *Love and Liberty*, he came in with the linking passages. Tanner Hunter, Wee Smith and John Rankine sang in turn, and he was much gratified to observe how well they had committed his songs to memory.

But as they sang and as he recited, he could not help reflecting that it was across the gap of the Cowgate that the gangrels had first met and had provided him with the inspiration that had determined the form of his cantata; and that he had had to take their defiance, and the bold philosophical line he had given them, out of the doss-house into the ken of normal men so that they might be inspired to reach out to a higher and freer form of life . . .

And when at last they reached the final chorus and the thundering voice of John Rankine almost brought down the walls (it attracted Holy Willie to cock an inquiring ear at the window outside), it seemed that the love of liberty was in their hearts and heads. He had never heard "a fig for those by law protected, liberty's a glorious feast," rendered with such tempestuous spirit.

Holy Willie scurried away from the window in mortal terror. The devil himself must be in the body of that terrible man Burns. The Lord would strike, and strike hard, for such blood-curdling blasphemy. Willie got out his horse and cantered home to Montgarswood, lest somehow the devil or Burns or both came after him. But beneath his fear was the realisation that he had failed in his duty to the Lord in not boldly entering Dow's house and clearing out the devil's spawn. He would go home and wrestle with them in prayer: that was the surest and best way of defeating them and all their works.

When the company had refreshed themselves and patted each other on the back and voiced their approval of the Bard, Rankine rose and made a statement. The Bard had a new poem for them and they were fortunate and honoured in having the opportunity to hear it. It seemed that the time would come when he would leave them to go over the ocean to seek his fortune in the region of the Indies: especially that fabulous place where so many fortunes had been made—Jamaica. It would be a sad day when the Bard left them. He claimed to have enjoyed a longer acquaintance with him than any of them. And right from the beginning of their acquaintanceship he had recognised the poet in him and had watched the fire of his genius grow brighter and brighter. He had not the slightest doubt that when the Poems were printed and the book came out from Kilmarnock that everyone in the West would immediately recognise that a great poet was leaving their midst. And he hoped that as a result of the reception his verses would get that he might somehow or other be induced to remain among them.

No: he wasn't going to make a speech: though, by God! if it came to making a speech about the Bard then he would make a speech with the best man living . . . But he wanted the company gathered here to-night, gathered as they were in their usual un-rehearsed way of good-fellowship, not to take the occasion too lightly. And he wanted the Bard to know that even if he had to go to the Indies, he would leave behind him friends in the West who would never forget him, and who would meet from time to time—the way they had met tonight—in Ayr, Tarbolton, Kilmarnock and Machlin, or wherever they might find themselves, and that they would sing his songs and recite his verses and keep his memory green till the day when he was once more back amongst them. Aye; and whether he had made his fortune or not: fortune did not matter to them so far as friendship was concerned. His going would be bad fortune for all of them: his coming back would be a greater fortune than all the fortunes that had ever been made in the Indies—East or West. He, John Rankine, his old friend and brother-farmer—and brother of the mystic tie—would remember that on his own behalf and on behalf of all of them gathered here—aye, and of many who had not the good fortune to be gathered here to-night . . . What the Bard had to say to them he didn't know; but anything that bore the imprint of his genius would be more than welcome . . .

Robert arose to a storm of welcome. He was moved; but he showed no trace of emotion on his face, which was calm to the point of distance.

"Thank you, John: my thanks to you one and all . . . If there is a greater thing in this life than honest friendship then I do not know what it is. When my appointed hour comes to say farewell to Scotland, it won't be easy . . . But I'm not away yet; and before then I hope to enjoy many nights of good-fellowship with you. Now, about my new verses: those of you who read the prints will have seen how the Highland Society met the other day in London.

"Some of you may think that it's a far cry frae Glengary to Machlin; but however far it is, it is still the same cry. And for me, as for the Highlanders of the North, it is a gey bitter cry: the cry for liberty that we cannot have answered in our native land. Aye; and there is bitterness enough here. We may breathe the air; and we may lift up our eyes, when we straighten our backs, to the hills . . . We may even till the soil if we have rent enough to pay for the privilege. But the glorious feast of liberty is not for us to enjoy: not in our native land. That is why so many of our sons are driven, year after year, to leave our native shores and to seek freedom in distant lands—but especially that land where our cousins and kinsmen have struck such a valiant blow for liberty—the Americas. But those poor devils of our Highland countrymen are not to be allowed the freedom to seek freedom; and that's irony enough for any man. And who, pray, is not to allow them freedom to emigrate? Not German Geordie, as we might expect. Once on a day not so far distant, the Chief was the father of the Clan: now he is the feudal lord treating his children like a herd of stirks to be disposed of as he thinks best and without any consideration of their feelings. It was on this theme that I threw these lines together in the white heat of anger. You are to imagine Beelzebub addressing the gallant Highland gentry in the person of the President, the Right Honourable the Earl of Breadalbane.

"Long life, my lord, an' health be yours, unskaithed by hungered Highland boors! Lord grant nae duddie, desperate beggar, wi' dirk, claymore, or rusty trigger, may twin auld Scotland o' a life she likes—as lambkins like a knife!

"Faith! you and Applecross were right to keep the Highland hounds in sight! I doubt na! they wad bid nae better than let them ance put owre the water! Then up amang thae lakes and seas, they'll mak' what rules and laws they please: some daring Hancock, or a Franklin, may set their Highland bluid a-ranklin'; some Washington again may head them or some Montgomerie, fearless, lead them; till (God knows what may be effected when by such heads and hearts directed) poor dunghill sons of dirt an' mire may to Patrician rights aspire! Nae sage North now, nor sager Sackville, to watch and premier owre the pack vile! An' whare will ye get Howes and Clintons to bring them to a right repentance? To cowe the rebel generation, an' save the honour o' the nation? They, an' be damned! what right hae they to meat or sleep or light o' day, far less to riches, power, or freedom, but what your lordship likes to gie them?

"But hear, my lord! Glengary, hear! Your hand's owre light on them, I fear: your factors, grieves, trustees and bailies, I canna say but they do gaylies: they lay aside a' tender mercies, an' tirl the hullions to the birses. Yet while they're only poind and herriet, they'll keep their stubborn Highland spirit. But smash them! crush them a' to spails, an' rot the dyvors i' the gaols! The young dogs, swinge them to the labour: let wark an' hunger mak' them sober! The hizzies, if they're aughtlins fawsont, let them in Drury Lane be lessoned! An' if the wives an' dirty brats come thigging at your doors an' yetts, flaffin' wi' duds, an' grey wi' beas', frightin' awa your deuks an' geese, get out a horsewhip or a jowler, the langest thong, the fiercest growler, an' gar the tattered gypsies pack wi' a' their bastards on their back!

"Go on, my Lord! I lang to meet you, an' in my 'house at hame' to greet you. Wi' common lords ye shanna mingle: the benmost neuk beside the ingle, at my right han' assigned your seat 'tween Herod's hip an' Polycrate, or (if you on your station tarrow) between Almagro and Pizarro, a seat, I'm sure ye're weel deserv-in't; an' till ye come—your humble servant."

As he had spoken his lines, in a voice of tremendous edge and irony, he had grown away from the howff till he seemed only to be a voice speaking there and not a presence. Rather was his presence beyond their knowledge and understanding. Only John Rankine followed him in his mental voyage: Lapraik would have liked to have followed, but he was too old, and liberty, though dear to him who had known incarceration in Ayr gaol through the failure of the Douglas and Heron Bank, was not such a glorious feast now. But men like Tabaccy Ronald and the Tanner and Mattha Morison, the joiner, though they could understand every line of the poem, could not follow the thought that lay behind the lines. The Bard here was beyond their ken: he was much too big for them.

Only John Rankine knew that he was fit to address the parlia-ment of the world when he was in this mood. A strange lad, he thought, as he listened; and there was no getting to the bottom of his strangeness. A moment ago he had been one of themselves, laughing and joking and singing and making fun with the best.

And now he stood there in the corner of the room speaking in a different voice with a different intonation and looking a different man: a man remote and austere; a man it would be difficult to approach and almost impossible to make contact with. He had seen him in this mood before. Even at his ingle-cheek he had watched the transformation. It was, he supposed, the transformation of the man into the poet; when the everyday exterior of the man fell away and the inner man began to shine through, began to take control . . .

At his own level Wee Smith also understood. But his under-standing was not as deep as Rankine's. For Rankine too, as he had already explained to Robert, had once been a poet and had had the poet suppressed in him by the turn of event and circum-stance; and he had a much deeper experience of life than Smith had or could have had.

And the Bard, though he appeared to be distant from the room, was held there only by the contact of John Rankine: for his was the only presence of which he was conscious.

And so, when the *Address* was over, it was Adamhill that bounded to his feet and came over and shook his hand.

"I doubt nor Wilson will let that gae into print, Rab; but let me hae a copy o' that, for it's the best thing o' its kind ye hae ever done. God Almighty! what a pity the Highland Society hadna been present the nicht to hae heard that: they would hae filled their blunderbuses wi' roosty nails and gaen out to the midden and blawn their rotten brains out!"

But the Bauld Lapraik was cautious. "Canny, Mossgiel: if that gets abroad they'll clap ye in the gaol on some pretext or ither and that's a' the Indies ye'll ever see. Ye've a skill there that beats a'; but oh, laddie, ye canna flay the gentry—even the Highland gentry—like that and expect them to dae nocht about it! Ye've enough fire there to cause anither Rebellion . . ."

"Exactly, Muirkirk. And maybe another Rebellion is what Scotland is needing. Maybe I'll send a copy to Henry Dundas himself with my warmest compliments."

"Maybe the same Henry Dundas will get his copy without you troubling him wi' the expense o' the postage. Henry the Ninth's no' sleeping and neither are his agents. I tell ye, Mossgiel, Scotland has seen a' the rebellions she'll ever see."

"And a good job too, Mr. Lapraik," said Tabaccy Ronald. "Another rebellion wad unsettle the country completely."

John Rankine looked at him with curiosity. "Ah weel, Maister Ronald, it wad tak' a damned sma' rebellion to unsettle you."

But Ronald was not to be put out: "The country has nae stammick for ony mair rebellions, Maister Rankine; and neither hae I."

"G'wa' to hell: I've seen a better stammick on a grey louse cracked on my thumb nail!"

It was Johnnie Dow who sprang to the rescue. "Gentlemen! while ye've been enjoying yoursel's there's been a meikle haggis stoiterin' i' the pat. What d'ye say?"

But there was no need to say anything. Whisky-hunger was sharp on most of them. There was an immediate roar of approval.

STILL CLOSER KNIT

Jean Armour had given herself neither to Robert Wilson nor to any other lad in Paisley. It hadn't been easy to resist; and she had allowed Wilson more liberties than had been prudent. But she had been unable to forget Robert Burns.

And so it happened that she could no longer bear the separation from Machlin, and decided that it would be better to go home and face whatever music there was to face. She would have her bairn at home; and if she delayed much longer, not only would travel be difficult, but she would be a greater object of scandal when she mounted the cutty stool: already she was becoming self-conscious of the weight she was carrying . . .

On Friday evening, the 9th of June, she came back to the Cowgate and noted in a quick apprehensive glance how the house cast a black shadow against the rear of Johnnie Dow's, across the window from which Rab had so often made signals to her in the past . . . She almost imagined she saw his face at the window now . . .

As soon as he saw that his sister was home, Adam, a brother in his early teens, made quickly for Mossgiel. Robert Burns was one of his heroes: indeed he was his only hero; for Adam was a steering, dare-devil lad with a hearty contempt for all authority, and especially the authority of his father and the discipline of Daddy Auld.

Adam whistled softly to the Bard where he was working in the close, and the pair of them retired behind the barn. As soon as they had secured privacy, Adam blurted out:

"Jean's hame, Mr. Burns: Sandy Dow drapped her aff half an hour ago."

His heart began to race. "And why do you come to tell me this, Adam?"

"I knew you'd want to ken. Oh . . . and she's gey big i' the belly."

He could not help smiling at Adam's earnest expression. He was a small hard-set wiry fellow, with a puckish intelligence screwed on to his sharp freckled features. A grave countenance did not become him.

"Did she ask you to come and tell me?"

"No . . . Ah, but she would if she'd gotten the chance! My mither chased me out whenever she cam' in."

"And what d'you think I should do, Adam?"

"I'll carry a message to her: you can trust me, Mr. Burns: the way you have often trusted me in the past . . . afore Jean went to Paisley."

"I suppose you know why Jean's . . . big in the belly?"

"Aye, fine." Here Adam's face broke up in a mass of freckled lines.

"You're no' heading for salvation, Adam . . ."

"They say a' the best company gaes to hell, Mr. Burns."

"You're an imp o' hell already! Away hame; and if you get a chance o' that sister o' yours, tell her I'll ca' in the nicht some time. On you go, you daft deil, afore I plant my brogan in your doup."

But Adam's news greatly excited him . . . especially that remark of his about the bigness of Jean's belly. Paternity was never a subject he could treat with indifference. And the knowledge that Jean had come home with his child in her womb sent great waves of sympathetic response surging through him. It was easy for him, in this mood, to forgive all the bitterness that had passed between them: easy to forget all about Mary Campbell . . . And as he went about his work in a state of trance, he found himself singing the song he ever associated with Jean and that green thorn tree by the banks of the river Ayr . . .

As soon as working time was by, he washed and tidied himself with some care and went down the hill to Machlin. First he called in at Dow's and surveyed the house from the back window. All was quiet: the place looked deserted. He waited some time, hoping to see Jean's face at the window. And then, remembering that Adam had told him how his father was from home, he finished his caup of ale and went round and knocked on the door.

Mrs. Armour admitted him; but only for the reason that she did not want him to be seen standing on the doorstep: otherwise she would more gladly have received the devil himself. But once she had admitted him into the dimness of the dull spence, she unleashed her venomous tongue.

"I thocht you understood that we wanted nothing to dae wi' you? Ye hae a brazen impidence to show your face here. You'd better understand once and for all that we want nothing frae you."

"I called to inquire how Jean was."

"Nae doubt; but we're no' interested. Sae I maun ask you to cut your stay short and never to darken this door again. Mr. Armour's no' at hame the now or he wad hae sorted you and sent you packing."

"I can see that civility's lost on you, Mrs. Armour. I want to see Jean for a moment: there is some business we have to discuss." He hesitated for a moment and then fired a random shot. "Unless you want the matter discussed before the Session: in which case it would be idle for me to object."

The shot found its mark.

Mrs. Armour went to the spence door and called her daughter. When Jean came ben, as she did almost immediately, he was touched to see the difference in her. Overnight she had become a mother and a matron. She was exceptionally heavy with child and her breasts were full and weighted: only about her eyes was there the soft backward innocence of maidenhood. He would have stepped forward and embraced her; but her mother stood between them, tight-lipped and bitter.

"How are you feeling, Jean?" The words were hopelessly inadequate; but they were the only intelligible ones he could muster on his lips.

Jean did not respond. She had met his eyes with a dull, far-away response. Now she lowered her gaze to the floor and said nothing.

Her mother's voice cracked like a whip: "What's the nature o' the business you had to discuss?"

"Jean! will you come with me to Mr. Auld and we can make a clean breast of the business? As far as the Session's concerned, we're in this together."

But Jean, with her gaze still lowered, said: "There's nothing I can do until I hae seen my father. I maun do whatever he says."

"But have we no duty to one another?"

"Little enough you care about duty! You've heard what Jean says; and that's all the duty there is to it. Maybe you'll go now?"

"If I go this time, Jean, you canna expect me to come back."

"I can only dae what my father says, Rab."

There was the finality of resignation in her voice. And the damnable harridan of a mother stood between them.

He moved slowly towards the door. "Very well, Jean: if that's how you wish things to be atween us . . ."

It was easy to see what had come between them. Jean was not a fighter. She was pregnant and in the hands of her damnable parents. Her nature was far too soft to withstand them. And because he had no home to which he might have taken her, he had to submit to their control. He was no longer angry, no longer bitter: only weary and depressed. The hell was that he loved Jean as much as he had ever done: there was no escaping this. No escaping the response to her of his blood and his heart. And here he was, married to Mary Campbell . . . Soon enough she, too, would be big in the belly like Jean!

His thoughtless follies and indiscretions were coming home to roost now; and there was no one to blame but himself. He had acted too impulsively with Jean in that matter of the marriage lines, thinking that they solved all his problems instead of raising ones he had never dreamed of.

He had fallen into the arms of Mary Campbell on the rebound from Jean Armour. But if it hadn't been Mary Campbell, it might have been Eliza Miller or some other lass.

In his weariness he was able to review his position with a cold objectivity. The essence of his trouble (as he had always known) was that he was capable of loving more than one lass at a time. Loving them, not lusting after them: though he had his share of bygoing passion to contend with. He loved Jean Armour and he loved Mary Campbell: he had married the one and now he was married to the other. And he was leaving Scotland to go to the Indies with Mary Campbell even while Jean would be giving birth to his child: even as he was leaving dear-bought Bess in the care of his mother and under the protection of his brother.

The blackguard's road out would have been easy enough. Plenty took it and were thought little less of at the hinderend. He could have denied Jean and Mary, satisfied the Session and then gone his own way with as much rejoicing as he could muster.

But he was no blackguard; and he loved them. He hadn't loved Betty Paton as he loved Mary or Jean, yet he hadn't acted the blackguard with Betty, was incapable of acting the blackguard with her. But where was all this leading him? Leading him into a tangle of emotion from which it would be difficult to escape—even though he went round the world trying to escape.

But why was it that Mary was already receding into the background while Jean, with her load of mischief and her downcast eyes, was dominating the foreground? Hadn't he already decided that Jean had forfeited any right to his affection or consideration?

Aye: as if what he decided in his head could determine the response of his heart . . .

THE REVEREND SAGE

William Auld stood with his back to the empty fire-place in the Cowgate spence. Jean Armour sat with bowed head in a chair in front of him.

The priest spoke in a low voice.

"You have disappointed me sorely, Jean; and you have dishonoured and wounded your parents deeply. I married your father and your mother; I baptised you; I watched you grow up through childhood into girlhood; I watched you blossoming into a fine young woman. I was proud of you—though you didna ken that. I looked on you as one of the fairest flowers in my vineyard: a great credit to us all . . . Maybe you can understand how grievously disappointed I am to find you in this shameful state of sin?

"Tell me—and it will be easier to tell me than tell the Session—did Burns force himself upon you? Did he seduce you? You understand me? Now, you mustn't try to hide your head in shame. Your time for shame is past. I must hae the truth of this."

"I . . . I loved him, Mr. Auld."

"Ah, Jean, Jean! Beware o' the lusts o' the flesh. Surely you kenned it was sin to yield before your union had been blessed and sanctified? Surely you hae heard me rebuking the sin o' fornication often enough . . .?"

"I ken now I did wrang, Mr. Auld."

335

"Aye . . . and like most sinners, when it's ower late. And do you still . . . love . . . Robert Burns? Now you maun answer me. I'm here to help you what I can."

"My father says I've to hae nae mair to do wi' him."

"Aye . . . And you'll do what your father bids?"

"Whatever my father and you say, Mr. Auld."

"That's a good lass. But—eh—you didna answer my question—do you still hanker after Robert Burns?"

"I canna blame him, Mr. Auld—though my father would kill me gin he heard me say that."

"You've had a sair time wi' your father! Aye . . . Mr. Armour is a stern and upright parent, and this has been a sore blow to him. No: I'll no' tell on you, lass: what passes atween you and me doesna pass beyond the four walls here . . . You still hae a fondness for him! Ah well: you'll need to forget that, Jean lass. Burns is no' the man for you—indeed he is a maist dangerous man for ony young woman to hae dealings wi'. A clever man, Burns: aye, and a tongue on him that would wile the bird frae the bush, for Satan's behind that tongue. Your parents are wise to forbid you ony further association wi' him—verra wise."

"I canna think he's a bad man, Mr. Auld—and he's had a lot o' trouble."

"Well . . . he's a bad man for you. There are degrees o' badness, I'll admit. But Burns is treading a dangerous path—and I fear much for his immortal soul. Gin he doesna mend his ways, he'll come to a bad end—bad as his beginning has been. Na, na: ye maun look about ye for a quiet, steady-going, God-fearing lad—when your troubles are by. Ah, but you're no' by wi' your troubles, lass. But I'll ease your path for you. You've the Session to face . . . but you needna face them the now. Hand me in a letter to the Session on our next Sabbath meeting. You need say nae mair for the present, but that you admit your condition—and that Robert Burns is the father. And that you're heartily sorry that you have given . . . and must give the . . . Session . . . trouble . . . on your account. Aye: that will meet the case. Such a letter will save you from an ordeal that I would fain spare ony lass that has made a mistake through trusting ower much in a man.

"Aye, Jean: men are no' to be trusted in matters o' the flesh. I hae seen much sin in my day and mony lassies ruined by trusting a man when they should hae trusted in the Lord and remembered their catechism and His commandments. Aye . . . ye'll cry mair afore you're done; and ye'll weep mony a salt tear that you didna hearken till your duty. But in so far as I can lighten the hand o' the Kirk on you, then I will.

"But though it can be lightened it canna be lifted—ye'll need to stand i' the kirk and be rebuked. I could dae nae less to my ain dochter gin I had been blessed wi' one . . .

"Now I'll need to hae a word o' advice and consolation wi' your parents. Dinna grieve too much; but pray night and day to Almighty God for forgiveness. Humble yourself before Him . . . and never forget how you have defiled yourself in abomination—and think nae mair o' this Burns and the evil o' his wicked influence . . . that ye may come to the Lord's house in a proper state o' repentance. I'll be praying for you myself—and maybe the Lord will answer our prayers . . ."

THE GOSPEL HORN

Mr. Auld leaned back in his chair.

"Seat yourself, Mr. Burns. It is the custom to have men like you stand . . . considering the circumstances. But we have much to say: so be seated. You ken why I have sent for you?"

"I have to appear before the Session on Sunday?"

"You have that. It's not an experience you are likely to enjoy."

"I can't say I enjoyed my previous experience, Mr. Auld."

"That was when I indulged you in standing in Tarbolton: Mr. MacMath was it? Aye: Mr. MacMath is inclined to leniency in dealing with the sin of fornication. In Machlin we have a greater respect for the Lord's commandments."

He recalled a phrase of Jean Glover's, spoken in Irvine long ago.

"Fornication is an ugly word, Mr. Auld."

"Fornication is an ugly sin, Mr. Burns. I am painfully aware that some of you modern folk are minded to make light of it; but the Lord will not make light of it."

"Has Jean Armour admitted that I am the father of her child?"

"Do you intend to deny it?"

"There is a touch of ironic humour about a situation wherein a woman will accept a man as the father of her child and at the same time will refuse to countenance him as her husband."

"You offered marriage to Jean Armour?"

"I was *married* to Jean Armour."

"That, sir, is a bold statement to make to my face."

"I'm not given to trade in lies, Mr. Auld. I was married to Jean Armour; but the marriage did not suit the proud stomachs of her parents; and so the marriage was nullified by an Ayr lawyer who had my name cut out of the paper. In the eyes of the law, Mr. Auld, I am no fornicator."

"God's law and Scots law are two different things, Mr. Burns."

"Aye; but we render unto Cæsar that which is Cæsar's and unto God that which is God's."

"I trust, Mr. Burns, that you are not going to prove stiff-necked in this business. I have indulged you in this matter of a private talk so that I might have a better understanding before your case comes up before the Session—the officer will summon you as is the custom. I have no desire to be unjust to you: or to Jean Armour. Jean has admitted to me privately that you are the father of her child: do you admit her claim?"

The priest and the poet were fencing. The Bard, with his secret knowledge of Mary Campbell locked in his heart, wondered if he had been wise in telling Auld of his marriage to Jean Armour. Auld, hearing for the first time of the irregular union, wondered if it might not be best to insist on its solemnisation— or to pretend that it had never existed. His sympathy was all for Jean. There was little doubt in his mind that Burns was not the husband for her; but it was a pity to see her branded as a fornicator.

"There is talk about you sailing to the Indies, Mr. Burns?"

"I hope to sail before the end of the summer."

"And since Jean Armour wishes nothing to do with you, am I to presume that you wish to have nothing to do with her?"

"I am given to understand that there is some possibility of her marrying a weaver in Paisley . . . At least, when I called on her on her return from that town, her mother promptly showed me the door. There is nothing else for me but to compear before the Session and to stand rebuked in the Kirk."

"I have heard nothing about a Paisley weaver: I trust you are sure of your facts, sir."

"Robert Wilson's his name: I believe he once sat under you here, Mr. Auld: seeing he has a claut o' siller, I don't suppose there will be any objection to him."

"The Kirk cares nocht for a man's siller, Mr. Burns: it's sad to see a young man like you sae bitter."

"There's little need for you and me to beat about the bush, Mr. Auld. If I were Claude Alexander o' Ballochmyle, I wouldna be asked to thole any dribbing from Willie Fisher or James Lamie. Not that any of your worthy lay-shepherds would have the boldness to set themselves up before the gentry."

"That will do, sir! Remember my office. I have already indulged you beyond your merit; but don't be minded to presume on that. You are no common sinner, common though your sin may be. You are a headstrong man; and you are a man with an uncommonly strong head. I am not content to see you compeared and rebuked, as you think. It is my duty before God to wrestle with you and to bring you to a sense of your sin and the enormity of your guilt. Judgment must be tempered with mercy; and both with understanding. There is not the shadow of repentance in you for your sin with Jean Armour: there is no sense of guilt. This weighs heavier with me than you realise. Is it nothing to you that the child Jean Armour is carrying to you will be born into sin? It is nothing to you that its parents will be branded with the shame of that sin? Do you think for a foolish moment that by going to the Indies you will escape from the consequences of this sin? Is it nothing to you that some day, sooner or later, you will be ushered into the presence of your Maker with all the ugliness of that sin black upon you? Aye: and that you may be too polluted in sin to be received into His presence but cast forthwith into the everlasting pit of hell-fire and damnation? Bethink yourself, sir; and humble yourself in the thought of His awful presence. Pride, Mr. Burns, pride: that is your curse and your undoing. Pray, day and night, to be saved from the headstrong folly of a stiff-necked pride. Weighed in the scales of my parish here, you have all the elements of greatness; but greatness that is not firmly founded in the fear of the Lord can be a terrible curse to a man: aye, a terrible curse. Your spiritual welfare is in my hands, Mr. Burns. I would be guilty of mortal sin were I to treat my responsibility lightly . . . And then, Mr. Burns, you are young. And the path of youth is strewn with terrible and clamorous temptations: especially the temptations of the flesh. You see: ye canna put an old head on young shoulders: it just canna be done. But then youth thinks it kens sae much better than age. Youth lacks experience: experience that comes only with the years and the fullness of God's own time. Age must therefore guide youth through the difficulties that beset it. That is where the Kirk in its wisdom is like the ancient of days; for it has an age-long experience and it is bigged on the bed-rock of the Lord. And so, if it becomes necessary, the Kirk must chastise. The Kirk must not be squeamish in sparing the rod that the child be spoiled. No young man that I have known, Mr. Burns, is better fitted to under-stand all this than you. I have told you before that the Lord has lavished gifts on you in a great abundance. Certain of your poems have come into my hands and I will confess to you now that I have been deeply impressed with the power of them. But their power for evil is as great as their power for good. And great gifts can lead a great man to great destruction as the history of the world well proves. So if I say hard things to you, things that give great offence to your proud spirit, dinna think that I say them to give you offence only—but because I think more of your immortal soul than I think of your temporal welfare . . .

"But: you have made up your mind to go to the Indies: very well then. That will place a lasting barrier between you and Jean Armour, and there would be no point in trying to reconcile you and her . . .

"As for this foolish talk of marriage with her in the past: I'll forget about that. Since that is the Armours' wish and your own wish, and since you say the paper has been destroyed, there is no point in raking it up to cause further scandal: especially since it is a secular matter and of little consequence. Jean Armour may want to marry this weaver you speak of; and you may have your own plans when you get out to the Americas. But the ordinances of the Kirk will require to be satisfied; and it will be necessary to wrestle with the pair of you still further; and to bring you into a state of grace . . ."

The Bard made no attempt to interrupt the flow of Daddy Auld's eloquence. He had talked to him in this strain before, and he had to confess that he was not a little impressed by it. There could be no question: Auld was by far the most astute of the Old Light clergy; and there was equally no doubt that, somewhere in the man, there was a hard rock of sincerity and uprightness. But his arguments were without validity; and it was equal folly to believe that the entire wisdom of the Almighty resided in the safe-keeping of the Kirk of Scotland.

It was natural that Auld should seek to protect the Armours, to take their side against him: as far as that was concerned, he was only an incomer to Machlin parish. So he had no bitterness in his heart against Auld for this: only bitterness for the circumstances that so ordained it.

But if Auld was determined to play his cards carefully, he must be prepared to do likewise. He must learn to match cunning with cunning, to counter move against move, and to emerge in the end with as little skaith as possible. It was clear he had only Auld to deal with: clear that Auld had no intention of risking Holy Willie or any other of his elders in debate with him. It was clear that Auld feared him and was anxious to avoid any inflammation of the scandal. But he would take no advantage of this. There was nothing to be gained by crossing Daddy Auld: there might be plenty to be gained by allowing his fear of him to rest where it was.

But it wasn't so much that Auld feared him as he feared his influence in the parish. The best thing that could possibly happen was for Burns to sail for the Indies. He would be out of harm's way there . . . and Jean Armour would be free to marry her weaver . . .

Long after the Bard had gone, Daddy Auld sat and ruminated on their interview. It was strange to think that this tenant-farmer carried about him such an air of independence and authority. Mostly when he had had occasion to interview sinners on a moral lapse they professed extreme repentance and begged humbly for his forgiveness. Some tried to brazen out their sin with vehement denials; but as soon as their guilt was brought home to them they collapsed more abjectly than the others. But Burns was different: vastly different. He had never had to interview a man like him.

And he had sat there, a hand firmly placed on either knee, his great eyes smouldering and burning, his head held at a stiff-necked angle of stubborn pride . . . Aye, a great pity that he could not get at him on a common level of understanding. And yet how wrong and wide of the mark were the reports of him he got from Fisher and Lamie. Neither of them had the slightest inkling of the man they were dealing with. No doubt Burns gave them a hot time of it: they were gey tame fowls for him to pluck . . .

Aye: and little wonder that he had got round Jean Armour: Jean would be a gey tame pullet under his hands . . . Ah, but that marriage now: strange that the Armours had been silent on that. Still, it proved, if it proved anything, that Jean was not the abandoned lass his elders, against his own better judgment, had made her out to be. Jean had not yielded till there had been some sort of marriage.

He wondered for a moment who the lawyer in Ayr might be who had destroyed the marriage line. This would be another of lawyer Aiken's tricks . . . and as like as not Hamilton would have a finger in the pie somewhere.

Ah well, they would see how Burns behaved with the Session. He would have to be very careful that Fisher didn't take it into his head to make any remarks calculated to enrage the Mossgiel poet: he didn't want another *Holy Fair* or a *Holy Willie's Prayer*.

Finally Daddy Auld opened the drawer of his table, adjusted his finely-balanced tortoise-shell rimmed glasses, and read again the letter he had received from Jean Armour: "I am heartily sorry that I have given and must give your Session trouble on my account. I acknowledge that I am with child, and Robert Burns in Mossgiel is the father. I am, with great respect, your most humble servant, Jean Armour."

What he had prayed and hoped against had come to pass—and neither Fisher nor Lamie had availed him anything.

APOSTLE AULD

On the 25th of June he compeared before the Session. There were others compearing that evening and for the same offence, and they wandered ill at ease about the kirkyard waiting till Robin Gibb, the officer, summoned them before Mr. Auld and his lay-shepherds.

The Bard did not feel ill at ease, however. He was in a grand mood to deal with the Session should they try to cross-examine him beyond what he was prepared to tolerate.

But Daddy Auld had the Session well in hand: he knew the combustible material with which he was dealing. But however tight his hand, he could not ride too roughly over them, and he knew how each and all of them were ready for Burns the moment he appeared.

Soon auld Robin Gibb came hirpling to the door and called for the Bard. As he approached the long table he noted that there was a full attendance of the elders: Hugh Aird, Tam Guthrie, John Siller, James Smith, James Lamie, William Fisher. Each and all of them eyed him keenly as he approached the table. Those who had never spoken to him and had only seen him in the streets or at the service knew him well by reputation. They looked forward to his ordeal with keen satisfaction. But they also noted with some inward alarm that he came towards the table with his head held high and with a firm and manly step.

Willie Fisher, at the right hand of Auld, fidgeted on his seat. He was not only ill at ease: he was a riot of indecision. He did not know whether to revenge himself for all the indignities he had suffered at the Bard's hands or whether it would be better to play safe in case he wrote another and perhaps more terrible poem about him. He had felt safe enough as he had sat with his colleagues. And it had seemed a pretty safe vantage point from which to launch an attack; but now that he saw his enemy approach he knew misgiving. The black-guard looked as if he didn't give a damn for either God or the devil, to say nothing of Mr. Auld and the members of the Session.

Auld wasted no time in opening the case.

"Robert Burns, tenant-farmer in Mossgiel: you are summoned to appear before this Session to-night to answer for the sin of fornication with Jean Armour, who is presently with child to you. Do you admit this charge?"

"I do."

"Do you express sorrow for your sin and ask forgiveness from the Lord in the presence of this Session and within the sacred walls of His house?"

"In so far as I have sinned against the Lord I express sorrow and seek His forgiveness."

"This being so, you will require to stand in this house three several Sundays that you may be rebuked for your sin, and, having been thus rebuked, that you may be absolved from scandal in all time coming. Does the Session wish to ask any questions?"

But the Session was flabbergasted. Never had they heard a compearing rushed through at this break-neck speed. This was beyond any use and wont they could ever remember, except in the case of one of the gentry, when, of course, it would have been indecent to have acted otherwise . . . Holy Willie's teeth rattled in his head with impotent wrath: he had no idea where to begin. But James Lamie, very red about the gills, came to the rescue.

"By your leave, Mr. Auld, I think there are some questions that micht well be askit. This is not the first offence Mr. Burns has given the Session."

"It is the first offence that we as a Session are concerned with, Mr. Lamie. The previous occasion to which I think you are referring was taken over by Doctor Woodrow in Tarbolton Parish. As

Mr. Burns stood there his three several Sundays and was rebuked and freed from scandal in all time coming for that offence . . ."

But a breach had been made in Auld's authority, and the Session made at the gap like a flock of sheep. Unfortunately for the Session, several of them began to speak at once, and in a moment they were reduced to ragged incoherence . . . This played into Auld's hands.

"As Moderator of this Session, I will have no disorder: neither will I have any unseemly conduct. Mr. Fisher, sir! will you have the decency to sit still in your seat and cease from bobbing up and down as if you were on fire! And will you, Mr. Lamie, have the respect due to me as Moderator not to roar: I am not yet deaf! If you have no further questions to ask, I propose to dismiss Mr. Burns in the meantime and to proceed with our agenda, which is full enough in all conscience without this unnecessary haranguing."

Since Fisher had again bobbed involuntarily in his seat, he now felt that he must justify himself. "I agree wi' Mr. Auld and move accordingly."

James Lamie glared at him with ill-concealed anger: "Haud on, Mr. Fisher! I desire to ken—and I hae the right to demand an answer to my question—I demand to ken how long this sin of fornication has been going on with Jean Armour. There are degrees o' fornication, and the Session has the right, before it pronounces its findings, to ken just whatna degrees are involved here. Is this a sin hardened by lang standin', Mr. Auld? This is a bi-lapse already: how are we to ken that there's no a tri-lapse on the road and that the accused is in a proper frame o' mind to give due consideration to his offence? That is as much our duty here as any other: we maun see to it that sinners are brought into a full and proper state o' repentance."

"Aye: there's an unco byornar crap o' bastard bairns bein' sown i' the parish, Mr. Auld; and it behooves the Session to root out this sin amang the young fowk so that we dinna run the danger o' becomin' the Sodom o' the West . . ."

By this time Auld was beside himself with rage.

"Please to withdraw yourself, Mr. Burns, while the Session goes into a private deliberation. Robin! see Mr. Burns to the door and stand guard till you are called."

When the officer had retired with the Bard, Daddy Auld fairly let himself go.

"I will not have the dignity of my office as Minister in this Parish and Moderator of this Session challenged in front of one of my congregation. It is scandalous: it is outrageous: it is intolerable!"

But James Lamie was also beyond himself with rage. "Haud on there, Mr. Auld: the Session has its rights, its privileges and its duties; and it's no' the job o' the Moderator to ride rough-shod over us the way you are doing. It looks suspicious-like that you have some reason for dealing leniently wi' this kenned sinner . . ."

"Will you have the goodness to put that charge down in writing, Mr. Lamie, so that it can be taken before a higher court—and so that you may be examined in your fitness for your office? Have you taken leave of your senses, the lot of you? This Burns, as you are all aware, is no ordinary sinner, common enough though his sin may be. We must deal with this man in a way that will bring no discredit upon us. We must be doubly on our guard not to overstep the limits of what we may do and what we may not do—and what it may be seemly to do, having regard to all the antecedents and ultimate consequences of our acts! The discipline of the Kirk lays it down that a sinner must be compeared and that the sinner must express proper repentance for his sin. If necessary the Session may wrestle with an obdurate sinner in prayer; and the Minister is ever in his right to wrestle with a sinner in prayer and by exhortation. But neither the Session nor the Minister may browbeat a sinner who has made proper confession of his guilt and has expressed his sorrow and repentance! I have wrestled with this man Burns; and the Lord has privileged me to see something into his heart. He is no ordinary hardened sinner. He kens well the sin he has committed . . . But handle this repentant sinner the wrong way and we will send him out into the outer darkness—there to sin again! And that is a heavy responsibility for any man to have on his soul. Besides, in thus sending him out into the darkness, we would be kindling a fire of unrighteousness to burn in the minds of evil-doers against the Kirk; and this is an equally heavy responsibility. I ken what is in your minds. You have heard many evil things against this man. To some of you he has been a sore and suppurating thorn in your flesh . . . And you think I am letting him off lightly! May God forgive you the shame of your thoughts; *and may He grant that I keep my peace with some of you.*

"And now let us pray that His abiding Grace may sweeten our counsels and that His divine hand may guide our deliberations and that we, the unworthy instruments of His purpose, may not be led into vanity or uncharitableness; but that we may come to judge the sins of our fellows with pure hearts and clean minds; and that we let no mean or unworthy motive or consideration cause us to swerve from the clear path of our duty, knowing that He seest into the inmost corners of our hearts, and that nothing is hid from His knowing . . ."

And thus, ultimately, did Daddy Auld cowe his Session and bring them to his way of thinking. He was too great a man for them singly or collectively; and when he raised himself to his full stature they wilted away before him.

It was a cowed and beaten Session the Bard faced when Robin Gibb again summoned him. Auld dealt with him briefly—and summarily dismissed him.

The other delinquents followed in rapid order: it was the briefest session in the history of Daddy Auld's ministry. But Holy Willie and James Lamie were strangers to each other from that night.

BEFORE THE CONGREGATION

July 9th was the date fixed for his first penitential appearance in the kirk. He had learned from Jeannie Smith and Eliza Miller that they were annoyed with him for not arranging to stand with Jean in her hour of trouble; and he had some difficulty in assuring them that he had nothing to do with this arrangement, and that Daddy Auld was not the man to allow him to dictate where and how he would stand. Moreover, there were so many delinquents standing that day that it was quite impossible to arrange for all of them to mount the cutty stool, and therefore they were being conceded the privilege of standing in their own places in the kirk.

What he did not tell them was that he was certain Daddy Auld had so arranged matters that it would be impossible for Jean and him to mount the cutty stool together. Nor did he tell them that he was suffering the indignity of being publicly rebuked by Auld in order to get a certificate of bachelorhood from him. He had long learned in the hard school of experience that there were many things it was better to keep from folks' kenning. Only the great challenging truths were to be told from the house-tops and shouted in the market-places: private truths were not necessarily matters of public concern. Indeed, private truths were all the better for being restricted to private ears.

It interested him, nevertheless, to find Jean's friends were still his friends and that they still took an equal interest in their mutual welfare. What he did not know was that Jean, in her intimate talks

349

with Jeannie Smith, had revealed that she was more in love with him than she had ever been, and that only the terrible anger of her father and the bitter opposition of her mother prevented her from getting in touch with him and assuring him of her true feelings.

And there was the burden of her unborn child. She could not afford to risk the displeasure of her parents in any way; for she had now become a burden to herself; and she was beginning to fear the ordeal of childbirth.

She suffered deeply from the talk of his going to the Indies. It seemed that he would be going almost any day now: almost certainly before her child was born. Her dilemma was indeed pitiful; but there was no road out. Her first concern was to be delivered safely and to be brought through her lying-in period without mishap. After that she would see . . . But the idea of bringing up her fatherless bairn in Machlin while the father she loved so deeply was a thousand miles across the ocean, and that in all probability she would never see him again, was almost more than she could bear; and it was to Jeannie Smith that she confided her inmost thoughts.

Jeannie, who knew nothing about Mary Campbell, had thought it hard that Robin wouldn't even consent to stand with Jean in the public gaze of the kirk when her parents could not possibly have raised any objection. She was only partially satisfied with Robin's explanation. She had never known Daddy Auld to be so lenient with fornicators. And she knew what all Machlin knew: that Robert Burns did not stand well in the eyes of the Kirk Session.

Knowing this, Machlin made a good turn out on the Sunday to witness the humiliation of the Mossgiel poet who was so notorious for his bawdy heresies and sallies against the Old Light herds for miles around. It would be glorious fun to see him get his ditty from Daddy Auld, since no one was so expert in giving a cutty-stool ditty.

It was a very different story at Mossgiel. The family were deeply ashamed and outraged. They decided (without any decision having been taken) that they would absent themselves from the service.

Robin's mother had long ago resigned herself to his fate. He would go his own road no matter what anybody said; and she was convinced, though sadly convinced, that the road he was travelling would lead him to disaster. She no longer hid her head in shame for him. In this matter of shame he was not her son; and he was even less the son of William Burns. Whose son he was she could not fathom. It seemed now that she had never borne him nor suckled him at the same breasts that had suckled Gilbert. He had grown up and grown away from her from the moment he had been able to toddle across the beaten earthen floor of the Alloway cottage. He had given her pain and heartbreak many a night even as he had given many an anxious moment to his father. But she no longer grieved for him. Only occasionally did anger mount in her; and then she was sorry afterwards for the sharpness of her tongue.

She found it was better for her peace of mind to leave him alone and to interfere with his goings-out and his comings-in as little as possible.

And this, in more or less degree, was the attitude that had been adopted by his sisters. But neither Nancy nor Bell had lost pride in him. He was still their brother, and their highly-gifted brother, no matter what he did. The shame was that he did so many shameful things. First Betty Paton and now Jean Armour. They knew he was no blackguard; but how could they hold up their heads in the parish or how could they hope to get decent husbands when their eldest brother behaved in such a way? They had blamed Betty Paton for the first offence. They were still inclined to lay a lot of blame at the door of Jean Armour. But two bastard bairns within a year could not easily be explained away.

Willie, of course, was too young to realise the full implications of his eldest brother's moral lapses: he doted on Robert and would have done anything for him. So if he got a lassie with bairn, that was natural and not to be questioned. Different with other folk maybe; but whatever Robin did was right; and that was an end of it as far as Willie was concerned.

Gilbert had suffered all that he could suffer. He found that none of his own friends and none of Robin's friends thought very much about it. In the matter of the Armours they were one and all on Robin's side. Gilbert was uneasy. But at least in the case of Jean Armour, Robin had married her before she had conceived; and there was moral strength here. If the Armours had cared to break off the marriage, then the odour of immorality was about them and not about his brother.

In any case Robin was going to the Indies; and he was publishing his poems. The poems were more important than Jean Armour and all the bastard bairns that could ever be born. And if the poems were a great success . . . But Gilbert was cautious. He had worked all he knew to ensure they would be a success. But he would count no chickens until they were hatched . . . indeed, until they were running about and looking like the world.

But he would not go to the kirk and see his brother rebuked. This was something he could not be asked to endure. If Mr. Auld and the Machlin Session didn't like it, then for once they would just need to lump it.

Robin did not like having to stand in the kirk. But at least he had won a partial victory over Auld and a resounding one over Holy Willie and the members of the Session: it would be a bitter pill for them to swallow to see him stand in his place to-day . . . and stand by himself.

But for all that, it hurt his pride to have to endure the ordeal. It was against his most fundamental belief in the dignity of man and the inherent dignity of man in his relationship with woman. He would have welcomed, in other circumstances, to have taken a stand in the matter and to have incurred the full wrath of the Kirk, even though it had meant formal banning in the end. To have risked excommunication would have been a big thing to have risked. But if Jean had stood by her promise, there was nothing he would not have stood against rather than have submitted to a degrading ritual that cast a slur on his manhood and the grace of his child.

But he had much more to worry him than indulgence in moral attitudes. He was at grips with life in all its inexorability; and life was much more grim and unrelenting in its discipline than the Kirk. To fight the outmoded morality of the Kirk was one thing: here the fight was an intellectual one and needed only strength of mind and spiritual courage. But to fight the morality of society in practice was quite another matter, and it called for the additional courage and strength that is born of economic independence. He wasn't fighting this battle alone: he was fighting it with the burdened bodies of Mary Campbell and Jean Armour. Here it would have been madness to have come into the open and given battle. His battle had to be fought from every available piece of protective covering. Here he had to fight a battle of retreat; and it was incumbent on him that he lose none of his forces. He would have to fight Daddy Auld—and the world—with every weapon that he knew.

But the sun was shining and there was gladness in his heart. His health was good and his poems were making progress. By the end of the month he would have commenced poet in print. What did it matter that he had to appear before Daddy Auld and the whole parish? Let them take a good look at him; and let them take a good look at Jean Armour. She had rejected him. But did she seem any the happier for that? Aye: let them look at him. He could stand their looks, could stand the looks of anyone. He owed no man anything. None of his friends had rejected him. He stood higher with them than ever he had stood. When men like John Rankine and Gavin Hamilton and Doctor MacKenzie and others stood by him in his trouble, what had he to fear? When men in the great town of Ayr like Robert Aiken and John Ballantine and Major Logan and Doctor Douglas and William Chalmers stood firm in their friendship, why should he be afraid of the Machlin bodies? When sterling good fellows in Kilmarnock like Robert Muir and Tam Samson and John Gowdie and Major Parker were proud to claim him as their friend, why should he worry about his petty Machlin enemies?

Far from reckoning this a day of defeat and humiliation, he would turn it into a day of victory.

Let them look at him; and let them look long. They were looking at a poet and a man of independent mind who was not afraid of any of them.

And indeed his friends had stood by him. Neither Hamilton nor MacKenzie nor Wee Smith nor Tanner Hunter attended the service that day. And it was a serious step for them to take. Their absence would be noted and they would have to give an account to the Session . . .

But just as the men absented themselves in respect for him, so the lassies attended in strength to give their moral support to Jean. The Machlin belles were there in full muster. Even Jenny Surgeoner, broken in body and cowed in spirit, was there with head bowed in sympathy and understanding.

The Armours were present in force. James Armour, his face harsh and red, looked neither to the right nor to the left, but fixed his eye on a vacant target on the wall. He was in a bitter mood. This was indeed public humiliation for him. But at least he would let the parish see that he would rather be humiliated than have a blackguard like Burns for a son-in-law. Aye: let them look; and let them note how a God-fearing, respectable father could bear up to the outraging of fortune and maintain his respectability through it all.

But the rest of the Armours were by no means so sure of themselves. All of them had a hang-dog look, and the lads seemed downright sulky. The diminutive Adam scowled defiance at every eye he caught; and he caught many.

Jean's mother, white and tight-lipped, looked as if she might burst into a flood of petulant tears: it was obvious to all that she was playing the martyred-mother part and that she was enjoying the publicity she was receiving. To maintain her part, it was essential to keep her eyes lidded as much as possible. The mocking glance in a neighbour's eyes would have shattered her confidence . . .

The light from the north window struck directly on the pulpit; and when Daddy Auld raised himself to his full height he presented an imposing presence against a harsh and gloomy background.

The north light, though it clearly revealed the white-haired dignity of the priest, cast no glare in his eyes, and he was able to survey his congregation without strain. Daddy Auld had a fine voice (though its chords were a trifle gaunt now) and the steep-raked roof of the kirk provided him with a perfect sounding-board. When he raised his voice in supplication or in exhortation, when he uncoiled a great moaning sigh from his pythonising innards, the echo of the words Ooooh Looorrd went booming and bumming and soughing under the lofts and sighed their way upwards in soft reverberations along the musty roof-beams until they were finally dissipated in the sacerdotal shadows.

The Armours' desk was in front of the pulpit, slightly to the left of Daddy Auld. It was one of the most expensively-rented desks in the kirk. For the privilege of a prominent position, James Armour paid the Session the sum of ten shillings and ninepence yearly.

The Mossgiel desk was well behind Armours', and to the right.

The Bard sat squarely to his desk. Few desks gave more accommodation than for three persons: such other persons as might be attached to it sat as near as they could, on stools or chairs.

Mr. Auld noted immediately he cast his eye over his flock that Burns sat alone. But he did no more than note the fact as he noted many others. In due time he would review these mental notes and draw the necessary conclusions.

The sermon lasted a little longer than two half-hour turns of the sand-glass; but Daddy was far from being at his oratorical or theological best. At first Robin listened with some show of interest, but very soon that interest died away and he sank, arms folded, head drooping forwards, in one of his dwams. Even the numerous noises that began to hum around him failed to distract him.

The congregation was restless. There was a dank thundery warmth in the air and many folks began to sweat profusely under the Sabbath cleadings. They shuffled and fidgeted, leaned forward and leaned backward, moved their seats this way and that. A dog-fight started outside and there was a sudden explosion of snarls, yelps, howls, gurlings, yowlings, gurrings, gowlings and all manner of ungodly barkings. Robin Gibb, the beadle, slipped from his desk and went out to see what could be done to quieten them. Everybody in the congregation waited to hear how he would succeed. Daddy Auld might as well have been preaching to the Ailsa Craig . . .

But the snarling curs were not to be put off by the mere appearance among the tombstones of the Machlin Kirk beadle. And when one mangy brute bared its yellow fangs at Robin, he returned quickly to the vestry, seized a collecting ladle, and sallied out again to the fray, with the result that the disturbance increased in ferocity and volume. But Robin knew what he was about; and presently, when the crescendo had suddenly broken off, he returned with the bits of the broken box and handle, placed them quietly in the corner of the vestry, and resumed his seat as if nothing untoward had happened.

The dog-fight amused the younger elements of the flock. Adam Armour sat with a grin of impish delight on his hitherto sulky face.

But Robert Burns heard nothing of the dog-fight. There were many of the unco guid who nudged each other and made signs that he was fast asleep. His apparent sleeping outraged them deeply. Not only was it disrespectful: it showed he had little concern for the sin for which he was about to be rebuked . . .

The Bard was thinking about his Kilmarnock volume. Wilson had promised it for the end of the month. He had rejected many of his happiest efforts, but he was setting *The Twa Dogs* first in the volume, and this was some compensation. He was not anxious to have many songs—indeed he had had a struggle to get him to accept *Corn Rigs*. Maybe some day he would have the opportunity of seeing his words printed with the music. This was the only way a song should be set forth to the public. But maybe this was hoping too much. It seemed that printing music was a difficult and expensive business.

Always there was this vexed question of expense. Because of expense, how many beautiful airs had been lost to Scotland? He knew a good hundred himself that had never been set forth in print. These melodies were fast dying out since even the words were forgotten; and without words to sing to it, a melody soon perished.

But why was he worrying himself about the songs of Scotland when soon enough he would be bidding farewell to her shores?

Maybe in the Indies . . . Maybe once he was settled there he would be able to spare some time to prick down the old melodies and set new verses to them. Maybe he could leave behind him a manuscript volume, so that when the day came when it was not an expensive business to print a song his manuscript might fall into the hands of someone who would understand its value and significance. Aye: even in the Indies it might still be possible for him to work on a book that would eventually bring some honour to his country and show to generations yet unborn how the old folks in the Scottish highways and byways had sung their days in deathless melody.

As long as he had access to pen and ink and paper there was no reason why he should not.

Then came the penultimate act of the service. In a deep and solemn voice William Auld said: "The following sinners, who have compeared before the Session, and who have made confession of their guilt, will be upstanding before the congregation: Robert Burns; John Smith; Jean Armour; Agnes Auld; Mary Lindsay."

First named, the Bard was first to his feet. He stood squarely to his desk and looked straight into Auld's eyes. His face was passive and expressionless. But his heart began to race. It was an ordeal to have to rise and stand forth as a sinner who had confessed and admitted guilt, and who was now in the act of asking that his sin might be forgiven him.

Jean Armour rose awkwardly and stood with bowed head.

A wave of excited curiosity spread through the kirk, and the minister allowed himself sufficient pause before he spoke.

The folks in the Common Loft above the schoolroom craned their necks upwards and forwards so that they could get a good view of the penitents. Alone, of them, Mary Lindsay stood in the front seat of the opposite West Loft. There was much whispering in the back seats, and not a few smothered sniggers.

But the cynosure of the congregation's collective eye was Robert Burns, for he was the best known and by far the most colourful personality there.

Even the gentry were interested. Thomas Miller (Lord Barskimming) on one of his rare visits to Machlin Kirk (he was in his eightieth year) sat in the perch of the Barskimming Loft on the same wall as Auld. He watched the Bard with some curiosity. He had heard from Doctor John MacKenzie that he was something of a poet. Indeed, he seemed to recall that when Doctor Hugh Blair had been visiting Barskimming lately, MacKenzie had read them some verses on Machlin Holy Fair and that Blair— ever a keen and seldom a kindly critic—had thought them to be not wanting in merit. Well . . . the man standing there was certainly no ordinary individual—and he might be a poet as well as a fornicator.

He cast a side-long glance at the pulpit, and the Lord Justice Clerk of Scotland wondered how Mr. Auld would address them. It wasn't a task he himself would have enjoyed. And though Kirk discipline didn't seem to do much good, he agreed on the necessity of rebuke and admonition, for it would never do for fornicators to get it into their heads that their offences were trivial in any way. Indeed it was a crime that, by striking at legitimacy, struck at the root of succession, and hence at the root of property. That, thought the Lord Justice Clerk, as he waited for Auld to begin, was probably the basis of the seventh commandment.

James Boswell, of Auchinleck House, paying one of his courtesy visits to Auld's kirk, was in the company of Lord Barskimming. (The old Auchinleck Loft in the west wall had been extended to cover the vestry, and, as the West Loft, was now rented to sundry parishioners.)

Boswell and Auld were friends of long acquaintance. His interest in Robert Burns, as in the other sinners, was satisfied by a bleary-eyed glance. His mind dwelt on the days when Willie Auld had been something of a dandy. He could not help regretting that he had discarded the sumptuous wigs of those days.

He must remember to twit him at dinner about the really stupendous wig he had worn the last time he had visited him at St. James's Court in the Lawnmarket of Edinburgh.

Boswell could now see that wig, fantastic upon Willie's fantastic head, the great mass of perpendicular curls swinging and bobbing across his shoulders every time he moved his head—it must have been a brute to carry for any length of time.

He had seen Willie down the West Bow to his inn in the Grassmarket. He could hear the voice of a shocked bystander even now. The amazed townsman had gaped at the wig with open mouth, and then had said to his companion in a voice that rang across the narrow street: "By God, sir, there's a wig awa' by like the hunner-and-nineteenth psalm!"

Aye: Old Sammy would have found the Reverend Mr. Auld of Machlin a much tougher and formidable exponent of Calvinism than the Reverend Mr. Dun of Auchinleck.

He must remember to ask the Reverend Willie how many verses there were in the hundred-and-nineteenth psalm—and what had become of the wig!

Claude Alexander, and his sister Wilhelmina, sitting in the Ballochmyle Loft diagonally opposite, could not see the face of Robert Burns; but they could tell from the tilt of his head that he most certainly hung it in no shame. Miss Alexander, who was no beauty and was now on the sunny side of thirty, wondered what her reactions would have been had she ever found herself in the embarrassing position of the three wretched women who now stood with bowed heads and white faces. But, of course, such rebukes were only for the common herd. Had she ever conceived, she would have gone to Edinburgh or York or Bath.

But, alas, the genteel and haughty lass of Ballochmyle had never been involved in such a possibility—and it was unlikely, for all her brother's vast wealth, that she would ever tempt a man now. The common herd certainly had to pay (as was but proper) for their pleasures; but it did seem that they had pleasures to pay for.

Her brother Claude, on the other hand, thought differently. He had spent many fruitful and enjoyable years in India. All this fuss about fornication was ridiculous. Far better to let the lower orders breed like rabbits if they wanted: thus they would provide the country with a plentiful reserve of cheap labour . . . It was obvious that that fellow Burns there was openly enjoying his brief moment of notoriety and was not at all repentant.

In the adjacent Patrons' Loft across the window-gap, John Arnot of Dalquhatswood, paying one of his periodic visits as deputy for the Earl of Loudon, whose factor he was, watched the Bard with great interest. Robert Burns was the most remarkable man he had ever known, and, at the beginning of his trouble with Jean Armour, had written him what he could not help considering one of the most remarkable letters ever written. It was a fantastic, incredible letter, packed with wit and pathos and scholarship; but so characteristic of the man who had written it that it seemed to Arnot most unfitting that he should now be standing with the ruck of everyday sinners. John Arnot remembered how one day when he had visited Mossgiel on a factorial visit of inspection, Robert Burns had assured him that he had indeed married Jean Armour. And he could not help wondering how he had got round that bit of business with Auld and his Session of inquisitors: he would need to make a point of asking him about it when next he visited Mossgiel—or met him in Gavin Hamilton's.

John Arnot could not help but feel sorry that the "hough-magandie pack" had at last got the Mossgiel Bard in their clutches. For a certainty, there would be a blistering poem from his pen to celebrate the occasion.

Arnot was a man of the utmost respectability or he would not otherwise have been the Loudon factor. But like many another man in his position, he was prone to the luxury of private thoughts; and Robert Burns came very near to giving public expression to them.

But if the gentry and their representatives were interested in the proceedings, the ordinary folks of Machlin were absorbed.

The endless stream of penitents that flowed to the breakwater of the stool of repentance always fascinated them.

The men and the women were often sharply divided in their responses. Sometimes the men found their sympathies softening towards a lass they thought unfortunate, only to find their women-folks denouncing her as a shameless hizzie and a brazen bitch.

George Markland and his wife Agnes Shaw, for example, were particularly sympathetic to Jean Armour. They realised only too well that it might have been their own daughter Jean whom Burns might have ruined. And yet, though their sympathies were all for Jean Armour, they could not bring themselves to hate Robert Burns. They had always found him considerate and civil, and their own daughter spoke highly of him. Mrs. Markland whispered in her husband's ear that James Armour would have been better advised to have allowed them to set up as man and wife. And George Markland, knowing they had often courted in his barn, nodded his head and began to feel uneasy: damned but it was an uneasy ordeal for young folks to go through with, and Rab Burns was bound to be feeling his position keenly.

Nance Tinnock, on the other hand, had little sympathy for Jean. Her own son Robert had once been compelled to mount the stool and stand his rebuke from Daddy Auld. And though Robert Burns was an infrequent visitor to her ale-house, she had a soft heart to him, as she had to all young lads whose feet slipped with the tempting Jezebels of the parish. Nance was firmly convinced that it was the Jezebels who led the lads into temptation, even though she knew how little temptation they needed . . .

Hugh Woodrow, the smith, looked keenly from Robert Burns to Jean Armour. He was well acquainted with both of them. And the smith thought, as so many men thought, that he wouldn't have minded standing in the kirk for a year of Sundays for the pleasure of having put Jean Armour in the family way.

But throughout the congregation the fight was being joined in the minds of the worshippers; and busy tongues would flail the chaff of censure from the grain of merit for weeks to come.

For Jean Armour, conscious of the excitement in the congregation, conscious that Rab was standing there behind her, the ordeal was almost beyond bearing. It was the bitterest moment of her life. She knew she should not be standing to be rebuked and censured for fornication: at worst she should be standing here with Rab at her side for the sin of an irregular marriage. And yet, in the clutch of circumstance, she felt so weak and helpless that she had no bitterness and resentment to offset her shame. All she wanted was that Mr. Auld would be quick and brief with his censuring and so let her escape to the partial sanctity of the Cowgate.

Auld coughed and a hush instantly settled on the congregation. He looked from the face of one penitent to another. Then in a cold clear voice he said:

"You appear there to be rebuked, and at the same time making profession of repentance for the sin of fornication.

"The frequency of this sin is just matter of lamentation among Christians, and affords just ground of deep humiliation to the guilty persons themselves.

"We call you to reflect seriously in contrition of heart on all the instances of your sin and guilt, in the numbers, high aggravation and unhappy consequences, and say, having done foolishly, we will do so no more.

"Beware of returning again to your sin as some of you have done, like the dog to his vomit, or like the sow that is washed to her wallowing in the mire."

There was a general shuffling in the kirk as they resumed their several places; and there was much whispering among those who sat in the shadows and in the rear. Daddy Auld had come down on them with a very light hand indeed. Auld was getting past his best. Some of them could mind the day, not so very long ago, when he would have dressed them down till they would have been sobbing fit to break their hearts. Aye! and up on the cutty stool too: even if it took all day to give them a thorough dribbing . . .

But the service was nearly over. Auld had lifted up his voice and his countenance in the last prayer: soon he would be raising his long arm and extending his great hand in blessing over them . . .

As the kirk dispersed he made his way out, looked to neither hand but made straight across to Gavin Hamilton's. He had arranged to meet his landlord and MacKenzie there.

After they had discussed his ordeal, Gavin Hamilton said:

"I understand, Robert, that James Armour has been inquiring as to what siller you are likely to make out of your poems: does this not appear to you as being strange?"

"Strange? In what way, Mr. Hamilton? I doubt if he can be thinking of having me as a son-in-law after destroying my marriage lines . . ."

"No: I think he's even less disposed to that idea than ever. But he kens that you're going to the Indies and he kens that John Wilson is about to put your poems on the market. He passed the remark to a good friend of mine that if you could make enough money out of a lousy book o' stinkin' verses to pay your passage to Jamaica, you could damn well pay for the expense of throwing his dochter wi' one of your ill-gotten gets . . . Save your anger, Robert: I'm only reporting exactly what has been reported to me!"

"You don't think he could clap me in gaol, do you?"

"Easy enough: all he needs to do is to get Sheriff Wallace to issue a writ. You have admitted paternity: what can you deny? It's done day and daily as you well ken."

"But I've no money; and it is doubtful if there will be any profit to speak of from my poems. Indeed I have mortgaged enough of that in gathering together my kit for the voyage. God damnit! am I never to be left alone——"

"Steady, steady: a calm head at a time like this is absolutely essential. And I'm not telling you all this merely to enrage you: I'm not your friend for nothing. There is a way James Armour can be bested in an affair like this. All you have got to do is to make assignation of all your property and your rights to your brother Gilbert . . . or to whomsoever you think would be best. Say you decided on Gilbert: he would understand that the assignation was purely legal. The money would still be in the family: only Armour couldna touch a penny of it."

"But he could still throw me into gaol?"

"He could. But what good would that do him? Satisfy his spite maybe. But he would rather have the money. And, of course, the complaint would need to be lodged in Jean's name and over her signature . . . But what's to prevent you going into hiding for a week or two? Is there anywhere you ken you could go? Somewhere the sheriff's officers would never think of looking for you?"

"Will you draw up the necessary deed for me to sign, Mr. Hamilton?"

"Certainly, Robert. There will be no difficulty in that. You'll want it drawn out in favour of Gilbert: in fact I would need to insist that it was in Gilbert's favour since he has equal rights wi' you in my farm."

"Yes, yes: I agree to Gilbert. But there's a little bit o' poetic justice I would like to mete out here. Armour wants my money for Jean's bairn: I want it to go to Betty Paton's lass. She'll be coming to Mossgiel any day now. I promised her mother I would look after her; and we never ken how things will fare about Mossgiel when I'm away. I'd like some provision made for her."

"There's justice in that, Robert; and wisdom too. There's nothing to prevent Miss Paton filing a claim against you as well as Armour . . . But here again you see the need to assign your money in trust to Gilbert . . . I'll tell you what. Fetch Gilbert down here wi' you the nicht and we'll no' be long in drafting out a deed. Syne, Willie Chalmers or somebody can have it read out at the Cross o' Ayr; and that'll mak' everything fully legal and binding. But you'll need to go into hiding the moment we discover that Armour has taken out a writ. Don't worry: the moment he puts his nose in Mr. Wallace's chamber, intelligence will be brought to me here. We writers hae got to have our pulse on every siccan ongaun, or our clients would seldom get the satisfaction they do. In law, you see, the important thing is not justice so much as aey being a step ahead o' your enemy."

And in the case of Burns *v.* Armour, Gavin Hamilton had no intention of having to whistle for the rent of Mossgiel. But there was added satisfaction in the knowledge that in helping himself he was also helping the Bard, for he had a very genuine regard for him.

Doctor MacKenzie said: "Troubles never come by themselves, Robert; but you'll get over them. When you've settled down in the Indies, you'll look back on all this and laugh. Aye: you'll have the laugh on them yet. But I maun say I think James Armour is behaving very foolishly—and I canna but feel sorry for Jean Armour. I wouldna think she would have any hand in issuing a writ against you—indeed I doubt if she would ever be consulted."

THE WARRANT

Word having reached Mossgiel that the ship *Nancy* was at Greenock and that he would receive orders any day from the captain to proceed there and take up his berth, there was feverish activity to finish the packing of his sea-chest.

He wrote to Mary Campbell that she, too, might be ready to sail. It worried him that he had only had one note from her saying that she was well, that she was coming to Greenock, and that he could write her there in the care of her relation, Peter MacPherson. But the fact that she had had to dictate the letter to another would no doubt account for its stilted and unemotional brevity.

On the evening of Saturday, the 29th of July, St. James's Lodge from Tarbolton held a visitation meeting in Machlin. As depute-master, he had never missed a meeting of his Lodge, and he had the feeling that this might very well be the last he would preside over. As junior warden, Gilbert, too, was in attendance.

As soon as the business of the meeting was over and the Lodge had passed to refreshment, he meant to let himself go in grand style: he would let the brethren see how the social hour should be enjoyed.

It was at this point that Gilbert came to him with a sealed note and a verbal message that it was secret and urgent.

He retired to a corner and broke the seal. He recognised Jamie Smith's writing. The note read:

"My sister has just had word with your Jean. She is in sore trouble and pleads that you be informed immediately that the warrant you spoke of will be issued for your apprehension by Monday morning. The poor girl is in great distress for your sake—and in mortal terror lest her father discover that she has blabbed. She would give anything to meet you and explain. Destroy this note. Let me hear from you when you have safely grounded as arranged. The Lord look after you is the wish of yours, through thick and thin, J. S."

He had a hurried word with John Wilson the secretary, bade a hasty farewell to the brethren, and left the meeting with Gilbert. When he was gone, the secretary noticed that he had not touched his drink. It must indeed have been urgent business that had called him away. But, reflected the canny John, it wasn't lost what a friend got; and he drained the glass.

In the evening, when the gloaming had settled down over the land, a light cart emerged from the Mossgiel road-end and presently turned along the Kilmarnock road.

He lay in the bottom of the cart beside his sea-chest. Gilbert led the pony. A quarter of a mile ahead, William acted as advance scout. Cousin Robert Allan had gone off earlier to prepare against his arrival at Old Rome Forest on the Fairlie estate, lying a little beyond Kilmarnock.

He had thought of many other retreats before he had finally decided on Fairlie. He believed he would be safe there. At the worst, it would be a good place to escape from; and he could spend alternate nights in Irvine or Kilmarnock . . . But the publication of his poems on the coming Monday finally decided him in favour of proximity to Kilmarnock. He had plenty of good friends there who would shelter him in his need.

Robert Muir had got his message from Bob Allan; and when they rumbled into Auld Killie he was waiting for them with a hot bite and a glass of wine. The chest was unloaded; the cart was put in the yard; and after a hasty meal and a rehearsal of plans, Gilbert rode back to Mossgiel. Willie had only come half-way—when they had been certain there would be no Machlin travellers on the road. Bob Allan would bring home the cart when he rode back through the town on the Monday morning.

"Tell your folks not to worry," said Muir as he bade Gilbert good-night. "They'll never have the audacity to arrest Robin; and even if they do, we'll not be long in raising a subscription here, and in Ayr, as will give him his freedom. Armour must be mad."

"Aye," said Gilbert. "But when you're dealing wi' mad dogs you have to be careful . . . But I shall ever remember your kindness, Mr. Muir."

"It's a great privilege to be able to be of any assistance to your brother. Have no fear: once his poems are before the public, not even Henry Dundas will dare to clap him behind the bars . . ."

"You're no' thinking of pushing on to Fairlie the night, Robin? The idea's impossible. Come out with me to Loanfoot and you can slip away in the morning."

"Sunday morning! So that I'll be a conspicuous figure on the road! No: I must get there under the cover of darkness. I've arranged that. If I don't arrive, the Allans will think something has happened to me. What a mess, Robert! Running away like a hunted animal! And my poems coming from the press on Monday! Thank God I managed to get all my proofs corrected and all my arrangements made wi' Wilson before this broke. But it'll upset my arrangements with the subscriptions. I had intended delivering the bulk of the copies to my friends. But it canna be helped now: my friends will just have to make allowances . . .

"How did it all happen? That's a long story, Robert. I was sailing along fine. Stood two Sundays in the kirk. Just my usual luck: I have only another Sunday to stand and then I am a free man . . . and a certified bachelor. Now I may never have the opportunity of standing—before I sail. I suppose I ought to go mad, since that's about all any reasonable man could do in the circumstances . . . I don't even know that I'll manage to settle with Wilson: I may even be in gaol . . . And what the hell am I to do between now and sailing? All my many good friends to say farewell to before I go! And how can I do that? I might be picked up anywhere.

"And I must sail. I can't go back on that now. Everything's been arranged and I've signed everything over to Gilbert. And Betty Paton's bringing her bairn to Mossgiel . . .

"As a matter of sober truth, Robert, I'll share a secret wi' you; but I must have your solemn promise that the secret will lie between you and the grave . . . I've a wife waiting for me in Greenock! Mary Campbell . . . Aye: the same Highland Mary . . .

"Ah, don't tell me: since ever my father died it's been one damned folly after another . . . And me acting from the highest principles! I should have known that men like me canna afford to have principles. This world doesna allow a poor man to have principles: you need money for that, plenty of money. And yet, such is the irony of life, you canna have money and principles too. Strange, is it not?

"No: Mary's child shouldn't be born till we get to Jamaica. She's due about the end of the year. You see: I just had to get a certificate from Daddy Auld. We may need to get married officially when we get there. So I'll need to go back and stand another Sunday in Machlin. I don't suppose the sheriff's men will be out looking for me on the Lord's Day. Gilbert will be spying out the land for me. I could dash in next Sunday—and dash out again.

"I'll be damned if I'll let them beat me. Whiles I get bitter about Jean; but I can never keep up my anger. Now that her time is coming near, I just canna be angry wi' her. I suppose I still love her: I suppose I'll always love her. The times I had wi' Jean! There never was a sweeter armful. I can't smother my natural feelings and say that because I'm married to Mary Campbell I should have no feelings for Jean Armour. You canna say no to your deepest feelings. I love Mary. I'm more than happy to think we'll settle down together in Jamaica as man and wife. I don't suppose I could settle down wi' Jean Armour now even if there was no Mary Campbell: there's been too much bad blood spilled atween us for that. In any case I haven't the means to settle down wi' Jean. And she wouldn't come wi' me to the Indies: not unless she poisoned her father and mother . . . though they both deserve a worse death . . .

"There was nothing else for it. Take my brother Gilbert: he doesna care if he never puts his arms round a lass: it just doesna worry him. At least it doesna drive him mad. But I have had to face the issue wi' myself. I just canna live without a lass. I've always been that way. Don't think I would change places wi' Gilbert: not even at this unfortunate moment. If it was just a case o' lifting my leg and saying fare-you-well, life would be easy and pleasant enough. But I've got to be in love.

"And then I can't look upon paternity as something to be shunned or denied. I have feelings as a parent. That's what worries me about Jean. I'll never see the bairn. Yet I ken well enough that I'll be thinking about it for the rest o' my days. Damnit! it will have my blood in it as well as hers. It'll be a Burns as well as an Armour. It'll maybe be more Burns than Armour: it's happened before and it can well happen again. It may even be a boy! And how do you think I'll feel in Jamaica wi' a son growing up in Machlin? And maybe Jean married to some rotten-hearted beggar that'll be bad to him? All very well to say that I should have thought about that before I fathered him. Hell! I married Jean: didn't I? I was thrown over in the damnedest way—and then I married Mary Campbell. I do penance; and Daddy Auld says: 'Go and sin no more'—as if that was the end of it. Go and sin no more! It must make the angels weep to hear such bluidy cant. He might as well tell folk to go and cough no more . . .

"And if I am wrong, then, by Heavens, I'm being made to pay for it! And so is Jean; and so will the bairn yet to be born . . .

"What a mockery it all is. God created us with desires and with wills to resist those desires. But some of us He created with too strong desires and wills too weak to resist them. And when we behave as He has given us the constitution to behave, along comes the Kirk and says that we have sinned in the sight of God and must suffer accordingly. But what does this make God? A monster who takes a delight in torturing His creatures for the mere sake of enjoying the torture!

"I refuse to accept it, Robert. I can think only of the Creator in terms of Benevolence; and Benevolence and suffering don't flow from the same fountain-source. I can recognise no suffering in this world that comes from God; but I see plenty of suffering all around me that comes from man.

"And I believe that we will work our redemption when we eliminate man-made suffering from the world . . . Aye: we've discussed all this before: only the idea of it all has hit me with unusual force these last days . . . I've had time and plenty to think about the fate that awaits me at the hands of men—and the mischances of fortune . . ."

Robert Muir had let him talk himself out. But he would not have minded if he had taken the whole night to do so. He could imagine nothing more inspiring than to listen to his friend when he was in talking fettle. And to-night, with the strain of events tensed upon him, his talk was gloriously nervous, pursuing with lightning flashes the thoughts that came into his mind . . . flashes that lit up the dark corners of doubt and uncertainty . . .

But there was a practical side to his friendship; and since Robin was determined to push forward to the Fairlie estate he would at least accompany him to his residence at Loanfoot that lay in that direction. They could talk as well outside as inside; and they could discuss the practical business of the poems being published on Monday. Whatever he could do, he would be only too glad to do. He was certain that once the poems were before the public that the public would acclaim him. Once he was acclaimed there would be little need for him to remain in hiding or to suffer the indignity of being hunted like a felon. Not knowing James Armour, he had some difficulty in taking his writ as seriously as Robin did.

On the Sunday he wrote to several friends telling them of the position he now found himself in.

To John Richmond in Edinburgh he wrote:

"My hour is now come. You and I will never meet in Britain more. I have orders within three weeks at farthest to repair aboard the *Nancy*, Captain Smith, from Clyde to Jamaica, and to call at

Antigua. This, except to our friend Smith, whom God long preserve, is a secret about Machlin. Would you believe it? Armour has got a warrant to throw me in gaol till I find security for an enormous sum. This they keep an entire secret, but I got it by a channel they little dream of; and I am wandering from one friend's house to another, and like a true son of the Gospel 'have nowhere to lay my head.' I know you will pour an execration on her head, but spare the poor, ill-advised girl for my sake, though may all the Furies that rend the injured, enraged Lover's bosom await the old harridan, her Mother, until her latest hour! May Hell string the arm of Death to throw the fatal dart, and all the winds of warring elements rouse the infernal flames to welcome her approach! For Heaven's sake burn this letter, and never show it to a living creature. I write it in a moment of rage, reflecting on my miserable situation—exiled, abandoned, forlorn—I can write no more—let me hear from you by the return of Connel—I will write you ere I go."

In the quiet of the afternoon he took a turn round the parks of the Fairlie estate he knew so well, since many a happy hour he had spent here. He reflected that when his father had first come to the West from Edinburgh it had been to Fairlie he had come . . . Fate played many a strange trick. Fairlie was like to be the last place he would rest in before he made Greenock and left Scotland.

Greenock! Mary Campbell was waiting for him there. Well: Mary would have had his letter by this time and she wouldn't have long to wait. As like as not she would be able to see the *Nancy* lying about the harbour . . .

But what a way to be leaving Scotland! He was twenty-seven: in the prime of manhood. And what had he to show for it? Years of hard and grinding toil; years of hard reading and hard studying. Yet he stood now as he had once stood in Irvine: without a spare sixpence in his pocket.

True, he had made many fine friends; and he had known many glorious hours with the lassies. He had paid for these hours and was still paying for them. But he had always had to pay the hindmost price . . .

Yet for all his friends and his glorious hours he was being driven to leave Scotland like a criminal. Instead of enjoying his last days in Scotland, enjoying the pleasurable task of distributing his printed verses, he had to skulk in hiding and wait for second- or third-hand reports of how they would be received. This was as bitter a pill as ever he had had to swallow: how bitter nobody but himself could know.

All this was to be laid at the door of the Armours. Their stinking pride had been his undoing. It was all very well for Jean to see the folly of her ways. She was seeing that folly too late.

Would she not have been happier to-day as his wife—even if she had been the wife of a labouring hind? But maybe the blame was as much his. He should have insisted that she come with him as soon as she discovered she was pregnant; and he should have insisted that she come to Mossgiel until such time as he got some kind of labouring work and, with it, a roof to shelter them. No doubt to-day she would be only too pleased to crawl under any kind of a roof, provided she could do so as his wife.

But recrimination was profitless. Jean belonged to the tragic past. His future lay with Mary Campbell and the spicy islands of the far distant West . . .

He would have to watch himself or he would fall to pieces. He had more to worry about than he could cope with. At least he couldn't cope with it in isolation. As soon as it was dark, he would have to get into Kilmarnock and have a drink with Robert Muir. Maybe it would be possible, Sunday or no Sunday, to forgather with Tam Samson, Willie Parker, Charles Samson, John Gowdie, Gavin Turnbull . . . anybody who would provide an audience and set the bowl flowing so that the terrible tensions within him might be released. He couldn't go on chasing the tail of his worries like this.

But to get to the Indies he would need money. Wilson would be in no hurry to collect any. He would wait till the money came in in the usual way of business. Somehow or other he would need to get round the outlying districts himself and get the money in his own hand: he would know it was safe then. Without money he daren't show face in Greenock—supposing he could dodge the sheriff's men. Even Mary Campbell, if she discovered how desperately poor he was, might think twice about sailing with him. But would anyone believe that he, as tenant-farmer in the twenty-eighth year of his life, could be so utterly destitute?

And then it dawned upon him that probably nobody really did believe he was so desperately poor. Men like Wilson probably thought he made a poor mouth as so many people did. Maybe they thought he pled poverty merely to gain greater sympathy and consideration.

When he came to think of it, none of his friends treated him as though he were on the brink of destitution. And perhaps he had never acted as though he were. He had always had a proud stomach where money was concerned; and he had never really revealed to anyone how he actually stood—except in general terms.

Well: was he to go round his friends at this late date and tell them that he was without a penny? Could he insist that they believe him? At worst they would only put him down for a liar: at best they would think that he wanted to cadge from them. Either way the idea was unbearable. He would have to continue to put the same face on life as he had always put. A poor man, yes; but honest and independent and asking nothing but friendship and good company and the warmth of a kindly heart . . .

As he walked round the Fairlie parks where his father had first broken bread—and soil—in the West, he found that he could not escape from the coils of his own thoughts.

He determined he would risk walking over to Robert Muir's residence at Loanfoot. Together they might risk a jaunt into Killie and see how things stood in Sandy Patrick's howff. If Tam Samson was enjoying a caup of ale he was almost certain to be enjoying it with his good-son Sandy. It would be folly for him to spend any of his last precious hours in Scotland skulking by himself when such company was to be had for a few miles of walking . . .

And in Sandy Patrick's howff, behind a barred door, a few of Auld Killie's sons presided over by Tam Samson passed such a night as the Reverend John Russell never imagined took place in the town even on the merriest fair-night. But then these sons were not of the Old Light persuasion: indeed the only light that some of them worshipped was the light that lay in a caup of good Scots ale when it was laced with a gill of good Scots whisky. With a guard outside to look out for the elders on their rounds (or any other enemy of social mirth and glee) it wasn't long till they had thrown decorum to the winds and were singing how Duncan MacLearie and Janet his wife came to Kilmarnock to buy a new knife . . . And how the night it was a holy night, the day had been a holy day: Kilmarnock gleamed wi' candlelight as Girzie hameward took her way . . .

But though they told many stories and sang many bawdy songs (in conscious as well as unconscious defiance of the Kirk's age-long subversion of the flesh to theological abstraction and death-fixated dogma), the poet was unable to drive either Jean or Mary completely from his mind. In the din of the drink-merry hour, he remained painfully sober. Indeed the drink only served to sharpen his sorrow and tangle his thoughts by releasing the springs of his emotion. He entertained notions of borrowing a horse and riding forthwith into Greenock in order to hear from her own lips how Mary Campbell was faring; what reception she had got from her parents and how they viewed her voyage to the Indies; what preparations she had made against the privations and rigours of the voyage: for he had heard they could be many . . . Above all he wanted to take her once more in his arms and experience the quiver of her responding flesh and hear from her own lips, in that quaint accent of hers, that she loved him, that she needed him, and would follow him to the ends of the earth . . .

But no sooner did he see himself riding towards Greenock than he was turning the horse and riding post-haste back along the familiar road that led to Machlin and to Jean . . . And there and then he could have laid his head on his arms on the ale-wet table and mingled the ale with his tears . . .

Surely Jean and he had known a love that is given to few lovers to know; surely those late summer nights by the banks of the river Ayr, beneath the green thorn tree, had been happier than they had had a right to be? Happier than the happiest moments that had gladdened Eden's garden. For a thousand years before the Fall there could have been no greater happiness than he had shared with Jean. Man could not know greater happiness and live: even now the memory of it was crazing his senses.

No: it wasn't the caup-ale and the Kilbagie that was making him feel this way. He might have been drinking milk for all the effect it had on him. Or maybe he was drunk, drunk as he had never been drunk in his life before. He knew only that there was something far wrong with him: or something far right. He was seeing some things now with a clarity he had never known . . . The very thought of Jean was as intense and immediate as a physical orgasm; her physical vibrations annihilated space; the chemistry of her blood sent time reeling backwards; the great all-embracing waves of her love sucked him down in the darkness of physical sleep, replacing the harshness of the physical world with the unconscious harmonies of the dream world, where the mind is blotted out and sensation, like a rose, folds her petals upon the dewdrops of awareness . . .

With Mary he had never known such love. Mary's love played like a bow on the strings of sensation. It was music; but it was music of awareness. The mind sharpened to a pain-point of sensitivity. It brought the intellect in higher and higher relief. It cried for affirmation; it called for statement; it demanded confirmation. Even in the quiver of her flesh was the quiver of the ideal: quivering against the fear of denial and the outrage of betrayal. It was love in all the poignancy of its pain. It sent forth agonising shoots of tenderness and wept for the pity of unresponse. It made love sentry the night and guard the darkness. It was a wound that bled and had ever to be staunched . . .

Mary Campbell needed him: he needed Jean Armour. They were the split halves of the whole that should be life. But he couldn't tear himself apart, mind from heart, ideal from sensation, learning from knowledge. He was united in all his opposites. He was torn only in the conflict of opposing desires. But his desires must not oppose: he must fight for his own wholeness. If he didn't he would be destroyed in mind and in body and he would never know laughter again: laughter that healed the body and cooled the mind . . .

Laughter!

His fist crashed down on the table.

"Laugh, damn ye! This is the Lord's night: we'll hae a' eternity to weep and wail and gnash our black stumps o' rotten teeth. Laugh, Tam Samson: you great bluidy barrel o' tripes and puddins! Laugh, damn ye, for ye hae the loudest laugh this side o' the Earl o' Hell's supper-table . . . And you, Robert: my worthy frien' and brither dear: get haud o' a big strappin' sonsy hizzie wi' a meikle wame on her like a c'aff bed—wi' a couple o' meikle saft bowsters for your head to rest atween. And row and roll and laugh there till ye fa' asleep . . . You weep wi' sorrow an' you weep wi' laughter. You shed tears ony the ways o't. But since there maun be tears, let them be tears o' laughter. When I get to the bluidy Indies I'll laugh and laugh and laugh till I hae nae tears left for weeping . . . To-morrow morning my poems will come out. And will folk laugh! Black Rab Burns a poet! The Lord God haud us up! He's only half a tenant-farmer o' a hunner an' auchteen acres o' wat sour clay that wadna grow a crap o' decent thristles for a cadger's cuddy. What did I tell ye? You're laughing already afore the bluidy poems are out . . . A poet! Send the poor gowk to the Indies to get sunstroke, for he's moonstruck here. A poet marry my dochter! Not if he knocked a bairn out o' her every twal-month. What! Ye dinna see onything to laugh at? Well, turn the hell-hounds o' justice after him till he hands over the gowden guineas that'll pay for my dochter's virginity—and my decorum! If you canna laugh at that there's nae laughter in you. For me: I'll laugh and sing and shake my leg as lang's I dow . . . Perish the drop o' bluid in me that fears them. Aye: Kilmarnock wabsters fidge and claw . . . And you Sandy, that's stan'in' there a' mouth an' een: fill up the caups wi' that glorious ale o' yours and let's sing Guid-Nicht and Joy be wi' ye a'. For that's how I'd like to leave you. That's how I'd like to remember you across the Atlantic's roar . . . Only laugh—so that I winna hear the roar o' the waters, for I've hated the sea a' my days and a watery grave's an ill grave for a lad that was bred to the plough . . ."

But instead of laughing, Tam Samson, helped by Robert Muir, oxtered him round to Rosebank, his house on the Braeside. Tam put him to bed . . .

And Tam wept tears; but what kind and for what was beyond his knowing . . .

GOOD BLACK PRINT

The sun was nearly in the mid-day sky before he stirred from the bed in Tam Samson's house. But apart from a touch of nausea he felt reasonably well. Tam came to waken him with a caup of strong ale and insisted that he drink it no matter how he felt.

And then Tam placed a volume of his *Poems* in his hand. "I was round at Wilson's and cadged it frae him: I kent the sicht o' it wad cheer ye up. Lie there and read your book till the ale works through you: by that time there'll be a bite on the table."

He had scarcely words to thank Tam; but Tam wasn't waiting for thanks: with a wave of his arm he left the room.

He had corrected the sheets for his poems and he was familiar with the type and the setting; but this was the first stitched copy he had handled. He turned over the pages to get the feel of the book. There was no doubt Wilson had made a fine job of it: there wasn't a handsomer volume of poems printed in Scotland. An elegant job first to last: well worth every penny of the three shillings the subscribers would pay for it.

He turned again to the title page: *Poems*, Chiefly in the Scottish Dialect, by Robert Burns . . . He was indeed a Bard now and fully justified in using the title: the proudest title any man could earn. The Bard of Ayrshire: a proud title! God be praised that he had lived to see this day and that he had seen it while his foot was still on Scottish soil . . .

He turned the page and read his Preface.

"The following trifles are not the production of the Poet who, with all the advantages of learned art, and perhaps amid the elegancies and idlenesses of upper life, looks down for a rural theme, with an eye to Theocrites or Virgil. To the Author of this, these and other celebrated names their countrymen are, in their original languages, 'A fountain shut up, and a book sealed.' Unacquainted with the necessary requisites for commencing Poet by rule, he sings the sentiments and manners, he felt and saw in himself and his rustic compeers around him, in his and their native language. Though a Rhymer from his earliest years, at least from the earliest impulses of the softer passions, it was not till very lately that the applause, perhaps the partiality, of Friendship, wakened his vanity so far as to make him think anything of his was worth showing; and none of the following works were ever composed with a view to the press. To amuse himself with the little creations of his own fancy, amid the toil and fatigues of a laborious life; to transcribe the various feelings, the loves, the griefs, the hopes, the fears, in his own breast; to find some kind of counterpoise to the struggles of a world, always an alien scene, a task uncouth to the poetical mind; these were his motives for courting the Muses, and in these he found Poetry to be its own reward.

"Now that he appears in the public character of an Author, he does it with fear and trembling. So dear is fame to the rhyming tribe, that even he, an obscure, nameless Bard, shrinks aghast at the thought of being branded as 'An impertinent blockhead, obtruding his nonsense on the world; and because he can make a shift to jingle a few doggerel, Scotch rhymes together, looks upon himself as a Poet of no small consequence forsooth.'

"It is an observation of that celebrated Poet, whose divine Elegies do honour to our language, our nation, and our species, that 'Humility has depressed many a genius to a hermit, but never raised one to fame.' If any Critic catches at the word genius, the Author tells him, once for all, that he certainly looks upon himself as possessed of some poetic abilities, otherwise his publishing in the manner he has done would be a manœuvre below the worst character, which, he hopes, his worst enemy will ever give him:

but to the genius of a Ramsay, or the glorious dawnings of the poor, unfortunate Fergusson, he, with equal unaffected sincerity, declares that, even in his highest pulse of vanity, he has not the most distant pretensions. These two justly admired Scotch Poets he has often had in his eye in the following pieces; but rather with a view to kindle at their flame than for servile imitation.

"To his Subscribers, the Author returns his most sincere thanks. Not the mercenary bow over a counter, but the heart-throbbing gratitude of the Bard, conscious how much he is indebted to Benevolence and Friendship for gratifying him, if he deserves it, in that dearest wish of every poetic bosom—to be distinguished. He begs his readers, particularly the Learned and the Polite, who may honour him with a perusal, that they will make every allowance for Education and Circumstances of Life: but if after a fair, candid and impartial criticism he shall stand convicted of Dulness and Nonsense, let him be done by, as he would in that case do by others—let him be condemned, without mercy, to contempt and oblivion."

After this there was no lying in bed: he must find out what his Kilmarnock friends were thinking.

And then he remembered that the warrant for his arrest would also make its public appearance to-day. Even now the sheriff's men would be calling at Mossgiel. No: they would have been there by now. Maybe they would make a swoop on Kilmarnock . . .

Hell roast and blast them! When he should be receiving his honours as a Bard he was being hunted like a badger.

Tam Samson was sympathetic. "It's a bad business this warrant. There's nae point in you vaiging about the toon since you never ken when the officers might spring out on ye. Ye canna risk that just when your book's coming aff the press and Wilson's men are hard at the stitching. Bide a wee and I'll get some o' the laddies to scour the toon and see how the land's lying. We'll soon ken if ony strangers hae made their way intil the toon—and just exactly what their business is. But, Robin lad, I maun say that I'm ta'en on wi' the look o' your book. I read the Twa Dogs afore I cam' ben to wauken ye; and by God but it reads weel in print. And mind ye:

print mak's a difference: a great improvement. No' that I could sit doon and read stracht through. Na, na: poems are like a measure o' guid wine: ye canna slooch it doon at a gulp the wey ye wad a bicker o' tippenny. Ye maun sip denty-like to relish the full flavour. Aha: I'll be mony a lang nicht at your book, Rab. An' I see ye havena got Holy Willie intil't. But that wad be fully strong for Johnnie Wilson. Ah! but bi-God ye ken Johnnie's no' strait-laced: he can gie and tak' a coorse story wi' the best o' us. Damned, Rab, but folk are narrow: ye can say onything that comes into your head; but ye canna print what comes into your head. Now if a thing can be said, surely it can be printed? I just canna see the reason for the hypocrisy."

"There's good enough reason too, Tam: when you put words down in print they become the property of everybody who can read. But I fully agree with you about the narrow limits that are set by the self-appointed critics as to where the lines should be drawn. It's usually hypocrisy that decides where the line shall be drawn; and that's what irks me and has irked me sore wi' Wilson."

"I ken what you mean fine; but could we no' hae private books for private reading as weel as public books for public reading."

"Aye: there's something in your idea, Tam. But I wish I knew how my book was being received. I ken it's too early yet. Folk are no' waiting for my book to appear so that they can throw their work aside and no' look up till they have finished it. But you ken how I feel?"

"Fine I ken Rab; but you've no' to worry. You've been worrying ower much lately. No' that you havena had cause and mair to worry you. But you'll need to be mair careful, lad, and look after your health. When your nerves get worn thin they can play the devil wi' you."

"I suppose they played the devil wi' me last night? But you'll need to forgive me for last night. I don't know what I said——"

"Never mind what you said or what you didna say. You said nothing that onybody could tak' offence wi'. And naebody took offence. Mind ye, Rab: drunk or sober you're aey worth listening to. Aye: ye had us a' spell-bound last nicht. And a bit feared."

"I hope Mistress Samson wasn't annoyed with my conduct?"

"Man, the wife's gotten a saft side to ye. She's out for a bit message the noo; but she'll no' be lang and then ye'll hear frae hersel' what she thinks o' you. It was me got the warm side o' her tongue last nicht. No' that she worries about me. But she blamed me for getting you into the state you were in. Damned! it wasna what you drank, Rab. I've seen you rise frae twice as much again without turning a hair. That's what I mean by telling you to look after yoursel'; nerves, laddie, nerves. Too much worry and no' enough sleep. It gets the better o' you in the hinderend."

"Tam . . . I may need to borrow a horse——"

"I've twa at the grass the noo, Rab. You can hae your pick whenever you tak' the notion. Same wi' the saddles . . . tak' your fancy. Dinna let a horse worry you."

"Thanks, Tam: I'll repay the debt wi' a swatch o' rhyming-ware some day. And you ken I'll no' abuse the horse."

"You'd abuse a bairn quicker. There's none o' us aboot Killie but wad dae onything for you. You've only to say the word. Mind that! We're brithers by obligation; but what's mair to the point, we're brithers by inclination."

Despite the years that separated them, he felt very close to Tam Samson. Some day, and some day soon, he would repay his kindness in verse. For the moment, he had no words with which to convey his deep gratitude.

Kilmarnock was rich in the character of her sons. She had a hard core of hard-thinking, hard-swearing and hard-drinking mechanics—weavers of carpets, makers of leather goods, knitters of bonnets and hose, dyers of cloths, and makers of plaidings.

More than Ayr or Machlin was she rich in human personality, for her mean streets were tightly packed and her small houses overcrowded . . .

Machlin was but a country village snuggling round the kirk. Ayr was the county town and a seaport; always there was a keen wind blowing in from the sea dispelling the stinks and stenches, and bringing a salt-tanged freshness into its meanest corners.

But Kilmarnock was a rabbit-warren of a town and there was no sea-freshness in its breezes. The place stank of filth and poverty and vermin-infested humanity huddled in wretched hovels. There were many fine dwellings lying here and there, protected by a plot of garden; but the better houses were on the outskirts of the town. The seven mean streets that radiated from the Cross were narrow and ill-paved, and spoke loudly of the hugger-mugger of clarty folks compelled to crowd ever closer upon each other because they were allowed nowhere else to live.

But the Kilmarnock folks were tough with a wizened toughness. Their compactness gave them a clannish stolidity that was not to be found in Ayr. Wit sharpened wit in the struggle to attain personality and individuality within the framework of the clan. The struggle threw up its philosophers, its theologians and its poets—and a tough, quaint, heady lot they were.

Gavin Turnbull was a worthy character and the leader of the local poets. As such, he sometimes drank in the Bard's company in Sandy Patrick's howff.

To-night he was holding court with two brother-poets who had called on him to discuss the *Poems*.

Gavin was indeed a minor poet. But he had all the atmosphere around him of a traditional one. His attic room contained neither chair nor table. An open bed of loose straw stood in the corner, a stone by the grateless fire served as a stool, the ledge of the window-frame did for desk and table, just as the lid of his tin kettle provided plate and bowl.

The brother-poets sat on the edge of the bed while Gavin, from the stone, looked up to them.

John Andrews, the elder of the two visitors, was an ancient weaver who, like Gavin, had seen better days: he was an expert, when sufficiently sober, at loom-making and repairing.

His companion was as young as Gavin; but he was harder bitten and more realistic in his poetic values.

Andrews said: "How is it that I've never heard tell o' this man Burns? Ye say he's weel-kenned about Killie; but, dod! I never kenned him——"

"And there's damned few you dinna ken, Jock!" interrupted his companion, Peter Scott.

"I ken him weel," replied Gavin. "Of coorse, he chooses his company——"

"By certes, and he chooses his verses! How in God's name a farmer frae Machlin can rhyme like this is astonishin': astonishin'! The mair I read—and I've been sitting up for twa strucken nichts reading—the mair I'm astonished. I'm prodigious astonished, Gavin!"

"They're no' bad verses, Jock—here and there."

"Here and there! Damn ye—everywhere! Every bluidy line——"

"Every bluidy word!"

"There you are noo, Gavin; and ye ken Peter here's no' easily astonished."

Gavin clawed at the lice in his oxter. "Aye . . . they're good. A bit coorse here and there and wantin' a genteel polish——"

Peter Scott spat on the floor.

"Polish! What the hell are you gabbing about? Thir's no' verses for your ladies or pious priests. Thir's verses for men—no' college monkeys. And gin I fell in wi' this man Burns, I'd ask for the privilege o' shaking him by the hand. I didna need to sit up twa nichts like Auld Jock here. I feenished them at ae sittin'——"

"Of coorse, Peter, my een's no' what they were. But I thocht you were a great admirer o' this bard, Gavin?"

"Admire, yes. Having the honour o' his acquaintance, I count myself his admirer. Yes; but I am not only a poet myself but something of a critic of the craft. And I submit that the poems lack elegance——"

"And what the hell d'you ken aboot elegance?" Peter eyed the attic disdainfully and again spat on the floor.

"A man may have nothing but rags to his back and yet have the riches of fine thoughts stored in his mind."

The old bard became impatient. "Aye, aye, Gavin: we ken a' aboot your fine thoughts——"

"Aye; but we'd be a better judge o' that gin they were put down wi' the quill."

"Weel, a' I've got to say is that this poem here on The Twa Dogs clean beats onything I've ever imagined—far less onything I've ever seen in print—an' I hae an astonishing imagination, drunk or sober; and be damned to the baith o' ye!"

"Be damned to you!" snarled Peter Scott. "Wha was the first to say thir verses were supreme—viewed frae ony point? There's nae imagination needed. They're as plain as daylight. And daylight's nae use to a critic. A critic can only work by candlelicht—the daylight's ower sair on his bits o' bleary een. But in the weavin' shed where I work it's a different story. We got twa copies o' the poems: we split them up among us just as we'd split the cost among us. And every man yonder has a page nailed up beside his loom. An' when he's got a poem memorised he passes his sheet on till the next man. And I tell you, the men hae read nocht like it—and we hae some o' the best-read men in Scotland in our weaving-shed.

"Critics, be damned, and their damned elegance! There's naebody reads their damned elegant poetry but their elegant damned sel's. I cam' here the nicht wi' Jock Andrews no' to learn aboot elegance, but to hear about this man Robert Burns that bides about Machlin; that ploughs by day and writes poetry by night; that has set the Kilmarnock wabsters fidgin' and clawin' for ony scrap o' information about him; that has set them by the lugs as Black Jock Russell has never been able to dae . . . What like a man is he; how auld is he; if he's married, how mony weans has he gotten; if he's no' married, wha's he likely to marry and what's her name; where did he get his education—for he's got a learning he never got at the plough——? Has he gotten brithers and sisters— and hae ony o' them gotten his gift . . .? A' this an' mair, Gavin— that's what we want to ken. When a poet can pass muster in a Killie weaving-shed, he can pass muster onywhaur—Sae forget your bluidy learned jaw aboot elegance and what-not and tell us what you ken. And if you ken nocht, say so and we'll awa' up to Sandy Patrick's richt now."

Gavin Turnbull rose with a jerk from the stone.

"Now, now, now! There's nae need for ony high words, Peter. We'll go up thegither to Sandy Patrick's; and if Mr. Burns is aboot,

I'll see what I can do to let ye meet him—just for a minute, of coorse: just for a minute. And you've no' to take me up wrongly, Peter. Naebody has a greater admiration for Mr. Burns than I hae. Maybe I was a wee hasty, Peter, about the elegance—but I meant no offence. No, no: it was just maybe—seeing that the verses are so good—that I was ower anxious to see them a wee better as it were: just a wee shadie better . . . ye ken?"

But Peter Scott only spat towards the fire as he made for the door.

John Andrews wagged a dirty forefinger at Gavin as a signal for silence; and then they followed Peter down the creaking, rickety stairs.

Major William Parker lit his pipe and puffed vigorously. "I understand, Doctor Hamilton, that you kent Burns in Irvine when he was learning the heckling trade there?"

"I did, Major; mony a grand hour we had thegither in a wee ale-house in the Glasgow Vennel . . . Let me see now: oh, just a matter o' four or five years ago! I mind lending him Henry MacKenzie's Man o' Feeling—and I put him onto Robert Fergusson the Embro poet. I told him then that he was nearer to Fergusson than ony other poet I kenned."

"Maist interesting, Doctor. And did he show signs of his poetic genius then? He would be about twenty-three at that time?"

"Oh, you wad hae kenned he was a byornar lad. He was mair serious then, of course. And shy. At times there was a gentleness about him you associate mair wi' the women; but aey manly enough. Oh, and damned independent. I mind what amazed me maist was the byornar amount o' reading he'd put in. There wasna a poet or an author you could mention but he kenned about them: Milton and Pope and Shakespeare—and a' thae kind o' fellows. I was a medical student at the time—but I must say it staggered me. And his speech! By God, Major, but he had a richt elegant way o' talking at times. Just the verra best o' English that you wouldna hear onywhere else—no' even at the college. And syne he micht break into Ayrshire; and there he was equally at hame wi' the mither tongue."

"Yes, I've noticed that, Doctor. He's quite an exceptional fellow Robert—and a heart of gold: nothing mean or petty about him. In company he positively outshines everybody—and we have some very fine wits in Kilmarnock. We're all very happy about his poems here. We'll do all we can to ensure their success. But, for myself, I have no fear on that score. It's unfortunate that he's got himself into trouble with that girl in Machlin. The father issuing a writ has upset him greatly."

"Aye: it couldna hae fallen at a worse time for him. Ah, but this volume'll put him on his feet."

"Yes—for Jamaica. He's very foolish venturing out there. The trouble, Doctor, is that he's much too big for a hole like Machlin. He has a giant's intellect, y'know. What do those pygmies in Machlin know about genius?"

"What does onybody ken aboot genius, Major?"

"True; but he should be in Edinburgh or London. It's a tragedy that he should have to go and bury himself in the Indies. He's most unsuited for the venture. I've tried to think how we could keep him at home. But as you say, Doctor, he's so damnably independent."

"His mind's made up. I had a talk wi' him mysel' aboot that. But maybe the success o' the poems will alter his mind. There's nae doubt that they'll be a success. I expected they would be good. But damned, Major, when I opened the volume and read The Twa Dogs I was bowled over. There just never has been poetry written like this. I'm no critic; but I ken what I like and what I don't like; and now that I've gotten the flavour o' Burns I'll waste gey little time reading ony other stuff. Damnit, Major, the whole toon's talking about them—Aye, and I hear the mechanics are coming to blows ower the respective merits o' the verses. And when did you ever hear o' mechanics fechting ower a swatch o' verses afore?"

"It's certainly a maist unusual way of appreciating poetry, Doctor."

"Ah, but the richt way, Major. When folks fecht about poetry then the poetry maun mean something. And up till now, ony poetry I've read's meant damned little—when it meant onything."

Johnnie Wilson, for all that he was ages with the Bard, seemed to grow more wizened and shrivelled every day. He rubbed the palms of his thin black hands vigorously together and then clutched at his snuff-mull. When he had sufficiently doped himself, he threw the mull from him among his papers and repeated his palm-rubbing gesture.

"Yes, Mr. Burns: the Poems are coming along nicely. It will take time, of coorse, to get round all the subscribers. But you're doing well to think of calling on such of them as live about Cumnock way. I'll look out the list and lay aside the volumes for you. Patience, of coorse, patience—a grand virtue, Mr. Burns. For a'bodies, Mr. Burns: maist suitable for a'bodies: priests and poets, publicans and sinners. Printers, of coorse, unlike the rest o' human cattle, are born wi' patience . . .

"Notwithstanding, Mr. Burns: notwithstanding, sir, I made one fell mistake wi' your volume. I should hae set your Cottager at the beginning o' the buik. Aye: I thocht the Dogs wad hae done it; but I was mistaken. But The Cotter's Saturday Night—aha, that's gotten them, Mr. Burns. That's a cloak will cover a' your shortcomings and your bits o' lapses.

"I met Mr. Russell this mornin' in the Strand. 'Mr. Wilson,' roars he, 'that's a blackguardly volume o' verses ye hae putten out frae your press.' 'Blackguardly, Mr. Russell?' says I, looking like an innocent babe. 'That's a strong word, Mr. Russell.' And wi' that he gars yon meikle staff o' his dirl on the causeway. 'My cloth, sir,' says he, 'doesna allow me to use a fuller expression.'

"Mind you, Mr. Burns, you're the better to keep to the offside o' yon staff when you're speaking to Mr. Russell. So I ventured respectfully to suggest to him that maybe he hadna read your Cottager.

" 'No, sir,' says he, 'that I didna. But I did read a wheen blethers about twa dogs; an' siccan impident trashery I ne'er saw printed. Then sir,' says he—and by this time he was bellowin' fully loud for the public highway and a wheen auld wives were cocking their lugs at their doors, 'then sir, I read twa-three staves o' The Holy Fair afore I sent the buik fleeing to the back o' the fire. But gin I ever meet wi' your poet Burns, I'll gie him a holy fair that'll put the fear o' God through him!'—and wi' that he played swipe wi' the meikle stick till the wind frae it near blew my hat aff.

"But you see what I mean, Mr. Burns? Had I prefixed the buik wi' your Cottager it wad hae made a' the difference . . . Of coorse, where Mr. Russell got the copy to throw i' the fire I've nae idea: he didna get it here . . .

"But, patience, Mr. Burns, patience—and I'll hae mair news for you gin Saturday. But keep your een peeled for thae officers o' the sheriff: I canna hae my poets thrown i' the gaol at a time like this."

By the end of the week the Bard felt more calm in his mind. He had decided on his plan of action. He would risk standing in Machlin Kirk the next day. Then he would see Daddy Auld and get his certificate. Later he would ride into Cumnock by way of Glenconner, and collect such monies for his book as were due him on the way.

Gilbert arrived on the Saturday evening with the Machlin news. It seemed that the sheriff's men had called several times at Mossgiel but that they had spent most of their time sitting drinking in the Whitefoord Arms, much to Johnnie Dow's disgust. They had told Johnnie that they were going back to Ayr for fresh instructions and that they would probably not be back unless Armour could tell them definitely where the Mossgiel farmer could be found. They had a damned sight more to do than ride up and down the country looking for the man that had bairned his dochter: for all they knew or cared to know it might have been the best thing that could have happened to her.

Gilbert agreed it would be safe enough for him to stand in Machlin Kirk. If the sheriff's men didn't make any appearance the following week, it would mean as likely as not that they had given up the chase.

And then there was his book. It was going well. Wonderfully well. The reports he had had were enthusiastic. Everybody was delighted with their money's worth. What were the reports from Killie?

Robin assured him that the reports from his end were equally enthusiastic, even though the distribution of copies was only now beginning to get fully under way. But, so far, reports were excellent.

Robert Muir said: "How could it be otherwise? I said from the beginning, Gilbert, that the Bard had nothing to fear once his poems got circulated, and that if he didn't make his fortune, at least his fame would be secure. The only difficulty is getting the copies delivered to the subscribers. That's bound to take time. I'm more nor certain that by the end of the month there won't be a copy left on Wilson's hands."

"And how does it feel to be an author?" Gilbert inquired.

"It's too early to say, Gibby: I wish I hadn't to go to the Indies: not for a while yet. I'd like fine to hear what all my friends have to say; and I'd like to hear what my enemies have to say: that's even more important. But by Monday, Gibby, I'll be on my way through to Cumnock and all that lies between Machlin and Glenconner. I've been tied up here all week. And what a week! I've nothing left o' the grace o' God about me. Maybe I've disappointed my friends in Auld Killie: what wi' my drinking and my unorthodox opinions . . . But I've had a grand time wi' Tam Samson, Willie Parker, Gavin Turnbull . . . But how are they taking things at Mossgiel?"

"Well, the least said about that the better, Robin. They're upset, of course; but then it could hardly be otherwise; they don't understand and maybe it's just as well they don't. My mother's very bitter. I've done what I could to pacify her. But you ken well what her ideas are and how neither you nor me could shift them."

"What did she say when she saw my book?"

"You'd better wait till you see her yourself. Only try and remember that she doesna belong to our generation . . ."

"Aye: the only poem o' mine she ever said she liked was the Auld Farmer's Salutation . . ."

"And the Cotter's Saturday Night?"

"No: all she ever said about that was that here and there it wasna bad . . . Ah well: what does it matter? Do you ken the best poem in the book, Gibby? It's a toss up atween twa o' them: The Mouse or the Address to the Deil . . ."

"The Cotter's Saturday Night for me."

"What do you say, Robert?"

Robert Muir did not hesitate for a moment. "To me, Robin, your best poem is no' in the book: I mean Love and Liberty. But the best in the book is The Twa Dogs."

"Aye: that was Wilson's opinion to begin with. But though I agree wi' you about Love and Liberty, I've seen enough of the smoking bowl this week to last me a lifetime . . . And to-morrow I'll see the last o' the churches built to please the priest . . . When I've done my penance wi' the priest o' Machlin, it'll be a long time before I do any more."

"Amen to that," said Gilbert. "And may the time be long enough to be never."

FREE FROM SCANDAL

Daddy Auld polished his spectacles on his linen napkin.

"And now, Mr. Burns, having done your penance and made public profession of repentance, perhaps you will sign the Session minute here that acknowledges how everything has been properly carried out?"

The Bard looked straight into Mr. Auld's emotionless eyes. "Is this custom, Mr. Auld?"

"It should be custom. Maybe I don't like embarrassing folk that canna sign their name. But you have a very bold signature, Mr. Burns; and in your case I would like everything to be in the best order so that no matter who had occasion to pry into the niceties of the business would find that everything was beyond dispute. On reflection, Mr. Burns, I trust you will agree with me."

"I never had any hesitation in putting my name to the truth, Mr. Auld."

He took the quill that the priest offered to him and added his name to the foot of the minute.

"And now, Mr. Auld, might I ask for my certificate?"

"You are in some haste, Mr. Burns?"

"I may receive word any day to proceed to Greenock to join my boat for Jamaica."

"So you are sailing?"

"Had you any doubt on that point, sir?"

"No . . . No . . . This may be the last time I will see you then?"

"That is so."

Auld straightened himself in his chair; but the mask of his expression seemed to soften.

"I have been looking at your book of poems. You ken what I think of your Holy Fair? On the other hand I have read your Cotter's Saturday Night! I am somewhat at a loss to explain how it is that in the one brain there can exist such extremes. The one gave me infinite pleasure: the other gave me infinite pain . . . But you are leaving us, Mr. Burns, and you want your certificate. By the way: I understand that Mr. Armour has issued a warrant for your arrest against the payment of a large sum for the child that Jean Armour has yet to bring forth . . . I understand that you are at the moment in hiding from that writ: is this so?"

"Mr. Auld: you and I have bandied many words; but we won't bandy any more. We've had our differences and our disagreements. I want to ask you an open question and I would like you to give it a fair and honest answer. Do you think that Armour, in pursuing me the way he is, is behaving like a good Christian—or that you approve of his conduct?"

"I could answer you in a variety of ways, Mr. Burns; and without equivocation. But I know the ground you are on. My answer is: no! I do not think that Mr. Armour is doing right in the sense you mean. I will go further and have a word with Mr. Armour about this. As you are leaving the country, freed from all scandal, I think Mr. Armour would do well to forget that he has a legal claim on you in respect of his daughter's unborn child. Had you still been remaining amongst us the circumstances would have been rather different. No, Mr. Burns: I dinna like to see a man harried."

"Thank you, Mr. Auld: I appreciate what you have said. I am not asking you to intercede with Armour on my behalf. But if you think that speaking to him will do any good then, sir, I stand, as always, your obliged and humble servant."

"I'm glad, Mr. Burns, that we are not parting with bitter feelings between us. I hope you do appreciate that my work here is not easy and that I have to hold the scales of justice as evenly as, with the grace of God, I can. You are not wanting your critics in this parish, Mr. Burns; and I am not wanting in my critics either. And though there is much in your actions of which I have disapproved, I am convinced, especially from the last poem in your book, that your better feelings will triumph in the end, and that you will be a credit to your Christian upbringing.

"Here is the certificate that you are entitled to; and I fervently pray that the minister into whose hands you will deliver it will never have cause to censure you the way I have had . . . And may God guide you and lead you always in the paths of virtue; may He be with you always. Good-bye, Mr. Burns."

Auld rose and extended his long bony hand. It looked cold and lifeless; but there was surprising strength in its grip. The Bard grasped it firmly.

"Good-bye, Mr. Auld; and may I wish you continued good health and a long and happy ministry in Machlin?"

As he walked down the Bellman's Vennel he was conscious of a feeling of loss. Auld and he had little or nothing in common: indeed they were in opposition. Yet there was something about Auld that commanded respect. Beneath his rigid and unbending exterior there was a quality of understanding that he had found altogether lacking in such other Old Light practitioners as he had met. Aye, and in certain of the New Lights too. Nearly everything that Auld stood for was hateful to him; and he could not help thinking that his persecution of Gavin Hamilton was as near to harrying a man as could be; but it was quite impossible to hate Auld or to believe that he was insincere. Wrong, undoubtedly, he was; but he held to his wrongness with a rare integrity. But, right or wrong, integrity was so rare a quality he hoped he would always be able to recognise and honour it wherever it appeared.

GUID AULD GLEN

That evening he rode into Glenconner and spent the night under the hospitable roof of Auld Glen.

The old man was delighted to see him and to lay his hand on a copy of his poems. But when he learned that he was virtually on the run from Armour's writ, he became indignant. The family shared his indignation. But John Tennant would not have it that this was his last visit to them.

"Na, na, Rab: you canna flee awa' to the Indies like this. And it's a silly-like thing to be doing anyway. What the hell's there for you in an outlandish foreign place like that? Bide a wee, Rab: something's bound to turn up for you. This book o' yours is certain to bring you to the notice o' some o' the gentry—I'll see that it gets to her lady-ship here—and as like as no' one or other o' them will see their way to do something for you. Oh, it's a' verra well being independent. But you've got to work at something. Wi' the knowledge you hae and the head you hae on your shoulders, you could factor an estate to ane o' the gentry as weel as the next—and a damned sicht better than some o' them that are doing it the now. Na, na: dinna be in ony hurry to set sail. Get round the countryside wi' your book and you'll see something will turn up for you."

Good friend as Auld Glen was, the Bard did not feel like telling him about Mary Campbell. Glen was a rough old Scot; and had half a dozen of the lassies been pregnant to him he would not have thought any the less of him: indeed he might have thought more. Glen was now enjoying his third wife and he had fathered more children than he could count on the fingers of both his hands. But there was something that prevented him telling about Mary Campbell. Auld Glen looked upon love as a weakness when it wasn't a piece of foolishness. A young lad in the heat of his blood might ride into the next parish to get his arms round a lass. But nobody but a crazed fool or an idiot would think of going to the Indies because of one. A man had to be as sensible about women as he was about a horse.

It was not that Glen was a gross old lecher. He was a man of the most sterling worth; a man William Burns had been proud to acclaim; a man with a warm heart and animated by the kindliest and most generous sentiments. But where the female sex was concerned, he was utterly lacking in any romantic illusions.

So Glen would hear nothing of his going to the Indies, and they spent the night discussing his verses and the prospects of the book being a success. And as always when they got talking about his verses, he would end up with the observation that had his father lived, he would have been proud of him. Glen's admiration for William Burns increased with the passing years.

"It wasna only that he was proud o' you, Rab, as a man has every richt to be proud o' a weel-doing son. Man, he had faith in you! Aye: richt frae the earliest. Maybe you don't believe that, Rab. But I'm telling you; and I ken. I used to say to him when he was in the Mount and I was in Laigh Corton and you were only a bit laddie, no' to build his hopes on you ower high. I've heard your mither getting on to him too. But he must hae seen something in you that nae other body saw: at that time I mean.

"Aye: he wad hae been a proud man the day gin he had lived to lay hands on this book. And mind you: there was naebody i' the West kent a book better nor William Burns. You get your sangs and your ready wit frae your mither; and by certes when your mither was in the Mount she had a sang to her voice and a rare lilt to her tongue. Her and me used to get on like a thatch on fire. But it's frae your father that you get the depth and the insight. Aye; it was frae William Burns that you got the learning and the politics and the religion. A' the wark in the head cam' frae William Burns. But you see: whaur you hae got them a' beat is that you hae the best o' both sides: aye, and wi' a benison added baith ways. That's a combination that canna be beaten.

"Sae think ower what I'm telling you and bide at hame in the meantime till the book mak's its ain way! Oho! mind you: folk'll hae plenty to say agin it. But dinna let that worry you. Sae mony folk are eaten up wi' jealousy. Aye, they'll run you doon to the lowest: that's the way o' the warld. But for a' that, gin you hae patience to gie the book time, it'll mak' friens whaur friens count: that's wi' folks that hae nae occasion to be jealous o' ye. But ony ill thae kind o' folk say aboot ye, Rab: tak' that as an honour. For when a'bodies hae a guid word to say aboot you, it means that it's no' worth while saying onything aboot you. I mind a man saying to me ae day at the mart: 'Weel, John: I'm surprised to hear that ye've gotten married for the third time.' 'Ah, well,' says I: 'gin the first wife had lived there wad hae been little need.' Of coorse, Rab: I ken you've a tongue i' your head and that you don't need me to tell you what to say. And I ken weel that you'll say something. But don't ever be frightened to say it, even if it's to the highest in the land. For ony man that had William Burns for a father and Agnes Broun for a mither doesna need to look far for his pedigree: least of a' to hang his head for it . . ."

It seemed that everyone about Glenconner was in the fullest agreement with their patriarchal father in his assessment of the Bard and his parents. And he was touched by their tribute . . .

THAT HAPPY NIGHT

The next day found the Bard collecting money and delivering copies among his many friends and acquaintances in the Cumnock district, lying some half-dozen of miles south of Machlin. That night found him seeking shelter in John Merry's Inn at New Cumnock.

He had stabled his pony and had entered the Inn quietly and called for a drink. As he had hoped, it was Mrs. Merry who answered his call. She stood for a moment in the doorway of the room and stared incredulously at him.

"God bless and keep us a'! Is it you, Rab?"

"And who would you rather see than me, Annie?"

Annie Rankine ran forward and threw her arms round his neck and gave him a powerful hug and a kiss on either cheek.

"God, Rab, but I'm glad to see you. What are you doing down this length? You're no' down wi' your Poems, are you?"

"Down wi' the Poems, Annie, and desperate for the cash! I'm just as you kent me, Annie: without a penny to bless me. But no' lacking a penny to drink your health! Where's John Merry till I shake him by the hand? This'll be the third time I've seen you since you were married?"

"You should hae come oftener, Rab: you ken you wad hae been welcome ony time o' the nicht or day. John's out aboot the kye somewhaur: it'll no' be lang till he's in. But what's this I'm hearing aboot ye?"

"And what are you hearing about me, Annie?"

"I'm hearing that you hae been on the cutty stool for a Machlin jad and that you're thinking o' sailing for Jamaica."

"Well: you've heard correctly, Annie. You don't mind the Machlin lass: do you?"

"She must hae been a silly bitch frae a' I hear. You wanted to marry her and she wadna hae you! As I said to John when I heard o't: gin I had had the chance three or four year ago, you wadna hae stood on ony cutty stool. Aye: John kens fine you're an auld sweetheart o' mine, Rab; and he kens that's a' by wi' now."

"But you're happy enough in your marriage, Annie?"

"Happy enough, Rab. When I couldna get you, I had to do the next best thing! Och, dinna heed what I say, Rab; you ken I'm still John Rankine's daughter. But I'm sorry to hear aboot this Machlin lass. Were you fond o' her?"

"To tell the truth, Annie, I was; and still am. I made my last appearance in Machlin Kirk on Sunday there, and I got my certificate from Mr. Auld stating that I leave Machlin free from scandal . . . and a single man. Now I'm taking a last look round my friends, delivering copies of my Poems to those who were so kind as to subscribe. And if I can collect the cash while I'm here, so much the better. You can understand it will not be easy for me to get together my passage-money and the hundred and one things that I need before I sail."

"Och, we'll no' be long in helping you to get in the money for your book. There's folk in here every day asking when it's coming; and a lot o' them left their money wi' John . . . But tell me: what's come ower you that you maun flee awa' to the Indies? Now that you're freed o' your Machlin nonsense, what possesses you to leave us?"

"I'm sailing, Annie, in search of that fantastic thing—liberty."

"You're a blether, Rab! But what's your real reason: if it's no' too private?"

"That is my real reason, Annie. But like a lot o' things I hae done, I suppose it does seem fantastic."

"Weel: I suppose you ken your own business best. But if it had been ony trouble that John and me could have helped you wi', you ken you have only to say the word."

"No: it's nothing like that, Annie. Just the usual Burns luck. Mossgiel hasna turned out a damn bit better nor Lochlea . . . But never mind my worries: here's a copy of my book: tell me what you think of it!"

Annie took the book gently in her hand and stared at it for a long time. Her eyes were full of wonder.

"Oh . . . it's a grand book, Rab: far better than I thocht it wad be."

"Turn to page two hundred and twenty-two."

Annie rubbed her hand on her apron and turned the pages.

"Oh, you're a deil! You've printed my sang! That's real good o' you, Rab. Wait till John sees this. I'm aey asked to sing it when there's ony singing going. He said to me when we got your subscription bill: 'I wonder if Rab Burns'll print your sang, Annie?' But I didna ken what to say . . . and I was feared that maybe you wouldna. Maybe you had another lass that wouldna like to see a sang that was wrote for some other lass. But you ken: it gives me quite a turn to see the words set down in print. I wonder how many folk'll ken it's my sang?"

"The Epistle that precedes it is to your worthy father: they'll be able to put one and one together. But what the stranger thinks is of little consequence to us. We ken whose sang it is and so do our friends." He put his arm round her and gave her an honest kiss full on the lips. "Aye; and I still mean every word o't, Annie. That happy night was worth them a', amang the rigs o' barley."

"Oh wheesht, Rab, and dinna set me goin': John Merry kens nocht aboot what happened yon nicht."

"And if you're wise he never will." He gave her a playful smack across her ample hips. "But come on, landlady: what about a sup o' kail or something: I'm as hungry as a hawk."

It was a glorious night they had in John Merry's Inn. There was singing; and Annie sent everybody's blood leaping with her rendering of *Corn Rigs*.

Some of the lads present were known to him; but many others were strangers. But kent faces or strange faces, they gave him a hearty reception.

He should have taken advantage of the evening and ridden up the water of the Afton some three miles to Pencloe to pay his respects to Tom Campbell, a warm admirer of his verses; and to have called, on his way back, on John Logan of Knockshinnoch. But some of the younger lads had gone out and rounded up a bevy of New Cumnock lassies. With the aid of a fiddler and feet-stamping and hand-clapping (to say nothing of the singing of an odd verse of a Cumnock "psalm") they began to dance. The temptation to join them proved irresistible.

It was a long while since the Bard had danced with such light-hearted abandon. He looked somewhat stiff and heavy as he sat at the table or moved around. But whenever the fiddler entered into his rhythm and stroked the *Reel o' Stumpie* from the thairms, he fairly leapt to his feet and had Annie swept to the middle of the floor.

"D'you mind o' you night when we first went to the dancing class in Tarbolton and Anra MacAslan played for us? D'you mind the time we had at the ball the time o' the races . . .? Weel, Annie, there's a wheen o' lads and lassies here the nicht think they ken what dancing is. Get ready and we'll let them see something. If this is to be the last dance I'm to have in Scotland then let it be a dance I'll never forget."

"God, Rab, I dinna think I could gie you a dance like I gave you in Tarbolton. But mind you: if I get warmed up you'd better look out—I'm no' the genteel twal stanes I was then . . ."

David Gaw, the fiddler, arched his eyebrows and watched them. He knew by the way they squared up to the dance they were going to enjoy themselves. He was aware of the animation passing between them. He sensed that if they were not lovers they had once loved. And as music was still a powerful aphrodisiac to his mature blood, his bow swept across his fiddle in such a way that the physical throbs he drew from it electrified his hearers. The room became charged with passion. Desire leapt and flickered on the snap of the melody.

By common consent the others left the Bard and Annie to improvise a set themselves. Already the lads were singing: "Wrap and row, wrap and row, wrap and row the feetie o't; I thocht I was a maiden fair until I heard the greetie o't . . ."

They were on their toes; they were leaping in the air; they were stepping to the right and stepping to the left; they were in the linked-arm birl; out of the birl and into the side step; the dashing swerve of the figure; arms above the head; arms angled from spanned waists: elbow edging to elbow; heads cast to the side but eyes never leaving eyes and both pairs of them flashing, breaking, fusing . . .

The sweat ran down the fiddler's nose. The dancers were in a lather; but they knew no discomfort. They were no longer in Cumnock. They were back in Tarbolton, in Lochlea, in Adamhill; down in the oak-tree bawk beside the waving rigs of corn and barley . . .

The stamping onlookers were singing: "My father was a fiddler fine, my mother she made mantie O; and I mysel' a thumping quean and danced the Reel o' Stumpie O . . ."

His arms folded across his chest, the Bard passed the fiddler on leaping toes. The fiddler winked. The Bard said: "Green Grow the Rashes;" and the fiddler nodded as if he had thought of the tune himself. When the beat of the measure changed and the thumping, even measure of the reel gave place to the drawn-out note of the strathspey, the room went mad.

Annie knew the old words and she flushed a deeper red—if that were possible; flushed deeper because the words put an intellectual meaning to the measure and the rhythm that she had not needed . . .

And then she realised that the Bard was paying no attention to the words: he was completely absorbed in the music and the dance; and in her.

Rab Burns! Why had he not fulfilled the promise of that Lammas night among the rigs of barley? Why was he dancing there with such vigorous abandon, still a man unmarried? Would he ever marry? Or would he dance from lass to lass till he could dance no more?

And what kind of lassies would there be to dance with in the foreign parts to which he was going? And what kind of measure would they dance?

He knew that he might never have another night like this before he sailed. He knew that if John Merry had not been a friend and a man whose friendship he valued, that Annie and he might well have had a night between the blankets that would have eclipsed the night they had had among the corn rigs . . .

But everything has its end as well as its beginning; and the lads and lassies of New Cumnock had to get to their beds sometime. They departed, wishing him the best of luck and voting the happy night one of the finest they had ever experienced.

Annie and her husband sat down for a last drink before they retired. John Merry was proud of the Bard and expressed his sorrow that he found it necessary to sail to the Indies. Annie also expressed her sorrow. An old lover is always a source of sorrow. But she did not eat out her heart. She was happily enough married, even though John Merry was woefully lacking in physical passion. But he was kind and considerate. Maybe it was that a man could not have everything; and she knew well enough that she could never have held Rab Burns to her skirt tails.

"Maybe you'll meet wi' a lass in the Indies? What kind o' lassies are they oot there?"

When she spoke, he thought immediately of Mary Campbell waiting in Greenock. His face clouded and he knew that he could no longer sit and discuss things with his friends. He asked for another drink and went off to his chamber in the attic.

When he was gone, John Merry said to his wife: "I dinna think you should hae mentioned the lassies in the Indies, Annie. Did you notice how his brows came down? I'm afeared that he's still in love wi' that Machlin lass Jean Armour . . ."

"Aye, maybe: the trouble wi' Rab Burns is that he must always be in love wi' some lass or anither . . . It wad be a blessing if he could fa' in wi' the right one: one that could mak' him happy."

"That was mair nor you could dae, Annie."

"Ah, weel: mony a happy hour the twa o' us had when we were aboot Adamhill . . ."

"I could see that when you were dancin'."

"Could you?"

"The whole room could see that, Annie. But I'm no' jealous. God lass! if it wad mak' ony difference you could go up to his room the nicht . . . But Rab Burns is the only man I wad dae that for."

"And you wadna think ony the less o' me if I did, John? Come on to your bed, you silly man, for you dinna ken what you're saying."

"There's no' a silly bit about me; and fine you ken that. When I saw you dancing wi' him there and when I heard you singing Corn Rigs, I thought to mysel' that it was a pity fate had ever separated the pair o' you. For by God! if ever a couple were made for one anither, it was you and Rab Burns."

"Maybe we were, John: maybe we were; but Rab had other ideas. Let's talk no more about it, John, or I'll need to forbid him the hoose; and I wadna like that."

John Merry saw that his wife was near to crying. He rose and put his arm round her: "Come on, lass: I didna mean to hurt your feelings: I was but joking."

And Annie Rankine, who was still in her heart the Annie of the Corn Rigs but was now in fact Mistress John Merry, put her arms round her husband and wept tears on his shoulder. But the tears came from a source that lay deeper than the wells of joy or sorrow: deep below the surface of conscious awareness . . .

AUTUMN'S PLEASANT WEATHER

The next day the Bard was riding through the countryside making his way back to Fairlie. He had sold all the copies his saddle-bags could carry. And he was the richer by a few pounds.

But he hadn't made enough of his visit to the Cumnock district. There were still many good friends he had not found time to visit.

As soon as he was settled down again in Fairlie and had resumed contact with Wilson and his Killie friends, he sat down and wrote to Kennedy and Logan. To Logan he wrote:

"I gratefully thank you for your kind offices in promoting my subscription, and still more for your very friendly letter. The first was doing me a Favour, but the last was doing me an Honour. I am in such a bustle at present, preparing for my West-India voyage, as I expect a letter every day from the Master of the vessel, to repair directly to Greenock; that I am under a necessity to return you the subscription bills, and trouble you with the quantum of Copies till called for, or otherwise transmitted to the Gentlemen who have subscribed. Mr. Bruce Campbell is already supplied with two copies, and I here send you 20 copies more. If any of the Gentlemen are supplied from any other quarter, 'tis no matter; the copies can be returned.

"If orders from Greenock do not hinder, I intend doing myself the honour of waiting on you, Wednesday, the 16th inst.

"I am much hurt, Sir, that I must trouble you with the Copies; but circumstanced as I am, I know no other way your friends can be supplied."

It was going to be difficult to get all his copies delivered and the money gathered before he sailed. He would have to risk offending some of his subscribers by sending them the whole of the copies that had been signed for on their subscription sheets and to let them do the delivering and collecting as best they could. There was nothing else for it; and he had to get money . . .

He had little time for drinking or leave-taking now. All his time was taken up with Wilson, getting the copies arranged for delivery . . .

On Sunday the 13th he rode into Ayr, for he was anxious to hear what intelligence Doctor Douglas had about the *Nancy* and Captain Smith . . .

As it happened, the Doctor had friends visiting him from Jamaica, and the news they had was far from encouraging.

So depressing indeed was their news that he broke his journey and called on Willie Logan of Park. The Major was sitting gloomily in his villa, nursing the effects of the Saturday debauch with his Ayr cronies. But his face lifted the moment his sister Susan admitted the Bard to his den.

Susan Logan was a good-natured woman who doted on her brother.

"I havena had the chance to do more nor keek at your Poems, Robert: he'll no' let the volume out o' his hands. He even carries it about wi' him. But I hear plenty talk about them. And I'm glad to learn they're catching on so well . . . But there he is, Robert—wi' the big black sheep on his back. I've told him that one day it'll stay there. Maybe you could write a verse or twa on that theme."

"I'd rather write a verse on his fiddling, Susie."

"Ah, damned, Robert, I fuddle more nor I fiddle nowadays."

"That's true enough," said Susan. "I'll away and see about a bite o' food."

"Ease your shanks on the chair there, Robert. I've a bitch o' a head, a proper bitch. I've been waiting an excuse to start on the bottle—though I'll need to hold my nose till I get the first dram down . . . Aye, I'm sorry I missed you the last time you called . . . And now I hear you're finally settled on Jamaica wi' Charlie Douglas . . . What's that? The Whites said that, did they? I'd a wide variety o' fevers when I was in America. Man, if you've gotten the right constitution you can stand onything."

"I had an idea you might feel like the fiddle—for, by heaven, I need something to cheer me up, Major."

"Man, there's no' a tune in me the now. And my dear auld mother fair grues when she hears me scraping on the Sabbath. No: you'll need to cheer me, Robert—else we'll baith drown our sorrows. That's the beauty o' sorrow—it puts moral justice and a rational theology in the bottle. Aye, and the doctor says since the coating's burned off my stammick I'll need to go easy. But I told him gin the waistcoat stood up as weel as the coat had done, there was no need for alarm till the sark came through."

"I'm afraid, Major, my stomach's aey been in its waistcoat, for I've never been able to lay in any reasonable cargo o' spirit."

"Keep it that way, Robert. It's a damned silly way to live as I do. But then, there's nothing else left for me. You're no' at the prime o' your life yet—and you've got your poetry. What need has a man for fire-water when he can get drunk on visions? And, by God, sir, you've gotten the vision . . . No: I don't know how to advise wi' you. You see: I was hot on the physical side o' life—a born soldier—and I got my fill o' it. You're no' that kind o' a man at all. You carry the world in your head. Whether you go to the Indies or no', you'll still have that head wi' a' its fancies. All I ken is that I'll be damned sorry when you go, for I've had some rare times in your company—and I used to fiddle for you when I wadna fiddle for myself . . . You could understand what it was I was trying to put into my scraping. When you go I'll put the fiddle by me . . . But dinna ask my advice. Bob Aiken's the man to advise you—that's both his nature and his profession. But wait till I get another drink or twa in me and maybe I'll play for you yet. And I'm saying nothing about your book till I feel better. I've plenty to say. Only I don't want the sour bitch o' melancholy to spoil my saying o' it. Come on, lad: you're no' touching your drink. Aye, you're a poor fiddler, Robert; but you have more music in you than ony man I've met. You've gotten the ear and you've gotten the heart for it—all you lack is the fingers. But that's nothing. I'll tell you what I'll do. I'll play you what I think o' your book—and you'll ken from my playing just what I think o' it . . .

"Aye; but no' just yet, Robert. I'll need to wait till the drink loosens up the joints o' my fingers and supples my wrist for the bow. And you want Miss Gordon's Strathspey for one d'you no'? Aye; and Soldier's Joy and Whistle Ower the Lave o't! Oh, I ken the tunes you want, Robert. God! and gin the drink gets round the cockles o' my heart I'll play them as I've never played them. Certes, I'll kittle the bow-hair on the thairms for you—aye; and my mither'll just need to grue . . ."

And as he rode back from Willie Logan's he experienced a longing to have an intimate crack with Jamie Smith and to learn the news of Machlin: especially as it concerned Jean . . .

Maybe he should throw everything to the winds and ride into Greenock and see Mary and tell her the news. But Greenock was a far ride of some fifty miles away. It wouldn't be long now till the beginning of September, and it would be fine to be sailing under a Captain who was known to Gavin Hamilton.

In the morning he wrote to Smith:

"I went to Dr. Douglas yesterday fully resolved to take the opportunity of Captain Smith; but I found the Doctor with Mr. and Mrs. White, both Jamaicans, and they have deranged my plans altogether. They assure him that to send me from Savannah-la-Mar to Port Antonio will cost my master, Charles Douglas, upwards of fifty pounds; besides running the risk of throwing myself into a pleuritic fever in consequence of hard travelling in the sun. On these accounts, he refuses sending me with Smith; but a vessel sails from Greenock the first of September, right for the place of my destination; the Captain is an intimate friend of Mr. Gavin Hamilton's, and as good a fellow as heart could wish:

with him I am destined to go. Where I shall shelter I know not, but I hope to weather the storm. Perish the drop of blood of mine that fears them! I know their worst, and am prepared to meet it—

> 'I'll laugh, an' sing, an' shake my leg,
> As lang's I dow.'

"Thursday morning, if you can muster as much self-denial as to be out of bed about seven o'clock, I shall see you as I ride through to Cumnock. I could not write to Richmond by Connel, but I will write by the Kilmarnock Carrier. After all, Heaven bless the Sex! I feel there is still happiness for me among them.

> 'O Woman, lovely woman! sure Heaven designed you,
> To Temper Man! we had been brutes without you!' "

And when he did ride through Machlin in the early morning, Smith was there to welcome him.

Smith had excellent news for him: the *Poems* were going better than even he had hoped. There was the possibility that he might sell fifty copies before he had exhausted his friends and acquaintances.

About Jean Armour he had little news that was fresh. She had been much reassured when told that he was safe and likely to remain so. And she was delighted that the *Poems* were selling so well. But things were still bad with her folks and her father's anger showed little signs of abating. There was only one hopeful ray in the general greyness. James Armour was not so sure now that it would be a good thing to have the Bard apprehended. Several folks had been talking to him (or so Jean gathered) and they had been advising him against the warrant. Even Daddy Auld had told him that the idea was foolish and little becoming to a man in his position. Of course they both knew what Armour was like: he had become stiff-necked. But as the sheriff's men had not come back to Machlin, it seemed that his stiff neck would do him little good.

It was when the Bard was riding down the Cowgate after his talk with Smith that Armour saw him. He went in to his wife in a black rage.

"There's that damned scoundrel frae Mossgiel awa' doon the Gate. What the hell's the guid o' the law when he can go riding through the countryside like one o' the gentles? And where d'you think he'll be awa' to? Aye, but naebody'll tell that at Machlin Cross."

"Noo, James, there's nae guid in you gettin' yoursel' worked up. And you ken fine that we're only getting clashed about when he's goin' scot-free. In ony case: even though you did nab him you ken he has his money settled on his brither and that get o' his frae Largieside. Nae wonder he got round our Jean wi' his marriage lines: there's no' a mair sleekit polished blackguard in the country. Nae wonder he has to flee to the Indies. Mark my words: time will show that our Jean's no' the only one that has suffered . . . I told Mr. Auld that; and I didna miss him and hit the wa' either——"

"Ah: clap your jaws thegither and put a steek in your gab. I'll get even wi' him yet. But it's damned galling to see a beggar like that riding past your door as if you were in the wrong and no' him. The only justice I'll get is if I lie in wait for him wi' a stick and lay on his back and sides what I'm able. That wad be aboot the only justice I wad get and it wad be the only punishment he wad understand."

Later, when Jean had a chance of her mother alone, she asked what the trouble had been and her mother told her how "that black deil Burns" had rode down the Gate and near rode her father down without as much as a nod of his head. Jean said nothing. To hear any word of him was a great relief. To know that he had been in the Cowgate that very morning! To have seen him and to have heard the sound of his voice would have been unspeakable joy. But maybe Jeannie Smith would come round: maybe she would have some fresh word of him. And then her heart leapt within her as she heard her mother continue.

"I don't think your father's gan on wi' that warrant. There's nae guid in your father being made a laughing stock by that worthless scart. Your father has been too sair worked a' his days to be upsides wi' the like o' him that has plenty time to write blackguard verses for blackguards like himsel' to laugh at in Johnnie Dow's. We'll just take nae notice o' him, that's what we'll dae. Your father has mair to dae than tak' up ony o' his time wi' cadgers' brocks that havena a penny to their names . . ."

In the afternoon Jeannie Smith called and they had an hour to themselves.

"My father's no' goin' to worry ony mair aboot that warrant, Jeannie. D'you think Jamie could get word to him so that he'll no' need to run aboot the country ony mair but'll be able to lie in his bed at nights and no' worry?"

"That's grand news, Jean. Rab was in seeing James as he rode through to Cumnock. He's collecting the money for his book and delivering the copies. He'll be away for about a week, James says. He's going away doon into Maybole and Kirkoswald: it seems he's a lot o' friends that way."

"Aye, he's plenty o' friends. He used to tell me how he went to a school there to learn how to measure land and what not."

"Ah weel: it's no' likely the sheriff's men will be looking for him doon there. But I'll tell James and I ken he'll pass on the news if he can . . . And he's no' for the Indies till about the beginning o' September. It seems that he was doon in Ayr talking wi' Doctor Douglas and he was advised no' to go wi' that boat the Nancy . . . James says he's looking fine and in good spirits—what wi' everybody liking his book . . ."

"I'm glad his book's a success. I wad like to have a copy. But you ken what would happen if a copy was to come in here. Of coorse, Jeannie, you and me havena the education; and maybe we wadna understand . . ."

"Maybe we wadna, Jean. That frightens me when I think of James Candlish: you ken whatna scholar he is. But ach! women are no' expectit to be scholars. They're only expectit to cook and wash and mend . . . and hae weans. And if we couldna hae weans I dinna expect the men wad hae ocht to do wi' us."

"And sometimes after we hae weans they dinna want onything to do wi' us."

"Aye: that's true, Jean. Men can be an awfa' heartbreak . . . but maybe that's what we've gotten hearts for."

"But if we are to tell the truth, Jeannie, we'll just need to confess that we canna do without the men."

"You're missing Rab sair, Jean?"

"Aye: I'm missing him. My mither says that my hour will come onytime now. If I could only see him and speak wi' him without my father kennin' I would be able to face my ordeal better."

"Och, you'll be all right: you're big and strong and you'll have little trouble bringing a bairn hame to the world."

"I dinna ken, Jeannie; but I've seen my mither suffering terrible wi' the young ones when she was lying in. Sometimes I used to be crying myself and me trying to help what I could. And puir Jenny Surgeoner told me o' the terrible time she had."

"You'll be a' richt, Jean: Jenny's only a slip o' a lass compared wi' you: I wish I had half your constitution . . . But I'll need to run now. I'll tell James about the warrant; and I'll tak' a run in and see you the morn . . ."

The Bard had not seen James Armour in the Cowgate; and he rode on as fast as his pony and the state of the roads would allow him. There was much to do and many people to visit.

He called in at Dumfries House and said good-bye to factor John Kennedy, collected his money on the subscription sheets, and, despite much entreaty to stay over night, rode on to Merry's Inn. After refreshing himself and his beast, he pushed on up the water of the Afton some three miles to Pencloe, to call on Thomas Campbell, another good friend to his subscription. He retraced his steps and called upon John Logan of Knockshinnoch . . .

By this time he was becoming inured to farewells. Everybody had the same thing to say: that it was a great pity he had to go to the Indies; that his loss to Scotland would be a great loss; was it not possible for him to find some kind of employment that would enable him to settle down in his native land and marry and have children, prosper and know happiness . . . One expressed himself one way and one another; but this was the burden of all their plaints . . .

His mood alternated between anger and despondency as he rode along by the Water of Afton. Anger came from the poverty of his lot when he compared himself with others. His friends were good friends, honest sterling fellows. But what had they done to deserve more their security and independence? True, they were not rich; but they had more than enough to satisfy their wants and supply them with many small luxuries. He had not enough to supply his wants. Economically he belonged to that class of tenant-farmers who were below the average of their class . . . And this angered him as it had always angered him. But it angered him more to see the fine mansions of the wealthy gentles. No family had worked harder or were working harder than his family; but for all their work they only managed to keep their heads above starvation level . . .

But his anger burned itself out and he thought how generous had been the help given him by his friends—however rich and influential. Had it not been for Aiken and Ballantine in Ayr; Muir, Samson and Parker in Kilmarnock; and Hamilton and MacKenzie in Machlin, where would he have been to-day? Without their backing, and the backing of their friends, there would have been no printed collection of poems . . . His fame would never have been higher than that of a local rhymster.

No sooner did he feel gratitude for his friends than sentiment began to gain ascendancy of his emotions. He began to see them as more kind and generous than he had any right to expect any human beings to be. But he had so long suffered the reverses of fortune that anyone who showed him a kindness was looked upon as a friend for life. In his likes, as in his dislikes, he knew no half measures . . .

In the morning he said good-bye to Annie Rankine and they kissed and wept together, for they had known great happiness and were parting in the bloom of their youth never to meet again. It was this knowledge that was unbearable, and caused the heart to break and the tension of emotion to dissolve in the release of tears . . .

It took him a long time to recover from the emotional strain of parting from Annie Rankine. It was not only the parting from Annie as an old love and constant friend: the parting from Annie was the parting from everything that he held dear and that had come to mean as much to him as life itself. But indeed this was life. Life that merely breathed was life without mind and, therefore, without that most precious of all life's gifts: memory. But of what use was memory if it did not carry the mind forward in anticipation? He had said good-bye to all the sweet memories that Annie Rankine embodied; but more painful was the parting from the promise of the future. No matter what happened, the future could hold no anticipation of Annie Rankine: or men like Campbell of Pencloe or Logan of Knockshinnoch. But somehow his parting with the men had not brought to his mind so sharply just what parting meant as had the sudden tears trickling down the honest face of Annie.

He was making across country to Maybole. The hill-road from New Cumnock to Dalmellington was as bad a road as he could remember having travelled. And wild and lonely as were many of the Ayrshire roads, he doubted, on this dull August day, if there was a lonelier. At the end of ten or twelve damnably hard miles he was glad to rest his buttocks in one of the few seats in the Dalmellington Inn that boasted a calf-skin cushion stuffed with wool . . .

But after an ill bite served by as grim and cross-eyed a servant-lass as he had ever clapped eyes on and he had rescued his pony from as surly a landlord as could have been found in the West, he resumed the cross-country journey to Maybole by way of the hill-track to Straiton. As he rode down into Straiton, the land became more pleasant and there was greater evidence of cultivation. It had been a great disappointment to him to find that the Doon, the beloved river of his boyhood, was such a poor stream in such a bleak country as Dalmellington; but now he was coming down into the land that was kindlier and more like the land he had known about Alloway.

At Maybole he met Willie Niven, his old school-fellow of the Kirkoswald days. That night there was a gathering of the Maybole friends of Niven, who was now coming to the fore as a prosperous merchant, and they gave the Bard a welcome that gladdened his heart. It seemed, now that he was leaving, that there was no end to his friends and well-wishers: it was also apparent that while people could be impressed with a length of verses written out in a bold hand of write, a volume of the same verses set out in good black print and stitched up into covers was something so impressive that it awed folks—even from the outside. There was one set of values for a poet with a bundle of manuscript in his pocket and quite another for one with a well-printed volume at his disposal. The merit of the poems was secondary.

The Bard had time to notice all this and time to note that there was more than a touch of sycophancy in some of the well-doing folks of Maybole. He noted a trace of jealousy underlying the sycophancy. Willie Niven was quite genuine in his regard; but he did not fail to let it be known that he was a most successful merchant, and that while poetry was a very fine thing to have at one's disposal, it was equally fine to be a prosperous merchant. But the Bard stored these impression for use against another day when he would have time to sort them out and test their true meaning and significance . . . For the moment it was enough that there were many good fellows wishing him well. Their little vanities were harmless enough . . .

The deepest pleasure of his Maybole-Kirkoswald trip came when he visited his old Kirkoswald love, the sweetest and most innocent love he had known: Peggy Thomson. But Peggy dear the evening's clear, thick flies the skimming swallow . . . He had loved Peggy with all the fervid innocence of inexperienced youth . . . Always he had thought of Peggy as he had known her in those early days; sweet-tempered, soft-spoken, shy-smiling . . .

She was wife to Willie Neilson of Minnybee now. He remembered Willie too from his Kirkoswald adolescent sojourn. Willie, if he had developed the bent of those youthful days, would be the right husband for Peggy.

So he rode up to the farm of Minnybee with the anticipation of meeting with old friends who would be as pleased to see him as he to see them. And he was not disappointed. They received him with a simple friendliness that touched him in a way that Annie Rankine had not touched him. Everything about Annie was robust, healthy and natural. There was no fragile delicacy about her: nothing calling for his protecting instincts . . . But Peggy was different, for his memories of her were different: purer in their origin: refined and distilled by the years . . .

In truth Peggy was a simple lass with no pretentions to being anything but an honest wife to a good husband. If she had a sweet disposition she was not conscious of it, and certainly made no effort to exploit it. Nor had Willie Neilson any desire to be other than a sober industrious husband and a good father. He wanted nothing from life but to be allowed to work out his own destiny with as little let or hindrance as possible.

But Peggy, like Annie Rankine, had once hoped that he would marry her . . .

Like Annie, she was sad at the thought of parting. She felt Robin was embarking on a voyage that would bring him no happiness . . .

In the evening when they were sitting round the ingle, he produced his volume and handed it to Peggy.

"Do you remember this song when it was still in manuscript, Peggy? Tell me how you like the look of it in print?"

She looked where his finger indicated: Song, composed in August. She read the poem while Willie came and looked over her shoulder. "Now westlin winds and slaught'ring guns bring Autumn's pleasant weather; the gorcock springs on whirring wings amang the blooming heather: now wavin' grain, wide o'er the plain, delights the weary farmer; the moon shines bright, as I rove by night to muse upon my charmer.

"The paitrick lo'es the fruitfu' fells, the plover lo'es the mountains; the woodcock haunts the lonely dells, the soaring hern the fountains; through lofty groves the cushat roves, the path o' man to shun it; the hazel bush o'erhangs the thrush, the spreading thorn the linnet.

"Thus ev'ry kind their pleasure find, the savage and the tender; some social join, and leagues combine, some solitary wander:

avaunt, away, the cruel sway! tyrannic man's dominion! the sportsman's joy, the murd'ring cry, the flutt'ring, gory pinion!

"But, Peggy dear, the evening's clear, thick flies the skimming swallow, the sky is blue, the fields in view all fading-green and yellow: come let us stray our gladsome way, and view the charms of Nature; the rustling corn, the fruited thorn, and ilka happy creature.

"We'll gently walk, and sweetly talk, while the silent moon shines clearly; I'll clasp thy waist, and, fondly prest, swear how I lo'e thee dearly: not vernal show'rs to budding flow'rs, not Autumn to the farmer, so dear can be as thou to me, my fair, my lovely charmer!"

When they had finished reading, Willie turned and said: "So you wrote that for my Peggy?"

"Well . . . I didna ken she was going to be your Peggy. Had I kent, Willie, I believe I could have made it a better sang. But when I'm in the Indies and thinking on the quiet happiness of the pair of you here, I'm more than certain I'll compose a better sang."

"Man, Robert, it's a bonnie sang: something Peggy and me'll cherish a' our days. Aye, and hand it on to them that come after us. Will we no', Peggy?"

"It's like you, Robin, to remember me wi' a sang and I wadna ask to be remembered ony other way."

"You couldna have paid my bardship a higher compliment, Peggy, wi' that speech. But seeing that I'm leaving, I've put in a special line or two for you on the fly-leaf. It's a poem no other copy of my verses can boast."

Peggy turned to the fly-leaf and scanned the lines. But emotion seemed to overcome her. "You read the verse, Robin: you aey had a way o' reading verses . . ."

So he read the verses to them in a quiet voice. "Once fondly loved and still remembered dear, sweet early object of my youthful vows, accept this mark of friendship, warm sincere: friendship! 'tis all cold duty now allows.

"And when you read the simple artless rhymes, one friendly sigh for him, he asks no more, who, distant, burns in flaming torrid climes, or haply lies beneath the Atlantic roar."

He well knew that the lines had no literary value. But to him, as to Peggy and her husband, their value in sentiment was high. To them the lines were charged with immediate emotion, and there was no escape from it. He watched Peggy across the light of the fire. Her face was suffused with heightened feeling: strange that she was the lass he had held to him in the shade of the lea-rig some seven or eight years ago when he had thought the lassies existed only to be kissed chastely and cuddled delicately . . . He had not been a fool then: he had loved as a boy and a girl had a right to love: the right dictated by their emotional experience. And he was glad, as he looked at Peggy, that their love had never been consummated; glad that he would carry the innocence of this friendship into the unknown future.

And Willie Neilson, knowing that his wife had come to him a virgin, felt proud that his Peggy had once been loved by a man like Robert Burns: a man who could write such wonderful poetry and yet could come and sit at their fireside as one of themselves. And this was the mystery: he was one of themselves while he remained a being distinct and apart: secret and unfathomable. But always likeable: there was no escaping the warmth and richness of his personality . . .

Willie Neilson walked with the Bard towards the top of the brae. There they stood and looked around them. It was autumn's pleasant weather. Where the rigs of grain caught the sunlight there was evidence that it ripened towards a full harvest.

"Whatever comes, Willie, I hope you have a good hairst. Men may come and go and women wi' them; but a good harvest means everything to a farmer; aye, and to the country at large. For the folks in the towns that sometimes look down on the poor farmer would very soon starve if he didn't manage to salvage something from the wreck of bad hairsts. Bad hairsts have been my downfall: first bad seed and then bad weather . . . Aye, it's as simple as that, Willie, when you havena as much siller laid by you as will see you tided over a rainy day. Strange, is it not, that a rainy day can make all the difference to our moods and our fortunes? Maybe it has always been so for those who depend solely upon their labour and whether or not the sun ripens the fruits of their labour or leaves them to rot where they grow . . . Ah well, Willie: where I'm going there will be no lack of sunshine . . ."

"No . . . I dinna suppose that there'll be ony lack o' sunshine, Robert . . ."

"Except the sunshine o' friendship, Willie."

"And maybe that's the best sunshine a body can hae."

"I don't think there's ony doubt about that. The longer I live the more I prove that friendship is the finest flower o' human existence. And if I had not known it before, then this farewell tour o' mine would have convinced me."

"Aye: it's hard on folk when they hae to part. And when folk go abroad there's little hope o' their friends ever meeting them again on this earth."

"If we could be sure that we would meet in the life to come . . ."

"Naebody ever cam' back to tell us . . . And maybe there's naething to tell . . ."

"Well, while we live we'll hold to our memories, and hope for the best. Here's my hand on that, Willie; and may you and Peggy live to see a hundred and know health and happiness every minute o' your lives . . ."

They parted on the brow of the hill. Neither of them was ashamed that there were tears in their eyes at the emotion of parting. They had been boyhood friends; they had heard little of each other in the intervening years; but they had met for a night round the ingle and the friendship that had flowed between them had been deep and touching. They knew that each would carry the memory of the other to the grave.

But perhaps the finest hour he had on this journey was spent with his uncle, Samuel Broun.

There had ever been a curious bond of affection between them. It was a rough affection. His uncle had nothing of his mother's simple piety. Sam'l may not have been an unbeliever; but he was no orthodox Presbyterian. He acted pretty much as his wants dictated. And he had a rough natural bawdy approach to life. The Bard was sure he had inherited many valuable traits from his maternal uncle.

They went down to the Kirkton Inn together and had a drink. In the Kirkoswald days they had spent many a happy hour in Kirkton Jean's howff and had seen many a strange and violent scene.

There was a touch of apology in his uncle's voice as he told him how the smuggling was not what it had been. There was still some activity; but the lousy gaugers were quick and keen on the scent nowadays, and folk had to be damned careful. Still, there were ways of beating them and running a cargo if it wasn't too big and the runners weren't too greedy. It was greed that undid most of them in the end. Enough was as good as a feast any day; and in the smuggling, where things were liable to be either a hunger or a burst, it was fatally easy for a man to over-reach himself and land straight into the hands of the excisemen.

"But damn you, Rab, wi' a head like yours, you could have done well about here. You've plenty o' brains and native wit and plenty o' your father's North-country shrewdness; and that's what damn few o' your gaugers hae gotten. Poetry's a' richt: naebody likes a swatch o' guid-gan verse better nor me: especially the grand stuff that you can throw aff. But where has it got you? Driven you to the bluidy Indies! That's a fine-like reward for a' your pains. And you hae got about as much for your farming. Na, na, Rab: honesty's the best policy when it pays. But when it doesna . . . Well, you've got to do the next best thing. I never kenned a rich man to be an honest man; but then the rich hae laws to govern their dishonesty so that they dinna ruin the trade a' thegither. You'll see the truth o' that when you get to the Indies. They don't bother wi' laws there. Ah! but when things get eaten up there, they'll no' be lang in introducin' laws to regulate the scramble for fortunes. The nabobs o' India didna fash themselves wi' ony laws, did they? Damn the fear . . . until it became a wee difficult to grab a fortune. But the trouble wi' you, Rab, is that you hae gotten ower much o' your father's stubborn honesty. And you ken what your father got for his pains. Oh, you're no' so stubborn as your father was; and I'm no' saying ocht but that your father was a hantle sicht too good for this world. Only I don't want to see you gan abroad wi' ony silly ideas in your head. Mind that it's every man for himself. Your idea is to mak' a fortune. So be quick about it and get back here. When you've made ten thousand pounds, dinna be tempted to wait and mak' anither ten. As like as no' you'll tak' ane o' thae fevers and some other body'll enjoy the benefit o' your siller. Mind you: if you watch your step and mind what I've told you, a trip to Jamaica will do you no harm, and damned, it might do you a lot o' good."

The Bard laughed at his uncle. He had heard this philosophy before from him. But it was not a philosophy he practised except in relation to some small point of the law. There wasn't a kinder-hearted man in the parish; nor was there a man who was more kind and considerate to those less fortunate than himself. Perhaps that was why he was successful in his small smuggling ploys: no one about the parish would have dreamed of informing on him: even the gaugers looked on him with a not unfriendly eye.

The Bard realised only too well that his uncle was trying to offset the dangers of an unselfish idealism; was trying to tell him that a man could be foolishly disinterested in his own welfare and especially the welfare of those who depended on him. And he was wise enough to realise that this trait in his family did need a little watching. What warmed him to his uncle was his anxiety to be certain that he would succeed after so many failures that were not of his own making.

"And are you no' taking a lass wi' you: or are you waiting to see what they're like in the Indies? Ah, damned, I've nae doubt that there'll be some fell hizzies oot there. Oh, and nae bother wi' the kirk session. Fill in and fetch mair: that'll be a' the cry yonder. Ah, damnt, Rab: I've had the notion o' a black hizzie mysel'. I'll warrant they'll hae a way wi' them. Black as the Earl o' Hell's nicht-gown, and the bluid in them running like molten brass. And a fresh ane to cool the bed for you every nicht! They tell me the half-breeds out yonder are hotchin like vermin . . . An' the missionaries . . . Man, I've heard some queer stories . . .!

422

"Ah weel, lad, it'll no' be lang noo till you'll be putting the salt sea leagues atween you and hame; and you'll hae mony a sair heart thinking back on the auld places and the folks you hae kenned. But you'll get ower that. Just keep in mind that you went out there to mak' your fortune and let nothin' stop you. Least o' a' the black hizzies . . ."

"If I make my fortune, uncle, I'll send you a brace o' black beauties."

"By certes, Rab, they would earn their keep hereabouts; nae question: they wad never be idle."

There could be no question either, thought the Bard, life was an inexplicable mixty-maxty. His mother would never have understood such talk, and she would never have recognised that it was her own brother who was talking. Yet they were of the same flesh and blood and had been reared together. But for that matter, would any of his sisters recognise him? Not only did men keep secrets from women, but they kept secrets from each other: each man acting his part according to circumstances, and only bringing to his part what he thought the circumstances demanded. In this respect, every man and woman was a strolling player through life: only some were more gifted in the number of parts they could play. His uncle here played a small part and he seldom changed it; but he played it well, and it was always a pleasure to enjoy his performance . . . The wild Shakespeare, who had been an actor in every respect, had thought so: and no doubt with good cause. But life was tragedy and comedy, and it had never been possible to separate the strands . . . Here he was at his old game of catching manners living as they rose . . . It was more than time he was getting back to Mossgiel and finding out how the land lay. It had been fine to get that letter from Jamie Smith telling him that Armour was beginning to change his mind about the warrant. Better still to learn that Jean had not fully deserted him but still had his interest at heart . . .

He would go home by Ayr and see his patrons there, and have the benefit of their advice. If his book was selling as well there as it was doing here, then they would no doubt be glad to welcome him. And Doctor Douglas might have some more word about Jamaica . . .

"Well, uncle: I'll need to be getting on my journey . . . Maybe you'll manage to ride into Machlin an odd time and see how my mother fares. Gilbert could do wi' a word of advice and encouragement now and again: like me he gets easily depressed. My mother and me don't just see eye to eye; but you ken that. She thinks I'm completely lost to grace, and that I'm heading for hell wi' a' the speed I can muster. Oh, I understand her fine: if she understood me half as well it would make all the difference. But I would feel better if you would try and keep in touch wi' them."

"Certainly, Robert my boy, I'll do what I can for them. I ken how to handle Aggie. Your mither had a hard life . . . Aye, a damned sight too hard. You ken as weel as me how poverty bites into the bane; and Aggie's had to be gey near the bane a' her days. She'll never change now, you ken: you just canna expect that. But mind you, Rab: you hae bits o' her about you . . ."

"She once told me that I was a Broun as weel as a Burns."

"And she never spoke a truer word. A' that rich tang o' life aboot you: that's the Brouns. The brains, nae doubt, come frae your father, for the Brouns were never scholars, even if they were never fools. But by God, Rab! the Brouns hae kent how to enjoy life even when the sourest o' the grue and the grim was smacked across their gabs . . . What is it you say? I'll laugh and sing and shak' my leg as lang's I dow? That's the real Broun spirit; and wi' that spirit you hae nae need to fear where you may go . . . And if I'm no' much good at writing, dinna let that prevent you frae sending us ane o' your grand letters, back and forrit: damned, we'll aey be thinking o' you; aye, and in our ain way praying for you . . ."

Never had Robert Aiken been more enthusiastic in his welcome as when he received the Bard on his journey up from Kirkoswald. He insisted that he dine with him that night and be toasted by a gathering of his Ayr friends.

"I've sold nearly a hundred and fifty copies o' your poems, Robin. Everybody's talking about them: delighted, delighted! Never saw folk as enthusiastic about onything. Raving mad, some of them. You're a great success, Robin, and there's nothing for you to fear now. Armour's writ? You'll hear nothing more about that. In ony case, there's enough good folk in Ayr to see that you'll come to no harm that airt. And I don't see why you should sail now. There must be something here for you. How would you like to go into the Excise? There's worse jobs; and you could rise there—in time. Gauger? Aye: you would need to start at the bottom first. It would be security for you; and it would give you time to write your verses. Mind you: this is just the start o' you as a poet. From what I hear, your book's as good as sold out. There'll need to be another edition. And what's to hinder you, wi' a sheaf o' new verses, to bring out an edition every year?"

This good news seemed to have a depressing effect on the Bard. He shook his head slowly.

"You're forgetting Mary Campbell, Mr. Aiken."

"It's a bad business that, Robin. You're going through wi' it?"

"My honour, if you'll grant me any, wouldna allow me to do onything else. And cold prudence, for once in my life, tells me it's the wisest thing to do."

"You've got your certificate from Auld? Well: you went through an irregular marriage wi' Mary Campbell and you gave her twa Bibles wi' wrote-out declarations on them . . . There's no doubt she could mak' things hot for you if she cared, and I've no doubt but she'd care: or her parents would onyway. Aye: so you think there's nothing for it but the Indies after all? You see: you will go and do the daftest things, Robin."

"Maybe you're forgetting, Mr. Aiken, that I love Mary. When I was at the height of my Armour trouble, she was a great comfort to me. Indeed she was the only person who stuck to me and had faith in me. And now in the hour of my bardship's triumph, I canna desert her. I just canna do it, Mr. Aiken; and I don't think you would ask me to do it."

"The trouble wi' you, Robin, is that you can love too many . . . How do you ken that you'll settle wi' this Mary Campbell?"

"A man has got to settle some time. And a wife and a home and children is the best way to settle him: it was how we were meant to settle."

"Weel: why no' settle here in the West? Need you go to the ends o' the earth to do that?"

"Jean Armour's bairn will be born any day now. Do you think I could go about Mossgiel wi' Mary—and Jean nursing my bairn in the Cowgate? But there wasn't room for Jean at Mossgiel, and there's less for Mary now that they're saddled wi' Bessie Paton's bairn. I've worried about this night and day, Mr. Aiken: even when I didn't seem to be worrying. But I see no escape. It's the Indies: or a shameful and humiliating dishonour that I don't choose to face or to ask Mary to face . . . Everybody kens I'm going. I've said farewell and parted wi' my friends in several parishes . . . And I'm not going to stand and be rebuked by Daddy Auld again . . . No, Mr. Aiken: your news about my book is glorious, wonderful, and more than I had any right to expect; but if I have committed follies then I must pay for my follies . . ."

"You're tired, Robin; and all this excitement has got the better o' you. You could do waur nor go round to John Simson's and sup a coggie o' broth and lip a drop o' Kilbagie. You maun get above your low spirits. You're the Bard o' Ayrshire now: mind that. Folks o' quality are on your side. You'll be getting invites from some o' the best homes i' the West before long. You're something more nor a tenant-farmer in Mossgiel. You've plenty o' good friends here; and among us we'll no' see you stuck—or onything like it. On you go: I'll be down to Simson's later on . . ."

He had ridden into Ayr elated and filled with the highest expectations. The news he had received from Bob Aiken couldn't have been better. How was it, then, that he now felt empty and sad? It was difficult for him to explain. Maybe it was the shattering realisation that though he had won for himself his dearest ambition, the honour of being the Bard of Ayrshire, it had come at the very moment of his greatest defeat. The defeat he had brought on himself. He had nobody to blame but himself. Mary Campbell had turned out to be the greatest disaster in his life. If only he had waited . . . If only he had done everything different from what he had done: if only he had been born a different person . . . For this was what it amounted to: he had done what he had done and he couldn't have done otherwise. There was no good in trying to evade what he had done: there was no good in trying to avoid what he now must do. Having set his foot on the road, there was nothing to do but follow it. And at least Mary Campbell had never hesitated to follow the road with him . . . and without counting the cost.

Robert Aiken's estate of Whitehill lay on the outskirts of Ayr. It was a pleasant place, and the Bard had visited it once before: but tonight there were several visitors in his honour. He was introduced to his patron's three sons, Andrew (whom he had already met), John and Robert, and his only daughter, Grace, a child of some nine summers. There were some kent faces in Ballantine, MacWhinnie, Willie Chalmers, Major Logan and Doctor Douglas; and there were folks he met for the first time.

Robert Aiken, apart from the wealth he had acquired as a lawyer, was well connected. Through his mother, Sarah Dalrymple, he was related to the Reverend William Dalrymple, the parish minister who had baptised the Bard at Alloway; and he was related to a nobler connection, James Dalrymple, Esquire, who had the previous year come into possession of the considerable estate of Orangefield, to the north of Ayr. This Dalrymple was cousin germain to no less a nobleman than James Cunningham, Earl of Glencairn.

It took some time for the Bard to become familiar with all the genealogical details of Bob Aiken's family-tree; and because of this, he moved with some caution among the representatives, until he was able to place them without fear of mistake.

He found James Dalrymple a man without any great learning, but without any great snobbery. Indeed the gentleman was of an extremely sociable disposition and liked nothing better than good company and plenty of lively conversation. He showed little disposition to treat the Bard as a markedly social inferior, and very soon had him at his ease.

"You don't hunt, Mr. Burns? You should follow the hounds. Greatest sport in the country . . . Any time you are about Orangefield, have the goodness to call on me. I have an excellent stable there; and I can put a hunter at your disposal. Damnit, Mr. Burns: all poets should hunt. It would give them a glorious appetite for life. Clears the mind: keeps the kidneys and liver in order. Eat better and drink better for it. Aye, damnit, and write better poetry for it. I never feel I'm living unless I'm in the saddle—with a beast of mettle under me."

"In these matters, perhaps it is better for the poet to remain a spectator. But my humble bardship is much honoured by your goodness, sir."

"Any time I can render you a service, Mr. Burns, I shall consider it a privilege. Your Poems have done Ayrshire a great honour. I shall see that they are taken notice of in the Capital."

James Dalrymple raised his glass: "To your health, Mr. Burns— to your very good health, sir."

The gathering, however, was too big and too formal to allow of any real intimacy; and as he realised he was the show-piece of the evening, he revealed only the outward shell of his personality.

He was sensitive to the fact that these good people had no need to flatter him with their attentions, and that they might just as easily have ignored him. That they didn't ignore him, but sought rather to show their appreciation of his worth as a poet, did not fail to register with him or make him feel other than deeply in their debt.

But beneath all their kindness he could not escape the fact that he was, poet or no poet, a poor tenant-farmer about to sail to the Indies because there was no place for him in his native country; and that, but for the accident of his poetry, he was not worthy of a lift of their eyebrows.

For Aiken and Ballantine his feelings were deep and genuine; they were based on years of solid friendship: it was the social excrescences around them that cautioned him to withdraw . . .

It was only towards the close of the evening that he managed to have a more friendly word with his host and Ballantine. Both reiterated their feeling that there should be another edition of the

Poems and urged him to see what Wilson in Kilmarnock was prepared to do about it.

But the idea of another edition had never crossed his mind. He had aspired to no more than a modest and local fame; he had hoped for no more than to be remembered as a Scots Bard gone to the West Indies.

And now, within a month of the publication of his book, it was sold out and people were clamouring for copies that were not there.

"Maybe if I were to postpone my voyage for a few weeks: until such time as I saw Wilson and found out what the position was . . ."

"By all means postpone your visit, Robin: another edition will certainly bring you more money so that your voyage will not suffer and your prospects made the brighter."

"I agree, John: there's nothing to be lost by waiting to see what Wilson can do. It would be folly to let an opportunity like this slip. Who knows: there might be an opportunity yet for an edition in Edinburgh. I don't think it would be too much to hope that your fame might spread as far as the Capital."

Ballantine agreed. "Yes, Robin: I think that when news of your work reaches the Capital, they will think just as highly of it there as we do here. And this is maybe the best reason of all for thinking over your voyage."

"Anyway: you have a word wi' Wilson and let's hear of the outcome," said Aiken.

But the Bard's mind was numb with speculation. He could no longer think clearly about anything. He was anxious to get home and discuss the matter with Gilbert. There were some things he could discuss with his brother he could discuss with no other living soul. And though he knew that he had no better friends in Ayr, he felt a sudden overwhelming longing to be away from them all and back among folk with whom he could be completely natural.

THE ANSWERED PRAYER

He was coming into Machlin one day at the end of August when he met Jenny Surgeoner.

"Hullo, Rab . . ."

"Hullo, Jenny: and how are you after all these months? What! Is this the bairn?"

Jenny Surgeoner eased the shawl from the baby's face. "Wha d'you think she's like, Rab?"

"Damnit, Jenny, it's hard to say. I was never ony good at telling who a bairn took after until it was grown up . . . and sometimes no' even then. But she's got your eyes and nose. Maybe there's a touch o' Jock Richmond about the forehead. But she's a bonnie bairn, Jenny, so what does it matter who she looks like?"

"Oh, I think she looks like Jock!"

"Well: she couldna look like a better man, could she? When had you word last from Jock?"

"I've never had ony word, Rab."

The tears began to show in her eyes. He could hardly believe her. It seemed incredible that John Richmond could have failed in his duty to write her all these long months.

"D'you mean to tell me that he has never written you, Jenny: not even a sheet to ask for your health?"

"Not a note o' ony kind, Rab. And when I was in Paisley I used to spend hours learning to write so that when I got a letter I could answer it. You've had word, haven't you? D'you think there'll be onything wrang? D'you think he's forgotten me?"

"Damnit, Jenny, he couldna hae forgotten you. I know Richmond well enough to say that. He told me that he would come back and marry you: whatever else may happen I'm sure he'll keep his promise to you. Richmond's no' much of a hand at writing letters. Maybe he writes too much in the way o' his work to be bothered writing in his idle time; and maybe he has little enough o' that."

"If you think he'll come back, Rab, that's a' that matters . . . I was in seeing Jean this afternoon: she's wearying on you sair, Rab. D'you no' think you might manage in to see her for a wee while? She said you werena to worry about the warrant. Old Armour doesna want to pursue you ony mair."

"Little I'm caring what he wants. He's done a' the damage he can do. He came between Jean and me."

"Jean's breaking her heart about that now, Rab."

"Aye: when it's too late."

"Och, it's no' too late, Rab. She's aey loved you: it was her father . . . You've nae idea what she cam' through. If it had been me I wad hae done away wi' mysel'. He's a terrible man."

"Aye: and her auld mither's no' a damned bit better."

"But parents are a' the same, Rab, when a lass gets into trouble."

"But to hell, Jenny: you ken that I gave Jean lines . . . But don't let's go over all that again. How's Jean keeping?"

"Her pains might be on her now. Oh God, Rab: she's a terrible size: I couldna stop wi' her for thinking what she'll have to come through. I think you should look in when you're passing: it makes a' the difference to a lass to ken that she's no' deserted. At a time like this differences should be forgotten about."

"D'you think they'll let me in? I've had a lot to thole from them, Jenny."

"I ken, Rab; but what you've had to thole is nothing to what Jean's having to thole now."

"I'll see, Jenny. And be good to that bairn; for if Jock Richmond could see her just now, he would have you married right away."

They had sauntered back from Netherplace and they were now almost opposite the Whitefoord Arms. He took his leave of her and went in for a drink.

Her news was disturbing. It was unbearable to think that Jean was lying there in the Cowgate: maybe in labour; maybe at this very moment giving birth to their child! Maybe he should risk the wrath of Armour and do as Jenny had suggested. Jean was breaking her heart for him? Well she might: they had had many happy hours together. Too happy. But there was no doubt: women had a hard time of it; and when a lass was in labour it was hard to keep up spite . . .

John Dow saw he was distraught. "What's the matter, Rab? Wi' a' thae books you hae sellt, you should feel like a dog wi' twa tails. There was a traveller in here the ither day and he said that your verses were the finest that had ever come out o' Scotland. God! and he seemed to be weel up in verses . . ."

But the Bard wasn't listening to John Dow. He was thinking of Jean lying in that upstairs bedroom. The room from which she had so often made signs to him . . .

He finished his drink hurriedly and turned and left the room.

Mrs. Armour did not receive him graciously. But she received him. James Armour came ben the spence and he appeared to be a very worried man.

"I canna say that I'm glad to see you, sir. That's speaking for mysel'. But we're gey worried about Jean."

"It's Jean I'm worried about. Don't imagine I came here to plead my cause, for you ken fine I have no cause to plead. But I ken Jean wants to see me. So we'll bandy no words, Mr. Armour: she's your daughter and she was my wife and it's my bairn she's lying in wi' now."

"We'll say nae mair about that, Mr. Burns. Up the stair, wife, and see that Jean's in a fit state to be seen . . . Aye: it's a sair time for a parent. Maybe you'll hae a dochter yoursel' some day. And maybe she'll come hame some nicht and tell you that she's wi' bairn to a man that canna provide her wi' house or hame . . .

But I'll say nae mair about that. You'll just need to excuse my feelings."

He looked at Armour closely. The man was not lying. He was indeed distressed. Every ounce of combativeness seemed to have oozed from him and left him empty. He realised that he must be feeling for his daughter in her ordeal.

But the truth, apart from this, was that James Armour realised he had made a mistake in destroying the marriage lines. He had made a very wrong estimation of Robert Burns. From being locally notorious, he had sprung almost overnight to being a man of local fame. What he had thought would be a disastrous liability in his family looked like turning out to be a very considerable asset. But who could have guessed that gentles like Mrs. Stewart of Stair and Mr. Dalrymple of Orange-field would have taken up a beggarly tenant-farmer in Mossgiel and spoken well of him merely because he had published a volume of verses? It was damned hard that years of patient work could be overtopped by a common blackguard merely because he had the gift of the goose-quill. And it was a damned ill turn the world had taken when a man, in seeking redress for his daughter's dishonour, was to be told that he was at fault for using the machinery of the law.

James Armour was puzzled, distressed and sorely out of his depth. He didn't know what to think; and he was afraid to think in case he found himself once more in the wrong. It was a blow to his pride and his confidence to feel that his own judgment, which had hitherto served him so well, was no longer to be trusted . . .

Jean's relief at seeing him beside her bed was touching to witness. Robin had great difficulty in restraining himself. He steeled himself into remembering that she was no longer his wife; that as far as she was concerned he was a single man with a letter from the priest to certify his singleness and his freedom from scandal.

"I'm glad you've come, Rab. It's been terrible a' this time having to do without you."

"That's hardly my fault, Jean."

"I ken it's no' your fault, Rab. And if you only kent the whole story, it's no' a' my fault either."

"We'll let that flea stick to the wa': how are you feeling now, lass?"

"I wish it was a' ower, Rab: this waiting's terrible."

"Your mother says you havena lang to wait now. If there's onything I could do . . . onything I could get you?"

"A' my prayers were answered, Rab, when my mither came up to tell me you were waiting to see me. You ken I never wanted our lines destroyed? You ken, as far as I'm concerned, that nothing could destroy what came atween us . . ."

"We'll talk about a' this when you're safely through your ordeal, Jean. But you must remember that while it's easy enough to destroy a line, it's no' so easy putting it thegither again."

"Whatever you say, Rab . . . I'm glad to hear your Poems hae been a success. Will you need to go to the Indies now, Rab?"

What she would say or think when she learned that he had sailed for the Indies with Mary Campbell as his wife troubled him greatly. He knew well that she had no legal claim on him, that morality allowed that she had no claim on him. But he also knew that neither legality nor morality had more than the shallowest bearing on his real feelings, and that emotion could not be governed by such superficial trumperies. Every ounce of his real being told him that he loved Jean Armour now as deeply as ever he had loved her. He knew, even as she spoke, that he must lie to her.

"Maybe I'll no' need to go to the Indies, Jean. But whether I do or don't depends on many things independent o' you or me . . . If we were free creatures, Jean, and not shackled and chained by the irons of poverty and circumstance, it would be easy to say what I would do. But a' that matters for the moment is that you bring your bairn safely into the world, and that you yourself come through the ordeal unscathed: as I ken you will. You've nothing to fear, lass. You're big and strong and wi' the constitution . . . Well, you've got a better chance than ony woman I ken. And when your hour comes, I'll no' be far away."

"I'll be fine, Rab: dinna worry about me. As lang as I ken you're no' angry wi' me I'll face onything. It's just that lying here waiting . . ."

"You're on the last lap now: so hold fast and everything'll turn out all right. And mind: if you want me at ony time tell Adam and he'll find me."

"Adam likes you, Rab; and so does my sister Nelly. It was just my folks; and they didna understand."

He leaned over the bed and kissed her gently. Sweat-beads glistened on her brow. Beneath the thin coverlet she seemed enormously swollen. She took his great rough paw in her damp hand.

"It's a boy, Rab! Put your hand there and you'll feel him kicking."

He felt. The shock of the movement, unbelievably vigorous, went through him like an electric impact. Jean's dark eyes swam with happiness.

"Wait till you see him, Rab: you'll be real proud o' him."

He staggered from Jean's door round to Dow's, his emotions in a maelstrom of conflict. Betty Paton's wee lass had given him a deep thrill. But this was beyond any mere thrill. This was shattering, devastating. This sent his father-heart swelling and thumping in his breast so that it hammered on his ribs with physical discomfort. If he had gone to the Indies without knowing this . . . But to hell with the Indies! Here he was about to become the greatest father in all Scotland. There wasn't another lass in the kingdom who could throw him such a boy . . . What was a book of verse compared to this? This was life: great and glorious life . . . Of course: it might be another girl. Betty Paton had been sure of a boy. Maybe they wanted boys. Maybe he wanted a boy. Did he? Yes: he wanted a boy and Jean wanted a boy: well, maybe it would be a boy. Maybe for once in his life he would get what he wanted . . .

But he would need to pull himself together. There was no point in letting folks see how he cared: or that he cared anything. After all that had happened they wouldn't understand: they hadn't enough blood in them to understand. That was what was wrong with folks: their blood was watered down, dammed, lying in stagnant pools . . . Their feelings were but poor scum floating on thin emotion.

Otherwise their blood would well up and break down all the dams that had been built to thwart and confine human instincts and blight the free flowering of the human spirit . . .

The following day he took pen and wrote to John Richmond:

Mossgiel,
1st Sept. 1786

My Dear Sir,

I am still here in statu quo, though I well expected to have been on my way over the Atlantic by this time. The *Nancy*, in which I was to have gone, did not give me warning enough. Two days notice was too little for me to wind up my affairs and go for Greenock. I now am to be a passenger aboard the *Bell*, Captain Cathcart, who sails at the end of this month. I am under little apprehension now about Armour. The warrant is still in existence, but some of the first Gentlemen in the country have offered to befriend me; and besides, Jean will not take any step against me, without letting me know, as nothing but the most violent menaces could have forced her to sign the petition. I have called on her once and again, of late; as she, at this moment, is threatened with the pangs of approaching travail; and I assure you, my dear friend, I cannot help being anxious, very anxious, for her situation. She would gladly now embrace that offer she once rejected, but it shall never more be in her power.

I saw Jenny Surgeoner of late, and she complains bitterly against you. You are acting very wrong, my friend; her happiness or misery is bound up in your affection or unkindness. Poor girl! she told me with tears in her eyes that she had been at great pains since she went to Paisley, learning to write better; just on purpose to be able to correspond with you; and had promised herself great pleasure in your letters. Richmond, I know you to be a man of honour, but this conduct of yours to a poor girl who distractedly loves you, and whom you have ruined—forgive me, my friend, when I say it is highly inconsistent with that manly Integrity that

I know your bosom glows with. Your little, sweet Innocent too—
but I beg your pardon; 'tis taking an improper liberty.

> "He would not have done a shameful thing, but once,
> Tho' hid from all the world and none had known it
> He could not have forgiven it to himself."

I do not know if Smith wrote you along with my book; but I tell
you now, I present you with that Copy, as a memento of an old
friend, on these conditions—you must bind it in the neatest
manner and never lend it, but keep it for my sake.

I shall certainly expect to hear from you by the return of
Connel and you shall hear from me yet before I go.

I am, My Dear Sir, your ever faithful friend.

THE THIRD OF LIBRA

On Sunday, the third of September, Mr. Auld being absent on a visitation, the Reverend James Steven preached. He took for his text the second verse of the fourth chapter of Malachi: "And ye shall go forth, and grow up, as calves of the stall."

No sooner had he announced his text than the Bard found comment on this tripping through his mind in rhyme: Right, sir! your text I'll prove it true, though Heretics may laugh; for instance there's yoursel' just now, God knows an unco Calf!

And should some Patron be so kind as bless you wi' a kirk, I doubt na, sir, but then we'll find, you're still as great a Stirk!

But if the Lover's raptured hour shall ever be your lot, forbid it, every heavenly Power, you e'er should be a Stot!

And when your numbered wi' the dead, below a grassy hillock, wi' justice they may mark your head—Here lies a famous Bullock!

As soon as the service was over he would call on Gavin Hamilton and regale him with this little effort. For if ever a bullock, calf or stot had erected itself in a pulpit, then its name was Jamie Steven. No wonder the poor wooden-tongued creature couldn't get settled in a kirk. He would be a sore trial on any congregation that had to sit under him. At very least, a man of God should have some human dignity about him and should be able to put some dignity to his mouthing of Holy Writ.

But underneath his superficial contempt for the Reverend Jamie was a deep anxiety for Jean Armour. Three days had passed since he had seen her and there was still no news of the birth. But he noticed that Mrs. Armour and Helen were absent from the Armour desk this morning, and that James Armour was looking more worried than ever. Had not Adam winked and grinned to him, he would have feared that something had gone wrong.

But even while he sat under the fat and florid priest, listening with only half an ear and sometimes with no ear at all to his ham-tongued habbering, Jean was in the throes of a hard and difficult labour.

They kept the news from him till late in the evening. It took several hours for them to redd up the place and for Jean to compose herself sufficiently to be able to receive him. It took the Armours even longer to compose themselves after the first initial effects of the shock . . .

When Adam Armour came to him with the news he literally leapt into the air.

Jean had been delivered safely of a fine boy and a fine girl.

When he had recovered himself, he looked out the gold guinea he had saved for the occasion, wrapped up a pound of tea and a small cheese and set off for the Cowgate.

His sisters stared at him in open-eyed wonder and his mother shook her head. What was humiliation to them seemed glorious triumph to him. It was beyond their understanding. Hadn't the Armours despised and rejected him?

But they had long given up any attempt to understand him. He was as far removed from their understanding as he was from their influence.

Gilbert, perplexed, scratched his thin hair and said nothing, for he could think of nothing to say. But when he followed him out into the close the Bard rocked him back on his heels.

"Don't be surprised, Gibby, if I come back wi' my son in my arms."

"Back here?"

"Where else, man? A bouncing son's a gift-horse you don't look i' the mouth. By God, Gibby, when you get a lass to land you a bouncin' brace at a throw, you'll be able to announce yoursel' man and father in the one breath—if you've ony breath left in you."

In the Cowgate spence, James Armour was reduced to the impotency of wringing his hands.

"My God, Mr. Burns, but this is a terrible calamity to befall us. One was bad enough; but twa! How in God's name is Jean to rear twa weans the way we're placed here? Man, Burns, my cup's filled to overflowing."

"Damn the fear, sir. If twa's too many for Jean, I'll tak' the boy off her hands. He can be reared, pap and spoon, at Mossgiel."

James Armour allowed his usually tight jaw to sag. The man must be mad to tie such a load of responsibility round his own neck. But you only had to look at him to see he was mad. But he was mad the right way for them; and he would have to be encouraged in his madness. By God! this was a piece of good fortune he hadn't expected.

"Of coorse, Mr. Burns, I would expect a man like you to come forward at a time like this and do the right thing. And of coorse you hae some claim to the boy that we canna deny you . . . But you'll want to see them! The wife'll be doon in a minute and then you'll get up the stair . . . Aye: Jean had a sair time, puir lass. Oh, but she's a' richt noo. Worn oot, you ken; but she's had a wee sleep and a bit sup o' warm gruel and she's coming round brawly. Oh, but God, sir, twins are an awfa' armfu'. When I came back ower frae the kirk and heard the news, you could hae knockit me doon. I hinna gotten ower the shock yet. But I'm forgetting my manners, sir. Here's a drop o' the best for you. And if you need it as bad as I do, then you're ower bad."

He expected to find her pale and wan; but she was surprisingly normal in her colouring. He did not know that she was in a slight fever.

Her mother had arranged things expertly. A damp-faced, black-downed twin lay in either oxter. Jean's smile was weak and her voice incredibly tired.

"God, lass: so you paid me double! And how are you feeling now?"

"I'm feeling fine . . . Rab. They're . . . bonnie . . ."

He stood beside the bed and looked down on them. It seemed almost that they had not come to life. They slept; and their pale bluish eyelids seemed as if they would never open on the world; their breathing was imperceptible . . .

"Just let them sleep the now, Rab. Maybe . . . the morn . . . you'll can tak' . . . them . . . in your arms . . ."

"Lie still, lass, and dinna disturb yoursel': I'll no' touch the precious dears . . . God, but it gives you a queer feeling. Aye, they're bonnie, Jean: as bonnie a set o' twins as heaven ever blessed."

"This . . . is . . . Jean . . . and this is . . . Robert."

"May the lass grow up to be as bonnie and sweet as you, Jean."

"And if Robert . . . If he's half . . . as guid . . . as you, Rab, he'll . . . be fine."

"Oh, he'll need to do a damn sight better nor me. He'll need to grow up and write poems that the world'll tak' notice o', and no' only the West here."

But Mrs. Armour was back in the room.

"Maybe you'll no' bide ower lang, Mr. Burns? You'll understand that Jean's had a sair time. And what dae you think, Jean, of Mr. Burns offering to tak' the boy and bring him up at Mossgiel?"

"Did you, Rab?"

"If it'll ease your burden, Jean."

But Jean closed her eyes and great pearly tears began to trickle down her cheeks.

Mrs. Armour laid her hand on his arm and beckoned him from the room. But he freed himself and went over to the bed, bent down and kissed her. He whispered softly in her ear: "Never mind, lass: I'll come and see you the morn; and we'll talk things ower when you're feeling liker yourself."

4

DEATH AND DELIVERANCE

LETTER TO AIKEN

About the beginning of October he began drafting a letter to Bob Aiken:

I was with Wilson, my printer, t'other day, and settled all our bygone matters between us. After I had paid him all demands, I made him the offer of the second edition, on the hazard of being paid out of *the first and readiest*, which he declines. By his account, the paper of a thousand copies would cost about twenty-seven pounds, and the printing about fifteen or sixteen: he offers to agree to this for the printing, if I will advance for the paper, but this you know is out of my power; so farewell hopes of a second edition till I grow richer! an epocha which, I think, will arrive at the payment of the British national debt.

There is scarcely anything hurts me so much in being disappointed of my second edition, as not having it in my power to show my gratitude to Mr. Ballantine, by publishing my poem of *The Brigs of Ayr*. I would detest myself as a wretch, if I thought I were capable in a very long life of forgetting the honest, warm, and tender delicacy with which he enters into my interests. I am sometimes pleased with myself in my grateful sensations; but I believe, on the whole, I have very little merit in it, as my gratitude is not a virtue, the consequence of reflection; but sheerly the instinctive emotion of my heart, too inattentive to allow wordly maxims and views to settle into selfish habits.

I have been feeling all the various rotations and movements within, respecting the Excise. There are many things plead strongly against it; the uncertainty of getting soon into business; the consequences of my follies, which may perhaps make it impracticable for me to stay at home; and besides I have for some time been pining under secret wretchedness, from causes which you pretty well know—the pang of disappointment, the sting of pride, with some wandering stabs of remorse, which never fail to settle on my vitals like vultures, when attention is not called away by the calls of society, or the vagaries of the Muse. Even in the hour of social mirth, my gaiety is the madness of an intoxicated criminal under the hands of the executioner. All these reasons urge me to go abroad, and to all these reasons I have only one answer—the feelings of a father. This, in the present mood I am in, over-balances everything that can be laid in the scale against it . . .

You may perhaps think it an extravagant fancy, but it is a sentiment which strikes home to my very soul: though sceptical in some points of our current belief, yet, I think, I have every evidence for the reality of a life beyond the stinted bourne of our present existence; if so, then, how should I, in the presence of that tremendous Being, the Author of existence, how should I meet the reproaches of those who stand to me in the dear relation of children, whom I deserted in the smiling innocency of helpless infancy? O Thou great unknown Power! Thou almighty God! who hast lighted up reason in my breast, and blessed me with immortality! I have frequently wandered from that order and regularity necessary for the perfection of Thy works, yet Thou has never left me nor forsaken me . . .!

Since I wrote the foregoing sheet, I have seen something of the storm of mischief thickening over my folly-devoted head. Should you, my friends, my benefactors, be successful in your applications for me, perhaps it may not be in my power in that way to reap the fruit of your friendly efforts. What I have written in the preceding pages is the settled tenor of my present resolution; but should inimical circumstances forbid me closing with your kind offer, or enjoying it only threaten to entail farther misery——

To tell the truth, I have little reason for complaint; as the world, in general, has been kind to me fully up to my deserts. I was, for some time past, fast getting into the pining distrustful snarl of the misanthrope. I saw myself alone, unfit for the struggle of life, shrinking at every rising cloud in the chance-directed atmosphere of fortune, while, all defenceless, I looked about in vain for a cover. It never occurred to me, at least never with the force it deserved, that this world is a busy scene, and man, a creature destined for a progressive struggle; and that, however I might possess a warm heart and inoffensive manners (which last, by the bye, was rather more than I could well boast), still, more than these passive qualities, there was something to be *done*. When all my school-fellows and youthful compeers (those misguided few excepted who joined, to use a Gentoo phrase, the *hallachores* of the human race) were striking off with eager hope and earnest intent, in some one or other of the many paths of busy life, I was "standing idle in the market-place," or only left the chase of the butterfly from flower to flower, to hunt fancy from whim to whim . . .

You see, sir, that if to *know* one's errors were a probability of *mending* them, I stand a fair chance: but, according to the reverend Westminster divines, though conviction must precede conversion, it is very far from always implying it . . .

ROBERT . . . ROBERT . . .

Unlike Jean Armour, Mary Campbell was able to conceal the swelling of her womb. But then she had not the rich blood of Jean and the forming child was small. She had not told her parents much. She had not told them she was pregnant. She had not told them she was sailing to the Indies . . . She hadn't told them because she couldn't. The longer she was away from Robert, the more depressed she became, the less certain of her future.

She told her parents that she had the promise of a good job in Glasgow . . .

Finally she came to Greenock. Her young brother was staying with the MacPhersons: he was taking up the trade of his uncle, and was about to be entered upon the carpentering craft.

But under the keen eye of the MacPhersons it became impossible to hide her condition. And then there were the letters from Robert Burns to explain.

Mrs. Campbell was sent for . . .

But before her mother arrived, and before she could offer any explanation, her brother went down with fever: the putrid, purple fever. There was no one to nurse him but Mary; and she did not hesitate. She was very fond of her brother.

The MacPhersons were anxious. They were angry too. But it was not possible to have any bitter hatred of Mary, for she was quiet and gentle and infinitely patient. Night and day she nursed her brother. The MacPhersons knew when to suspend judgment.

She pulled Robert through the crisis. But the strain was too much for her. She collapsed. Her vitality reduced to the lowest ebb, the fever assailed her with terrible violence.

She raved. She raved of Robert Burns and the Indies and of many things that scandalised the MacPhersons. But only in bits and snatches was her raving intelligible.

Mary had lucid intervals. She knew she was dying. She called her brother to her side (when she was free for the moment of the MacPhersons) and told him to write to Robert Burns if anything should happen to her. He was too young to understand everything; but he understood the importance of this Robert Burns to his sister. There was nothing he would have denied her. She extracted his promise; and a death-bed promise was sacred . . .

And so, on Friday the 20th of October, Mary Campbell died; died raving, cruelly wasted and disfigured with typhus; died in a foul-smelling box-bed in a small, ill-ventilated room encased in a height of grim tenements in Greenock.

She raved. But in the swirl of shattered images, a broken fragment would embed itself in the sub-stratum of her consciousness . . . The dank darkness of Machlin Tower, a darkness that seeped from the ancient stones and whispered a prayer from the monkish days; a darkness in which the soft vibrant whispers of her lover went whispering into the dark void of eternity, for the darkness there was the darkness that had been before the cry "Let there be light" had been uttered. In the timeless void of the darkness she heard the soft, vibrant whispers from her lover's lips; and she cried out from the darkness within her into the darkness that was without . . .

Robert . . . Robert . . .

And sometimes the voice of Father Auld spoke from the darkness of Jean Armour's hair into the smoke-filmed eyes of her lover. And she cried from the broken pain within her into the broken pain of the world without.

Robert . . . Robert . . .

And the darkness was shot with golden shafts and her lover came down a golden beam. Like a young god he came with a lover's soft call in his throat and a wave of his arm . . . striding down the golden beam that shot through the darkness.

Robert . . . Robert . . .

And he came to where she lay stricken in the tortured shadows and he lifted her up in his strong arms. But she broke in his grasp and fell for a thousand years through chaos. And she cried from the broken fragments of her broken soul—after a thousand years of falling—against the broken fragments of the external world.

Robert . . . Robert . . .

And there broke from her agonised fragments the fragment of her child, and they rolled the fragment in a sheet and laid it under the bed.

And she shrieked and shrieked, trying to collect the broken fragments of herself about her.

Her brother Robert drummed his weak fists against the bare wall and squealed like a rabbit in a snare.

MacPherson's teeth bit into his nether lip and he spat the blood into the fire. Nothing could have satisfied him short of tearing asunder every joint in the carcase of Robert Burns.

His wife sat trembling with her shawl tightly drawn over her head that Mary's cries might not lacerate her open nerves. Father in Heaven—hallowed be Thy name—have mercy on poor Mary and ease her going from the world of sin and suffering and the long dark nights of endless sorrow.

Sometimes Mary lay still in the foul stench of her suffering, falling through a thousand years of darkness.

But at last the rampant raging fever invaded the last cell of her physical being. The darkness shrieked the victory; blood dripped from the old stones of the Machlin Tower; and the bosky banks of the Machlin Burn withered away into grey-winnowed ash and the birds fell lifeless from the sky . . .

But the spirit rallied even on the knife-edged chasm of annihilation.

Mary Campbell parted the blaeberry-stained lids of her eyes upon the mottled-grey face of her brother, and cried from a strangled throat:

"Robert . . . Robert . . ."

And the Robert she cried for to the end was not her brother Robert . . .

And the waters that sang in her ears were not the waters of the river Ayr, where gurgling, they kissed the pebbled shore; but the waters of death's dark stream . . .

Robert Campbell wept and cursed, for the meaning of life and of death was beyond him.

But he kept his death-bed promise to his sister . . .

DINNER WITH A LORD

On Monday, the 23rd of October, the Bard spruced himself up and rode into Machlin and collected Doctor MacKenzie at the Sun Inn.

This was to be a momentous day for him, according to MacKenzie. Professor Dugald Stewart, who held the Chair of Moral Philosophy at Edinburgh University, had his country house at the nearby hamlet of Catrine. Doctor MacKenzie had introduced him to the *Poems* and the worthy Professor was anxious to meet the Bard. So, too, was one of his aristocratic pupils, the young Lord Daer.

As they rode out to Catrine, MacKenzie explained the background of Stewart and Daer.

"You needna be afraid of Mr. Stewart, Robin. He's not one of your ordinary pedagogues. He's a charming and modest man for all his great wealth of learning. And, believe me, he's one of the most learned men in Europe. He was Professor of Mathematics until last year: it's only this last winter he's been in the Chair of Moral Philosophy; and he's only in his early thirties now. A most brilliant man. The fact that he's invited you to dinner with him is a very signal mark of his appreciation. I'm very pleased for your sake, Robin; for if the Professor takes a liking to you he'll go back to Edinburgh this winter and talk about you. And maybe it'll not end at that . . . Lord Daer I've never met: he's one of the younger sons of the Earl o' Selkirk. The Professor's tutoring him up during the vacation: that's quite usual. But he must be a decent fellow for all that, or the Professor wouldn't be wasting his time on him. You see: he can pick and choose his pupils as he likes when outside his official duties . . ."

"I confess to a trifle of trepidation on account of Mr. Stewart's great learning. But as for His Lordship: well, I have never set up to be other than I am. And if he doesna like my bardship I won't lose any sleep about it."

The Professor leaned back in his chair and Lord Daer leaned forward.

"Well, Mr. Burns; and what do you think of the late American War?"

"The American peoples' gain, sir, is certainly our loss. But we deserved to lose, as everyone deserves to lose whose cause is not just. And I think, sir, that the day may well come when the American people will be a great people, and we may be a very small people indeed."

"You are a keen student of politics, Mr. Burns?"

"I am a keen student of life, sir; and life, as I see it, cannot be separated from politics."

Lord Daer's thin pale face flushed with emotion: "Exactly, my dear sir: exactly! And politics to be of any use in the land must be politics of liberality and conscious humanism."

"His Lordship, I should explain, Mr. Burns, has lately returned from France, where there is a growing tendency to give expression to libertarian sentiments inimical to the rule—or perhaps it would be more correct to say misrule—of the present not-too-happy monarchy. But, of course, there the parliamentary check on the absolutism of the crown is lacking. You will agree, will you not, Mr. Burns, that that lack is to be deplored?"

"Unquestionably, sir. But on the other hand: where corruption can exist between the crown and the legislative body, the lack may be no more than nominal."

"Moreover," broke in his Lordship, who was delighted at the turn of the argument, "where the election of the legislative body is itself attended with venal and corrupt practices, we may find ourselves in a more doubtful position."

"You are not a Pittite then, Mr. Burns?"

"Pitt is an able man. But I would rather at this moment that we had the leadership of a more able man: Charles James Fox."

"And less Henry Dundas!" said Lord Daer.

"I heartily endorse that sentiment, my Lord."

"You are indeed a very hearty man altogether, Mr. Burns; and you give very hearty expression to your sentiments. No, no: I did not intend that as a censure: heaven forbid! The hearty expression of opinion is the sign of a strong mind and a well-held opinion. I take it, Mr. Burns, that you have little difficulty in making up your mind on these complex issues?"

"When you are between the shafts of the plough, sir, and turning over the furrow, certain complex problems—that quite properly appear so to the schools of thought—have a way of appearing quite simple and yielding to simple solution. But no doubt this is where the simple and unlettered ploughman is at a disadvantage. Lacking the jargon of the schools, he is unable to make two blades of speculation grow where only one grew formerly."

With this reply the Bard saw that he had discomfited the company. MacKenzie coughed uncomfortably. Lord Daer looked slightly out of his depth. The Professor rose and filled up their glasses . . .

When MacKenzie and the Bard had taken their leave, the Professor summed up the experience for the benefit of his pupil, who, he saw, was deeply impressed.

"There, Basil my boy, you see the workings of strong and original genius of the poetic order. Mr. Burns has indeed very great gifts. The very purity of his language, the absence of Scotticisms, here, in this secluded and rural retreat from all learning, displays a most meritorious application of original genius working on what must have been, to ordinary people, very inadequate, not to say discouraging material. What ordinarily is unreadable—such as the execrable Harvey and his dreary Meditations among the

Tombs—he has, and in his extreme youth do not forget, read with avidity. But what a grounding, my dear Basil!"

"But what ground, sir, on which to build!"

"Very true. But do not forget that it carries great dangers. What Mr. Burns lacks is a sound classical grounding, carefully proportioned and supervised. Such a grounding would provide that essential balance to the forming of opinions, concepts, ideas . . . Of course: it might happen that he would lose some of his vitality, his raw and elemental source of power: his inspiration. Let us be honest with ourselves, Basil: to-day we have been in the presence of very remarkable talent."

"Would you go so far as to say genius, sir?"

"Well, of course, there are degrees of genius as well as of talent. But in so far as Burns is a ploughman—actually, Doctor MacKenzie informs me, he is a small tenant-farmer in partnership with a brother—in so far as he is a farmer, then, I think, we might use the term genius. But rough and unpolished, and largely uninformed in the best academic sense. A genius of an as yet unknown degree. And a great credit to himself and his family."

"I'm afraid, sir, that I have no pretension to such brilliant powers of discretion and analysis. I wish I had; but I'm afraid I have not the brain. And certainly, sir, I could never as much as aspire to have your extraordinary powers. But I must say that I thought Burns a good fellow with an ability altogether uncommon in one of his rank and station in life."

"Why, Basil my boy, that's exactly what I've been saying the long way round."

"I must crave your pardon, sir, I'm sure."

"No, no: how else do any of us learn except by imitation?"

"Yes, sir; but who did Burns imitate?"

Professor Dugald Stewart looked sharply at the young Lord Daer. Then he looked away. There was no doubt but that the earnest young fellow, with the hectic flush on his cheek-bones, was genuinely puzzled and had no presumptious ideas in his head.

COMMENT IN RHYME AND PROSE

This wot ye all whom it concerns:
    I, Rhymer Rab, alias Burns,
        October twenty-third,
A ne'er-to-be-forgotten day,
Sae far I sprachled up the brae
        I dinnered wi' a Lord.

I've been at drucken Writers' feasts,
Nay, been bitch-fou 'mang godly Priests—
        Wi' rev'rence be it spoken!
I've even join'd the honoured jorum,
When mighty Squireships o' the Quorum
        Their hydra drouth did sloken.

But wi' a Lord!—stand out my shin!
A Lord, a Peer, an' Earl's son!—
        Up higher yet, my bonnet!
An' sic a Lord!—lang Scotch ell twa
Our Peerage he looks o'er them a',
        As I look o'er my sonnet.

But O, for Hogarth's magic pow'r
To show Sir Bardie's willyart glow'r,
        An' how he stared an' stammered,
When goavin's he'd been led wi' branks,

456

An' stumpin' on his ploughman shanks,
   He in the parlour hammered!

To meet good Stewart little pain is,
Or Scotia's sacred Demosthénes:
     Thinks I: "They are but men!"
But "Burns!"—"My Lord!"—Good God! I doited,
My knees on ane anither knoited
     As faultering I gaed ben.

I sidling sheltered in a neuk,
An' at his Lordship staw a leuk,
     Like some portentous omen:
Except good sense and social glee
An' (what surprised me) modesty,
     I markèd nought uncommon.

I watched the symptoms o' the great—
The gentle pride, the lordly state,
     The arrogant assuming:
The fient a pride, nae pride had he,
Nor sauce, nor state, that I could see,
     Mair than an honest ploughman!

Then from his Lordship I shall learn
Henceforth to meet with unconcern
     One rank as well's another;
Nae honest, worthy man need care
To meet with noble youthfu' Daer,
     For he but meets a brother.

Doctor MacKenzie: Dear Sir,

I never spent an afternoon among great folks with half that pleasure as when, in company with you, I had the honour of paying my devoirs to that plain, honest, worthy man, the Professor. I would be delighted to see him perform acts of kindness and friendship, though I were not the object; he does it with such a grace. I think his character, divided into ten parts, stands thus—four parts

Socrates—four parts Nathaniel—and two parts Shakespeare's Brutus.

The foregoing verses were really extempore, but a little corrected since. They may entertain you a little with the help of that partiality with which you are so good as to favour the performances of,

Dear Sir, Your very humble Servant . . .

LOWLY LAID

The following day a letter came from Robert Campbell in Greenock. The shaky scrawl was scarcely literate. There was no heading on the paper; no date or salutation. It merely said:

"Mary Campbell, my sister, died here this month twenty days with a bad fever. It was her dying wish that you should be wrote to which I have now done. Robert Campbell."

The letter had been waiting for him when he had come in from the harvest-field for a meal. The light in the room being poor, the writing poorer, he had taken it over to benefit from the light of the window. The family watched him critically, for the letter had been franked from Greenock, and they wondered what news it might contain about his arrangements for sailing.

But the moment he had read the letter he crushed it in his hand; and, with a look on his face such as none of them had ever seen before, he went quickly from the room.

He thought he would never stop crying: the tears burned and squirted from his eyes and great convulsive sobs tore from his chest. He lay in a hollow of the damp ground; but he did not know where he lay.

No thoughts would come to him. The only consciousness he had was the consciousness of the unbearable pain of remorse. He knew he had done Mary Campbell a terrible wrong: a wrong that no tears and no sorrow and no regrets could ever expiate.

And because he knew that no tears could ever wipe out the past, he cried the more.

Never before in his life had he cried like this. Perhaps only once in a lifetime can a human being be so torn with grief.

He had cursed and reviled Gilbert with savage despair. But still Gilbert did not retaliate: he had waited patiently for his opportunity; and when it came he did not abuse it. For over an hour he pleaded with him. He did so very gently, for he knew how deeply hurt his brother was.

"For God's sake, Robin, realise that you were not responsible for what has happened. Even if you had been in Greenock you couldn't have saved Mary's life. You might have taken the first boat to the Indies, and you ken fine you might have been dead by now: Doctor Douglas's friends told you that. It wasn't you who made that decision. You waited till you got a better boat going by a better route. You were doing the best you could for the both of you. And it was the same when you went round the country collecting the money on your subscriptions: you had to get in the money before you sailed— both for Mary and yourself. You had no time to ride into Greenock. And you ken how the sheriff's men had a watch on the port so that the moment you had tried to step on board you would have been arrested. I'm looking at the case as dispassionately as I can . . . It was unfortunate that Mary couldn't write. It was unfortunate that you couldn't write freely to her. But here again: what possible blame can attach to you? If she was pregnant, at least you married her before she left . . . Maybe she didn't tell her parents. We don't know that; but it was her affair: not yours. I know I don't understand everything. I know I didna love Mary. But I know the difference atween right and wrong for all that. You've aey accused me of blaming you for things. And I'd still be the first to blame you if you did what I think to be wrong—even though you are my brother. I'm telling you now that if I thought you were in any degree responsible for her death I would blame you: and without hesitation . . .

"I know you're grieved and sair grieved: you wouldna be who you are were it otherwise. But to grieve is one thing and to accept guilt for something you haven't done and couldn't have prevented is a different thing. Indeed, if there's any sin in the affair, this is just where it lies . . .

"The first chance you get you can ride into Greenock and find out for yourself exactly what happened. If you would like me to go for you, then say the word and I'll go now: if you think it'll do you ony good.

"All right: I'll leave you. But spare a thought, if you can, for your living responsibilities. You've got Bess to think about, and soon enough wee Robert will be coming . . . At least they deserve, if they don't demand, some of your pity . . .

"You can depend on me. Not a word of this will escape my lips to anyone living. It's buried atween you and me for ever. Yes: I agree that the family must ken nothing whatever about it: just you and me. I understand better than you think, Robin. Man, if I could break my heart for you I would do that too. And it will break my heart if you go on like this . . ."

Gilbert pleaded himself dry. In the end he had to walk away and leave his brother sunk in his leaden stupor of grief.

He buried the grief of Mary Campbell's death deep within him; and he placed on the grave of her memory the knowledge that the Fates were against him.

He knew better than most that the cup of life had to be drained to the lees. He knew too that his appetite for life was the greatest instinct he had: his deepest instinct and his finest asset. Already on the grave of Mary Campbell the green grass of life was beginning to appear.

But he knew he would have to get away from Mossgiel, from Machlin, from every scene that brought back to him her memory. Not otherwise would life be bearable.

But it did not seem possible that life would ever be bearable again.

THE VISION OF THE BLIND

They were sitting together in the back premises of Robert Muir. They had much to talk about before they went round to see Tam Samson and other friends, and before he was made an honorary member of the Masonic Lodge there.

"I was paying a visit, Robert, to that excellent man George Laurie, minister at Newmilns——"

"I know him fine: I didn't know you were acquaint?"

"He was on Gavin Hamilton's subscription list and he wrote Gavin that he wanted to see me. However: here's a letter that Mr. Laurie got from Doctor Blacklock, a blind poet in Edinburgh. Laurie had sent him a copy of my verses. I'll read it to you:

" 'Reverend and Dear Sir,

I ought to have acknowledged your favour long ago, not only as a testimony of your kind remembrance, but as it gave me an opportunity of sharing one of the finest, and, perhaps, one of the most genuine entertainments, of which the human mind is susceptible. A number of avocations retarded my progress in reading the poems; at last, however, I have finished that pleasing perusal. Many instances have I seen of Nature's force and bene-ficence, exerted under numerous and formidable disadvantages; but none equal to that with which you have been kind enough to present me. There is a pathos and delicacy in his serious poems; a vein of wit and humour in those of a more festive turn, which cannot be too much admired, nor too warmly approved; and I think I shall never open the book without feeling my astonishment renewed and increased. It was my wish to have expressed my approbation in verse; but whether from declining life or a temporary depression of spirits, it is at present out of my power to accomplish that agreeable intention.

'Mr. Dugald Stewart, professor of morals in this university, had formerly read me three of the poems, and I had desired him to get my name inserted among the subscribers: but whether this was done or not I never could learn. I have little intercourse with Dr. Blair, but will take care to have the poems communicated to him by the intervention of some mutual friend. It has been told me by a gentleman, to whom I shewed the performances, and who sought a copy with diligence and ardour, that the whole impression is already exhausted. It were therefore much to be wished, for the sake of the young man, that a second edition, more numerous than the former, could immediately be printed; as it appears certain that its intrinsic merit, and the exertion of the author's friends, might give it a more universal circulation than anything of the kind which has been published within my memory.   T. Blacklock.' "

Robert Muir's reaction was electric. On being informed that Blacklock had already published a volume of poetry and that he was one of the leading critics in Edinburgh, his enthusiasm was boundless.

"There's no question: you must set out for Edinburgh. I told you that from the beginning. You had only to get into print for your fame to be secured. Now that you've decided against the Indies, what is there to prevent you? The harvest's by now: you could be spared easily for a week or two. You could try out the ground there at worst. You've already met this Dugald Stewart and Lord Daer: you know Dalrymple of Orangefield and Sir John Whitefoord: you've a valuable masonic connection there . . . I canna think of a brighter prospect, Robin. You've achieved fame; but go through to Edinburgh and, if you can bring out another edition there, your fame will be secure for all time."

"I'm almost persuaded, Robert. Aiken and Ballantine in Ayr are of the same opinion. Aiken thinks he can get me introduced to one of the best printers there. And since Wilson was so mean about the paper, I have no compunction in that quarter. I would like another edition. I have many new pieces I would like to print, and I would put in Love and Liberty and The Prophet and God's Complaint . . . Aye: my mind's almost made up; but I don't want anything said about it till I'm certain: in fact, till I'm there . . .

"And what d'you think of Mrs. Dunlop of Dunlop sending a carriage all the way from Stewarton to pay her respects to my bardship and to purchase six copies?"

"I tell you, Robin: if you get an Edinburgh edition, the printing presses there will be kept busy for the next hundred years."

"You don't think I should go in for the Excise?"

"You could do worse; but you could do a lot better. Somehow I canna see you as a gauger. It has compensations, of course; and if you could get someone to push you on . . . But don't think about that just now. Go through to Edinburgh and you'll like as not get the offer of a dozen good jobs. And jobs where you won't have to work. Hell, man: the half o' Enbro lives off government sinecures o' one sort or another . . ."

THE SONS OF AULD KILLIE

The Right Worshipful Master, Major William Parker, closed the Lodge and passed it to refreshment. When the Bard had been welcomed and congratulated on all hands and his health had been drunk a dozen times, the Major rose and said:

"Now that Brother Robert Burns is one of the 'Sons of Auld Killie,' to use his own words, I propose that we do not let him depart the Lodge till he has given us one more proof that he is indeed one of ourselves. Not that we need that proof; but I would like Brother Burns to leave us some poetic token of the honour he has bestowed on us here to-night with his presence. For if the Craft has honoured Brother Burns, we must not forget that Brother Burns has honoured the Craft."

When the applause had died down, the Bard rose and addressed the company.

"I had a dream the other night of how a much-loved and deeply-respected brother of Lodge Kilwinning met his lamented end. The following lines came to me in my dream. And while a Bard does well to cast his critical eye over the productions of his waking hours, he may be excused for allowing to pass, uncensored, his unpremeditated night-thoughts. And now, if the Brethren will bear with me . . .

"Has auld Kilmarnock seen the Deil? Or great MacKinlay thrawn his heel? Or Robertson again grown weel to preach an' read? 'Na, waur than a'!' cries ilka chiel, 'Tam Samson's dead!'

"Kilmarnock lang may grunt an' grane, an' sigh, an' sab, an' greet her lane, an' cleed her bairns—man, wife an' wean, in mourning weed; to Death she's dearly pay'd the kain: Tam Samson's dead!"

"The Brethren o' the mystic level may hing their head in woefu' bevel, while by their nose the tears will revel, like ony bead; Death's gien the Lodge an unco devel: Tam Samson's dead!"

And the Bard had already given the Lodge an unco devel: they were almost petrified with expectancy. Hugh Parker, brother to Major William, looked from the Bard's distant face to the top of Tam's bald, bowed head.

What was there about Tam Samson that, hitherto, he had missed? Tam was a worthy-enough merchant, no doubt; but how came it that the Bard had this faculty of seeing beneath the homespun worthiness of the merchant?

Many others thought likewise. John Gowdie—terror of the Whigs—who had been as insistent as any in persuading the Bard to publish his verses, wondered why Tam had been selected out of all the Kilmarnock worthies for this distinctive honour. Gowdie could find nothing remarkable in him. He was a good fellow, though a little tinctured with theological ribaldry; rough in his wit though always ready; but a man of no intellectual distinction. Why, then, had Robert Burns chosen Tam Samson?

But there was no opportunity for detailed questioning: the elegy had opened so well that no word was to be missed.

"When Winter muffles up his cloak, and binds the mire like a rock; when to the lochs the curlers flock, wi' gleesome speed, wha will they station at the cock?—Tam Samson's dead!

"He was the king of a' the core, to guard, or draw, or wick a bore or up the rink like Jehu roar in time o' need; but now he lags on Death's hog-score: Tam Samson's dead!"

Sensation melted in Tam's bosom. Some day he would be dead. It might not be long now. But when had Rab seen him at the curling pond? How came it that he knew how he roared up the rink in time o' need? Damnit, he could read the past as well as he could read the present that lay before him like an open book.

His brother John looked across the table at him and thought: "That's you to the life, Tam. And I've lived with you all my days and never really seen you till I see you now dressed in Rab's words. By God, and the words fit you, Tam: smugly and brawly they fit your fat, round sides . . ."

"Now safe the stately sawmont sail, and trouts bedropp'd wi' crimson hail, and eels, weel-kend for souple tail, and geds for greed, since, dark in Death's fish-creel, we wail Tam Samson dead!

"Rejoice, ye birring paitricks a'; ye cootie moorcocks, crousely craw; ye maukins, cock your fud fu' braw withouten dread; your mortal fae is now awa: Tam Samson's dead!

"That woefu' morn be ever mourn'd, saw him in shootin' graith adorn'd, while pointers round impatient burn'd, frae couples free'd; but och! he gaed and ne'er return'd: Tam Samson's dead.

"In vain auld-age his body batters, in vain the gout his ankles fetters, in vain the burns cam down like waters an acre, braid! Now ev'ry auld wife, greeting', clatters: 'Tam Samson's dead!'

"Owre monie a weary hag he limpit, an' ay the tither shot he thumpit, till coward Death behint him jumpit, wi' deadly feide; now he proclaims wi' tout o' trumpet: 'Tam Samson's dead!'

"When at his heart he felt the dagger, he reel'd his wonted bottle-swagger, but yet he drew the mortal trigger wi' weel-aim'd heed; 'Lord, five!' he cried, an' owre did stagger—Tam Samson's dead!

"Ilk hoary hunter mourn'd a brither; ilk sportsman-youth bemoan'd a father; you auld grey stane, amang the heather, marks out his head; Whare Burns has wrote, in rhyming blether: 'Tam Samson's dead!'

"There low he lies in lasting rest; perhaps upon his mould'ring breast some spitefu' moorfowl bigs her nest, to hatch an' breed: Alas! nae mair he'll them molest: Tam Samson's dead!

"When August winds the heather wave, and sportsmen wander by yon grave, three volleys let his memory crave o' pouther an' lead, till Echo answers frae her cave: 'Tam Samson's dead!'

" 'Heav'n rest his saul whare'er he be!' is th' wish o' monie mae than me: he had twa fauts, or maybe three, yet what remead? Ae social, honest man want we: Tam Samson's dead!"

The reading had been punctuated with much laughter and applause. Tam Samson sat with bowed head and honest tears of emotion trickled down his wrinkled, weathered face. He did not shed tears for sorrow. He shed tears for a happiness so intense that it could not otherwise be endured. It was an uncanny tribute; and how Rab Burns could have seen so deeply into his life, and so clearly comprehended the significance of his inner emotions, was touchingly wonderful.

And then the Brethren held their breaths as the Bard's spell enchanted them. No one wanted to miss a syllable. The picture of Tam was so rich and vital in its utter perfection that Tam, in the Bard's lines, stood forth more clear and lifelike, more instant-aneously perceptible in all his intriguing highlights, than he appeared in the solid flesh, sitting there with slightly-bowed head at the left hand of the speaker.

And when the Bard had finished and the long, low-ceilinged room had reverberated in an applause that sent the mellow light of a dozen candles wavering across their enraptured, upturned faces, Tam Samson rose slowly and extended a shaking hand towards him.

"Ah Rab, Rab," he said, when he found his voice, "I'm no' dead yet. But gin I was, and I could hear ye lay that aff frae the other side, then, damned, but I'd be a happier man dead than I hae been alive."

"Aye, Tam—and while there's a Brither living that can speak our hamely Westland tongue, you'll never be dead."

The Bard faced his audience. "But I must ask you to bear wi' me for a little. I have told you of my dream. In the morning when I had committed my dream to paper, I added an epitaph: 'Tam Samson's weel-worn clay here lies: ye canting zealots, spare him! If honest worth in Heaven rise, ye'll mend or ye win near him.'

"And then I headed the sheet with the line from Pope: 'An honest man's the noblest work of God'; and in the full light of grateful consciousness, added the following, per contra. And it is with this last grateful remembrance of Auld Killie, her sons and my dear friend and Brither here, that I would leave you:

"Go, Fame, an' canter like a filly thro' a' the streets an' neuks o' Killie; tell ev'ry social honest billie to cease his grievin'; for, yet unskaith'd by Death's gleg gullie, Tam Samson's leevin'!"

But on this the Lodge went leaping mad and threw all restraint and decorum overboard. The hands of time had stopped; the sands of life had ceased to run in the glass of mortality; and eternity had crept in on them along the soft shadows.

To catch up on its lag, time danced a reel; and the Brethren leapt in a mad excess of relieved gratitude.

BROTHERS

At the rig-end he cast the plough on its side.

"I've made up my mind, Gilbert: I'm going to Edinburgh. I've written to John Richmond, and he's willing to let me share his bed for a shilling a week. When I'll come back depends on how I get on. If I get a publisher for my second edition, I'll wait and see that through the press. I'm sending my Jamaica chest on before me: if I don't get a publisher I'll maybe sail from Leith. Or I'll sell what I don't need: I don't know. I've left you enough money to see my labour replaced until I come back . . . if I come back."

"Whatever happens you'll come back. You'll promise me that now. I have made little demands on you, Robin; but I have the right to demand that."

"By what right?"

"You would stand there and ask me that? I'll tell you by what right. Because I'm taking your place. It wasna me stood penance for Lizzie Paton; it wasna me stood penance for Jean Armour; but I'll need to be father to their bairns for a' that. I'm taking that responsibility off you; but don't forget it's a heavy responsibility. I'm taking onto my shoulders your share of the burden as well as my own of providing a home for a mother, three sisters and a brother . . . And I'm doing all this not because you asked me; but because I think it's my duty; because I think that nothing should be allowed to stand in your road; because I think it's more important that you and your poems should be encouraged—even though it means that I'll never get my head above the mire; because I think I'm better able to be father to your bairns than have the chance to be father to my own . . . Aye: and I'm proud to do all this because I'm proud to have the privilege o' being your brother—even though you do think damn little o' me . . ."

The Bard's eyes had never left Gilbert's. At last Gilbert noticed that they were filmed over with pain; that his face was blanched and that his jaw twitched.

"I could answer you, Gilbert: nothing easier; but I don't want to hurt you more than you can stand being hurt. But there's not one o' you would have had Betty Paton or Jean Armour or Mary Campbell about the house. My mother wanted me to marry Betty; but she was the only one. She told me what would happen if I didna . . . Well: it's happened; and a lot more than she bargained on. Think that over when you have time and inclination. But I'll promise you this. I'll go through to Edinburgh and see what I can do; and I'll pay back every penny that ever I took out of the family since the day I was born. And there's no work will be too degrading for me to put my hand to. Aye, I'll come back. How or when I canna say. But when I do, don't think I'll come back as the Prodigal Son."

"For Godsake, Robin, dinna talk like that. I could cut out my tongue that I ever spoke."

"It's better to speak the bluidy truth than keep it festering in your guts. And hold up that long-suffering bluidy head o' yours; for I ken, if you dinna, that I'm not worthy to be your brother. I'm leaving you in charge o' the family because I'm not fit for that responsibility ony longer. I'm leaving you before I bring ony more disgrace on you; and I ken I've brought plenty . . . What the hell are you blubbering for? God Almighty! could I have made a bigger mess o' my life gin I'd been the biggest unhung blackguard in Scotland? Do you think I don't know what my mother and sisters are thinking every time I sit down to a meal? Do you think I canna read their eyes like a page o' print? And how much longer do you think I can bear it?"

"Maybe they don't understand, Robin; but sometimes neither do you. But every one o' us is proud of you though we canna always show it the way you would want. The lassies have taken to Bess, and they'll tak' to Robert too. But you ken as weel as me how they've been brought up . . . For God's sake, Robin, try and understand my feelings just as much as I try to understand yours . . ."

"Aye: I understand your feelings. That's my bluidy fault: I understand ower many folks' feelings. But I want no sympathy— and I want no moralising. I'll take what's coming to me without whining. You've never heard me whining—and, by God, I'll be gey bad if you ever do. You know as well as I do that I've ploughed my sweat and blood into this clay. Could you have hired onybody to do as much? You've ruined your life by not being a father— have you? Well: I've ruined mine—and a wheen others—by being only half a father. My sense o' duty's just as damn-well keen as yours—even though I don't tie it round my knees like wooers' babs. I'll take sympathy from nobody; but I'll take no bluidy censure either. I'll do all my own censuring."

"All right: do every damned thing yourself—and consider nobody. You've gone your own gate since ever I can mind; and I suppose you aey will. That's one o' the privileges o' being a genius, I suppose."

"You suppose! You're too bluidy sanctimonious to suppose anything. And anything you do suppose isn't worth your while—or any other body's. When you see me taking ony liberties on account o' being a genius, you'll be entitled to bandy that word; but not before. Genius! It would make a cuddy laugh. Soaked to the bluidy skin and laired in saft clay! When it comes to doing a day's darg you ken a hell o' a lot about genius. Clear to beggary the whole bluidy lot o' you—and see how you fare! Every day I've risen since I can mind I've earned my bite and sup—and mair. And the next time you tell me I'm a genius I'll tak' that coulter and knock that damned silly sheep's head aff your body. And that's the last time I'll hash mysel' atween the stilts o' that bluidy plough——"

"Are you gan mad or what?"

"Aye—or what? Genius, madman: what next?"

"Baith! And a bluidy eediot into the bargain."

"Eediot!"

"Aye, you're nothing but a bluidy senseless eediot to talk the way you're talking. I ken fine you can lash onybody to the ground wi' your tongue. We're only a lot o' puir gulls where you're concerned. When you got a' the fancy feathers, there was nane left for the rest o' us. But you'll maybe get a sair plucking in Embro afore you're done. There'll be a wheen o' hawks there'll gar you skulk to the ground. You'll no' strut up and down the Canongate without somebody'll tak' a swipe at you!"

"That'll please you, will it? Awa' and row in the midden and tak' some o' the sanctimonious stink aff yoursel': your upright-eousness is pollutin' the air . . . Aye: you're a puir gull wha sees you, Gibby; and I'm a puirer bluidy hawk to disturb your bits o' drookit feathers. Eediots you said, and eediots we are; and every Burns I ever heard tell o' was nae better . . ."

The storm between the brothers blew itself out. Ever since the death of Mary Campbell the Bard's nerves had been liable to break down into troughs of intense introspective depression. The troughs had always been there; but never had they been so deep. And when he was depressed, the talons of remorse fixed themselves deeply into his vitals. At such times he took upon his own shoulders the burden of all the misfortunes that fate had showered on him.

He could escape from himself only in company, in the company of congenial spirits; and such spirits were not always at hand. As he ploughed the ridge of Mossgiel in the grey November days, it was difficult not to feel depressed . . .

When he drew up the balance-sheet of his life to this point, the picture it presented was gloomy enough. He was in his twenty-eighth year. For twenty of these years he had toiled like a galley slave and he had nothing to show for it. He was no richer to-day than when he had moiled on Mount Oliphant for nothing better than a thin and watery gruel. As a farmer, his prospects were as gloomy as they had ever been . . .

In his relationship with women he had been equally unfortunate. One wife had denied him; and the other wife was dead. He faced the world as a single man. And in almost any sense of the term he had never been married, since he had never known the satisfaction of a marriage-bed.

It was a sorrowful position: twice a married man and never taken a wife to bed! And yet he was the father of three children: possibly four!

And he would ride into Edinburgh with a certificate of bachelorhood in his pocket! And free of any scandal!

Could he have made a bigger mess of his life if he had tried? Worse: he had made a mess of Betty Paton's life; brought deep unhappiness to Jean Armour, and, most unbearable of all, he had brought death and disillusion to the lass who had trusted him most. It was difficult to escape the conclusion that he was cursed at his source; that his baleful star was not otherwise than ever in the ascendant.

He had brought no happiness to his own family. He had been anything but a credit to them. He had caused them to hang their heads in shame for his misdeeds.

Against such a record of headlong folly, of what use was it to set a volume of poems that had brought in no more than twenty pounds of cash? And of what satisfaction were the plaudits of a handful of folks who wouldn't walk ten yards to his funeral if he were dead to-morrow?

They rested from their labours for a brief moment, and he wiped the sweat from his brow.

"Maybe I despair too much, Gibby; and maybe I'm not thankful enough. There's folk having a damned sight harder time than us . . . We haven't died a winter yet though others have."

Gilbert heaved a sigh of relief that his brother was at last coming out of the trough of depression. It had been a gruelling week; and they had cut each other to the bone in the sweat and torment of their arguments.

The faint smoke-film was clearing from the Bard's eyes; the black cloud was lifting from his brow; the resonant timbre of his voice was coming back . . .

In no time he was humming the tune Gilbert knew as Jean Armour's; for he had told him how it was from her he had first heard it. He had told him that one day he would put words to it: maybe he was thinking of the words now . . .

"Is Auld Glen going to lend you a pownie for your journey?"

"Aye: he's spoken to his good-son, Geordie Reid o' Barquharie: he's got a good beast: spank me into Embro in a couple o' days . . . Everything's turning out splendidly, Gibby. I feel that I'm on the high road to fame and fortune at last. Everybody's been more than kind . . . Bob Aiken, Ballantine, Mr. Laurie, John Arnot, Hamilton and MacKenzie . . . It seems there are many good Ayrshire folks in Edinburgh: especially for the winter. There seems no reason why my hopes shouldn't be high."

"Fine! Keep your hopes high and everything will turn out better than our best hopes: it canna be otherwise."

HANDS OF FRIENDSHIP

Bob Aiken said: "When you get to the Capital, Robin, you'll need to look out. It's no' like Ayr. There's sharpers, pimps and bawds yonder by the hundreds: especially bawds. You canna get turning for them. Baxter's Close in the Lawnmarket you're for biding at? I ken it fine: you'll be in the heart o' things there . . . As soon as you enter the toon, the caddies will be asking if they can be of ony service to you. Tell ane to lead you to the White Hart Inn. Put your beast in there; and then the caddie'll tak' you up the hill to Baxter's Close for a bawbee . . . Now I've written to Mr. Creech the bookseller there; but your fame's there afore you; so dinna be feared. And now, the best o' luck and God's blessing . . . and write and tell me how you get on, for we'll be itching to hear your news. Oh, and dinna forget Orangefield: Dalrymple will be your patron there . . . Or maybe the Earl o' Glencairn will take an interest in you."

John Arnot of Dalquhatswood said: "Gavin Hamilton tells me that Gilbert and your brother William are fully fit to carry on wi' Mossgiel. Well: that's a' the business I'm concerned wi' . . .

"But I wish you luck, Robert. Luck and health and happiness. But at the hinderend you'll find that life's a matter o' luck—or ill luck. I'm one o' the unlucky ones o' this world, Robert: so I ken what I'm talking about . . .

"If you have ony luck wi' your new edition, put my name down for a copy. And if you've time to fill up a sheet wi' your Edinburgh news . . ."

When he handed over the pony, George Reid of Barquharie said: "Auld Glen was telling me that he heard the Earl o' Glencairn has gotten haud o' your book, and that he's fell taen on wi' it."

His youngest brother waylaid him in the barn. Willie's quiet face was set and serious. "I was wondering, Robin . . ."

"You've been wondering for a day or twa, Willie: speak up, lad."

"I was wondering when you are in Edinburgh if you would look out for a job for me?"

"Oh? D'you want away frae here?"

"It'll no' be the same when you're away. And there's nae future in farming for me. Maybe you could get me apprenticed to a saddler . . . I would like that. And I would like to see a bit o' the world."

"You would like to see a bit o' the world, Willie? Aye: well, that's no sin. A saddler might suit you . . . Have you spoken to Gibby?"

Willie shook his head.

"Right: say nothing and I'll see what I can do, Willie. You'll need to give me time to get my feet; but I'll no' forget you."

"I didna think you would, Robin."

"And why d'you think I should forget you? God, lad, things havena been easy this while back; and you and me havena had the same chances o' a crack the way we used to; but I'm still your brother. Never you hesitate to tell me ony o' your worries; and if I can dae ocht to help you I'll dae it. Are you still courting Mary Fergusson? Weel, I'll gie you a bit o' advice here that'll be to your good: so listen carefully . . ."

His sister Bell came to him, her dun, soured face held sideways. "I've nearly three pounds saved: you can hae that for Edinburgh if it would help you."

The Bard swallowed hard and forced a laugh. "Aye: it would help me to get you a dress and a new bonnet and maybe a nice new shawl . . . Thank you, Bell; but if things go the way I hope, you'll get the best shawl money can buy—and Edinburgh fashion can provide."

"We'll miss you."

"Will you, Bell? I havena been much o' a brother to you, have I?"

"I mind when you went awa' to Irvine . . . and I can mind when you went awa' to Kirkoswald . . . and I can mind when you came back again. You'll come back again? You'll no' go awa' to the Indies?"

Nancy, bustling and efficient and growing more like her mother every day, came to him where he was tidying his papers in the attic.

"What sark are you travelling wi'? You maun be decent to mix wi' the folk in Edinburgh. And you needna fash wi' thae papers: naebody'll touch them till you come back. When d'you think you'll be back?"

"When I've made enough money to put a handsome dowry ahint the best housekeeper i' the West."

"Dinna rack yoursel'! Gin I canna get a man withouten your dowry, or onybody else's, I'll bide as I am . . . And see you and no' marry ane o' thae toon jads: a' frills and fancies and frizzed hair."

"D'you think I'm as daft as a' that?"

"You're daft enough for onything; and you're a saft gowk where a lass is concerned! And in Edinburgh they'll be fa'in' ower themselves to see the great Ayrshire poet."

"You never know, Nancy: maybe I'll marry an heiress."

"She'll no' hae her sorrows to seek; and neither will you . . . You'll see and write to us . . .?"

At the Cross of Machlin he ran into Jean Markland.

"I hear you're leaving us, Robert? Goin' to Edinburgh to print some more o' yon verses? I wish you the best o' luck then. I liked your book, Robert. I laughed at The Holy Fair till the tears ran doon my cheeks. You're no' frightened . . . But who would frighten you! You'll be back soon? Weel, I'm glad I ran into you: I wouldna hae liked you to have gone without saying good-bye. We'll be hearing frae Jean how you're getting on . . .?"

To Gavin Hamilton he said: "I hope your dispute with Auld and the Session comes to a satisfactory conclusion."

"Well: Auld has lain quiet this year, Robert; but he's a black-hearted devil, and, like as no', he'll be concocting some fresh charge to lay against me. But don't worry: I'll see day about wi' him. Now you'll keep me posted as to your success in the Capital, wi' details o' your exploits . . . And if you can send me full details o' MacLure's roup and who buys the land I'll be weel pleased . . . And hurry back: for I'd like fine to see you working some improvements on Mossgiel . . . You couldna do better than sink ony money you make in Edinburgh into the farm: it'll pay a lang dividend . . . Have you seen Loudon's factor?"

Doctor John MacKenzie was less self-interested.

"I've written to Sir John Whitefoord telling him that you will be in the Capital; and in so far as he may have the opportunity, you can be assured that he will speak up for you. I've also written to Captain Andrew Erskine. The Captain's a brother of the Earl of Kelly, and one of the first men in society there. He might not be able to do much for you; but in getting out a subscription for your second edition, he will be a useful man to have the right side of; and who knows: he may take up your interests more energetically. The point is, Robert, that you canna have enough friends in a business like this. And, of course, there's Dugald Stewart: you could mak' a call on him . . . I know that I can depend on you not to rush in on them; but to wait till the opportunity occurs . . . Take things quietly to begin with, Robert; and when in doubt trust to that excellent native sense of yours . . . And mind that your Ayrshire friends will be praying for your success . . ."

Eliza Miller was apparently distressed.

"You're really going this time, Robin? When are you coming back? You're no' going away for ever, are you? No' after putting my song in your book? You put nothing for Jean Armour in it . . . You'll no' forget me: promise you'll no' forget me? We've had a lot o' happy times thegither—and Machlin'll no' be the same without you." She put her arms round his neck. "You've never promised you would marry me, Robin. If you promised, I would wait . . ."

Wee Jamie Smith's cheery red face was clouded.

"I'll no' be lang after you, Rab. I've seen an agent o' the Avon Printworks in Linlithgow and I've offered a partnership . . . Machlin's finished wi' me and I'm finished wi' Machlin . . . When you decided to go to the Indies I decided to quit. That's the court o' equity burst up noo. Aweel: we had a grand time while it lasted, Rab; and I suppose a' good things maun come to an end. If I hadna bairned Kirsty Wilson, things might hae been different; but that was the last straw wi' the unco guid here. There's plenty havena been in my shop since . . . But you'll write me? And listen, Rab: if you come across ony good bawdy sangs or ballads, be sure and send me a copy . . . You never ken: maybe we'll meet in Edinburgh yet. You ken what to tell Richmond . . .

"Jean Armour was in here the other day. By God, Rab: she's dafter about you than ever. I dinna ken how the hell you do it . . . But, certes! there'll be some fine dames in the Capital . . ."

Jeannie Smith said: "You'll dae fine in Embro, Robin. I ken you will. James'll no' be that far from you in Linlithgow. And James Candlish said he would like to settle in the Capital.

"Aye . . . and what about Jean? You'll be settlin' down when you come back? Wi' twa bonnie bairns like that, the Capital'll no' haud you lang . . .

"I'm real glad everything's turning out for the best. Jean and you hae had a sair time . . .

"It wad be nae sin, Robin, to kiss me good-bye . . ."

John Rankine gave his hand a long hard grip. There was a serious look in his steel-grey eyes, and the fine lines that the years had engraved on his great brow and about his eyes and mouth seemed curiously graven.

"You've come to the cross-roads now, lad. You've conquered the West and it bows down at your feet. But you're setting off now to conquer the world. I've had the boldness to gie you a feck o' advice in my day, Rab: you'll ken whether that advice has been bad or guid. But I'm goin' to tell you something that maybe you ken already and maybe you don't. Your strength lies here; lies in the fields and the muirs and the streams and a' that live and wark aboot them. And roun' the tavern table where the same folk are gathered to enjoy a social glass! But in Embro you'll fa' in wi' a different set o' folk a'thegither. And different folk mean different manners and different values. Harken to them; but never be deceived by them. Tak' what they say to you and then go awa intil a corner and think it ower.

"As for the women! They'll tempt ye: aye, certes, and you'll tempt them. But mind Samson and Delilah: not one o' them but gin you gie her a chance'll ettle for to shear aff the locks o' your genius. For the bitches ken weel enough that as lang as you keep your genius intact, they'll never be able to nab you and haud you to their will. So it's up to you, Rab, whether you conquer the world or the world conquers you. As for the Great Folks you'll meet there: let them think they're conferring an honour on you and use them for a' they're worth. And, of coorse, there'll be some honest fellows amang them. But let the Great Folks see and hear; and keep your ain counsel . . . for you're a better man than the whole tribe o' them put thegither . . . Aye; and it's a God's pity Jean Armour and you didna hit it aff. When I think on the Babylonian temptations that await you in Embro, I'd raither that you had been safely yoked . . ."

Isa, grown into a douce wee lass, kept asking questions about the Capital. What kind of folks lived there; what they wore; what they ate; and how they spoke . . .

Mrs. Burns said nothing.

THE HIGH ROAD

The twenty-seventh of November—and a dull morning. Heavy clouds banked up from the sea. There was a snell bite in the wind as it swept across the bare uplands. As long as the wind held there would be no rain.

It had been hardest of all to say farewell to his mother. But at the final moment it seemed that she understood; and she had given him her blessing and had offered neither advice nor reproach.

He must not become excited. He must not allow his thoughts to race ahead and his thumping heart to race with them.

He was going to Edinburgh, his country's Capital. He must enter there without any fear. Who was there in Edinburgh to tell him he was any better or any worse than he knew himself to be?

He patted the neck of the pony and spoke softly in his ear. He liked to think that the beast sensed something of the momentous nature of the journey.

He went into the Whitefoord Arms and tossed back a stirrup-cup and said good-bye to his host and hostess. Then he went round the corner into the Cowgate, and, while Adam Armour held the pony, he went in and said good-bye to Jean.

She was sitting by the fire giving suck to the infant Robert. His gums held tightly to the nipple, and his snub nose was buried in the rich swell of sweet flesh.

They were left to themselves.

"Well, I'm off, Jean."

"And when'll we be seeing you again?"

"There's no saying. But och, it won't be so long. It's no' the Indies this time. Look after the bairns when I'm away." He poked a finger under Robert's chin. "Haud on, you wee guzzler: leave some for your sister."

He put his arm round her shoulder and kissed her. It was a kiss from the green thorn tree. Her spine shivered and her forearms rose in goose-flesh.

"I'll come back, Jean," he whispered. He turned suddenly and strode from the room. Before she could get to the window, she heard the clatter of the pony's hooves on the causeway. She clutched the child to her breast and sank slowly onto the creepie by the fire.

He went round by the Cross at an easy canter, waved and shouted farewell to Jamie Smith standing in his door, then eased the bridle and let the beast take its own pace on the long slow slope ahead. They had a hard couple of days' riding before they saw the lum-reek of the Capital.

Daddy Auld came round the corner of the Bellman's Vennel as he waved to Smith. So that was Robert Burns off to Edinburgh! And Jean Armour nursing his twins in the Cowgate! Aye: the Lord moved in a mysterious way His wonders to perform. A strange man, Robert Burns. May God forgive him that he hadn't wrestled with him to better purpose. He had been a sore responsibility . . . He was better away from Machlin. But Edinburgh . . .? Daddy Auld shook his head and wondered.

THE END